Echoing Hearts

Book 1 of The Echo Series

C. R. Alam

COVER DESIGN: DOT COVERS

EDITED BY JENNY GARDNER

Copyright © 2022 by C. R. Alam

ISBN: 979-8-9871399-0-5

All rights reserved. No part of this book may be reproduced in any form or by any electronic or mechanical means, including information storage and retrieval systems, without written permission from the author, except for the use of brief quotations in a book review.

This is a work of fiction. Names, characters, places, and incidents either are the products of the author's imagination or are used fictitiously, and any resemblance to actual persons, living or dead, businesses, companies, events, or locales is entirely coincidental. No portion of this book may be reproduced in any form without written permission from the publisher or author, except as permitted by U.S. copyright law.

This book is intended for mature, adult audiences only. It contains sexually explicit and graphic scenes and language which may be considered offensive by some readers.

This book is strictly intended for those over the age of 18.

All sexually active characters in this work are 18 years of age or older. All acts of a sexual nature are completely consensual.

To my family for all of their support, love, and faith in me

One

Manhattan, New York City—three years earlier

Dean Rowland checked his watch for the third time in ten minutes, then readjusted his tuxedo's sleeves to perfection again. He'd been standing by the altar with the minister and his groomsmen for over twenty minutes. His bride was supposed to make her entrance fifteen minutes ago.

Turning to his best man and older brother, he asked through gritted teeth, "Gene, could you find out what's keeping Leighton?"

"I'm sure she'll be out soon." Gene scanned the church floor for the wedding planner, who seemed to have disappeared.

"People are getting restless." Family members and guests from New York City's upper crust filled the pews of the large church. Whispers among them started to echo in the cavernous space.

Dean would've preferred a small, intimate wedding over the extravagant event Leighton's mother had planned for more than three hundred guests. When he'd first entered the church, thousands of roses, lilies, and other flowers he couldn't name seemed to have jumped at him. He'd thought they were competing against the church's beautiful stained-glass windows, and it had seemed wrong.

Something had been off since he'd woken up this morning. It might've been just a feeling in the air or his gut. But he always paid attention to his instinct. Well, almost always—he'd been ignoring this same hunch for a few months now. But this time, it was harder to ignore.

Dean shook off the sense of foreboding and returned to the present issue. "I know Leighton wants to make a splashing entrance, but tell her to make this one in five minutes."

"Fine. But smile, for crying out loud, or people will think you're not a happy groom."

Dean flashed Gene a pointed look. "I won't be happy until my bride stands beside me."

"I'm going." Gene started to move but turned back to Dean. "Hey, seriously, you are happy, right?"

"Having a ball here, Gene," Dean replied sarcastically.

Gene's concern was apparent on his face, but he didn't say anything else before he discreetly made his way out. Dean knew his brother was only looking out for him, so he plastered on a smile to cover his irritation. He turned to his parents, sitting in the first row, and saw questions on their faces. He gave them a reassuring nod. Though he wasn't sure whom he was really assuring, his parents or himself.

Chris Sullens, his good friend and groomsman, took Gene's abandoned spot and whispered, "Everything all right?"

"We'll find out soon enough." Dean kept his smile on while he faced the murmuring guests.

Dean's smile vanished when Gene returned moments later. As he handed a note to Dean, Gene's face confirmed what Dean already suspected. The only indication that the message's content affected Dean was the slight tightening of his jaw as he read it.

Murmurs in the crowd grew as they realized something was afoot.

Dean pocketed the note and asked Gene, "Do you mind making the announcement?"

Gene nodded. "Are you okay?"

Dean wasn't sure of the answer to that question. He simply thanked his brother before walking to his parents. He took his mother's arm and led his confused parents out of their seats. But instead of explaining, he turned to his assistant, Melanie, sitting behind his parents.

"Get Frank Heller and meet me in the hallway," he instructed in a steady voice.

"What's going on, son?" his father questioned as Dean led them through a side door to the hallway.

Once they were alone, he answered, "Leighton had a change of heart."

If it weren't for his parents, he wouldn't bother explaining it to anyone. "Apparently, she's felt differently about marrying me for a while but didn't have the courage to say it to my face."

The door that led to the main church floor suddenly banged open. Leighton's father, Samuel Heston, stormed into the hallway. Behind him, the church was in an uproar.

"What is the meaning of this, Dean?" Samuel Heston demanded. His face was red with rage.

Dean eyed the man who almost became his father-in-law. "You should ask your daughter."

"What are you talking about? She's on her way. I was just waiting for her up front—"

"You would've waited for a long time. She's not coming," Dean interrupted, his voice flat.

"Don't you know where your daughter is on her wedding day?" Dean's father jumped in, clearly upset with the news.

"Dad, I'll handle this. Why don't you and Mom find somewhere to sit?" Dean glanced at his sister, Kat, who had followed in Heston's wake. Understanding the silent request, she ushered their parents away without a word.

When his family was out of earshot, Dean turned to Heston. "Leighton could've ended this months ago instead of dragging us all through this fiasco. What are you playing at, Samuel?"

"I swear to God, she said she'd go through with the wedding..." Heston abruptly stopped as he realized he'd revealed too much.

Dean's hands fisted so tight he could feel his short nails piercing his palms. But he kept his anger in check. He didn't use brute strength to punish people who wronged him.

Dean's lead lawyer, Frank Heller, walked in with Melanie as if on cue. Without taking his eyes off Samuel, Dean addressed Frank, "Since my fiancée jilted me this afternoon, all agreements on the wedding expenses are void. Correct, Frank? I won't bother with the amount I've already paid, but make sure Heston gets the rest of the bills. I'll be damned if I have to spend another cent on this farce."

The blood drained from Samuel's face. Dean knew Samuel was on the brink of bankruptcy due to bad investments and uncontrolled spending on his wife and daughters' parts. He knew Samuel was counting on him, as a dutiful son-in-law, to bail him out.

"Oh, and cancel the credit I was going to extend to Heston since we won't be family after all," Dean added as he turned away.

"Wait for a second here, Dean." Samuel reached out a hand to stall Dean. "Let me talk to Leighton—"

"Don't bother." Without looking back, Dean walked out of the church.

"Damn."

Rae Allen heard one of her roommates, Brandon, muttering from their tiny apartment's living/dining room.

"What's that?" Rae peeked her head out of the small kitchen.

It might house three closet-sized bedrooms, but the apartment was still tiny enough that the roommates could hear every little sound the other made. Sometimes, it made things a little awkward. Thank goodness for earphones.

Brandon looked up from his phone. "You know Dean Rowland? He owns Aquarius Media, one of the most innovative companies in the country."

"Of course I know of him. What about him?" Rae walked out with a bowl of cereal and joined Brandon on the couch.

"He was stood up at the altar yesterday." Brandon showed the article he was reading on his phone.

Rae took the phone and read the gossip.

"Man, that's rough." Brandon reclined on the couch with his arms folded behind his head. "I mean, if a rich, successful, good-looking guy like Dean Rowland could get dumped, what's the chance for guys like me?"

Rae studied the picture accompanying the article. Dean Rowland posed with his runaway bride in his arms at some event. They looked beautiful together, but Rae didn't detect much chemistry between them. The way the couple stood rigidly next to each other didn't exactly scream love. Maybe that was why the fiancée had a change of mind.

"He might be all that, but it doesn't mean he's perfect," Rae rebutted. "What are you worrying about, anyway? Didn't you get three bras thrown at you at the last gig?"

Rae grinned, remembering Brandon's dumbstruck expression as one of those mentioned bras had hit him on the face. It'd been a double-D sheer number. She'd think by now he would've gotten used to that treatment, being the front man of a popular indie rock band.

"That's all fun, of course." Brandon grinned. "But I'm talking about love and that special someone you'd commit yourself to for the rest of your life."

Rae watched her friend's musing face and smiled. At twenty-seven years old, Brandon, with his slightly longer than normal wavy light brown hair, had that boy-next-door charm that every mother would love. Add in the rocker vibe, with his half-sleeve tattoos and a stylishly disheveled persona, and he was just too hard for many girls to resist. But the side of Brandon that had always fascinated her was his belief in love.

"Obviously, being rich, successful, and good-looking isn't the key to a happily-ever-after," Rae said with a shrug. "There is no guarantee. Period. It's all fairy tale. So, if you don't expect it, you won't get disappointed."

Brandon turned to her with a deep frown. "That's depressing, Rae."

"It's called managing expectations." Rae put a spoonful of her now soggy corn flakes into her mouth.

Brandon sat up and scrutinized Rae with a teasing smile. "You're telling me you don't have any desire to find that special someone who you just can't live without? Someone who will always have a special space in your heart? So special that your heart doesn't feel whole when that someone isn't there?"

"Is that what you're looking for? Waiting for?" Rae's eyebrow rose in skepticism. "From my experience, giving a big piece of your heart like that tends to lead to heartbreak."

Brandon's smile wavered slightly. And for a fleeting glimpse, Rae sensed that Brandon knew exactly what she was talking about. But in the next second, he recovered.

"Heartbreak is always a risk for the kind of love worth the wait," Brandon stated with a solemn smile that didn't quite reach his eyes.

The door to bedroom number three swung open, and a tall guy with a bad case of bedhead walked out in a T-shirt and boxer shorts.

"What are you guys yapping about out here so early?" Curtis complained as he yawned.

Brandon checked the time on his phone. "It's almost ten."

"It's fucking Saturday. What's so important that you had to interrupt my beauty sleep?" Curtis dropped into the only reading chair in the room, propped his feet on the coffee table, and promptly shut his eyes again.

"Oh, nothing. We were just talking about some rich guy who got dumped at the altar, which led to Brandon going on a tangent about forever love and all." Rae finished her cereal and got up to the kitchen.

Curtis groaned. "God."

"I know, right?" Rae shrugged as she put her bowl into the dishwasher. "I say why waste time searching, waiting for love, when you just get left behind and broken anyway?"

Rae closed the dishwasher door, turned back, and found Brandon studying her with a peculiar look.

"Not every love story gets a happy ending, but it doesn't mean you give up trying to find it," Brandon said.

"Well, some people just aren't meant for it."

"Everyone deserves love, Rae."

"But not everyone gets it. Or needs it." Rae gathered her bag with her laptop and notes. "Anyway, I gotta go do some work."

Brandon's eyebrow rose at her abrupt segue.

"I'll see you at your show tonight." Rae opened the door.

"People need love, Rae." Brandon tried to get the last word in.

"Oh, for crying out loud, would you stop?" Curtis rolled his eyes at Brandon.

"Agree to disagree. But you do you, boo." Rae grinned at Brandon before closing the door behind her.

Two

Somewhere in Tennessee—April, three years later

Rae Allen waited for the incoming traffic on US-411 to clear before steering her rental car to TN-68 toward Georgia.

"You owe me big time, Susan," Rae told her friend on the speakerphone.

Susan Adler, the editor-in-chief of *Homes* magazine, had reached out to her for an emergency project this morning. It had led Rae to change her plan from flying home to New York City to driving to a property about four hours away from where she'd been.

"Yes, I know," Susan replied. "But how was I supposed to anticipate Maggy getting a stomach bug? That poor woman. But lucky me, I found out my famous travel-blogger friend and former staff writer just happened to be hours away in Tennessee. How was the Farm, by the way? Is it worth all the hype?"

Rae had left the luxurious small resort and spa at the foothills of the Great Smoky Mountains earlier that morning. The exclusive vacation destination had invited her to spend a few days experiencing their beautiful setting and accommodations and enjoying the top-notch dining and spa experience. She'd chronicled her stay in snippets of video logs she shared with her numerous loyal followers. Then, she would detail her days in a few articles that her readers would use as a reference to plan their own travel.

"It is if you have money to throw around. The location is breathtaking. Just gorgeous and so quiet. But outside the Farm, other more economical options are just as great, minus some amenities, of course."

Rae always included other charming accommodations and affordable activities when writing about fancy places. She knew not everyone could afford a place that charged almost $1,000 a night for a room.

"Does the owner know I'll be coming in instead of Maggy?" Rae turned the conversation back to the current assignment.

"I've sent her an email. I'll try calling her again as soon as I get off with you," Susan assured Rae. "Thank you, again, for saving me from having to postpone this article."

"What's so special about this property anyway?" Rae had wondered about it since Susan had begged her to go to this house on Lake Lanier in Georgia.

"First of all, it's a beautifully designed home. The photography team already did their work last week. Maggy couldn't go for the interview at that time, hence it was scheduled for this weekend instead. Katherine Hamilton wanted the writer to spend a night in the house to showcase it fully."

"Weird."

"She mentions photos won't fully capture the house. She claims the writer will need to experience it."

"Ehm..." Rae tried to understand that. "Did you email me pics?"

"No. I want you to get your impression first hand."

"You're sending me blind?" Rae scoffed. "Look, I like being wowed when I go somewhere new, but I'd usually have some research done before going to a private property and meeting its owner."

"The brief is in your email," Susan told her. "When you meet Katherine, she'll fill you in. She is being rather mysterious, but I have a feeling about this one. For one thing, it has a gorgeous lake view, and it's surrounded by eighteen acres of woods. But what I find intriguing is that Lois Schwartz designed the whole interior."

The name of the world-renowned interior designer perked Rae's ears. "Lois Schwartz doesn't do work for just anybody."

"No, she doesn't," Susan confirmed.

"Now my interest is piqued." Rae tapped the steering wheel. "Did you reach out to Lois?"

"I get the runaround from her team."

"Curious."

"Right?" Susan said. "There might be a reason for the privacy, but it'll be good to know if there's some human interest angle we can highlight."

"Got it. I'll text you when I get there."

Gainesville, Georgia

Slowing her car, Rae scanned the side of the road. She could only see trees, not a building in sight. Yet, the GPS indicated that she'd passed her destination and was insistently telling her to make a legal U-turn.

Rae eyed the car's digital clock flashing *4:47* and groaned. Pulling over, she rechecked the GPS. She was on the right road, and the directions showed the address wasn't far from where she was. There was no other way but to trace her route back from that point.

Not far from where she doubled back, Rae spotted what might be a mailbox, and Stella—the name she gave the GPS lady—announced, "Your destination will be on the right." When she got nearer, she could see that it was actually a neat mailbox made from a tree stump, and next to it was a clearing that hardly anyone could spot. She could've sworn she hadn't seen it driving from the other way earlier.

Turning the car into the driveway, she drove for a couple of minutes before making out the one-level residence. She parked on the side of a circular drive and got out of the car. For a moment, she studied her surroundings. The house was tucked into the woods, but the foliage framed it perfectly. With its combination of wood, stone, and glass, the structure blended naturally with its surroundings. Her earlier weariness evaporated and was replaced by the thrill of exploring the rest of the property.

After ringing the doorbell, Rae looked around as she waited for someone to answer the door. The road wasn't visible from where she stood. If it was privacy the owners sought, they definitely got it.

Talking about quiet, she wondered why nobody answered the door. She rang the bell again and got the same result. She then dialed Katherine Hamilton's phone number, which Susan had included in her email brief. As the phone rang, she scanned the grounds and spotted a path around the side.

The call went to voicemail, and Rae weighed her options. Perhaps someone was around back and didn't hear the bell or the phone. It was a large property, after all. She decided to follow the path.

As she rounded the corner and came to a large green lawn, Lake Lanier came into view through a clearing. It was a marvelous view, but when she turned her attention to the back portion of the house, she stopped short.

"Wow," Rae breathed out as she took her first full look at the estate.

The clean lines of the mahogany, glass, and stone combination created a modern living space that exuded a homey feel. The house wasn't obnoxiously large like many estates she'd seen, but it was by no means small either. Instead of looming in height, it spread wide in a slight curve—like an embrace. She thought it was just perfect. It looked inviting, and she grew excited to spend the next two nights there. Though first, she must find her host.

Rae climbed the stone steps leading to the raised deck along the length of the back of the house. A steady splashing sound came from the beautiful freeform pool on one side of the large terrace. A masculine body gracefully sliced through the water.

Relieved she finally found someone, Rae proceeded toward the poolside and waited for the man to reach it. When his hand touched the stone, and his head emerged from the water, ready to make a turn, Rae immediately stepped closer to get his attention.

"Excuse me," she called out.

The man abruptly straightened up in mid-turn and looked up at her, whipping cold water at her feet. His face registered shock at her presence, but it immediately morphed into a look of annoyance—almost hostility.

Rae's smile wavered as she instinctively stepped back to lessen the intensity of the man's glare.

"Who the hell are you?" he demanded.

Three

The man's tone should've alerted Rae to tread cautiously, but somehow, she found herself staring at his chiseled face, shadowed by a couple of days' worth of growth. Water dripped from his hair, making it look like delicious melting dark chocolate.

Rae's eyes started wandering down to his broad shoulders, but she caught herself. She quickly looked up to meet sharp grey eyes growing harder as the seconds ticked by.

Clearing her throat, she answered, "I'm sorry to startle you. My name is Rae Allen. I'm here on behalf of Homes magazine. Are you Mr. Hamilton? I've been trying to contact Katherine Hamilton."

The annoyance level on the handsome face seemed to elevate instead of dissipating with her every word. Without responding to Rae, he pushed himself off to the other side of the pool. He pulled himself out in one smooth move.

Taken aback by the unwelcoming attitude, Rae could only follow his lithe movements. She got a good look at his swimmer's lean muscled upper body, a defined stomach that narrowed down to strong-looking hips, and a fine behind. She couldn't help but appreciate his well-toned long legs in clinging black swimming trunks before he grabbed a large white towel to dry himself off.

Realizing she was gawking, Rae averted her gaze to the sky and tried to fill the silence. "I rang the doorbell several times. When nobody answered, I thought I'd go—"

"Snoop around a private property?" he interrupted without even giving her a glance.

Sensing the quiet hostility in his otherwise intriguingly even voice, Rae was lost for words for a few seconds. The thought that Mrs. Hamilton was lucky to have both a beautiful home and a sexy husband evaporated from her mind.

She didn't just drive four hours for some man to accuse her of breaking and entering. She took several quick steps to confront him but stopped once he turned to her as if he had some invisible power to freeze her. But he didn't manage to suppress her rising temper.

"I've actually been requested to snoop around this property this weekend." Rae used her sweet-as-honey voice with a hint of a sting. "Mrs. Hamilton arranged it with *Homes* magazine. She must've forgotten to cc you on the memo."

This time, he merely raised his eyebrow at her. One eyebrow.

Rae stifled a groan of irritation as she watched him pick up a cellphone and walk away to make a call. She pulled out her own phone and dialed Susan.

"Hi, you've reached Susan Adler's phone. Please leave a message," the automated reply came on.

"Susan, I'm here at the property, but there's no Katherine Hamilton to meet me." Rae hissed into the phone. "Instead, there's a guy here who looks ready to chop my head off for trespassing. Call me back. Or better yet, please fix this."

She then tried calling the number for Katherine Hamilton once more. Another voicemail.

Rae sighed and tried to clamp down on her growing frustration. She reminded herself she was good at going with the flow and finding her way out of a jam. It was just a mix up. Nothing she hadn't handled before.

But boy, that Mr. Hamilton really got her goat without even trying. She swept her gaze to the lake's calm surface and took a deep breath. A spring afternoon in the south could get a bit toasty. But after spending her childhood in Minnesota, Rae would savor a sunny warm day in early April anytime.

But then a cool breeze blew in, and her nose tickled. "Haa...choo!"

The sneeze didn't stop with one. Another two followed consecutively.

"Pollen," the deep voice came from behind her and surprised Rae's sneezing to a stop.

Snatching a tissue from her purse, Rae quickly cleaned her nose as she muttered, "No shit."

Apparently, she misjudged the volume of her voice because when she turned, Mr. Hamilton's questioning raised eyebrow indicated he'd heard her. But at least he looked somewhat amused. Perhaps, she could still clear up any misunderstanding. She could swallow her pride for the sake of professionalism.

"Look, I'd like to apologize again. Obviously, you weren't informed of my arrival. There was a last-minute change, but I am supposed to be here," Rae started. "But if this weekend has become inconvenient, I'm sure *Homes* can arrange a new time."

Rae studied the infuriating man—still distractingly bare-chested, she noted—trying to gauge his reaction. But his mouth didn't even twitch to indicate that he'd accepted her explanation.

Fine. I don't need to take this crap. I tried.

Rae turned up her smile. "I will go. Thank you for your..." she paused before injecting a trace of venom into her voice, "...hospitality."

She spun around and was already halfway down the steps when his voice stopped her in her tracks.

"Kat is on her way," he said. "She asked if you'd wait."

Rae rolled her eyes and exhaled slowly to release her exasperation. He couldn't tell her that before she stomped away?

Turning toward the man yet again, Rae said through gritted teeth, "I really don't want to bother—"

"Too late," he deadpanned. "Have a seat. Kat will be here soon."

Without another word, he walked away to the far side of the house and vanished through a set of French doors.

Rae was left alone where she stood with her mouth open.

Rae stayed motionless for a full minute before she managed to swear under her breath. She'd canceled her weekend plans for this favor. She was tired from driving, and that arrogant man totally challenged her sense of decorum.

She was amazed that he'd triggered her with very few words in a few minutes. In truth, she hadn't expected his cold response when her first reaction to him was this inappropriate, instant blood-warming attraction. It was a rare sensation and had thrown her off-kilter.

And there was something familiar about him that she couldn't quite place.

No matter. It didn't give her an excuse to be unprofessional. She was here to do a job.

Rae shook her limbs deliberately and forced herself to shed her foul mood.

When she felt somewhat in control, Rae scanned the enormous deck. From where she was standing, facing the back of the house, she could see a raised slate whirlpool connected to the pool to her right. To her left, a spacious outdoor dining area bled into a set of comfortable sofa and chairs surrounding an outdoor fire pit. She decided to sit by the pool under the shade of an umbrella.

Not long after, Rae heard a door slamming and rushed footsteps approaching her. She looked to see a beaming woman coming through another glass door, beelining it to where she sat.

"Katherine Hamilton?" Rae inquired.

Offering her hand to Rae, the other woman's smile grew bigger. "Please, call me Kat."

Rae's immediate instinct was to like the woman and feel sorry that she had a jerk for a husband.

"Good to meet you, Kat." Rae shook the other woman's hand. "I'm Rae Allen. Susan Adler from *Homes* sent me."

"I'm pleased to meet you," Kat said. "I'm sorry, but I missed Susan's emails and calls. I thought this weekend was canceled when Maggy fell ill. I didn't think she could find someone to come on such short notice."

"Susan called me this morning. I happened to be only a few hours away, finishing another project," Rae explained.

Kat's eyes suddenly widened. "Wait. Are you Rae the Lone Wanderer?"

"Yes," Rae confirmed with a hesitant smile.

"Oh my god. I follow you on Instagram. I love your travel posts. You were just up at the Farm, weren't you? I've always wanted to stay there."

"Well, it's a beautiful spot, but I'm not here in that capacity. Since I was nearby, Susan asked if I could fill in. I used to write for *Homes*, but I understand if this arrangement isn't ideal. We could reschedule after Maggy feels better."

"Are you kidding? No! You're here now," Kat said. "I just wasn't expecting Dean to be here this weekend. I mean, the man hadn't been home for months. Of all the weekends in the year he could grace us with his presence, he decided to come this week. Unannounced." Kat laughed at the situation. "I didn't even know he was here until he called me just now."

Rae frowned, hearing her host's tangent. Why wouldn't Kat know her husband's whereabouts? Were they separated?

"I'll take care of it. We'll have the weekend talking about the house as planned. Dean just has to deal with it." Kat linked her arm around Rae's elbow as if they'd been best friends for years and led her to the door. "Let's go inside where it's cool."

"I'd love a glass of water if you don't mind. I'm parched." Rae realized it as she felt the chill of the air conditioner hit her skin.

"Goodness. He didn't offer you a drink?" Kat huffed, then stalked to the kitchen, dragging Rae along.

"Well, there was the confusion—" Rae tried to appease Kat.

"Dean may not have lived here for the past decade, but he shouldn't have forgotten southern hospitality." Kat detached herself from Rae and went to the refrigerator. "He probably didn't have much to offer. I was going to stock the fridge for Maggy, but y'know—"

"Water is fine," Rae insisted. But her thirst was temporarily forgotten as she made a full circle in the spacious, modern kitchen. "Wow, what a gorgeous kitchen."

"You like?" Kat beamed. "It's one of my favorite rooms."

"I love kitchens. You've done an amazing job with this one. Just look at that view from here." Rae stood by the breakfast table and looked out through the glass wall.

"Thank you. When I designed this house, I wanted to blend it naturally with its surroundings and bring the outside in," Kat explained.

"I can't wait to see the rest." Rae was eager to explore the house, but the thoughtful look on Kat's face dampened her enthusiasm.

Kat handed Rae a glass of icy water. "I just have to talk to my brother about you staying here for the weekend first."

Rae cocked her head, not following Kat's statement. "Your brother?"

Kat nodded absently. "It is his house, after all. I have his permission to have the house featured, but I didn't anticipate your visit clashing with him being here. Like I said, he's usually never here."

"Wait, sorry. The Dean you've been referring to is your brother?" Rae asked.

"Yeah."

"The man I met earlier? Tall, dark-haired, and..." Rae almost added 'rude' but stopped herself in time.

"Good looking?" Kat finished flippantly. "Don't let him hear that, but yes, that's him."

Oblivious to Rae's thoughts, Kat narrowed her eyes at Rae. "Who did you think he was?"

"She thought I was your husband," a masculine voice chimed in, making Rae jump.

Kat's gaze flew over Rae's head, and her face filled with mirth as she burst into laughter. "Oh, no!"

Rae realized she'd blundered, but she wasn't one to simply take the veiled mocking lying down. She faced her adversary, who leaned casually against a wall opening on the kitchen's opposite side. A grey T-shirt and jeans now covered his swimmer's frame. His arms crossed on his chest accentuated his biceps.

Rae focused on his face and challenged, "I wouldn't have made that mistake if you had just told me who you were."

His cool grey eyes locked on Rae's, and she didn't blink. *You don't scare me, buddy.*

"This is too funny." Kat curbed her laughter and reprimanded her brother, "Gosh, you're horrible. You didn't even introduce yourself? Have you totally lost your manners?"

Coming between her brother and Rae, who were still playing the staring game, Kat said, "Rae Allen, meet my usually pretty nice brother, Dean Rowland."

"Ah, it's a pleasure to finally get a name," Rae pointed out with a small smile to soften the gibe.

Still not uttering a word, the infuriating man barely inclined his head as an acknowledgment, but Rae could've sworn she saw the tiniest twinkle in his eyes. And maybe there was the barest hint of a smile on his lips.

"And Dean, this is Rae Allen," Kat announced, beaming sweetly at her brother. "Your houseguest for the weekend."

Four

Dean Rowland listened to the sound of nature as it prepared to welcome the break of dawn. He could still hear a lone owl hooting in the distance, but a choir of morning birds just started to fill in the earlier stillness.

Sitting on his deck in the dark with only embers glowing in the fire pit to illuminate the night, Dean watched the eastern sky for a glimpse of light.

Not just yet.

He didn't realize how much he missed the silence until he'd arrived here two days ago. After living in New York City for over a decade, he'd gotten used to hearing traffic, sirens, or tripped car alarms throughout the night. Still, the quiet didn't help him stay asleep longer.

Dean had never needed much sleep—a few hours tops—but those few hours hadn't been enough lately. For once in his thirty-four years of life, he'd felt fatigued enough to compel him to take a break.

He'd flown home to enjoy a few days of solitude in his barely lived-in new lake house. This was only his second time there since he'd commissioned his little sister to design and build it.

Kat did a tremendous job, Dean mused proudly as he studied the shadowed elegant lines of the multilevel roof. He did find some sense of peace back home, and he'd thought a few more days by the lake would probably fuel him enough to return to his monotone existence in New York.

But that serenity was interrupted when a woman with the clearest blue eyes he'd ever seen had trespassed onto his property. It was barely hanging by a thread in the first place. He'd never get that rest now that he had to play host to the prickly woman.

A quiet swish of a sliding door opening brought Dean's eyes to the poolside of the deck. Said woman stepped out into the night wrapped in a robe that flew around her legs as she moved. Her hair was loose in thick waves down her back. He hadn't noticed the abundance of it since she'd worn it wound in a bun when they'd first met yesterday.

She closed the door as quietly as she'd opened it and walked around the pool to stand by the deck's railing. Unaware of her audience, she set her eyes on the eastern sky and waited.

Saturday morning.

Scratch that. It was still pitch black when Rae dragged herself out of her wonderfully comfortable bed. She'd had to remind herself this wasn't the first time she'd gotten up before the rooster's crow.

Kat had urged her to be out on the deck before sunup. She'd explained the house enjoyed both sunrise and sunset due to its location, but the morning view was the best. So here Rae was, in her pajamas and robe, standing on the deck. Waiting.

The sky was still quite dark, but she could see dawn was about to break. Taking its time, fiery streaks started bursting from behind the tree line, and the sky developed a heavenly combination of colors.

Rae sighed when the streaks of sunshine reflected on the still lake. Her senses were entirely consumed by the images created by the sunrise. Though not a morning person, she still appreciated the beauty of the daily phenomenon.

To her surprise, everything about this place was breathtaking. From the property, the view, and the house, to the man who owned it. The memory of Dean Rowland emerging from the water suddenly appeared in her mind. Long, strong legs, lean muscles, and broad shoulders.

It was ridiculous for her to be so drawn to that rude man for no reason whatsoever. She liked nice, harmless, good-natured men. Whereas her host was unpleasant, curt, and apparently had no smile muscle whatsoever. Though Rae must admit he had a compelling face. Everything about it was sharp, especially his grey eyes. A shiver had run down her spine when she'd felt those eyes on her.

Rae almost laughed at herself for letting her mind stray. After Kat had dropped the bomb that Rae would stay for the weekend, Dean had dragged his sister away for a private conversation. She hadn't seen him since. Maybe he'd moved out for the weekend or something. She actually felt bad for driving him out of his own house.

Well, maybe not.

Last night, a quick internet search on Dean Rowland had filled the gap in her knowledge of her host. She'd known he looked familiar, but the unshaven look had thrown her off. He was the same Dean Rowland, the founder and CEO of Aquarius Media Corporation.

She recalled he'd been a favorite subject of *Page Six* since he was one of New York's most eligible bachelors. Then, he'd been left at the altar three years ago, and the gossip pages had swarmed him like maggots. There was a lot of speculation about what had broken up the high-profile engagement, but the most interesting question had been about his fiancée. Apparently, she'd disappeared from the face of the Earth. Nobody from the Manhattan elite had seen her since before the canceled wedding. Even her parents had kept mum about it.

Curious.

Outside of the old gossip news and business-oriented features, Dean Rowland had recently kept himself out of the limelight. Though Rae would've recognized him eventually. He was a visionary in media technology who revolutionized how people consumed their news, communications, and entertainment. And her best friend's band was under Aquarius Music, one of Dean's companies.

Yeah, her host—whom she'd probably pissed off—basically owned her best friend's band. Just her luck, she thought.

Absorbed, Rae belatedly realized the sun had continued to climb and started to light the lawn and deck in soft hues. She could stay there forever and enjoy the cool morning, but she probably should go back inside, get ready, and form a plan to smooth things over with her grumpy host. If she saw him again.

After taking a quick snap of the view with her phone, Rae turned toward the house, but she was startled to find his grumpiness himself sitting quietly on the other side of the deck.

His eyes met hers. And goose bumps prickled her skin.

Dean observed his houseguest as she stood on the edge of the deck. He hadn't been surprised when she'd come out. But he wondered why he'd found her more riveting than the rising sun. He noticed how the rays had highlighted the red streaks in her hair. Her skin was luminous in that soft morning glow, and she somehow seemed softer than the feisty woman he'd met yesterday.

A low hum ran through Dean's veins as he continued to study her.

Dean's lips pressed into a white slash at his reaction to the aggravating woman. He'd had enough of the female population lately. Since being jilted at the altar, there hadn't been a scarcity of ladies trying to comfort him—and he'd been willing to accept the offers for a time. But they were merely a distraction. And he'd decided he didn't need that anymore.

All his life, Dean had known precisely where he was going. Since high school, every achievement had been a stepping-stone to a higher goal. And it'd led him where he was, where he wanted to be. There was more yet to accomplish. But working to reach that next milestone for his company hadn't been as gratifying as it used to be.

Why? Dean had no clue. But when in doubt, his instinct was to return home. Being in the small town he'd grown up in and near his family tended to ground him. Even if they didn't necessarily provide the answers he sought, they helped him feel somewhat normal again.

"Good morning." A firm, clear feminine voice broke into Dean's musing.

Dean's gaze refocused on the Athena standing on his deck. During the split second when his mind had gone somewhere else, she'd turned away from the lake and now was looking straight at him. The morning rays behind her irradiated her features as if she were a goddess gracing him with her presence.

It rendered Dean speechless.

"Kat said not to miss the sunrise. It was spectacular," he heard her say further.

Even though her words were perfectly pleasant, he felt her bristle. But he still couldn't find his tongue—a first for him. He was a man of a few words, but usually by choice.

"Well, you have a good day," Rae pronounced in a veiled "screw you" tone, making Dean realize he'd only been staring at her without replying to anything she said.

What the hell is wrong with you? Dean cursed at himself.

"My favorite part is when the sunshine frames the mist on the lakeshore," he quickly announced when she started to move away. "You can still see it from here."

Miss Rae Allen looked at him with round eyes and didn't move when Dean gestured an invitation to his seating area. But she must've been intrigued enough to see what he was talking about that she hesitantly approached him. He motioned for her to sit on the other side of the couch and pointed to the lakeshore.

"Oh my goodness," she exclaimed under her breath. Her mouth shaped a smile of appreciation. Her eyes filled with wonder.

Rolls of mist lay just above the water with streaks of light shining through them. The image was surreal, as if they were transported to a fantasy world. It felt fitting to Dean after the picture she'd unknowingly presented seconds earlier.

"Thank you for showing me that." Rae beamed a genuine smile at him.

And she knocked Dean off-kilter for the second time.

What the hell? He could only nod in response.

The smile stayed, but her brows furrowed as she eyed him for a few moments before turning to the view again.

Dean bet she probably found him odd. After how he'd behaved yesterday and this morning, he wouldn't blame her. He thought he'd overreacted about her being there. And his primal reaction to seeing her this morning was disturbing. He decided it needed addressing.

"Coffee?" Dean asked.

She swung her head in surprise at him, as if he'd suggested a blood sacrifice or something.

"It's ready." He got up. "Cream or sugar?"

There was a glint of suspicion in her eyes. Perhaps sitting with a stranger at dawn made her uncomfortable. And after how he'd welcomed her yesterday, he couldn't really blame her for being uneasy. The least he could do now was help her relax. After all, she was there for his sister's benefit.

"I do offer guests beverages, contrary to popular belief," Dean assured her.

An amused twist at her mouth appeared, then she nodded. "I'd love a cup. White. With one sugar, please."

Dean went inside to prepare the coffee and resettle himself. While checking on the brew, he considered her preference for coffee interesting. He'd assumed a bold woman like Rae Allen would've liked her coffee dark, strong, and bitter. He should've known not to judge a book by its cover. After seeing her this morning alone, he believed Miss Allen might not be all sass. Perhaps the tough exterior was a shield for a softer and sweeter interior.

He brought the freshly brewed coffee on the tray that Kat had prepared the night before. He was grateful for her forward thinking because he hadn't prepared anything himself to entertain anyone for years.

Rae was still admiring nature waking up when he put down the tray. She thanked him when he poured her a mug of coffee and asked her to help herself to the cream and sugar. Then they sat, sipping their coffee in silence.

Dean was considering apologizing for his behavior yesterday when she suddenly said, "You're lucky to have this view every morning."

An easy, mild conversation was an excellent way to break the ice. He followed her lead. "I've only seen it twice. But it's much more interesting than the sunrises in New York City."

"I'll take your word for it. I'm not usually awake at this hour."

"I am." He surprised himself when he further revealed, "I don't sleep much."

"Oh." Rae gazed at him, her eyes lingering on his.

Dean wanted to know what was in her mind when she studied him like that. He didn't have to wonder long.

"Why are you suddenly being nice?" The direct question just flew out of her mouth.

It made him want to laugh. He managed to restrain the laugh and smirked instead. "Do you prefer me obnoxious?"

"That's not exactly the word I'd use. I'm thinking more along the line of arrogant—"

"Been called that," he interjected. It wasn't news that some would think of him as arrogant.

"...ass," she finished.

The last part caught him off guard, and he burst into laughter.

"And that," Dean submitted. "But usually not to my face. It's refreshing to hear an honest opinion of myself for a change."

There was a skeptical smile on her face. "Well, I'm glad to be of service."

"I was expecting a quiet weekend. Your arrival threw a wrench in that plan." Dean decided to level with her. "But here you are. I can't exactly ignore you, can I?"

"I totally expected you to ignore me my entire stay here."

Dean's lips twitched at her blatant honesty. "I may be an arrogant ass, but I'm not entirely unreasonable. I owe you an apology for being unpleasant yesterday after you trespassed onto my property."

Rae narrowed her eyes at him as if deciding something. "I suppose I owe you an apology for being equally rude after you falsely accused me of breaking and entering."

Dean saw the smile on her face as she sipped her coffee, and he couldn't help but smile himself. They both deliberately hadn't apologized outright, but he felt they'd reached an understanding. He'd gotten irrationally annoyed when Rae had shown up out of nowhere. Still, as the two of them sat in silence, he concluded that having her around wasn't unpleasant. He actually rather enjoyed exchanging jabs with her. They might just be enough to stop his disturbing reaction to her from growing.

Five

"This is basically a bachelor pad—a sophisticated and forward-thinking one—but essentially, that's what it is," Kat claimed as she led Rae around the house.

"I built it with my brother in mind. It's all about combination," she continued. "Dean is both a small-town Georgia boy and a New York mogul. He loves modern lines but respects the classic craftsmanship."

"I see that, though calling this house a bachelor pad seems to belittle your talent," Rae pointed out. "You brilliantly translated what you see in your brother into this house, with the fusion of wood and the glossy glass and the natural colors with simple lines. This house has a country feel, but it exudes elegance."

Kat beamed at Rae's observation. "Exactly."

"So, how come you never mentioned Dean owned the house when you first talked to Susan?" Rae asked.

"He doesn't think it's important. He prefers if his name is left out of the article," Kat answered. "Lois Schwartz's designing the whole interior, on the other hand, would garner more interest from *Homes*' readers."

"Absolutely. But your brother is the house. It'll be quite challenging to portray what you've done here without giving a clue to its inspiration."

"Dean's very private." Kat shook her head. "After all the skewed rumors those gossip pages wrote about him three years ago, he's been very selective of when he's featured in the media."

Private? Sure, she didn't see Dean's name often in gossip news anymore. But there were times when she'd happened to glimpse pictures of him in society pages with different women hanging on his arm—after the wedding debacle and his fiancée's disappearance.

"I'm not a gossip writer," Rae argued. "I'm not interested in writing about his private life. I'm after giving your hard work the accolades it deserves."

"I also don't want people to think that I am where I am because of my successful big brother," Kat insisted.

"I understand." Rae glanced at the woman walking next to her. Despite her effervescent demeanor, Kat took her work seriously. Rae imagined it wasn't an easy career path to pave for a young female architect.

"Anybody can see the cleverness of your design just from looking at this house," Rae reasoned. "I'd like to reference him to highlight the thoughts that went into the design."

Kat stopped in the middle of the lawn, studying the back of the house as she considered Rae's suggestion. "If you could mention his name as minimally as possible, I'd agree. But you'll also need to ask Dean's approval," Kat said with a wink.

That gave Rae pause. This morning, she and Dean had some kind of a truce, but would he grant her permission to reveal his ownership of the house?

"Here's a little feature nobody has seen yet," Kat continued, oblivious to Rae's thoughts. "I've designed it so it'd be easy to transform this into a family home."

"Wouldn't that be merely cosmetic?" Rae asked.

"There are things to consider when you have children—babies, toddlers. Safety, functional layout, room to grow, and storage, to name a few, which I've thoroughly considered from the first time I drew the plan.

"When he's ready to start a family, the house will accommodate the necessary changes," Kat elaborated. "Not that he's aware of it."

"I see," Rae said, doubting that Dean would be ready to start a family soon. He seemed too focused on expanding his company internationally. If she wasn't mistaken, Aquarius Media Corp. had extended its business to Europe and Asia.

"Ever since the unfortunate event three years ago, Dean has distanced himself as far from marriage as possible," Kat continued. "After being left at the altar, who could blame him? I'd have issues as well, I suppose."

Rae didn't respond, waiting for Kat to elaborate.

"I'm just hoping he'll find someone who will love him wholeheartedly, and I'll get to execute my plan," Kat said wistfully. "Oh, please don't mention that." She grimaced, belatedly realizing she'd revealed more than she should to a virtual stranger.

"I might only mention how you've considered the design for different phases of life," Rae assured her.

"Wonderful." Kat smiled, relieved.

At that moment, shouts and peals of laughter from Kat's twin nephews filled the air as they splashed around in the pool. The eldest Rowland sibling, Gene, and his family had arrived shortly after Kat and her husband, Matt, for a family cookout.

"You see, a bachelor pad, yet family-friendly," Kat proclaimed as they approached the deck.

The three men huddled around the grill, beer bottles in hand. The children were having fun in the pool. And Amanda, Gene's wife, was setting side dishes on the outdoor dining table.

"You're right," Rae agreed. "You have a wonderful family, Kat."

"Yes. Too bad our parents are still on their extended Greek vacation. It's not a full Rowland cookout without them. But you count your blessings, right? I wish Dean could be here more often. He's been...busy."

Rae detected a hint of sadness in the other woman's voice.

"I imagine his work would be quite demanding," she sympathized.

"Yes, but he used to come home regularly. This is where he'd return to get his bearings. Even before this house existed. This is where his family is. He knows all of our doors are open. When he was with Leighton, his ex-fiancée, he started missing some holidays. And when she left, he buried himself in his work."

Rae wasn't sure why Kat shared in-depth information about her private brother. But, somehow, she wanted to hear more about her host.

"That was why I wanted to build this house for him," Kat said.

"It's wonderful, Kat. And look, he's here, enjoying it." Rae looked over to the gentlemen grilling meat over hot coals.

"You're right, Rae." Delight returned to Kat's voice as she watched the men laugh together. "Thanks for pointing that out."

"Anytime."

"I should check if Amanda needs help. Do you have more questions?" Kat asked.

"None that can't wait," Rae said.

"I hope food's almost ready. I'm suddenly famished."

Rae enjoyed the Rowland cookout. At first, she was uncomfortable intruding on their family gathering, but this family was full of friendly, engaging people, and she didn't feel like an outsider. Gene was a funny guy and a very cool dad. Amanda, his wife, was a sweet woman with a quick wit that balanced Gene's sense of humor. Their two boys were a handful but nonetheless charming. Kat's husband, Matt, was also lovely but relatively quiet.

She couldn't see how Dean could be a part of this family. While everybody else was so warm and open, he was closer to tepid and an enigma. She could've sworn he was adopted. However, though Gene was just under six feet and slightly smaller built, while Dean stood much taller with his long legs and broad shoulders, there was an unmistakable resemblance between the two.

Maybe she'd judged too quickly. Even though he wasn't exactly talkative, Dean was unexpectedly agreeable today. Even if he still didn't talk much among his family, she could see the warmth in his eyes when he looked at them, which told her that this man couldn't be a complete jerk.

So who was Dean Rowland really, Rae wondered. The arrogant rich guy she'd first encountered yesterday? The quiet family man who just happened to be a workaholic as his sister described? Or was there something more sinister in his closet as the gossip pages had alluded to after the disappearance of his ex-fiancée Leighton Heston?

"So, to sum up, you left Minnesota, ended up in New York, and never looked back?" Gene asked Rae. "Sounds like our Dean here. What is it about that city that makes people forget their homes?"

Dean's brows furrowed at Gene's words. "I never forget where I come from."

But everyone ignored his protest.

"I went back a few times. I recently lost my last connection there, so I don't have any reason to return," Rae corrected. "I'd rather explore new places instead of visiting the past. There's a big world out there, and I'd like to see all of it—experience it."

"How are you doing on that front?" Matt asked.

"Pretty well. During college, I spent my summers traveling state to state, picking up jobs that gave me access to interesting experiences. I cataloged my travel on my blog and social media channels. It was my great escape. And as it turned out, people enjoy my stories."

"She wrote a book about it," Kat informed. "Titled *A Wandering Soul*."

"I think that's on my book club list," Amanda said. "Wow, now I can brag I've met the author."

Dean witnessed the blush on Rae's porcelain skin as his family laved her with attention. In the daylight, Miss Rae Allen again sported her casual but refined outfit, her hair tamed into an artful bun. She looked at ease surrounded by his clan, unlike yesterday when she'd jutted that little chin of hers at him and met his eyes out of pride.

A slow smile formed on his face as he recalled how she'd looked at dawn with her hair unbound and no trace of makeup. She'd been bewitching. He'd been captivated by her silhouette alone. Until she'd realized she wasn't alone and her guard had gone back up.

They'd returned to their separate corners of the house after coffee. Then Kat had whisked Rae away for breakfast and a tour of the town. Dean actually hadn't spoken with the woman since. And it suited him just fine.

After their morning conversation, he admitted he admired the woman's spunk. He was also acutely aware of her allure to him. He'd never been intrigued by a woman in such a short time in his entire adult life. It was a disturbance he didn't need.

Noticing a movement at the corner of his eye, Dean turned his attention to his sister. Kat was staring at him with an arched eyebrow. He raised one of his own in a silent question as Kat made an urgent head gesture signaling him to go inside.

"Looks like we're out of beer in the outside fridge. I'll re-stock it." Kat got up. "Anybody want anything?"

Dean smoothly offered to help and followed her inside as she took some requests. Once they entered the kitchen, Kat abruptly stopped him in his tracks.

"What are you doing?" Kat demanded.

Dean pondered the question before saying, "What do you think I'm doing?"

"You better get that thought out of your head." She pointed her forefinger at him as she started to the refrigerator.

"What thought would that be?"

"Whatever notion you have about Rae."

Dean cocked his head in surprise that somehow his sister was perceptive enough to read his mind. It took him a couple of seconds to utter, "Excuse me?"

"Don't even, Dean," she warned him fiercely. "I like her."

"I'm not sure what you're getting at. But if you're still concerned that I don't want her here, you can relax," Dean evaded. "She and I reached an understanding this morning."

"Did you now?" Kat scoffed. "I think you're getting too pleased to have her as a houseguest."

"What's that supposed to mean?"

"She's a beautiful woman."

Dean kept his face impassive at Kat's statement. Though he wouldn't say Rae was beautiful in the classical sense. Striking might be a more accurate word. He shrugged as if to say, *So?*

"I see how you look at her." Kat elaborated, "Normally, I'd be thrilled to see you interested in someone I like. Unfortunately, you don't date anyone for more than a few weeks before you move on. And from what I heard, you're not even dating at all lately."

The temper that Dean usually had a good hold on suddenly threatened to erupt. But he didn't raise his voice. It turned flat when he questioned, "How would you know about my dating life?"

"Uh...gossip sites." Kat stumbled but recovered quickly. "That's not important to this conversation. My point is your interest is usually fleeting, so I'd appreciate it if you leave Rae alone."

Kat opened the fridge door and took out a couple of mini cans of ginger ale for the twins. Then she found the six-pack of beer she'd brought earlier and shoved it onto Dean's arms.

"It's not your business whom I date, Kat." He only managed to keep his voice calm because he knew his sister.

"Well, with that logic, it wasn't your business who I dated, either. But it didn't stop you from chasing off Andy Duley at the homecoming dance," Kat pointed out.

Dean's jaw clenched at the memory. "Because I overheard him bragging he'd score with you by the end of the night."

"And that gave you the right to drag him out of the dance?" Kat retorted.

"I'm your big brother. Who else is going to look out for you? If Gene wasn't already at college, he would've been right there with me."

"Exactly, because you're my brother." Kat smiled at him. "And you care about me. So I'm asking you again to stay clear of Rae. She's writing about my work, Dean."

"Kat, I won't jeopardize this for you."

"Then it's settled. You'll stay courteous while she's our guest. Tomorrow, she'll go home and write the article, and that'll be the end of it."

"Why do you even think I'm interested? She has a tongue as sharp as a razor. She told me to my face that I was an arrogant ass."

Kat laughed. "Did she now? Well, she got you pegged. Maybe I didn't have to worry after all."

"Why's that?"

With a shrug, Kat answered, "Women tend to fall head over heels for you. Even when they don't win your heart, they still give you their devotion. Look at Melanie or Gayle. They're your most loyal followers."

"Melanie is my executive assistant and fifty-four years old." Dean almost rolled his eyes.

"And Gayle is one of your right hands and married with children. I know." Kat picked up the drink cans. "Just saying."

"Your theory is flawed. At least one woman didn't give her loyalty to me." He didn't expect the bitterness to still sting.

Kat's teasing smile faded. "Aww, I didn't mean to dig that up."

Dean brushed it off with an indifferent shake of his head.

"It's been three years, Dean. You've got to move on." Kat touched his arm with her free hand. "She was never right for you."

A short laugh escaped him. "And what kind of woman do you deem right for me?"

"Not our guest!" Kat doubled down on her first point. "She's too self-reliant. A loner. She carved a successful career out of solo traveling since she was eighteen. She's like the female version of you. You'd be butting heads constantly. I mean, you guys duked it out from the first second you laid eyes on each other."

Dean saw Kat's logic. But at the same time, no woman had pushed back at him like Rae had. And even for a man of very few words, no woman had rendered him speechless just for being.

It was probably best he stayed away from Miss Rae Allen.

"You have nothing to worry about, Kat." With his mind settled and the beer in his hands, Dean started heading back out. "I'm much too busy for a challenge. You know I like my women tamed and declawed."

Kat's eyes followed her brother as he slipped out of the kitchen and rejoined the family on the deck. He started chatting with their nephews.

Damn it. Did I blow it? Kat pursed her lips as she assessed the situation.

She'd felt the strong invisible current between Dean and Rae from the first time she'd been in the same room with them. And today, even though Dean barely said a word to Rae, Kat noticed his gaze would often land on her. The way he watched her movement had been one of fascination. But how long would it last?

Her concern about Dean's brief liaison with women was genuine. The man never had to work for a woman's affection. Kat thought perhaps it was why he easily moved on to the next girl. They didn't hold his interest long enough.

Dean was goal-oriented. He needed a constant challenge. A yes-sir-whatever-you-say type of a woman would never do for him. Kat was sure he'd almost married Leighton only because marriage had been his goal at that point. She didn't wish her brother humiliation, but thank god Leighton was smart enough to walk away from that. That union would've been a colossal mistake.

On the other hand, Rae had shown she could hold her own against Dean. Other women would trip on their feet to get on Dean's good side if they got the welcome he'd given Rae—even if the fault wasn't theirs. Rae had called him an ass. For some reason, Dean respected her for it. And by marking her forbidden, Kat had bolstered Rae's appeal even more.

With a grin, Kat walked out to the deck. She handed the ginger ale cans to Graham and Andrew and witnessed in real time how Dean's eyes were involuntarily drawn to Rae when she came out from a door on the other side of the deck.

The second their eyes clashed, electricity buzzed in the air. It felt somewhat volatile, Kat thought with a big smile.

You might say you're too busy for a challenge, brother. But I don't think you can resist.

Six

New York City, New York—July

"Your sister's on line one," Melanie, Dean's assistant, announced over the intercom.

Dean picked up the receiver without averting his eyes from the figures he was studying on his computer screen.

"Katherine," Dean said into the mouthpiece.

"Dean," Kat mockingly copied his tone on the other end of the line.

"Everything all right?" Dean assumed Kat had to inform him of something urgent if she was calling his office.

Kat knew unless it was an emergency, he preferred his family to call or text him on his cellphone outside of work hours. He'd be in one meeting or another most days, so he couldn't give them the appropriate attention. It just happened he'd blocked off this morning to do some desk work.

"More than all right," Kat claimed. "I wouldn't be so impertinent to disturb my loving brother if I didn't have anything important to share."

Dean ignored the sarcasm. "What is it?"

The excitement in Kat's voice traveled through the line clearly. "Have you read the article yet?"

"What article?" Dean replied, still studying the midyear financial report his CFO had just shared.

"On your house in *Homes* magazine," Kat said.

"Since I don't subscribe to that particular magazine, so no, I haven't," he replied distractedly.

"Well, get a copy!" she ordered. "It's fantastic, Dean! Rae completely got what I was trying to do with the house. I couldn't wish for a better feature."

The mention of Rae finally got Dean's attention, and a picture of a redhead at sunrise emerged in his mind.

"Listen to this." Kat read, "Hamilton utilized the best of all combinations in designing this house—from the sunrise and the sunset, the wood and the glass, the classic and the modern. Everything blends perfectly to suit its inspiration—a man who himself is the face of modern sophistication, yet claims his foundation on the simplicity of his hometown."

"She wrote that?" Dean forgot the spreadsheet and sat back in his chair. "That's an improvement from her initial impression of me."

"You were a jerk to her at first," Kat said. "I'm glad she managed to overlook that."

"She's a professional writer. I'm sure she'd dealt with more difficult people than me."

"I don't know. You could be pretty annoying sometimes." Without missing a beat, Kat added, "We need to send her a thank you note."

"We?"

"Yes. I'll mail her one today, and so should you. It is your house she wrote about."

"She was a guest in my house. I didn't get a thank you note," Dean protested.

"She wrote one to me. But then again, I was nice to her from the start." Kat then ordered, "Get a copy of the magazine. Read the article, and please, write the damn note. Don't disappoint me, brother."

Before Dean could tell Kat what he thought of her threat, she hung up. He blew an irritated breath and pushed a button to call Melanie.

"Yes, Dean?"

"Can you get me a copy of the newest issue of *Homes* magazine, please?"

"I'll send someone right away."

Melanie was nothing if not efficient. Dean was reading the article within the hour.

It was quite a feature, with full-page and whole-spread photos giving the best views of the house. There was also a picture of Kat looking proud and happy.

Kat was right. It was a glowing article. He supposed that when a property was featured in such a magazine, they would highlight what was great about it. However, Rae had successfully captured the feeling he knew Kat had wanted to portray. Without much detail, she'd also injected him into the article—just enough to give Kat the credibility he'd wished for.

He flipped the pages forward and found the contributors' page. There was a black and white photograph of Rae laughing next to a paragraph about her. He read:

Rae's love for travel has led her to appreciate architectural beauties worldwide. From her childhood home in the Midwest to the high-rises of Manhattan, or from a little cottage in Ireland to the Taj Mahal in Agra, she finds every structure tells a story. While she shares her travels directly with her millions of readers through her channels, she regularly contributes to Homes *and other lifestyle and travel publications.*

Miss Rae Allen was one busy woman. She was probably out exploring a different part of the globe right now. He reasoned that a note would get lost somewhere anyway. So, why bother?

Writing to Rae meant reestablishing their brief connection, and he didn't need that. He'd wondered about her only once or twice in the past two months. Buying a large share of a Korean-based company as a part of their expansion to Asia had occupied his time. Still, it was odd that she'd popped into his head at all after saying goodbye that weekend in Georgia.

Dean shook his head in disbelief. His mother taught him better.

Just write the damn note.

Dean took out a piece of his personal stationery and started writing. Five minutes later, he called Melanie in and gave her the sealed envelope.

"Please have this delivered to *Homes* magazine," he requested.

When Melanie left his office, Dean sat in his chair pondering if he'd broken his promise to his sister. He'd thanked Rae for the wonderful article, but he probably ought not to have suggested dinner.

He only extended the invitation so he could thank her on Kat's behalf in person.

The decision to accept was entirely up to her.

Rae was pleased to get a call from Katherine Hamilton yesterday. Kat had told her she was so excited that she'd needed to convey her gratitude directly. It was good to hear the joy in Kat's voice. She didn't hear that genuine happiness in a grown adult very often.

Kat's enthusiasm wasn't a surprise to Rae, but receiving an ivory envelope bearing Dean Rowland's name was. Inside, on beautiful linen-textured paper, he wrote a short appreciation of the write-up about his sister's work in a slanted bold script.

That was decent of him and would've been enough. The dinner invitation confused her. She honestly didn't expect to ever hear from Dean Rowland again after she'd left his house last April. She'd sworn he'd erased any memory of her from his mind to not waste any precious brain cells the minute she'd driven away. And he hadn't popped into Rae's head since, either.

Well...maybe once or twice, Rae grudgingly admitted.

Rae recalled her last night in Gainesville. His family had just left, and it was just the two of them in the house. She would've excused herself for the night if she hadn't needed his approval to use his name in the article. She'd been low-key miffed by a chat between Dean and Kat that she'd overheard earlier that afternoon.

The context of the conversation was lost to Rae, but she'd heard Kat saying something about her and Dean butting heads. Dean's flippant response had clarified what he'd really thought of her. And it'd stung. But she was a professional. So what if the man had nicked her ego? She'd show him that women like her got their jobs done.

Rae had been agreeable when she'd accepted the glass of bourbon Dean had offered as they'd sat for a nightcap. She'd also used her most amiable tone when she'd breached the subject of revealing him as property owner for the feature.

Dean had looked at her over the rim of his glass—his eyes sharp. "I don't want my name to overshadow Kat's accomplishment."

The man was irritating, but obviously, he cared a lot for his family.

"I think Kat's work speaks for itself," Rae had replied.

An amused smile had formed on his face. "You really think your editor won't focus the headline on me once they know I own this house?"

"I can't guarantee that," Rae had honestly answered. "But I can make sure your name will highlight Kat's work instead of dimming her shine."

His expression hadn't betrayed him, but she'd felt his skepticism. "Why do you need to mention my name at all? If you focus on Kat's design, it doesn't matter who owns the house."

"You're right. I can simply write about Kat's technical and aesthetic decisions, but it'll lack a soul."

Dean had half-smiled at her choice of word. "The house has a soul?"

"In a way, every house does. Construction on its own is only brick and mortar. Or, in this case, wood, steel, and glass. But Kat put her love and admiration for her brother—you—into every part of this house. She infused soul into the house with her vision of you, with what she hopes this house can be for you."

The jesting smile disappeared into a tightening of his jaw as Dean digested her words.

"I can see you love your sister," Rae had added. "And you're very proud of who she's become."

"Extremely."

"So, I assume you believe in her. In her ability and skills?"

"Absolutely."

"Then there's nothing wrong with lending your light to boost her in her earned spotlight. I'll thread you in delicately to bring out Kat's brilliant artistry. Not every architect could do what she did here."

Dean had shaken his head in doubt. Rae would also be skeptical about how the press would position him in coverage if she were him.

"I'm not salaried by *Homes*," Rae had reasoned. "I'm actually doing this for a favor for their editor-in-chief. We're good friends. You can trust me when I say that Kat and the house will be the stars."

"I don't trust many people, Miss Allen," Dean had retorted. "Especially someone I've been acquainted with for less than forty-eight hours."

Rae should've expected that response. But she hadn't given up.

"Fair enough. I suppose I could keep your name out of it. I'll hint at the characteristics of the unknown owner Kat pulled inspiration from as if I was writing about the castle in *Beauty and the Beast*." Rae had dramatically shrugged. "It would give an air of mystery to the whole thing instead of the wholesome family bond I was going for."

"You'll write me up as a secretive eccentric hermit?" Dean had pursed his lips, but his eyes had lit with amusement.

"Won't be my first choice. I prefer the supportive, loving, and inspiring brother angle myself."

"You play dirty, Miss Allen."

"I play smart, Mr. Rowland." Rae's eyes had been dead straight on his. "You see, having claws give me an edge."

Rae wouldn't have known her arrow had hit the bullseye if not for a flash of recognition in his eyes. He'd acknowledged it seconds later—not in words, but with a slow smile and his approval to reveal his ownership.

As he'd predicted, Susan had wanted to refocus the article with an additional feature on the media mogul. But Rae had managed to stay true to her promise and used all of her influence to keep Dean as more of a supporting cast to Kat's star while still satisfying Susan's needs. After the bravado she'd displayed with him, she'd better deliver.

And she did. So, why would Dean want to see her for dinner?

Despite her reservations, Rae was intrigued by Dean Rowland. It was apparent he cared for and loved his family. And Rae always had a soft spot for that kind of man. Even if he had his flaws and didn't even like her. But she'd been certain she'd earned a bit of respect that last night.

As a businesswoman, Rae believed in never burning bridges—especially with someone as prominent as Dean. But she was also sure meeting him for dinner was like flirting with a live wire.

Making her decision, Rae scribbled a reply. After arranging to have her note couriered back to him, she'd shelved Dean Rowland in her memory bank like all her exciting experiences.

Seven

Rae grabbed a flute of champagne from the bar and started patrolling Club Echo's sizeable main floor perimeter. The light was dim, the patrons were shoulder to shoulder on the floor swaying to the melodic music playing on stage, and Rae felt so out of place.

She stretched herself to full height on four-inch heels and scanned the mezzanine level, hoping to find her friends. But between the low lighting and the crowd, it was hopeless. They might be backstage anyhow.

Rae placed her champagne on the small standing table near her and checked her phone to see if Brandon had replied to her text telling him where she was waiting. Before she unlocked the device, an arm snaked around her waist from behind and pulled her against a male body. Rae squealed in surprise but stopped short of elbowing the man in the ribs when she recognized the laugh.

"Are you nuts? I could've hurt you!" Rae spun around to Brandon, who grinned at her.

"I missed you, too," Brandon replied with a laugh. "I've been away for two months, and I don't even get a hug?"

Rae jumped into his arms and squeezed her best friend. "How was the tour? The pictures look awesome. I almost wish I were with you guys."

"You could've come."

"I said almost." Rae stepped back. "Joining you guys on tour once was enough."

"Oh, c'mon. We had tons of fun then! If not for you sharing about our road trip and shows and mobilizing our fans to come out and support us two years ago, we wouldn't have caught the Aquarius deal. And we wouldn't be here tonight, celebrating their tenth anniversary."

Rae always thought Brandon exaggerated her role in the band's success. They'd accumulated an enormous fan base as an indie band, and their popularity had made the tour possible. Rae had thought it would be a cool collaboration if she'd traveled with them. And it'd been an epic trip. Their followers had tripled during that summer.

"The accommodations this time were much more comfortable." Brandon winked.

"Anything would be better than squeezing in a van with five guys," Rae retorted. The fifth guy was the band's manager, Martin. "Besides, you had Frances this time."

At the mention of his girlfriend's name, Brandon's smile wavered. "Well, she left when we were in Colorado."

Rae frowned. "What happened? That would've only been midway through the tour."

Brandon shrugged. "Maybe it was too much for her. Anyway, we broke up."

"What?"

"I knew it was coming. She said I wasn't there enough for her."

"What the hell? You were attached by the hips for six months straight."

"I think she meant emotionally, not physically." Brandon messed his hair with his fingers absently—a sign of his confusion.

"That's BS. You're the most emotionally available man I know," Rae vehemently stood up for her friend.

"Yeah, well...I thought inviting her on the tour would help us get closer, but it did the opposite."

The grin on Brandon's face didn't fool Rae. Despite his rocker image, Brandon wouldn't take a breakup lightly. Instinctively, Rae leaned in and hugged him. "I'm sorry, Brandon."

"Thanks. I'm fine."

She looked up at his face. "Are you really, though?"

"Yeah, definitely," he assured her with a grin. "You know me."

Yes, she did. Brandon had been as close to a brother as she'd ever had. Even after their band became a success, Brandon hadn't changed much. Except for the better haircut, he was still easygoing, good-natured, and never took himself too seriously.

Understanding that he didn't want to dwell on Frances, Rae changed the subject. "Where are the others?"

"They were just behind me." The three other members of Canis Major materialized from the crowd as if on cue.

"Hey, share some of that love." Curtis, the tallest guy in the band and Brandon's oldest friend, spread his arms to envelop Rae in them.

"I missed you guys." Rae kissed Curtis' cheek and then embraced Justin and Ram. "Life is pretty dull without you boys around."

"Oh, come on." Justin narrowed his eyes. "We heard you've been driving up and down the coast all month. You should've just come with us."

"All that driving by yourself couldn't be more fun than hanging out with us," Ram, the drummer, added.

"Of course not." Rae good-naturedly replied. "You're leaving again next Sunday, right?"

"Yeah, we have some promos to do this week. Then we'll be off to Europe for a month," Brandon replied.

"Europe, here we come again!" Curtis exclaimed. "Can't believe we're hitting Europe twice within ten months."

"You guys have worked hard for that," Rae pointed out.

"And thanks to these guys, we can conquer the world," Justin added.

"Before you do that, Marco Polo, we should get backstage," Ram reminded. "We're up soon."

"Right." The other three guys nodded. As Aquarius' current top band, naturally, Canis Major would take the stage tonight.

"You'll be alright?" Brandon asked Rae.

"Of course." Rae waved them off. "I'll just be here cheering you on."

Rae wished the guys had brought dates so she wouldn't have to stand alone. She looked around the room again. The place was more packed than it'd been ten minutes ago. Rae started feeling like a sardine in a can, but that wasn't why she was a little anxious. Or was it excited?

There was a big chance a certain man might be there. Aquarius Music was one of his companies, after all. But why would she care if Dean Rowland was here? Apart from the note he'd sent a couple of months ago, she'd had no more communications with the man. But somehow, knowing he might be at the same place made her both apprehensive and pumped simultaneously.

What the hell is wrong with you? Rae chastised herself and stopped scanning the room for him.

She was sure he wouldn't even remember her if she hit him with a brick.

On the mezzanine level, within one of the club's VIP sections, Dean Rowland stood with Gayle Harris, the head of Aquarius Music, and Robert Monroe, his VP of communications. Robert was in the middle of reminding him of the speech he was about to deliver. Dean half-tuned him out. He knew the key messages by heart; he could deliver them in his sleep.

He took a sip of his champagne and scanned the place decorated in black and light gold trims, the colors of Aquarius. There were two stages on opposite sides of the main floor. Bleu Collins, Aquarius' newest singer-songwriter, was on one of the stages, playing piano and singing from her newly released debut album. The mood on the floor was light. But the night was young still. The party would be filled with numerous performances of different sounds, and the atmosphere would change.

The soft lighting added to the ambiance. Guests in designer clothes and fancy baubles completed it. Dean was taking a mental note of people he'd need to personally say hello to when a familiar face caught his eye. A face he hadn't seen for some time but, for some reason, had stayed in his memory.

Standing among Aquarius Music's highest selling band was the sassy Rae Allen. She looked chummy with the band members, especially with the front man. Dean noted the affectionate body language between the two. The urge to march down to them—*to do what exactly?*—just came out of nowhere. He found it unsettling.

"Dean, good of you to grace my club with your business." The voice of his best friend, Chris, came from Dean's side.

Turning to the blond man dressed impeccably in a dark blue suit, Dean replied, "Thank Gayle. It's her show. I had nothing to do with this."

"Without your vision in the first place, we wouldn't be here." Gayle raised her champagne flute to Dean.

"And without Chris' initial investment in my wild idea more than a decade ago, we wouldn't have gotten ahead of the race and be where we are now." Dean tipped his flute to Chris.

They'd met at college. Two young men with different backgrounds and upbringing: Dean from a humble working-class family and Chris from a long line of wealthy hoteliers. They'd immediately clicked over their visions of the future.

"It was one of my best investments since it's returned ten times over. My grandfather—may he rest his soul—would've approved that I didn't squander my inheritance." Chris clinked his glass with the rest of them and drank.

"Yes, this is exactly the feeling you want to convey in your speeches," Robert interjected. "Tap on that sense of jubilee we all just share. It's almost time."

Dean's left eyebrow rose in question. "Are you trying to tell me something about my speech delivery, Robert?"

"I have notes. You can be a little flat sometimes." Robert nodded vigorously, not intimidated at all by Dean's scrutiny.

Dean laughed. "Fair enough. Let's do our job before Robert bursts an artery."

Before he followed his team and Chris out, Dean swept his gaze to where he'd seen Rae earlier, but she was gone. He quickly scanned the immediate vicinity, but she'd disappeared. Realizing what he was doing, he wondered when he'd become obsessed with a redhead he hardly knew?

"Dean, you're coming?" Gayle inquired.

"Right behind you."

Refocusing his head on his task tonight, Dean trailed after Gayle. He'd do his duty: a little speech, brief interviews with certain media, and smile toward the camera. Publicity was a part of the responsibilities and expectations that came with being the face of the company he'd built from the ground up. Unfortunately, sometimes it happened whether he liked it or not. But tonight, he let Robert usher him to where he was expected to be.

Eight

When Bleu wrapped up her set, the club got darker except for the soft golden glow of the ambiance lighting. A DJ pumped out an energetic number that picked up a roar from the audience, and the floor started to move with the music.

It was loud with an incessant beat that drove dancers to match their movement to it and drove Rae to the protection of the ladies' room. No offense to the DJ, but dance beats gave her a splitting headache. She'd rather listen to Ram's drumming all day than that.

Taking her time in the restroom, Rae returned to the main room only to find the lights now aimed at a stage where a tall, charismatic man was giving a light speech. He hardly resembled the man she'd met in Georgia. In jeans and a T-shirt, Dean Rowland had the devil-may-care brooding good looks, but wearing a sharp dark suit and clean-shaven, he was captivating. The crowd was riveted by his magnetism, and the ladies were particularly charmed by the hint of a southern drawl in his voice.

Rae couldn't take her eyes off him.

After delivering a brief, witty speech praising both the talent and executives of Aquarius, Dean passed the stage back to the host, who proceeded to get the crowd ready for the next performance. He disappeared from her sight, swallowed by his people, guests, entertainment media, and photographers.

With that many people between them, Rae reasoned she and Dean would never get close enough to where she'd be obligated to say hello. He'd definitely stick with the VIPs. Her shoulders relaxed at the thought.

When Canis Major got on the stage, Rae felt at ease enough to sway to the fun-loving fast number they were playing. The fine champagne flowing in her bloodstream likely helped.

She'd love to join the younger crowd closer to the stage, but with her high heels and short dress, she chose a safer distance. To her delight, Brandon cued her favorite song from their latest album. It had been on the top-ten list for the past few weeks. It was a beautiful song about being rescued by love. Watching him sing the song and remembering his recent breakup made her feel sad for him.

"I would've never pegged you as a groupie," a low voice spoke close to her ear, sending shivers down her spine in an involuntary response. Her head whipped around, and she found Dean next to her.

"Hello, Rae."

His presence rendered Rae speechless.

He cocked his chin at her. "What? No comeback?"

"I'm not a groupie." She said the first thing in her head rather indignantly. Being mistaken for a Canis Major groupie was a pet peeve of hers.

The man laughed. It only took him five seconds to remind Rae how infuriating he was.

Quickly pulling herself together, she started again with a steady voice, "Congratulations on your success. You throw quite a party."

Dean gave a graceful nod. "Thank you, but I can't take credit for the party. I just got dressed and went where they told me to go."

"Well, you clean up nicely."

"So do you. You look lovely." His eyes focused on her, making Rae suddenly warm.

They hadn't seen each other for months, but after only a minute, it felt like they had been transported back to his house again, just the two of them, sizing each other up. Except for this time, it felt intimate, though they were surrounded by people and loud music. Having to talk closer to each other's ears, feeling his breath against her cheek might have something to do with it.

Dean leaned into her. "It's a pleasant surprise to see you here."

Rae's brow cocked in disbelief. "That's progress, considering your feelings about my presence the last time."

He took the soft jab with a rueful smile but moved on. "Are you here with them then?" He gestured to her friends on stage.

"Yes. Since they've been on tour this summer, I haven't seen them much."

Dean's lips parted as if he was about to ask more, but they clamped closed.

Feeling compelled to fill in the void, Rae said, "I didn't think our paths would cross tonight."

"You wouldn't have said hi?"

"If I ran into you, maybe." Rae hesitated, then added, "Honestly, I didn't think you'd remember me."

Dean's sharp eyes rested on her face. "We spent a weekend together at my house. Of course I remember you."

Rae felt the blood rushing to her face. He made that weekend they spent in Georgia sound more intimate than it'd been. Or maybe she just read too much into his words.

Why the hell was she all flustered now? Just because he looked dapper and was standing close enough that she could feel his heat?

"I'm flattered you remembered me enough to say hello," Rae graciously replied. "But please don't let me hold you. You must be in demand tonight."

Suddenly, Dean made a quick move that placed her body into the crook of his arm. The abrupt close proximity surprised her, and she stumbled back, but he was fast to steady her and spun her with him as if they were waltzing. Startled by the maneuver, Rae looked up to his face, puzzled. She pushed a hand against his chest to create space between them. He was focused on something somewhere over his left shoulder. She followed his gaze, only to glimpse a photographer aiming his lens toward them before Dean once again pivoted and blocked her with his whole body.

"Are you shooing me away at my own party?" Without explaining what just happened, he continued the conversation.

"I wouldn't dare."

Looking down at her with a very sexy, barely-there smile, Dean retorted, "Yes, you would."

Almost awestruck by the warmth in his gaze, Rae broke eye contact and pushed against his chest—a very firm one, she noticed.

"Do you mind?" she asked. "What was that about?"

"Sorry. I was trying to avoid giving a curious photographer bait for gossip. Trust me, you wouldn't want to be caught in a picture with me." He stepped back, giving her space. "I have to take my leave of you for now. Duty calls."

Rae couldn't think of a response. As quietly as he'd appeared, he slipped away, leaving her unsure of what had happened. Noticing her heart beating faster, she decided she must've had too much champagne and better put something into her stomach. She stopped a passing waiter and munched on some delicious caviar-topped hamachi tartar on bib lettuce.

As she chewed her food, her brain digested the last few minutes. She'd thought there was a chance she might see Dean Rowland tonight. And there might've been a slim chance they'd run to each other. But she hadn't expected it to be that interesting. Or...dare she say...flirtatious?

Gayle Harris was chatting with Chris about his new venture when Robert rushed toward them. His type-A personality shone through.

"We should get over to the press room," Robert instructed without preamble. "Where's Dean?"

"He excused himself earlier but should be back shortly," Gayle answered.

Robert pursed his lips as he checked his watch. Gayle could virtually hear his internal monologue, going through the detailed event timeline he'd scheduled for Dean and her. Tonight's event ran smoothly due to Robert's almost general-like command and his team's excellent work.

"He's down there." Chris pointed to the main floor, not too far below where they stood. "He's talking to someone."

"Who?" Robert looked over the banister to check. "It better not be a stray reporter, I swear to God."

"Is that..." Chris started, then paused to take a better look. "I think that's Rae Allen."

"Why is that name familiar?" Robert frowned.

"Travel writer. Her debut solo-travel memoir hit the New York Times best-seller list last Christmas," Chris informed him. "I've been following her for years. I'd love to invite her to the resort."

Chris was just telling Gayle about the series of high-end boutique resorts he was developing in exotic parts of the globe. The first recently opened in a remote corner of Bali, the beautiful destination island in the Indonesian archipelago. She already planned her next family vacation there.

"Her writing is down to earth, relatable. She's covered everything from the best humble eatery to the most luxurious accommodations," Chris continued. "She doesn't simply portray the surface of the place she visits. She dives into the community. She talks to the people. You get more than pretty pictures when you read her work; you're immersed in it."

"Sounds like you're a fan," Gayle noted as she strained her neck to better look at the woman. She couldn't see her clearly as Dean's tall figure blocked most of Gayle's vantage point. But suddenly, Dean put his arm around the woman and spun. Gayle's eyes popped wide at what she witnessed.

Are they dancing? Dean, dancing? Who is this woman? Gayle's curiosity flipped into precautionary mode.

"Smooth," Chris commented as they watched the couple below.

"What is he doing?" Robert's scrunched brows showed he was as perplexed as Gayle by their boss' change of demeanor. "Is that a smile? Why can't he smile like that at the reporters?"

"Do any of the reporters look like that?" Chris glanced at Robert with a knowing smile.

"What did you say her name is again?" Gayle asked Chris.

"Rae Allen."

Suddenly the name clicked in Gayle's brain. Her road-trip-tour collaboration with Canis Major a few years back had put the band on their radar in the first place.

"Allen!" Robert exclaimed. "Yes, she wrote an article for *Homes* magazine on Dean's lake house in Georgia a couple of months ago. I saw it on the weekly coverage report. I asked Dean about it because it didn't go through my team, and every media interaction must go through my department. He said it was mainly his sister's deal, but he approved it personally.

"The article was excellent for Katherine, but it humanized our stoic leader, so I didn't mind it," he concluded.

"I wonder how she managed that?" Gayle thought out loud.

"Just look at him right now." Chris grinned.

There was an aura of protectiveness in how Dean's arms surrounded her. In their seven-year business relationship and friendship, Gayle had only seen Dean like that with his family, closest friends, and perhaps his ex-fiancée. But she'd never seen Dean look at a woman the way he was looking at this Rae Allen—with fascination. Not even at Leighton.

Maybe she was reading too much into it. It was pretty dim. Besides, wasn't this woman with Canis Major's front man, Brandon Rossi?

Gayle decided she better keep an eye on the situation. Since Leighton's betrayal, Gayle couldn't help feeling protective of Dean. She was, after all, the one who had introduced and pushed them together. When Leighton had abandoned Dean at the altar, it'd felt as if she'd betrayed Gayle, too.

Though Dean never blamed Gayle for the failed relationship, the guilt didn't escape her. She promised herself she'd never play matchmaker again. Still, she also vowed nobody would hurt her friend the way Leighton had ever again.

Nine

For a full hour, Dean had done interviews that Robert had slotted for him. For another hour, he'd chatted with artists, executives, producers, engineers, and technicians who made Aquarius run smoothly.

He especially enjoyed discussing technological ideas with the engineers because, at the end of the day, these geniuses were the backbone of Aquarius Media Corp. The way they delivered music and other media content directly to the consumers without a middleman had propelled them ahead of competitors a decade ago. Though they'd moved beyond that, Dean continued to push the boundaries.

He could go full geek mode with the engineers all night if half his mind wasn't preoccupied by a certain woman. His encounter with Rae, though brief, left a lasting impression. He found himself searching the crowd for her from time to time. However, as he kept spotting her at Brandon Rossi's side, he grew more curious and annoyed each time she touched the tattooed musician.

Perplexed by his reaction, Dean tried concentrating on the current conversation he was having with Chris. His friend was updating him on the progress of his first resort opening. It'd always been Chris' goal to make his own mark in the hospitality business instead of taking over his family's well-established and world-renowned hotels.

"Based on current reservations, we're averaging eighty percent occupancy through the end of next year." Chris took a sip from his drink with satisfaction. "Soon enough, I can focus on the resorts alone."

"You are selling the clubs, then?" Dean questioned.

"Eventually. They're cash producers, but they were never my main plan. I only got into them because my father would never approve."

Dean knew that. Chris was a hotelier born and bred. He'd spent most of his younger days going from one Sullens' hotel to another, tailing his grandparents and parents while they managed their empire. Until a tragedy had hit the family and he was shipped off to boarding school. Chris had never told him the whole story, but Dean knew Chris' relationship with his father had never been the same since.

"You're saying you're finally ready to embrace your heritage?"

"I've always embraced it. I just don't need to kowtow to my father's standards to do it. I don't want or need the Sullens' hotels. I'm building my own legacy."

Understanding his friend's ambition one hundred percent, Dean saluted Chris with his drink. "Here's to our own legacy."

Chris' smile returned to his always affable face. "Did I see you with Rae Allen earlier tonight?"

Dean stopped drinking his bourbon and eyed Chris from over the glass rim. "You know Rae?"

"I know of her. I'd really love to meet her in person."

He and Chris often shared social and business networks. It was as much an asset as money. Normally, Dean wouldn't hesitate to make an introduction.

"I'm surprised you haven't introduced yourself," Dean replied neutrally.

Chris looked down in the direction Dean had seen Rae last. "You won't mind?"

"Why would I?" Dean knew Chris was fishing.

Chris glanced at him with a half-challenging smile. "You won't have any problem if I go there right now and ask her out?"

Dean loosened his jaw that he'd unconsciously clenched and forced a smile. "I barely know her."

Chris burst into laughter. "You're slipping, old man. You've got to work on your poker face."

When Dean just stared at him, Chris added, "From what I witnessed earlier, I'd say you're more invested in her than you'd admit."

Dean shrugged. "She did a feature on the lake house. That's all."

"Right. That's why you can't keep your eyes off her," Chris shot with a smug, knowing smirk.

Dean couldn't help a small smile. Was he that obvious? *Damn it. I am losing my touch.*

"I hope you got her number. Looks like she's leaving." Chris gestured with his chin in the general direction of the exit.

Dean watched Rae in her deep-sapphire-colored dress with her flowing auburn hair weave through the throng of people. Soon enough, she'd vanish completely.

Crap. Sorry, Kat.

"You'll have to excuse me." Dean practically threw his glass to his grinning friend and bolted to the stairs.

Rae was already through the hallway leading to the main door by the time he descended the stairs. He barely caught a glimpse of her stealthily going around the crowd of paparazzi whose attention was on the late-comers arriving on a flashy Lambo.

Unlike Rae, Dean knew he couldn't slip out unnoticed. Fortunately, Chris had shown him out the side door enough times in the past. The question was, could he catch her before she disappeared for good?

Dean got to the hidden side door in no time. He cracked it open and checked the situation outside. But he hesitated.

What am I doing?

He'd gotten to where he was by being strategic and thoroughly considering every step he'd take. So why was he sneaking out of a club to go after a woman?

Rae had entered his life three months ago and knocked him off balance. He'd ignored the disturbing feeling at his sister's request and just watched Rae drive away. Now, she'd shown up out of nowhere again. There must be a reason for it. He didn't know what it was yet, but his instinct was telling him to find out.

Dean pushed the door open. The first thing he saw was Rae walking on the abandoned sidewalk across from his side of the street. If that wasn't a sign, he didn't know what was.

Rae breathed in relief when she escaped the wall of lenses and blinding flashes barricading her way out. She quickly crossed the partially blocked 50th Street and walked toward 11th Avenue. She couldn't leave behind the commotion of photographers trying to catch stars getting in and out of their rides fast enough.

She was used to sharing parts of her life with her readers, but she couldn't imagine being hounded daily by vultures looking for any scrap to sell to the tabloids. At least she had control of what she put out on her website and other channels.

The boys had their share of paparazzi following them since the band became a rock and roll sensation. Dating a high-demand model, in Brandon's case, also guaranteed the gossip mongers' attention. But his reaction to the breach of privacy was to laugh it off, as he did about almost everything.

Rae doubted Dean Rowland responded to gossip the same way. In fact, he evaded media exposure he or his team didn't control. She could see he didn't enjoy the attention that came with his position. How he'd shielded her from being photographed with him earlier still baffled her. In hindsight, she probably ought to thank him.

He probably just didn't want to be falsely linked to some woman he barely knew. *Don't overthink it.*

Rae shook her head to get rid of thoughts of Dean. She whipped out her cellphone and tapped on a rideshare app to get a car to pick her up a block over, away from the club traffic. But before she could do more, she caught the sound of steps coming behind her.

Traveling solo and living in New York City had taught her to stay vigilant. Palming her phone in her fist with her thumb ready by the emergency button, Rae glanced back to check if it was a threat coming toward her or just a harmless passerby. To her shock, it was neither.

"Please, keep walking and don't attract their attention." Dean Rowland fell into step next to her. His eyes darted toward the crowd still visible behind them.

Rae, flabbergasted, refused to budge. "I'd usually do the opposite if a strange man accosted me on the street in the middle of the night."

Dean turned to her, a frown forming on his face. "Under different circumstances, you definitely should. But you shouldn't be walking alone through Hell's Kitchen at midnight in the first place."

Her jaw dropped. "Excuse me?"

"Shouldn't your date take you home? The least he could do is get you a ride," he insisted.

Temper now flared on top of Rae's confusion. She stepped into Dean's personal space and confronted him. "First of all, I am perfectly able to get myself home. Second, who the hell are you telling me what I should and shouldn't do?"

He looked at her as if she was crazy. "It's not safe."

"This is a safe enough neighborhood. Besides, I can take care of myself. In fact, you better give me a damn good reason why I shouldn't Krav Maga your ass right now?"

Dean obviously didn't expect the physical threat because it was the first time Rae ever saw him fail to school his expression. The stunned look on his face was comical; she almost laughed.

His gaze flew back to the club in the background, then returned to her as if reassessing the situation.

"I'm sorry." Dean lifted his hands up, palms open in a peace offering. "This isn't what I meant to do when I saw you leaving. I swear I'm not trying to do anything funny."

"What are you doing then?" Rae demanded.

"Can we talk and walk, please?" He waved his arm toward the direction Rae was walking earlier.

"No. Not until you explain yourself."

He dropped his arm to his side and sighed in resignation. "I saw you leave alone. Call me old-fashioned, but I didn't think it was safe for a woman to walk by herself at this time of night. I thought I'd offer you a ride home."

Rae narrowed her eyes but relaxed her stance. "Next time, start with the ride offer and avoid being a chauvinistic ass while you're at it."

"You know this is the second time you called me an ass," Dean pointed out.

Moving around him, Rae started walking. "I must bring out this delightful side of you."

He laughed and caught up with her in two steps.

"Look, I appreciate the offer, but you'll be going the wrong way." Rae unlocked her phone again to order the Uber. "I'm going downtown. Don't you have a Park Avenue penthouse or something?"

"Actually, I'm also going downtown. I live in Tribeca."

Rae ignored that information while waiting for a ride option through the app. "Thanks, anyway. I'm getting a ride at the corner of 11th Avenue."

"Okay." Dean nodded, but Rae noticed he continued to walk with her.

"Seriously, I'll be fine."

"Humor me. I'll stay with you until you get your ride."

"It's unnecessary, but suit yourself." Rae shrugged.

They walked in silence while Rae returned her attention to the rideshare app.

"May I ask why are you going home without your date? You came with Brandon Rossi, didn't you?"

Rae's brows drew together. "Brandon knows I can take care of myself. Besides, they still have another set to play, and I'm tired."

"Why did you leave your own party early? As the host, don't you have to stay?" she counter-questioned.

"I've fulfilled my obligations. And technically, I'm not the host," Dean replied.

But Rae was only half listening and sighed in frustration. The app hadn't given her ride options yet.

"Let me get you home," Dean offered again as he pulled out his phone and tapped the face. "It's Saturday night. You could be waiting for a while."

Rae hesitated to accept a ride with Dean Rowland. It wasn't safety that worried her. He'd had several opportunities in Georgia if he'd wanted to harm her. She was reluctant because of the same reason she'd declined his dinner invitation before—self-preservation.

"Don't you trust me?" Dean asked, a challenging half-smile on his face.

Rae gave the question a short laugh. She'd told Dean he could trust her last spring, and he'd given it to her. Now, he was playing the same hand.

"I don't usually trust any man I've been acquainted with for less than forty-eight hours," Rae replied.

"Technically, we've known each other for months," Dean corrected. "And you've braved sleeping under the same roof with me for two nights. I think a fifteen-minute ride home is nothing, especially for a Krav Maga master."

A full laugh escaped Rae, and Dean's half-smile turned full.

"You play dirty, Mr. Rowland."

"Something I learned from a worthy opponent."

They reached 11th Avenue, and a large dark blue sedan was waiting at the curb. Dean opened the back door, and a white-haired gentleman at the driver's seat glanced back with a smile.

"That's Tom, my chauffeur extraordinaire," Dean introduced. "Your chaperone, if you still have concerns."

"Good morning, miss," Tom greeted since it was after midnight.

"Tom, this is Miss Rae Allen," Dean said. "We're going to drive her home."

"Excellent, sir." Tom beamed at Rae.

With a resigned smile, Rae slid into the plush car. This might turn out to be a simple ride, but somehow she had a feeling it might change her life.

Ten

"So, tell me, Tom. Is it your employer's habit to give strange women a ride home?" Rae inquired as the car started moving.

"Mr. Rowland lends me out to his female staff who need a ride home late all the time, miss," Tom said. "And you're no stranger, miss. You're the lady who wrote the wonderful article on Mr. Rowland's home in Georgia."

One corner of Dean's lips lifted when he saw Rae's expression. Obviously, she didn't expect Tom's answer.

And Tom, being Tom, kept going, "Mr. Rowland showed me the article. He was very proud. We were all excited for Miss Kat."

"Oh." Rae glanced at Dean, looking perplexed. "And you remember me from an article published a month ago?"

"Of course," Tom replied easily. "Where are we going, miss?"

"Uhm...the Village," Rae answered and rattled off a short direction.

Then she turned her head to Dean, her brows still drawn together.

"Besides being a great driver, Tom doesn't forget faces and names. It's incredible, really," Dean explained. "And apparently, you made an impression on him."

"Huh." Rae sat back, digesting the information.

It was entertaining to see Rae speechless for once. It also gave Dean a chance to think of a clever way to see her again. It was a "third strike, you're out" kinda thing. To his bafflement, he wasn't sure how to proceed because he was certain she'd reject him outright if he asked her on a date.

"This night has taken an unexpected turn." Dean heard Rae talking almost to herself as she looked out the window.

"I'd agree with that," Dean echoed her sentiment. "It's safe to say I didn't expect to run into you tonight."

She turned to look at him. "Well, it's safe to say I didn't expect to find you running after me on the street, either."

"I didn't run." Dean scoffed. "I might've walked swiftly, but only because you were far ahead of me."

Rae raised a brow at him with a smirk. "You were running."

"Rushing might be a better word," Dean allowed. "I didn't want the cameras to catch me leaving." A slight grin involuntarily broke on his face. "It felt good to give them the slip."

"Oh, I see. I thought you rushed after me because you were concerned for my safety." Rae narrowed her eyes at him.

"Well, you were the catalyst for the escape," Dean added.

"So, I'm an excuse?" she questioned.

Dean looked her in the eye. "No. The reason."

He could've sworn her pupils flared in reaction to his words.

Keep it light, Dean cautioned himself. The banter had gone from teasing to intense too fast. He didn't want to scare her when he'd barely gained any ground.

To his relief, Rae brushed over his last words and commented on his earlier statement instead. "I can understand the media's interest in you. I saw you on that stage earlier tonight. You have something that people pay attention to—a quiet charisma. It's a gift to have."

Dean's eyes widened. "Is that a compliment coming from you?"

"Just stating an observation," Rae gave a nonchalant shrug. "Though personally, I've experienced more of your hostility than charisma."

Dean let out a low groan. "Oh, I think you deserved that treatment. You were trespassing."

Rae laughed. "I had a good reason to be there."

"Let's reverse roles. What would you do if you were in the pool and I was looming over you out of nowhere?"

She pursed her lips at his question. But after a few seconds, she conceded, "Fine, I'll give you that."

Dean smiled at the little victory, but Rae wasn't finished. "But that weekend, I had the impression you didn't want me there. So, why do you suddenly even care about my safety tonight? A woman you didn't even particularly like."

Rae watched Dean's smile flatten to his more familiar pensive manner.

"Why do you think I didn't like you?" he returned the question.

"Oh, just from your welcoming demeanor."

"You weren't exactly warm and cuddly, Miss Allen," Dean countered.

No, Rae hadn't been particularly pleasant to him, either. His rudeness had triggered her defense mechanism. But she'd also felt such an instant strong pull toward him that she might've overcompensated in her effort to neutralize her attraction.

"I suggest we bury the hatchet and start over," Dean suggested, his tone diplomatic. "Friends?"

Rae tilted her head to the side. "You want to be friends with me?"

"Yes. I read up a little bit on you and find you—what you do—interesting."

Rae's left eyebrow rose with skepticism. "Why? What I do is no more special than what many others do."

"I disagree. You're one of the trailblazers who found ways to utilize the internet to carve a career out of it. And to have started at eighteen, that's admirable."

"Thank you. But if anyone deserves to be called a trailblazer, it'd be you. You've not only built a career out of your ingenious vision of tapping the internet, but you've also built an empire."

"Well, I've had help. But my company simply created a new marketplace on the web by creating technology highways to get content to consumers on demand. What you've done is different. You've attracted a following. It's rare for anyone to have such a loyal fanbase in our current attention-deficient society. People are fickle these days, but your engagement is stable, even continuously increasing. People just love you," Dean concluded.

There was admiration in his voice that Rae didn't expect. Her eyebrow rose even higher in suspicion. "Surprised that anyone could like me?"

Dean barked a short laugh. "No."

"Oh, c'mon. You can be honest. I mean, I was shocked to see that you could be charming."

"Oh, most women find Mr. Rowland very charming, miss," Tom chimed in.

"I'm not sure I can trust you as a character witness, Tom," Rae retorted. "You're on his payroll."

"Mind your own business, Tom," Dean chided the driver, but Rae noted his slight grin.

"Of course, sir." The older man winked at them through the rearview mirror.

"As I was saying," Dean continued, "people go to you for travel recommendations. They trust your opinion about a destination. And most importantly, they enjoy the way you tell the stories of the places you visit. I'm surprised you don't have a deal for a TV series with anyone yet."

Rae sat back and wondered where this conversation was going. She was actually in the middle of negotiating for a six-episode show with a streaming network. It wasn't with the Aquarius network, but she imagined if anyone could hear about it before it was signed, it'd be Dean Rowland. But why would he care?

"We should talk," Dean suggested.

Rae looked at him with an unsure smile. "About?"

"A possible collaboration."

Rae blinked. "You're kidding."

"I don't kid." Dean looked at her with what she imagined was his boardroom smile. It was confident, mysterious, and tempting.

Rae couldn't find the words to respond. Thankfully, the car stopped in front of her building and saved her from making rash comments. She pointed at the modest walkup she called home. "This is me."

Dean glanced out and scanned the little brick building. It was a well-maintained structure, with four fully refurbished apartments on a charming little street. She felt lucky to find the cute one-bedroom apartment in a city that was becoming more expensive by the minute. If not for her brilliant financial advisor, who had invested her hard-earned income for the past ten years, she would've never been able to afford to live in Manhattan all these years.

She'd saved plenty when she'd shared the three-bedroom flat with Brandon and Curtis. It'd been fun while it lasted, but the place had grown claustrophobic for her when the boys' girlfriends started coming around. She'd consulted her advisor, and they'd agreed she could more than afford to invest in a property. She wasn't a billionaire like Dean was, but she was comfortable in her own right.

Dean opened his door and stepped out onto the sidewalk. He held out the door open to let Rae slide out.

"Thank you for the ride, Tom." Rae touched the lovely gentleman on the shoulder.

"It was my pleasure, miss. I hope to see you again." Tom smiled politely.

Rae returned the smile with a noncommittal one as she exited the vehicle. She reluctantly accepted Dean's offered hand to assist her. The same sizzle she'd felt running down her spine earlier that night flowed through her arm. She snatched her hand away as soon as she stood steadily on the sidewalk.

"You're all right?" Dean inquired, his face innocent.

"Yes." Rae quickly nodded and rushed up to her door and unlocked it. "Thank you for getting me home safely."

She turned around and found herself literally face to face with Dean. Standing a step below, Dean was now at her eye level. She just managed to swallow a gasp.

"Anytime. About that talk…" Dean started in a slow, low voice.

Man, those intense grey eyes did a number on her balance at one in the morning. Rae couldn't look away. What the hell?

"Are you free tomorrow?" Dean asked.

Rae found she still had some wit within her and replied, "I don't think it's a good idea."

"What's not a good idea?" His brows dropped.

"Us, collaborating."

"Why?" His voice stayed quiet and low.

The simple question stumped Rae because she didn't have a good answer. She finally said, "I'm not interested."

"What are you not interested in? We haven't discussed anything yet." Dean challenged, "You don't strike me as a person who would dismiss something outright without exploring it."

He got her there. And the bastard knew it from the way one corner of his lips quirked. It injected steel back into Rae's spine.

"Fine." Rae used her professional voice. "We can talk, but please note that I've informed you upfront what my answer is."

"Duly noted." His eyes sparkled as he inclined his head to her. "Tomorrow morning."

With that declaration, he turned and skipped down the short stairs to the pavement without warning.

"Wait a minute." Rae reached an arm out, trying to stop him. "Tomorrow?"

Dean opened his car door and looked back at her. "Any prior plans?"

"No, but it's Sunday," she reflexively answered and immediately bit her lip in regret.

Damn it. Rae's nose pinched at her failure to grasp the opportunity to get out of the meet.

"Perfect. We'll do breakfast."

"What?"

"I'll see you bright and early. It'll be like old times." He slid into his car and flashed her a rare full smile.

Rae was flabbergasted that her mouth was forming unintelligible words trying to protest.

"Good night, Rae." Dean shut the car door, and the car started rolling.

With a big huff, Rae walked into her building. It took all of her control not to slam the door and wake up all her neighbors.

What the hell had just happened? The SOB steamrolled her to agree with him.

Oh, he's good.

Rae climbed the stairs to her top-floor apartment with a disgruntled scowl. Dean Rowland had bested her tonight, but tomorrow was another day. She'd blame her inability to outwit him on too much champagne. After a good night's sleep, she'd be back in shape to spar with him.

A smirk appeared on her lips as she entered her apartment.

Oh yeah, I'll be ready.

Eleven

Something was vibrating. The persistent pulsing brought a groan out of Rae, whose head was buried under her pillow. She reached out an arm to feel around for her phone on the nightstand. After knocking something to the floor, her hand found the offending device. She barely peeked from under the pillow to look at the display. With a sleepy sigh, she answered the summons.

"Why didn't you text me last night?" Brandon's voice demanded on the other end of the line.

Rae winced at the reprimand. "Are you seriously calling me this early on a Sunday morning?" She glanced at the clock on her phone display and grumpily added, "It's barely seven."

"I was worried. You didn't reply to my text."

"Sorry, I didn't see it. I must've crashed instantly."

In reality, she'd had difficulty falling asleep because of a certain someone.

"Why are you awake? You must've gotten in late." Rae stretched her limbs.

"Walking home from a diner as we speak. Got hungry, so we went for an early breakfast."

"You guys are crazy." She chuckled. "Glad you had fun."

"It was a great night. You should've stayed longer. You missed some awesome performances and a little drama. I guess the suits lost the big boss. Apparently, he went MIA or something."

Rae's half-asleep brain perked up at that piece of information.

"I'm home," Brandon announced. "I'm gonna crash now. Glad you're okay."

"Call me later so we can make plans before you go back on tour."

"Sure thing."

After hanging up, Rae laid flat on her back, staring at the ceiling with bleary eyes. She could try catching more Zs, but she'd probably just toss and turn while agonizing over what was to come.

I'm not ready.

Rae grumbled, but she kicked the covers off and headed for the shower. An hour later, still in her robe with her freshly washed and dried hair loose, she padded barefoot to the kitchen. Opening her cupboard for some fresh coffee beans, she found an empty jar instead.

Crap.

She opened the fridge. It was also barren of fresh food because she'd forgotten to get groceries after returning from a trip north on Friday. She dumped some unappetizing food past edibility into the trash.

Needing a shot of caffeine first thing in the morning, Rae decided on a quick coffee run. She slapped on some makeup and threw on a breezy white oversized shirt dress, tapered at the waist with a brown braided leather belt. After putting her favorite studs in her ears and a long delicate gold link necklace around her neck, she grabbed her purse, slipped on a pair of sandals, and headed down the stairs.

Rae's brain didn't fully function without that first sip of coffee, but she distinctly recalled Dean mentioning breakfast. What time exactly were they supposed to meet up? Where? He'd managed to befuddle her last night that she hadn't thought about asking for details.

"I'm not going to worry about it," Rae murmured gleefully as she opened the door leading to the street. "Won't be my fault if I miss it."

"Good morning," a masculine voice greeted her.

Rae's jaw dropped in disbelief when she spotted the man responsible for sleep eluding her last night standing at the bottom of her building steps. He looked too awake for her liking and too appealing in a pair of tan chinos and a fitted navy short-sleeved linen shirt. His closely cut hair looked damp and somehow darker, making the smokiness in his eyes shine more in the daylight. He hadn't bothered shaving this morning, leaving a layer of shadow accentuating his jaw. And worst of all, he had that barely-smile of his on his face as if it was natural for him to be there at nine in the morning.

"What are you doing here?" Rae found her voice.

"We have an appointment." He innocently handed her a paper cup. "I got you a latte with one sugar. I hope that's white enough to your liking."

A waft of the delicious aroma of java teased her nose, and Rae almost moaned in pleasure. She was stunned that he remembered how she liked her coffee, but she handed it back to him.

"You taste it first," Rae prompted.

"Pardon?" His forehead crinkled in confusion.

Rae cocked her head. "A girl can't be too careful."

Understanding flashed in his eyes, and she thought she'd finally managed to insult him. She just waited to see what he'd do. She traveled alone for years, and she took her safety seriously. She'd bent some of her rules for him because she didn't get a dangerous vibe from him—at least not the usual kind. But she wouldn't take a drink from a man she barely knew when she hadn't seen it prepared.

Though his exaggerated exhale showed his irritation, Dean took the cup from her and sipped. He cringed almost immediately after gulping a mouthful of coffee.

"Gahh! Yeah, I wouldn't drink that if I were you. I can't even taste the coffee anymore." He handed the cup back to her. "It's just milk."

"I'll ignore that comment because you didn't object to my request." Rae nodded her approval. "I would've bet a month's income that most men would've verbally cursed me and stomped away at this point."

"I'm not most men." He swigged his coffee, probably to wash off the taste of her latte.

I know. Rae pursed her lips, trying not to smile, and took her first sip of coffee with relish.

"Thank you for the coffee. I was just running out to get some," Rae explained.

"Oh, I thought you were trying to evade me."

Rae shrugged. "Hey, it's not my fault you didn't specify the time and place for us to meet."

"I said breakfast. Isn't this around the time when people eat their morning meal?"

"These days, people can eat breakfast whenever they want. Seven, eight, nine. Even midnight." Rae took the final step down to the sidewalk and stood next to him. "Though, on Sundays, people tend to stretch breakfast and call it a brunch instead. That's usually around eleven."

Dean shook his head with a slightly embarrassed smile. "I was gonna call you to nail down the details."

"But..." Rae looked at him expectantly.

He grudgingly admitted. "I forgot to ask for your number."

"These days, there are ways to connect with people without knowing their phone numbers."

"I don't have a personal social media account."

"I see. So you do it the old-fashioned way; you just showed up at a girl's doorstep. These days, people frown upon that."

"Okay, okay." He held up his free hand in surrender. "So, you're saying I'm a dinosaur when it comes to social connections."

"It is bizarre because you're such a tech guy."

"What can I say? I'm like two sides of a coin. I think you said it perfectly. I'm the face of modern sophistication who claims my foundation on the simplicity of my hometown. So, it's totally in line that I love everything about technology, but I prefer traditional methods of human interaction."

Rae laughed at him, quoting her description of him. "Touché."

"How about we continue this conversation at breakfast?" Dean suggested.

"I know just the place." Rae waved her arm forward to lead the way. "There's a great diner a couple of blocks up."

"Perfect." Dean stepped in next to her.

Rae glanced up at Dean as they walked side by side. As if he felt her studying him, he turned his eyes to meet hers with a hint of a smile—just a touch. Rae caught herself from abruptly diverting her eyes but instead returned to her coffee as nonchalantly as possible.

Damn. She was energized now but couldn't tell if the coffee or Dean Rowland had gotten her blood moving.

Twelve

Dean watched Rae bestow her full smile on their waiter as she finished ordering her meal. The guy called her by her first name and was familiar with her coffee order, but he'd waited for the food order. Dean would bet Rae had tried every item on the menu and ordered based on her mood.

When Patrick, the waiter, walked away to ring their order, Rae turned to face him across the small booth. "I love their French toast. I feel like something sweet. Though you can't go wrong with anything you order here. You'll love your omelet."

The neighborhood diner Rae had taken him to was small, and they were lucky they'd walked in when they had. People had flooded in not long after they'd been seated. Now, the place was packed.

"You come here often?" Dean asked.

Rae nodded as she doctored her fresh cup of joe. "It's near, convenient, and happens to be really good. What's your favorite breakfast spot?"

"I don't have one," he said. "I don't eat breakfast much—coffee mostly. A protein bar if I really need something."

She paused before bringing her cup to her mouth and stared at him with furrowed brows. "Really? Then why the sudden urge this morning?"

"Not sure. Seemed like a good idea last night."

Because I didn't want to wait until lunch or dinner to see you again.

"And you seemed to be someone who enjoys breakfast," Dean added.

"I enjoy all meals," Rae declared as if anyone who didn't was crazy. "But meal preference aside, breakfast on a Sunday is a rather unusual time for a business meeting. I don't normally work on Sundays. I have a rule about it."

"Then let's think of this more as a discovery session—an exploration. No business, just us getting to know each other." Dean looked straight into Rae's eyes.

It's not a lie, Dean tried to convince himself. *But still a half-truth*, he admitted.

Rae's expression didn't reveal much, but the clear light blue of her eyes lasered in on him. He should've expected what was to come. Rae Allen never pulled her punches.

"Tell me the truth. The CEO of Aquarius Media Corp doesn't explore a potential project with the likes of me. You have people doing that in their respective businesses. You're much too preoccupied deciding what businesses you could buy to expand your network," Rae deadpanned. "So, what's the real deal here?"

Sweat broke under his shirt a bit. It'd been a long time since anyone could do that. Dean weighed his options. He could continue to feed her his half-truths, but what would that lead to? It was never a good idea to start any relationship—business or otherwise—with duplicity, however innocent it might be. If anyone should've known that, it was him. A thought of Leighton flashed in his mind.

"What I told you is the truth," he started. "I think you can do a great show for a streaming network. Your approach is different. You appeal to the younger crowd dying to explore the world."

He paused and searched Rae for any kind of reaction. She kept her face neutral and waited for him to continue. Dean swallowed. The woman wasn't going to make this easy on him. She was a worthy opponent. But he knew that.

"But you're right. That was only an excuse when I suggested this morning's meeting," Dean admitted.

"So, it was a ruse."

Dean pulled back his shoulders an inch as if he was physically pushed by her words. "A ruse sounds—"

"About right?" Rae pointed out in a don't-bullshit-me tone.

Dean huffed with annoyance and stared straight at her. "The simple truth is I wanted to see you. After Georgia, I never thought we'd see each other again, but we did. Last night. And I believe it happened for a reason."

Rae's pink lips parted, and her pupils dilated with her surprise. This time, she didn't seem to have a snappy comeback to his confession.

Finally, she asked, "What reason would that be?"

"I haven't figured it out yet." He sounded more irritable than he intended.

"Our meetings were just coincidences," she stated.

"I don't believe in coincidences," Dean said. "I wasn't supposed to be in Georgia when you showed up. And if my memory serves me well, neither were you."

"I stepped in to help a friend. So what?" Rae rolled her eyes.

"What about last night? Of all events in this city, you ended up at my company's party."

"I was there to support my friends," Rae retorted. "I certainly didn't expect to see you or for you to even remember me. And before you make a big deal about it, I didn't ask you to run after me or drive me home either."

Dean flattened his lips and blew a breath through his nose. "What was I supposed to do? Ignore you and let you walk home alone?"

"I told you I was capable of getting myself home." There was a stubborn edge in her voice.

Shaking his head at their ridiculous argument, Dean sighed. "Did it ever occur to you that I wanted to say hi to you? That I *wanted* to get you home safely?"

Rae clamped her lips over whatever smart-ass retort she'd been ready to fling at Dean. After admitting to tricking her into seeing him this morning because he believed that their paths had crossed for a reason, he had the nerve to turn it back on her. As if it was her fault that she didn't understand what his intention was.

"No. Just as I didn't know Billy Wagner pulled my ponytail because he wanted to be my friend." Rae crossed her arms at her chest while glaring at the man sitting opposite her.

Dean's eyes widened, and he scoffed. "You're comparing me to a grade school bully?"

"Yes. Why would you resort to deception—"

"Now, I didn't exactly—" Dean cut in.

Rae ignored him and finished, "—when you could simply ask if I wanted to have breakfast with you?"

Dean blinked as he considered the question. His voice was much more controlled when he replied—no, resigned. "Would you say yes if I did?"

She hesitated for a beat. "I don't know."

"No, you wouldn't." A rueful twitch of his lips accompanied a shrug of his shoulders. "You already have a certain idea of me in your head."

"Oh, now you claim to know what I think?" Rae questioned.

"No. You told me in person that I'm an arrogant, chauvinistic ass."

Rae narrowed her eyes. "And tricking me is going to change that opinion?"

"Obviously a wrong strategy. I didn't think." Dean leveled his eyes with hers. "I apologize."

Rae studied Dean and felt the sincerity of his words. She really should walk away from the situation, but seeing a proud man like Dean Rowland owning up to his mistake and expressing regret softened her stance. Nobody was perfect.

"Apology accepted," she decided.

There was a flicker of relief in his gaze. "Thank you."

"Good." Rae nodded as Patrick came around the corner with their food. "Now, that's settled. Let's eat."

Thirteen

The waiter placed warm plates in front of them, and the smell of eggs, sugar, and berries teased Dean's nose.

"Do you need anything else for now?" Patrick asked.

"It looks like my friend here could use a Bloody Mary," Rae teased with a side glance at Dean.

"Hold the tomato juice and celery," Dean agreed. He wasn't even half-joking.

The waiter stammered, "Aah, we don't serve hard liquor."

"We're just joking, Patrick." Rae patted the waiter's arm. "We're all set. Thanks."

The waiter nodded and walked away, looking confused.

Dean fell back on his seat, still feeling like an ass. Across from him, Rae cut into one of the triangles on her plate and gathered it on her fork, topped with berry compote. Then, she handed it to him.

He just stared at her like a dumbass. To be fair, he was in a daze. One minute she'd been interrogating him, and the next she was feeding him.

"Try it." Rae turned the fork handle to him, encouraging him to take it. "They do it the right way. The bread is custardy, and the surface is caramelized to perfection. You don't need syrup for this."

Dean hesitated for another second, then took the bite. She was right. The toast had a crusty sugary exterior, while the interior melted in a creamy finish cut by the acidity of the berries. He'd never had French toast like it before—not that he'd had much of the dish. He found some breakfast items too sweet for his taste.

"You're right. It's delicious." He returned her fork.

"Their omelets are delicate. I find most places overcook them." Rae gestured to his plate, suggesting he should eat.

He took a forkful of omelet, and damn if she wasn't right. He tucked into the meal with gusto. He now wondered why he didn't eat breakfast more often.

"I guess you like it." Rae grinned at him.

Dean swallowed the food in his mouth and nodded. "It's excellent."

Taking a break from the meal, he drank coffee and watched Rae eat her breakfast with similar enthusiasm. Her earlier aura of disapproval had been replaced with simple pleasure. He was amazed at the change of mood.

"Are we good?" Dean couldn't help but ask. He might regret it in a second.

Rae eyed him in silence for a heartbeat. "You came clean. You apologized. So, yes."

"That's it?"

"Well, you're paying for this meal," Rae deadpanned.

"It'll be my pleasure." Dean started eating again.

"Tell me—" Rae started.

"Uh oh." Dean sat straight up.

Her lips twitched. "Tell me, why did you feel the need to come up with an excuse? It doesn't sound like you. Not that I know you that well, but from our previous interaction, you strike me as a direct person."

"You're right. I am." Dean let his gaze rest on Rae's face. She'd looked elegant in her cocktail dress last night, but she was as captivating in a casual dress. Was her hair glossier this morning?

"Last night was an aberration for me. Something about you puts me off-kilter. I'd like to find out why," Dean answered. That much was true.

Rae's perfect eyebrows arched. "Well, talking about direct."

"You don't hold your words, either," Dean pointed out.

"I don't." Rae tilted her head as if thinking. "But I have to say I tend to lose my filters around you. I'm not usually as confrontational as I've been with you."

"You mean you don't usually call people asses?" A corner of his lips rose in a half-smile.

"Oh, all the time. Just not to their faces."

"So, I'm special?"

"Must be." Rae pressed her lips, trying not to giggle, but she failed and let out a full laugh instead.

Dean's half-smile turned full, seeing her face bloom with mirth. He couldn't remember if he'd ever been fascinated by a woman's laughter in the past.

"So you admit there's something between us," Dean prompted.

"Exasperation? Vexation?" Rae suggested.

"Absolutely. You're the most infuriating woman I've ever met," Dean agreed. "But there's more, and I'd like to know what it is. I hate feeling off balance."

"Oh, wow." Rae's eyes rolled. "Okay, how do we figure this out?"

"Spend the day with me. I'm sure we'll flush it out of our systems—whatever it is—by the end of the day."

"Or we can split up after breakfast and go on with our separate lives," Rae counter-proposed.

"No. I'd be thinking of you."

Rae's heart skipped a beat.

She knew exactly what Dean was talking about. She felt the same way around him—as if she didn't have her feet under her. It was unnerving. Probably it was the reason why she exerted herself with him more. It was overcompensation for the loss of control.

Unlike Dean, Rae knew precisely why he unbalanced her. Despite his obvious flaws and blunders, he intrigued her. And the feeling was quite insistent, while her usual interest in the opposite sex tended to be fleeting. Even as he annoyed her, he fascinated her. It was actually rather insulting to hear that he was puzzled about her and wanted to flush her out of his system.

He and Rae were of the same mind about the latter part, though. She had no interest in exploring this further. She wanted to slam the door on it. But then, he had to drop a bomb on her.

He'd said, *I'd be thinking of you.*

And damn, if that didn't make her stomach flip.

"Spend today with me. We'll do whatever you want," Dean proposed again. "You said you don't work on Sundays. So, what do you do?"

Maybe I'll bore him with mundane errands.

"Groceries. I ran out of everything." Rae started listing stuff with her fingers. "Laundry. Probably, a nap since I didn't get much sleep last night—"

"We can do that," the maddening man interrupted with a suggestive glint in his eyes. "But those sound like third date type of things."

"Whoa. Let me stop you right there, buddy." Rae held up a hand. "Who said anything about dates?"

"Well, what would you call two people spending a day together?"

"Hanging out," Rae quickly replied.

"Hanging out?" He drawled out each syllable.

"Yes. That's what friends do. They hang out."

"We're now friends?" Dean questioned.

"Sure." Rae drew out the short response reluctantly.

"And what do you do when hanging out with friends?"

"Depends on the mood or the day. Eat, have coffee, go window-shopping, walk in a park, watch a movie, whatever. But basically, we just talk."

"That's perfect. We're two down already." A seemingly innocent smile formed on his lips. "Don't you want to figure this out? The more exposed we are to each other, the faster we'll get over whatever this pull is."

Rae was tired of Dean referring to their "connection" as akin to a virus. Fine, if he was so desperate for immunity from her, she'd give it to him. She didn't want him infecting her either.

"All right." Rae huffed. "I'm yours for the day."

Fourteen

"What do you usually do on Sundays?" Rae asked Dean as they meandered their way out of East Village toward Washington Square Park.

Rae bit her lip, fighting back a grin as if she was about to wisecrack. Dean waited to see if she'd manage to hold it in. After they agreed to stay in each other's company for the day, they came up with a few basic rules: play nice, no question is off limit, and give honest answers. The first person to break one would have to do what the other asked.

"You're okay there?" Dean gave her a side glance.

She nodded and schooled her expression. "I'm good. Go ahead."

Raising his gaze to scan the roofline of the NYU buildings lining Fourth Street, Dean pondered Rae's question. "I suppose I do whatever I do every day. I wake up, swim laps, check emails, listen to the news, do some work—"

"Wait. You work on Sundays?" Rae's incredulous blue gaze rested on him.

He shrugged. "If there's work to be done."

Rae twisted her lips. "Do you do anything that doesn't involve work?"

"I call my parents."

"Good son." She nodded her approval. "What else?"

"Maybe catch a game on TV. I get a lot of invitations most nights, but I tend to stay in on Sundays."

"So walking through downtown isn't usually in the schedule?" Rae questioned. "When was the last time you walked anyway? Not counting last night."

Dean laughed. "I do walk, Rae. You know how it is in this city. Sometimes, it's easier and faster walking somewhere rather than driving. But I can't say I've strolled the streets often."

His phone suddenly buzzed in his pocket. He checked the display—Robert, again. His VP of communications had called twice and left several texts since the previous night.

"Go ahead, pick it up." Rae tipped her chin toward his phone. "Whoever it is must really need you."

"Sorry." Dean halted in his tracks and answered the call. "Yes, Robert?"

Robert immediately started reading him the riot act for taking off without giving him a heads-up last night. Dean swore Robert sometimes thought he was the boss instead of Dean. So he missed a couple of interviews. It wasn't a big deal.

"Did you give them Gayle instead?" Dean interrupted him in a firm, calm voice.

"Of course. But I—"

"Perfect," Dean said. "That's what we want for last night anyway. We'll talk tomorrow. Gotta go."

He ended the call and looked up to find Rae studying him from a few feet away.

"Work issue?" she asked.

"Nothing important."

Rae eyed the phone still resting in his hand. "We should add another rule."

"What?"

"No phones," she suggested. "They're distracting. We're on a mission. We should put them on silent or don't-disturb mode until we part ways. The more focused we are, the faster this will go."

Dean shook his head. "What if there's an emergency?"

"When was the last time you had an emergency call?" Rae challenged.

Hardly ever. By this point, each of his businesses had leaders he trusted to handle most issues. And if it was a family emergency, he'd be the last person they'd call.

"Are you one of those people who can't part with their devices?" Rae questioned when Dean didn't answer right away.

"I'd think you are, doing what you do," Dean countered. "Don't you have to check your feeds or comments?"

Rae flashed him an indulgent smile. "I told you I don't work on Sundays. I had to set myself boundaries. If not, I wouldn't enjoy other parts of my life. Work can wait until tomorrow."

Making her point, she took out her phone and turned it to do-not-disturb mode. "What can happen on a Sunday?"

Dean could think of a dozen things that might go wrong. But none of them would immediately affect him or Rae.

"Here. Give me your phone for safekeeping." Rae reached an open palm to him. "Let's see how long we can stay off them."

He was still doubtful. Though he wasn't on any social media platforms, he was hardly ever without his phone. But he followed her lead and switched the do-not-disturb mode on. Halfway to handing the gadget to her, he pulled his arm back. "Why can't I keep it?"

"Out of sight, out of mind. Helps us from reaching for them." Rae dropped hers back into her purse.

Dean narrowed his gaze at her and reluctantly slid his lifeline into her open purse. "You do understand that giving someone my phone takes a lot of trust?"

"Do you have a trust issue?" Rae asked flippantly.

Dean scoffed. "I hope I won't regret this."

"I could say the same." Rae grinned at him as she strolled toward the Washington Square Arch. "You do understand that spending a day with a man I hardly know takes *a lot* of trust."

Dean laughed. *Well, I served that one right at her, didn't I?*

Of all the things Rae had thought she'd do today, walking up Fifth Avenue next to Dean Rowland wasn't one of them. She also hadn't expected to enjoy listening to him.

"So you were telling me about your connection with Canis Major," Dean picked up where they'd left their conversation before they ducked into a boba tea shop.

She took a sip of the cold, sweet milk tea concoction filled with tapioca pearls and sighed. Dean didn't get one. He'd better not ask her to share when the temperature kept rising.

"Oh, yeah. I've known them since they were indie," Rae answered.

"Ah. I see. That's why you seem close."

"We're tight. We collaborated on a tour just before Aquarius signed them. We had a lot of fun on the road trip across the country, finding gems along the way and chronicling the trip, the music, and the fans."

Dean looked at her as if something had just hit him. "Now I remember Gayle telling me about it when she decided to offer a contract to them. That vlog series received such attention that everyone was following the journey."

Rae smiled at the memories. "It was epic."

"Are you with one of those guys?" Dean asked.

"Um?" Rae glanced a questioning look at him as she drank her tea. "What do you mean?"

"You looked particularly cozy with Brandon Rossi last night."

Rae rolled her eyes. "Oh, god. Not you, too."

"What? I'm just telling you what I saw." Dean added, "So you're not an item?"

"Who still uses that term?" Rae chuckled. "No. We're good friends—best of friends."

"Huh." Dean glanced at her for a quick study, as if deciding if she was being truthful.

"Why does my relationship with Brandon matter?" Rae countered.

Dean shook his head. "Just trying to figure out the dynamics, that's all."

"Let me make it simple for you to understand." Rae held his eyes. "Those boys are my family. I'd do anything for them."

He gave her a slow nod, but she wasn't sure if he understood. He asked, "Who else thought you were dating?"

"The fans." Rae shrugged. "People just can't accept that people of the opposite sex can be friends."

Dean shrugged noncommittally. "I mean, I could see why people doubt you're just friends. You both are attractive people who are comfortable with each other. There's chemistry—"

"What? Uh-uh." Rae quickly shook her head. "No. Brandon and I have gone down that road before. We have very different perspectives about that kind of stuff. And no chemistry—not that way, anyhow."

"So, you've dated?"

This was getting way too personal. But she'd agreed to the rules. In fact, she'd made most of the rules.

"We went on a couple of coffee dates when we first met," Rae honestly answered. "And we clicked right away as friends."

He looked skeptical. "I find it hard to believe a guy like Brandon Rossi would settle for a friendship with a beautiful woman."

"Obviously, you don't know Brandon," Rae retorted.

Wait, did he just say I was beautiful?

Rae shook off the stray thought. And before Dean could ask follow-up questions on the matter, she threw the first question that popped into her head at him. "If I were dating Brandon, do you think I'd agree to today's crazy experiment? Wouldn't I rather spend my time off with my boyfriend?"

"Maybe you just find me more interesting than him." Dean winked with a flash of a grin.

Rae returned the wink with a speculative gaze. "It's more curiosity, methinks."

"What are you curious about?" he asked.

"Well, I read up on you for the article, so I'm well aware that you're brilliant at what you do. Then from what I've witnessed in Gainesville, I can conclude you're a family man. You're pleasant to look at, and I think you're a pretty decent guy when you're in a good mood."

"Oh wow, thanks." His eyes narrowed in doubt. "I'm waiting for the bomb to drop."

Don't do it, Rae. It's none of your business.

But Rae ignored her own caution. "I guess I'm wondering why any woman would leave you—this almost perfect man—at the altar."

Fifteen

Dean felt the automatic tightening in his jaw and his veins bulging at his temples. He'd expected Rae to say something outrageous, but not that. Nobody had dared mention the fiasco wedding or his ex-fiancée for almost three years. Six months after having a field day on his personal life, the media had finally gotten tired of questioning what had been the real cause of the nuptial cancelation. And everyone in his circle had decided it was safer to pretend it hadn't happened.

With a deep breath, Dean tried to loosen his facial muscles, but his voice sounded harsh when he spoke. "Gossips were part of your research?"

Rae had the decency to blush. She knew she'd dug herself into a hole. But she tipped her chin up. "Can't be avoided when one web-searches your name."

That much was true, to Dean's chagrin.

"Clearly, this is still a raw subject," Rae added. "I apologize if it's something you don't want to talk about."

Dean didn't respond because he didn't trust himself not to say something sharp. Rae seemed happy to oblige him, and they walked a block in silence.

At some point, Rae tipped her head at him and studied him with penetrating eyes. "You still can't talk about it even after three years? She must've hurt you deeply."

Dean whirled his head to her. *You're kidding me right now?*

As if reading his mind, Rae shrugged her shoulders. "You can't get past it if you can't talk about it."

"You're a shrink now?" Dean's voice was low and measured.

"No, but I've got an inkling of what you must've felt or still feel." She looked away. "I've experienced loss, too."

"And did you talk about it to death?" he questioned, sarcasm dripping in every word.

Rae grimaced. "Some. It helped, but it still weighs on me every time I think about it."

The trace of misery in her tone gave him a pause. But then, she shook her head as if doing it physically would dislodge some unwanted memory from her brain.

She then returned her focus to him. "So what happened?"

"Why would I tell you?" Dean rolled his eyes.

Rae's mouth formed into a smile that an adult would usually give a child they pitied. "Because you agreed to answer my questions honestly."

Damn it. I did.

"Don't sweat it, though. We'll ease into it," Rae said, as if that would assure him. "Or we don't have to do this at all. We can call it a day."

Dean tipped his head and studied Rae's not-so-innocent smile. *So that's your plan.*

"You're not wiggling out of this that easily," Dean snickered. "You think you can scare me by asking personal questions."

"Aren't you? A little scared?" she retorted.

Dean shook his head slightly and blew out a breath. "You're diabolical."

Rae burst into a laugh.

But I can handle you.

"So close!" Rae snapped her fingers at him.

"Am I that bad that you can't wait to escape me?" Dean grinned at her.

"It's the principle of it," she replied as they turned west at the next intersection. "So, are you gonna answer my question?"

Dean's calculating brain ran a quick risk assessment of how much he could trust her. For privacy's sake alone, he shouldn't tell her anything. But for some reason, he wanted to trust her.

As Dean pondered how to best answer, Rae asked, "Time hasn't dulled the pain, has it?" Her voice was unexpectedly understanding.

With a sigh, he replied, "Not pain. Betrayal. Topped with a sense of failure."

Rae glanced his way. "Betrayal, I get. Failure...?"

"It's the one thing I failed at. Couldn't take it to the finish line." He chuckled, though he found no humor in it.

"I'd think the wedding was the starting line," Rae quipped. "But maybe it was just not meant to be. Have you thought about it that way? See, if Brandon were here, he'd say if you were meant to be together, you'd find each other again someday and live happily ever after."

"Brandon Rossi?" Dean frowned.

"Yeah, Brandon is a romantic. He believes in true love and all that stuff. I, on the other hand, personally think you dodged a bullet. Or both of you did, depending on how you look at it."

"Really?"

Without registering the derision in his tone, Rae went on. "But you knew that. You had to sense something was wrong before the wedding."

Dean had but ignored it.

"The question is, why haven't you moved on? Are you still pining for her?" Rae speculated.

"I've moved on."

"Your sister doesn't think you have."

"My sister?" He whipped his head to Rae. "How would you know that?"

"Kat mentioned you went home less and less when you were with your ex. And when she left, you shut your family out and buried yourself into your work instead."

"Kat said that much to you?" Dean was flabbergasted.

Rae touched his arm. "I don't think she meant to say so much. But I felt her concern for you. She hopes you'll find your way home more often now that she's built you the perfect house."

Dean stared at her hand on his arm but wasn't seeing it. He was still processing the information Rae had just revealed.

"So." Rae tapped his arm and broke him out of his reverie. "I'd say it's time for you to snap out of it."

"Just like that?" Dean snapped his fingers like she did earlier. "Was it that easy for you?"

The corners of her mouth dropped slightly. "Different situations. But I did it. I found some closure. And it doesn't sound like you have."

"It's pretty challenging to get closure when my bride disappeared into thin air on the wedding day," he deadpanned.

Rae stopped in her tracks, making him look back at her. "You mean those tabloids told the truth that she just vanished?"

"They got some of the facts right," he confirmed. "Her parents knew something. But they were more worried about saving face than her disappearance."

"Why didn't you look for her?" Rae asked.

"Because she asked me not to."

Rae's jaw dropped.

"She wrote she couldn't marry me and told me not to look for her. I didn't know she meant that she was leaving everything—New York, her family, her life," Dean continued his story.

"How did you know she was safe?" Rae stammered. "What if someone abducted her and made her write that note?"

Dean frowned at her. "I doubt that."

"But how did you know?" Rae grabbed him by the arm to stop him from walking. "No one can just vanish. Weren't you even worried? I mean, you were going to marry this woman."

"Of course I was worried," Dean blurted.

Rae stepped back and felt rather than saw the mixed emotions swirling in the usually stoic man. It took him three seconds to pull himself together and look back at her. His expression might be neutral, but he couldn't completely shut his eyes. There was regret in them.

"What is it?" Rae prodded.

Dean hesitated before gesturing for them to continue walking. Rae complied since the motion seemed to grease the conversation gears.

"I didn't look for her," Dean started. "Because I knew she wasn't in harm's way."

"How?"

"She was in love with someone her parents didn't approve of and eloped with him."

Rae gasped. The information wasn't exactly mind-blowing. It was a classic love triangle, except one of the triangle sides—Dean, in this case—was completely blindsided. Her heart cracked a bit for him.

"And you had no idea about the other man?" Rae asked.

Dean just gave a short shake of his head.

"Why the hell did she agree to marry you in the first place?" Suddenly, the rage came deep from her belly. "You gotta know when you said yes to a proposal that's already half of the commitment. Why did she wait to break it off until the wedding day? Why did she put you through that...that humiliation?"

Rae abruptly stopped and turned to Dean. A couple of people sharing the sidewalk grumbled and walked around, cursing.

Dean urged her to turn back by her elbow and led her forward. "I don't know the answers to those questions. I've wondered about them myself."

"You never got a chance to confront her about it, did you?" Rae asked more calmly.

Dean blew out a breath as if he was tired. "No, I did not."

She glanced at him. He looked exasperated—his lips flat, his forehead lined, and a vein at his temple seemed ready to pop.

"You don't look too happy," Rae suggested.

"Should I be?" He didn't look at her. "You just dug up a whole thing that took me years to forget."

"But you never really forgot it. I could tell because it feels..." Rae raked her brain for the right word. "...unfinished."

Dean scoffed. "Pretty sure it was finished when she eloped with another man."

"Then why is it still affecting you this much?" asked Rae.

"Let it go, Rae." Dean sighed.

But it was hard for Rae to let something go once she'd latched on to it. She felt Dean deserved answers. And he needed a friend who wouldn't tiptoe around the issue. And then a light bulb went off in her head. He needed her.

"I think I figured out why the universe put us in each other's trajectory," she exclaimed.

Dean's gaze swept over her face, and he looked slightly alarmed.

Rae beamed at him. "I'm here to help you find closure."

Sixteen

Dean transferred the grocery bag to his left arm as he and Rae arrived back at her apartment. The sun had mellowed as the afternoon rolled into evening, but the August heat clung. They'd had a bit of respite in the store, but the two-block walk had them perspiring again. Carrying the heavy load also added to Dean's discomfort. He couldn't help but laugh at his pampered self.

He had to admit between the heat and today's walking, he was a bit tuckered out. Rae had them meandering through the streets while they chatted. She'd steered him into an Italian market at some point, and they'd enjoyed a light meal of charcuterie, cheese, Italian bread, and cooled rosé. It was a gratifying experience for him. For most of his adult life, he always had a purpose—a planned day—but today, he'd enjoyed doing nothing.

"Here, give me that." Dean took the other grocery bag from Rae so she could fish out her keys and open the front door.

They then climbed the stairs to her apartment. Yup, she had to live on the top floor. He should be glad she lived in a four-story building. He was actually embarrassed because Rae didn't even seem winded. And it wasn't as if he was out of shape. He still swam laps daily, maybe not at the same speed he had in college, but he kept a decent pace.

"You didn't have to walk me home, but thanks for helping with the groceries." Rae opened her apartment door and let him in.

"We've been walking all day. What are a few more blocks?" Dean followed her to the kitchen. "Besides, I always make sure a lady gets home safe when I take her out."

Rae whipped her head to him. "This wasn't a date. This was an ambush."

Dean laughed. "Whatever you want to call it. I still took you out."

Before their time ended, Dean didn't want Rae to mistake his interest in her. With each hour they spent together, the more fascinated he became. She might've claimed they'd met to find him closure for the debacle of his almost marriage, but to him, the reason was much more straightforward. He wanted her.

Unfortunately, once Rae had decided the reason for their acquaintance, she'd been difficult to distract from that purpose. She was convinced he was still hanging on to the past and couldn't move on until he dealt with it.

Oh, he could. And he wanted to, if she'd let him.

Dean had never felt at such ease with any woman in his life. They'd talked nonstop, from traveling to debating current world politics. Sometimes he'd serve a teaser, and she'd return it with a smart comeback. An argument could turn heated, then one of them doused it with a light retort, and they'd laugh it out. The conversation had flowed like a river, where it rolled at a comfortable, easy pace for a length and turned into more exciting rapids in some parts. As long they paid attention not to get sucked in by the eddies, they'd had a thrilling ride.

"You can put those down here." Rae tapped a spot on the kitchen countertop and went to the fridge.

Dean did as instructed and looked around the kitchen to the open-concept living and dining area. It was a decent-sized apartment by New York City standards. He could tell it'd been renovated recently, but it retained some of its older charms. Light shades and comfortable furniture balanced out the rustic exposed brick walls.

Rae poured some sparkling water into two tumblers she'd filled with ice cubes. She handed one to him and drank half of hers in seconds.

"I needed that." She pressed the cold glass to her temple and trailed it down to her neck. She closed her eyes and sighed.

Dean couldn't take his eyes off her—his need for water was replaced by a different thirst. She'd put up her hair in a loose bun hours earlier, and the way she tipped her head, exposing her long, shapely neck, made Dean wish he was that tumbler she was holding.

Gosh, it was hot out there. Rae silently praised the inventors of air conditioning and ice-makers as she relished the frosty sensation against her skin. She could imagine steam rising from her pores as the cool air hit her body. She couldn't wait to get into the shower. The water would feel so refreshing.

Rae blinked her eyes open with a shower in mind to find Dean studying her from across her tiny kitchen. Was that heat in his eyes, or did she imagine that, too? Because the way he was looking at her was turning the image of a shower into a more R-rated version, featuring a very wet and almost naked Dean. And damn, if she didn't remember how good he looked that way.

Rae quickly blinked the thought away and downed the rest of her water. *I must be waaaayyy overheated.*

"You have a comfortable place, Rae."

Rae turned her eyes back to him, feeling caught off guard. "Thank you. It is."

"You've lived here long?"

"About a year," she answered.

"You got a little red." Dean gestured with his chin at her. "Too much sun?"

Rae tried a casual shrug. "Probably. My skin is a bit sensitive."

"You should be more careful. Maybe up the SPF." A corner of his lips rose in a bemused half-smile, as if he knew he'd caused her rosiness.

"Thanks for the dermatological advice, doc." Ignoring the grin, she started putting away the groceries.

"Anytime. I will require a thorough examination before I can provide further recommendations," he drawled lazily.

Rae glanced at him with a short laugh. The man was leaning his well-shaped behind against the counter, drinking his water leisurely without taking his eyes off her. He was a tempting tall glass of water.

"Save the cheesy line for someone else." Rae waved his flirting off.

"But I thought you'd want to help me move on." He managed to look innocent, charming, with a hint of sexual promise in his grey gaze.

Rae exhaled heavily and turned slowly to face him. She had to squash this attraction between them. However well the day went, she could not get involved with Dean Rowland. Not in that way.

"You clearly didn't need any help in that department," she said knowingly. She'd seen some pictures of him with women on the gossip pages. Y'know...for research. "I was serious when I said you needed closure."

"Here we go again." Dean put his glass down and crossed his arms across his chest.

If that wasn't a defensive gesture, Rae didn't know what it was. He'd fight her at her every attempt to dig deeper to get to that goal. But she truly believed that was what she had to do for him because he wouldn't do it himself. She guessed he'd rather pretend that episode of his life had ever happened.

"You can't see it yet, but I'm meant to push you there because no one dares to do it," Rae said.

"Why would you want to do that?" Dean questioned.

"I don't know. I sense that you need me to get you there. But I can't make you want to do it." Rae dug into her purse and fished out Dean's forgotten phone. She extended her arm to him with his phone in her hand. "It's your choice."

"I'm not done exploring." Locking their gazes, Dean covered her hand in his larger one, with his phone between their palms. His thumb absently caressed the skin on the inside of her wrist and sent a shiver up her arm before he pulled his hand away, taking his phone with him.

Rae could tell from the little twitch of his lips that he knew precisely what his touch had done to her. She'd tamped down whatever sexual desire she had because she didn't care for what sex could entail—attachment and eventually heartbreak. But Dean proved he could easily ignite her cold inside with little effort from the first time she'd laid eyes on him. She might not be able to resist him if he turned on his full charm.

There was only one way to handle this.

Dean felt his senses heighten when he touched Rae. He heard her barely audible sharp intake of breath and saw the glimmer in her blue gaze. He was acutely aware that Rae wasn't as resistant to him as she claimed. He noted with a small smile how she discreetly rotated the wrist he'd caressed. He now knew how soft her skin was. And he'd love to explore more of her.

As if she knew exactly what was on his mind, Rae moved past him and walked out of the kitchen area. Not having much choice, Dean followed her, and she led him straight to the door. Damn.

"We've explored enough today," Rae said as she reached for the doorknob. "I think we proved we could actually be friends."

Friends. There's that word again.

Dean noticed Rae would throw the word between them as soon as the idea of a date or physical interest was hinted at—like a shield. And now, she was ready to push him out of the door after a slight innocent touch. Did he read her response to him wrong?

"I'm glad you didn't tell me to go to hell this morning." Dean paused by the door, biding his time before he had to leave.

"I had fun." She sounded genuine, and it gave Dean hope.

"When can we do this again?" he threw his shot. "Perhaps we cut the walking part by a half next time."

His joke got a small laugh out of her. "Are you sore? A big, strong man like you?"

"I'll need to ice my feet when I get home." Dean wasn't even kidding.

"Elevating your legs would help, too," she suggested.

"I'll do that." And without a pause, he asked, "So?"

"Are you ready to find some closure?" Rae returned.

Dean sighed. "I don't understand why you think I need this. I'm over Leighton. I haven't thought about her in years."

"I find that hard to believe."

"Today is the first time her name has come up because you brought it up," Dean argued.

"If you're over her, why did you get so worked up earlier?"

Dean threw up his hands in defeat. "Fine. Let's do it."

Rae pulled back in surprise. She didn't expect him to give in, did she? Neither did he. He needed to get out of this, quick. But then, a happy smile blossomed on her kissable lips, and he forgot everything.

"Give me your phone." Rae opened her hand.

Without hesitation, Dean handed it to her. She dialed a number briefly before disconnecting it and handing the device back to him.

"Text me. We'll start from there." Rae opened her door and urged him out. "Trust me. You won't regret it."

With a parting smile, she closed the door.

God, what did I agree to? Dean was already half-sorry about his knee-jerk decision.

Seventeen

Dean scanned through the last of his emails, noting anything he'd need to attend to either later tonight or first thing in the morning. His lead executive assistant, Melanie, gave him a quick verbal rundown of his schedule tomorrow before he left the office for the day. He had a date to go to.

Well, I'd call it a date. Rae might disagree.

He hadn't waited to text her. He dropped a short message that Sunday night. He'd told her he'd felt a million years old and had dunked himself into an ice bath, to which she'd replied, "That actually sounds awesome. But who has an ice bath?" He'd been happy to extend an invitation. She'd then answered, "That might come in handy when I prepare myself for a plunge in Antarctica. Future goal."

They'd texted briefly here and there since then, mostly at night. Nothing heavy, but enough to put a smile on his face. Dean realized he'd been smiling a lot lately. It could ruin his reputation, but he seemed to like it again.

"Gayle was already on her way up here when I called her assistant to cancel," Melanie informed as she exited his office. "She'll probably be here any minute."

"That's fine," Dean acknowledged.

Dean checked his watch. It was almost six, but his people were used to having access to him after hours. He didn't leave his office until seven most nights, then usually he'd have a semi-business dinner with someone. Their HR policy was about work-life balance, but honestly, he didn't have that much life to balance. Work was his life.

Though tonight, Rae had finally agreed to meet if he could come over at seven. It was on the early side for him, but he wasn't going to say no.

"Knock, knock." Gayle strolled into Dean's office. "What's this about rescheduling?"

"Yes, sorry for the last-minute cancellation, Gayle." Dean shut down everything and gathered his stuff. "Are you free in the morning? We can do breakfast."

Gayle stopped by his desk with a frown. "Sure. But you don't do breakfast."

"I found a new fondness for it."

"Where are you going now?" Gayle inquired.

Dean walked around his desk and glanced at her. "Ah, personal appointment."

"Must be important if you're ditching me." She eyed him curiously as they walked to the outer office where Melanie sat.

"It was implied it might affect my future," Dean replied vaguely. At least that was what Rae had said about this closure she was obsessed about.

"Are you okay?" Gayle's curiosity turned into concern.

"Yes. I'm good," Dean assured her.

"Okay. Can't wait to hear more about it."

Dean merely smiled at his colleague and friend. "Talk to Melanie about breakfast. I'll see you in the morning."

"Tom is standing by, Dean," Melanie informed.

"Thank you, Melanie. Go home as soon as you schedule the breakfast with Gayle."

"Breakfast?" Melanie, too, looked surprised.

Dean didn't realize his employees were that aware of his habits, but he didn't have time to wonder about that. He waved at them and headed to the elevators. His mission right now was to beat rush hour and get to Rae.

Gayle watched Dean disappear into one of the elevators with a massive smile on his face. Curious. He was excited to get to wherever he was going.

Returning to Dean's executive assistant's office, Gayle locked her gaze on Melanie. "He looks chipper. So unlike our fearless leader. Where's he going?"

"I don't know. He didn't tell me." Melanie shrugged.

"Oh, come on. You've managed Dean's life for a decade. You know his schedule inside out."

"Dean only asked me to reschedule your meeting." The efficient matron clicked on her computer. "Does eight-thirty tomorrow work for you? I'll make a reservation."

"That's fine." Gayle waved away the question dismissively and planted herself on the edge of Melanie's desk. She gave Melanie a conspiring look. "Go on, you can tell me. Is he seeing someone new?"

The older lady gave no expression. "I wouldn't know."

"Tom would." Gayle smirked. "And I know you and Tom talk to each other."

"Are you implying Tom and I gossip about our employer behind his back?" Melanie raised one stern eyebrow.

Dean hadn't hired Melanie over younger, though qualified, prospective assistants for her secretarial skills alone. She was like a dragon protecting her eggs when it came to Dean. Though Gayle was the head of one of Dean's businesses, Melanie was not intimidated. Maintaining a respectful relationship with Melanie Swanson was advisable if anyone needed anything from the big boss.

"I wouldn't use the word gossip." Gayle wiggled her brows knowingly. "Look, I only have the best interest for Dean. I just want to make sure he's okay. Didn't you see that big smile as he was leaving? And doing a breakfast meeting?"

Melanie's pursed lips betrayed her true feelings, and Gayle doubled down. "You can't tell me there isn't something going on with Dean."

"It is rather odd," Melanie agreed.

"We need to find out what it is," Gayle suggested.

"It is none of our business. Besides, if he's smiling, I'm happy for him."

"Of course. But we need to ensure it's not a short-lived type of happiness. If you know what I mean." Gayle's lips pressed together into a concerned line. "If he is seeing someone, I need to make sure she's the right woman for him."

"Like you did with the last one?" Melanie gave Gayle a pointed look.

Guilt clawed at Gayle as a memory of Dean's face on his wedding day flooded her mind. "I screwed up. I shouldn't have played matchmaker. He hasn't been the same since."

"Miss Heston was never the right person for Dean," Melanie said evenly.

"I see it now." Gayle sighed. "That's why we need to find out what's happening."

"I'm not spying on Dean for you, Gayle."

"Not spying," Gayle quickly replied. "Looking out for him."

"He's a grown man."

"You're right." Gayle stood up in surrender.

Melanie was one tough cookie. Gayle stopped pushing and started to leave the office but glanced back at the protective mother hen. "Just keep an eye on him, will you?"

"Always."

Eighteen

Rae poured a few tablespoons of water onto the pan of garlic and cherry tomatoes, turned down the heat, and left the whole lot to cook down. She whirled around to the standing vintage butcher block in the middle of her square kitchen and continued prepping the salad.

A muted sound of a cork popping out of a wine bottle made her look up. Dean stood across from her, putting down the bottle to breathe and unscrewing the cork. But his eyes were caught somewhere else. Rae followed his line of sight. He was staring at a side-profile portrait of a woman in white oil on black acrylic above her working desk.

"Brandon painted that," Rae informed him.

Dean glanced at her. "Did he? I didn't know he paints."

"Brandon's multitalented. He's been painting all his life." Rae sprinkled some crumbled goat cheese onto the salad. "I've been telling him he should showcase his paintings."

"Is that you?" Dean was still studying the painting.

"That's his interpretation of me."

"You look like..." Dean paused, "a forlorn deity."

Rae turned to the painting with a slight frown.

"There's something in the eye that's so haunting," he continued. "As if you're storing the world's sorrow inside."

Her gaze tracked back at him in bewilderment. Dean turned and met her eyes.

"Did you sit for this?" he asked.

"Yes. We did it when we were still living together. Mostly in the morning when the light was the way he wanted it."

Maybe it was just her imagination, but Rae thought Dean's eyes flashed with something she didn't understand.

"You lived together?" he questioned.

"For a few years." Rae shrugged. "I was traveling a lot, and it was nice to know there were other people in the apartment when you're away, y'know."

"People?"

"Curtis also lived with us. And between those two, there wasn't a shortage of girlfriends coming and going." Rae rolled her eyes, remembering the days. "Love those guys, but when I could afford my own place, I was out. I need my privacy."

Rae noticed Dean visibly relax. He reached for the wine and poured her a glass. She picked it up, brought it to her nose, and inhaled a hint of fruity yet earthy herbaceous aroma before taking a sip of the light-bodied red.

"Oh, lovely. That'll go perfectly with the sauce." Rae nodded her approval. She took the bottle from Dean and studied the label.

"You know your wine?" Dean asked while swirling his glass.

"Just enough for my own enjoyment and cooking. That's an excellent Sangiovese."

Dean nodded after he'd sampled the wine himself. "I've got a feeling you're being humble."

Rae gave a short laugh and drank a bit more. "I'm truly not. I learned a lot about wine—Italian, especially—when I spent a few months there, working my way down from Turin to Naples. I did some groundwork at vineyards along the way and picked up a thing or two."

"You worked at vineyards?" Dean gave her a look.

"Nothing technical." Rae shrugged. "Sometimes they needed extra hands during harvest. Other times, I did whatever work was available."

He looked at her as though he had so many questions. But Rae had cooking in mind. She checked on her sauce and saw the tomatoes had started bursting the way she wanted. Into the sauce, she mixed the gnocchi she'd sautéed in olive oil earlier. She took the pan off the heat, topped the dish with some ripped fresh mozzarella, and slid the whole thing under the broiler.

"That should be ready in two minutes." She tossed the salad with a lemon vinaigrette and handed the bowl to Dean. "Take that to the table, please."

Rae grabbed the ciabatta she'd picked up on her way home, sliced it, and pushed that to Dean when he returned. For a moment, they moved in unison to get dinner on the table.

Finally, they sat down.

"That smells wonderful." Dean eyed the steaming pan she'd placed on a trivet. "I can't wait to try it."

"Thanks. It's a simple, summery dish, but super tasty."

They served themselves and dug in.

"Tell me more about working your way through Italy." Dean mopped some of the sauce on his plate with a piece of bread. "You must've worked with some Italian nonnas in their kitchen, too, judging from your cooking. This is delicious, Rae."

"Thank you. I did charm some nice ladies into giving me cooking lessons." Rae smiled at the memories of that journey. It was something she'd always cherish. "They taught me a young girl on her own needed to be able to feed herself."

But those mamas and nonnas did more than teach her to cook. They gave her a taste of a family.

Dean frowned. "When did you do this trip?"

"Exactly a decade ago. I'd just turned twenty-one and graduated from college. I wanted to explore Europe, one country at a time."

"And how did you manage that?" Dean sat back in his chair, focusing solely on her now that he'd finished his serving.

"Initially, I got a job working on a yacht sailing along the French Riviera to Cinque Terre for a few months. That was an interesting gig, seeing how that demographic lives." Rae abruptly paused. It was easy to forget who Dean was when he was sitting in her little apartment, with his dress-shirt sleeves rolled up, eating dinner she'd just prepared.

As though he read her mind, Dean retorted, "I don't own a yacht."

"But you could if you wanted to?" Rae asked rhetorically.

"It's not the best investment," he replied levelly. "We have shares in Inter-jets. Much more practical."

Rae had to pick up her jaw before it hit the table and couldn't help but laugh. "Right. No yacht, just private jets."

"Hey, when someone travels for business the way my people and I do, it's just a good investment. It saves us a lot of time and money in the end."

"I'll take your word for it." Rae ate the last bite of her dinner. "I'm not gonna lie. Working on the yacht wasn't for the faint of heart. I had to put up with a lot, and it was hard work, but sailing those waters...unforgettable."

"And you brought people to share that experience with you." Dean's lips curved in admiration. "I'm impressed with your resourcefulness."

Oh, man. What was I thinking, inviting him here?

When he'd asked to meet, she was already on her way home. She'd been busy running around all day and had just wanted to chill at home. But having Dean smile at her that way didn't help her relax at all.

What happened to his theory that exposure would render them immune to each other? That immunity better kick in soon. Crushing on the man wasn't a part of the plan to find him closure over his ex-fiancée. But she didn't know where to start on that front. Dean had been evasive every time she steered the conversation that way.

"Have you been back since?" Dean kept asking him about her travels. That seemed to be his strategy to put her off her mission.

"To Italy, yes. And I'm going back this fall for a project in the works," Rae answered while thinking about how to turn the conversation back to him. "Have you?"

"Yes, to Rome and Milan for business."

"Only?" Rae questioned. "Do you ever travel for fun? Vacation? Where were you planning to go for a honeymoon?"

Dean's lips flattened. "We didn't plan one yet. It had to wait until some major dealings I was working on were finalized. I guess she didn't want to wait."

Rae's eyes were wide in shock. "You prioritized business dealings over your honeymoon?"

"No," Dean replied indignantly. "It's normal to schedule a honeymoon at a more convenient time."

"Sure, but you'd usually plan and schedule it. You didn't even know where you wanted to go." Rae leaned in over the table. "You must've talked about some dream destinations before."

Dean looked blank.

"Really?" Rae's brain spun to dig into Dean's memory about Leighton and any clue about where she might've run to. "Did she ever tell you about her favorite childhood vacations?"

This time, he seemed to be giving it a thought as he twiddled his wine glass. "Not sure if she had a favorite. I know they used to have a large estate up in the Cape where they spent their summers, and they wintered upstate."

"Okay." *This is a good start.* "You must've vacationed together. Did you two go—"

"Why are you asking these questions?" Dean copied her and leaned in toward her.

"Well, how else should I figure out where your ex-fiancée is?"

Dean abruptly straightened up. "Why do you want to do that?"

"How else can you get closure?"

Closure—the second word in Rae's vocabulary that annoyed Dean. The first one was *friends*.

"You're still hung up on that?" Dean said through gritted teeth.

Rae sat straighter in her chair. "You agreed to do this. If not, what are we doing?"

"I thought we were enjoying a wonderful dinner. I haven't had a home-cooked meal in forever. This is such a treat." Dean said. "The last time must've been when I was at Gene's house last spring."

"Spring?" Rae sounded skeptical. "When I was there? That's nearly four months ago."

Dean shrugged his shoulders. "I don't have many people offering me freshly made home-cooked meals very often."

"The same lesson I learned from the Italian nonnas applies to you, too, y'know. Young men on their own need to learn how to feed themselves."

"Oh, I know how to feed myself. I just can't cook a meal." Dean half-grinned, satisfied that he managed to distract Rae from her previous line of questioning.

Rae studied him with a side-eye. She probably thought he was hopeless.

"Do you always travel alone?" Dean asked her before she wised up to his strategy.

"That was how it started—a soul-searching journey. I wanted to see the world and find my place in it. When I began documenting it on my blog and sharing pictures of my experiences, I'd never thought it'd lead me to where I am today." Rae smiled with a faraway look in her eyes. "It's helped me through turbulence in my life. It's led me to wonderful friends who I collaborate with now. It's opened so many doors for me.

"Now, enough about me." Rae wiggled her brows at him with a knowing smile. "Let's get back to you."

Dean groaned.

Rae looked at him as though she was tolerating a petulant child. "The more you fight it, the more convinced I am that you need this intervention."

"Why do you care so much about this?" Dean asked wearily.

She inclined her head, thinking before answering. "Because I know how it feels to be abandoned."

"Abandoned?" Dean snorted. "She left. I got over it."

Rae fixed him with a particular look he recognized and despised.

"Don't do that," he told her.

"Do what?" She frowned.

"Pity me." Dean's grip around the stem of the wine glass tightened. "I endured it from my family, friends, and even my employees for months after the wedding. But I showed them that I moved on."

The look vanished in an instant, replaced by an eye roll. "Oh, I saw how you moved on. You paraded a different woman on your arm every other week. None of them you took out for more than a few dates. Even I could tell they were only for show."

Her assessment left him scrambling for a response, but Rae was on a roll.

"You may be a brilliant man, Dean, but I don't think you realize how much your fiancée's action affected you. My guess is you have kept such a close fist around your heart since she left that you'll never let anyone in. Those women you dated had no chance. They were merely props. And now three years have gone by, and it has become your way of life."

Dean had to take a deliberate breath before responding, but his voice sounded dangerously harsh when he spoke. "When did you earn your therapy license?"

"I speak from experience." Rae smiled, not even deterred by his rebuke. "See, Brandon said essentially the same thing to me. He told me I've built walls around myself and only let certain people I trust in. That's why I recognize what you're doing. The difference between us is that I'm self-aware and content this way. You, on the other hand..."

"What about me?"

Rae smiled kindly. "You're not me."

Dean must've looked perplexed because Rae chuckled. She reached out and gently loosened his fingers from the wine glass before he broke it.

"You came from a loving family. Your siblings are in happy relationships. Your parents' marriage is still strong after..." She looked inquiringly at him.

"Forty-two years," he supplied.

"Wow. Forty-two. That's a long time to be married."

"What's your point, Rae?" Dean demanded.

"You wanted that same happiness. You probably didn't expect any other outcome when you asked Leighton to marry you, but it didn't turn out the way you envisioned. Other people saw what happened as a misfortune. You saw it as a failure."

Rae locked her gaze on him as though she could see through him. "And you don't like to fail."

Rae watched the grey of Dean's eyes turn smokier while he digested her words. She knew he didn't like what she had to say. She hadn't taken it kindly when Brandon had given her the same assessment. But she'd fully embraced it over time, disappointing Brandon and his romantic view of life.

She considered the game of romance a waste of time. It took too much energy, too much mental load. It required putting her happiness in someone's hands and hoping they wouldn't crush it. Rae had seen and experienced too much heartache to entrust her heart to someone else. She'd tend to it herself, thank you very much.

But Rae wasn't so stubborn that she couldn't see there were people in the world who somehow made it work. Brandon's parents and, as she'd pointed out, Dean's parents and siblings were some examples. And she believed Dean still had a chance for the happily-ever-after many hoped for.

"Tell me there isn't at least a grain of truth in what I said," Rae prodded gently when Dean diverted his eyes and finished the wine in his glass.

"I don't know what you think this conversation would accomplish." He sounded more weary than upset, to Rae's surprise.

"Not everything has to have a goal, Dean. If you somehow get something out of this, that's great. But if I only manage to get you to listen to my unsolicited observations, that's fine, too."

Rae got up, took their empty dishes to the sink, rinsed them, and put them in the dishwasher to give Dean a moment. She stole a glance at him, and guilt bloomed inside her. The fine lines at the corner of his eyes had deepened while thinking.

He was probably wondering what he was doing there with this crazy woman. She had a tendency to be too direct. He'd known that, and she'd warned him. Still, perhaps he wasn't ready to let go of whatever he was holding on to. Who was she really to tell him anything?

She probably should start over and just try being a friend. That was what Brandon had done for her to gain her trust. He'd given her time and friendship. She could try that, and then perhaps Dean would open up to her.

Rae returned to the dining table and gathered the leftovers to store away. "I'm sorry if I pushed too far. I won't bring this up again unless you want to talk about it."

"Somehow, I doubt that." Dean glanced up at her. "You're relentless when you have a purpose. We're not so different, you and I."

"I'd agree with you. But I won't help you with anything if all I do is antagonize you." She cleared up the table. "Then we'll never be free of each other. That is still your goal, right?"

"Maybe I was wrong." Dean got up and followed her into the kitchen. "Maybe I changed my mind."

"Changed your mind about what?" Rae put away the last dishes.

"Maybe I don't want to be free of you."

Rae froze. She felt his baritone voice as well as she heard his words, like seductive fingers brushing against the back of her neck. All of a sudden, she was both warm and chilled.

"Maybe we missed a glaring clue," Dean suggested near her ear.

Trying to sound in control, Rae stayed still and asked, "What clue would that be?"

"This." He ran the tips of his fingers lightly down her bare arm, and her muscles tightened instantly in response. The gasp escaping her lips was also unmistakably audible. She felt that caress all the way down to her toes.

Rae clenched her jaw, annoyed by her body's betrayal. *For fuck's sake. One touch, and my knees are buckling?*

She spun to face Dean. He was close enough that she could feel his breath against her cheek, but she stood her ground and glared at him. No way would she let him see that he affected her. She would wipe that smug grin off his face.

"Did I say you could touch me?" she asked with a challenging smile.

The smugness dissolved fast, replaced by an innocent apologetic smile. Dean raised his hands in submission. "No. And I won't again until you ask me to."

Rae snorted. "Were you born this cocky?"

Shoving his hands into his pants pockets, the man inclined his head with an amused twist of his lips. "Interesting choice of word, but yes, I was."

Rae couldn't help but laugh and lost her bravado. The goddamn man could stir her mood all over the place. Jeez, she was hot, cold, and everything else in between in a span of a minute. And now she was laughing with him.

Oh, man. I'm in trouble.

Nineteen

Dean watched Rae slide out from between the sink and himself, carefully avoiding him. As promised, he didn't touch her. But he couldn't take responsibility if any part of her touched him. He barely could hide the pleased grin on his face.

"You should go home," Rae announced. She padded to where his suit jacket rested over the back of the couch and brought it to the door, expecting him to meet her there.

Dean stubbornly stayed leaning on the kitchen island, following her with his eyes. "I got a sense of déjà vu."

"Got kicked out of a woman's apartment a lot, huh?" Rae teased.

"Is that what you're doing? Kicking me out?" He straightened and sauntered toward her.

"Well, it seems we've reached an impasse. So why prolong this?" she said. "I can't help you find closure if you don't want to. And I'm not interested in whatever it is you're suggesting."

"Not interested, or afraid?" Dean poked.

"I'm not gonna be one of those women you parade around. Okay?" Rae shoved his jacket at him.

"I think you're afraid." He carelessly draped the jacket on his arm.

"Oh, enlighten me. What am I afraid of?" She stood with her hand on her cocked hip, challenging him.

Dean leaned close. "I think you're afraid you'll like it if I touch you."

There was a brief, tense pause before she pushed him back at the shoulder with the tip of her forefinger. "You're so full of yourself."

"Prove it," Dean challenged.

"Prove what?"

"Prove that you're not afraid." Dean slid a hand into a pocket, appearing nonchalant.

"I don't have to prove anything to you."

"Yes, because you know you can't," Dean provoked. "I barely touched you just now, and you sparked like the Empire State Building on the Fourth of July."

Rae's eyes widened, and her mouth opened with outrage. It was so comical he almost failed to keep his face even.

"Imagine if we kiss." One corner of Dean's lips quirked in a tease. "You'll probably erupt like New Year's fireworks."

"Why, you arrogant..." Rae seemed to have lost her skill with words.

Dean nodded lightly as though he understood her dilemma. "I could see why that would scare you. I do incite extreme reactions from you."

"You don't, you ass. I'll show you." In a move faster than Dean could ever anticipate, Rae grabbed fistfuls of his shirt and yanked him to her. Any other taunt from him was drowned by her lips as they fused almost forcefully against his. He'd goaded her on purpose to get a reaction out of her. But he didn't expect this.

Oh damn.

He'd underestimated their chemistry. He'd only focused on how she'd responded to his touch; he hadn't been prepared for his reaction. He felt as if he was a car she'd just hot-wired. And their bodies were the two coils of copper wires that finally fused to create a short circuit and ignite combustion inside him.

Then suddenly, it sputtered as Rae pulled back, looking horrified. Her rounded eyes darted from his lips to his eyes. Her breath was rapid, as if she'd just dashed a hundred-meter sprint.

Wanting—no, needing—that sputtering to reignite, Dean didn't think. He recaptured Rae's mouth with his. This time, one arm roped around her waist and pulled her flush to him.

Her hands that were still gripping his shirt were now trapped between them.

With a twist, Rae freed her arms, and in the split second it took, Dean expected her to push him away and even slap him for being too insistent. And he'd deserve it. But instead, she slid them around his neck and buried her hands into his hair. She gasped against his mouth as if grasping for air, and he took the opening to deepen their kiss.

Relief flooded his veins as Rae's body melted into his. The initial explosion leveled to a steady humming as he gentled each stroke of his tongue against hers, each graze of his teeth on her lower lip. They moved harmoniously together, as if they'd danced this choreography a thousand times before.

Lazily, Dean broke away to drag his nose along her jaw and nuzzled up just under her ear. He inhaled her intoxicating scent and smiled against her skin.

He whispered, "I told you. Explosive."

Damn it!

Rae lengthened her neck so Dean could explore it. She'd forgotten all arguments not to succumb to this temptation. There was still a little voice inside of her screaming, *No! Don't be weak. You don't want this!*

Oh, but this feels so good.

Either she'd forgotten how it felt to be touched by a man, or she just didn't know how this particular man's touch would make her insides catch fire. What was the word he'd used? Explosive.

"Now imagine me exploring the rest of you," Dean said, nibbling her earlobe. His hands now gently rubbed her back, supporting her weakened body. "I'm a thorough man. It might take me hours to properly cover every inch of you."

The picture he painted transformed colorfully in her imaginative mind, and Rae swallowed a groan of anticipation.

Come on, Rae. Don't let him have the upper hand here.

With great effort, she dislodged Dean's lips from her throat. Rae wasn't sure where she got the will to break out of his sensual vampire mind trick, but she did.

"This doesn't mean anything," Rae insisted weakly.

The insufferable man smiled slowly. "This means a lot."

"It just means we kissed."

"You kissed me," Dean reminded her with a smile.

Rae wanted to argue, but any rebuttal sounded hypocritical. But for some reason, there wasn't a demand in Dean's gaze. There was a trace of smugness from proving his point, but there was also restraint.

"I'm gonna go," he said after a lingering look.

That was a surprising move. Rae had thought he might push for more.

"I'm leaving for Georgia tomorrow night for the weekend," he informed her as he stepped back and straightened his clothes. "Can I call you when I get back?"

"You're going home?" For some odd reason, the news made her happy.

"After what you told me about what Kat said, I thought about how often I see my family. And you're right. Not nearly often enough. I'm going to surprise them." There was excitement in his smile.

"I'm so glad to hear that." Rae beamed at him.

"Will you think about us while I'm gone, Rae?" he asked with a light caress of his fingers on her cheek.

Rae didn't answer, but he probably knew that she would.

Dean tilted his head and lay a soft kiss on her lips. "Because I'll be doing much of that until I see you again."

With those last words, he stepped out of her apartment and closed the door behind him, leaving Rae no choice but to think about him.

Twenty

"So, you kissed him?" Brandon's eyebrow rose in question. "But you didn't want to?"

Rae was cooking dinner for Brandon before he left on Sunday morning for the European leg of Canis Major's summer tour. Like in old times, they were sitting on the couch, having tea and chatting while dinner was in the oven.

"He didn't force you, did he?" Brandon's voice turned fierce.

"No!" Rae quickly clarified, "I did it of my own will. He knew just the right button to push, and at first, I did it just to shut him up—"

"I'm so confused." He sipped his tea. "So, did you want or did you *not* want to kiss this guy?"

"I didn't want our relationship to go there."

"Oh, you tried to friend-zone him like you did me, didn't you?" Brandon grinned knowingly. "Except this time, he didn't let you."

"I didn't friend-zone you. We both knew we were better suited as friends," Rae defended herself.

Ignoring her, Brandon stayed on the subject. "Let me summarize: This guy managed to get you to spend a whole day with him, which you enjoyed. Then he got you cooking dinner for him. And one way or another, he persuaded you to kiss him instead of making a move himself. Am I correct?"

"I suppose. Though I wouldn't—"

"This guy is brilliant!" Brandon interrupted Rae with an impressed nod.

"Seriously?" Rae glared at him.

"You got to hand it to him, Rae. He approached you with an out-of-the-box strategy and kept you interested. Obviously, he did better than any of the few men you've gone out on a date with before." Brandon curiously asked, "When do I get to meet him?"

"Never." Rae scowled. "I'm not going to see him again. I won't be manipulated into...I'm not even sure what he wanted."

"You're scared," Brandon deadpanned, staring straight at her.

"Of what?" she scoffed.

"Of falling in love."

Rae laughed. "Absolutely not, because I know I'll never fall in love. I'm too jaded for love."

"Don't say that," Brandon sternly warned. "You're not jaded. You've just never experienced real love before."

"Oh, like you have?" she jeered in her defense.

Brandon hesitated a second. "Yes, I have."

"How did that work out for you?" Rae mocked.

His deep blue eyes clouded a bit. "Not well, but it hasn't stopped me from trying to find it again."

Rae immediately regretted her words. "I'm sorry, Brandon. I didn't mean—"

Brandon waved her apology away. "Never mind that. Look, this is the first time I've heard you talk about a guy like this."

"Like what?"

"Like you're equal. He's meeting your every evasion head-on, and he challenges you instead of trying to woo you."

"It's a game for him." Rae pursed her lips. "And I don't care to play."

"If you think that's all it is for him, then I don't blame you." Brandon nodded. "But what if it isn't? I find it hard to believe a guy would work that hard to get a woman's attention just for a game."

"You wouldn't?"

"Only if it felt right."

Rae drank her tea, pondering Brandon's words for a few seconds. "Then I definitely won't see him again."

"I knew you'd say that. I was right. You're afraid you might actually fall in love with him if you haven't already," Brandon provoked.

"Take that back!" Rae pointed a finger at him. "I'm not afraid of anything."

"Sure." Brandon winked.

"I'm not afraid because I know myself. I can have fun with the guy while it lasts, but it will end. If I calculate correctly, he started his move on me last Saturday. So, it's been almost a week. His affairs don't seem to last more than a couple of weeks, so it'll be over by next Saturday."

"Jeez, woman. That's a depressing way to look at things." Brandon stared at her as if she was crazy. "How did you know about his relationship history anyway?"

"I told you I did a feature on his house, and I had to research him. Dirt shows up in a web search as much as the shiny stuff," Rae said. "The thing is, he doesn't seem like the same man the gossip pages portrayed. He was especially different when he was with his family."

"Different how?" Brandon asked.

"It was obvious that his family was everything to him. How he played with his nephews and how proud he was of his sister."

"That sounds like good character to me—a family man."

"Yet he could be full of himself."

"Don't mistake confidence for arrogance," Brandon advised.

Rae scrunched her nose but reluctantly agreed. Initially, Dean might've come off as arrogant, but she'd observed the opposite. No real arrogant asshole would interact with their driver the way Dean did with Tom.

"So, when will I meet this man of yours?" Brandon asked again.

Shrugging her shoulder, Rae drank her tea to avoid answering. Technically, Brandon might have met Dean. She wasn't sure. And what was the point anyway? Brandon was leaving for a month. By the time he came home, Dean would be long forgotten.

"Let's not get your hopes up. You might believe in this romantic stuff, but you know me. I've seen too much suffering caused by this supposed love. I'm not falling into the same trap my parents did."

Brandon sighed. "You can't start a relationship thinking it will end in doom, Rae. If we did, we would cease to exist."

"Don't need the happily-ever-after to reproduce. I'm living proof." Rae grimaced.

"You're hopeless." Brandon put down his mug on the coffee table in frustration. But he then turned back to Rae with new conviction. "No, I refuse to believe that. Everybody can find love. Everybody deserves love. But they need to be open to it. As your friend, I implore you to be open to it, Rae. Even if you're not actively looking for it, don't close yourself up to its possibilities."

"What if I don't want it?" Rae stubbornly said.

Brandon huffed but didn't give up. "Okay, let's try it this way. When you go on one of your ramblings to a new place, you're always willing to try new things, aren't you?"

"Of course. But I always try to know what risk may be involved beforehand."

"Sure. That's smart. But sometimes, there's an adventure that's so epic, it comes with really high risk. But you know there's also a chance for ultimate triumph, like in rock climbing."

Rae laughed. "Really, Brandon?"

"Yeah." He got animated when he was on a roll. "Rock climbing is tough and risky, but you don't start by thinking you'll fall flat on your back or you'll never start."

"And what if I fell flat on my back when I took the risk and started climbing this rock?"

"You're forgetting one important thing." Brandon winked. "You have me on the other end of the rope. I'll never let you fall flat on your back. I'll help you back up, just like how you've done for me these past few years."

"Oh, B..." Rae smiled at her best friend. "You know you're the best guy friend a girl can have."

Brandon rolled his eyes. "Yeah, always the friend, never the lover."

"That is not true. You've had your share of girlfriends. It's not my fault if you can't find the one you're looking for."

Brandon sighed and picked up his tea again. "In time. I'll find her when the time is right."

Brandon had left after helping Rae with the dishes, but not before she'd told him to send her pictures from the tour. With the Italy project in the late-prepping phase, Rae hadn't traveled much this summer, and Brandon could tell she was edgy. Though it might not be the lack of travel that made her tense.

Solely based on Rae's story, this Dean person—Brandon at least got a first name—was really getting under his friend's skin. She might not want to admit it and had talked a tough game about not seeing him again, but Brandon could tell she was into this guy. And in almost four years of friendship, Rae had never been this flustered about a man.

Brandon had always been worried about Rae's stance on love and relationship. It was understandable with her background, but he'd wished it hadn't stopped her from letting herself be happy. Sure, he respected that people didn't always need to be with someone to find happiness, but he felt Rae had never given herself a chance.

He hoped she'd listen to his advice and embrace this possible adventure. She was an explorer at heart, so perhaps she was intrigued enough by Dean that she'd at least give him a chance to see what his intentions were. Brandon didn't have much to go on, but from what Rae had told him, he had a good feeling about this guy. He just hoped he wasn't wrong

Twenty-One

Early Saturday morning, Dean knocked on his parents' door. He could hear his mother's rushed footsteps coming in from the kitchen. At eight o'clock on a Saturday, Martha Rowland would be making breakfast for her husband and herself. He wondered what was on the menu.

Without checking who was behind the door—gotta love that small-town habit—Martha swung open the door with a smile. Her hands flew to her mouth when she saw Dean standing there. The look on her face was priceless.

"When did you get in?" Martha grabbed his face, pulled it down to meet her kisses, and hugged him tightly. "Oh, my goodness. What a surprise!"

She turned to call out to his father, "Douglas! Look who's at the door!"

"How are you, Mom?" Dean laughed. "I missed you."

"Who is ringing the doorbell this early?" Dean's father's booming voice came down the stairs.

"Oh, hush. It's past eight." Martha pulled Dean inside and hugged him again. "I'm so happy you're home."

"So am I, Mom." He smiled.

"Dean!" Douglas emerged from the stairs and into the small foyer. "Did we miss a memo or something? We didn't know you'd be in town."

"Funny, Dad." Dean stepped to his dad and was enveloped in a bear hug. "I'll make sure Melanie sends you an email next time."

"I prefer the surprise," Martha said, with a reprimanding look at her husband. "You never have to warn us you're coming home. We just want you to come home whenever you can."

"I'm thinking I'll be coming home more often from now on," Dean said.

"That'll be lovely, honey."

"What are we doing standing here?" Douglas asked. "Let's go to the den."

"Coffee, honey?" Martha asked.

"Please." Dean nodded. "I can get it myself."

"Go take your dad to the den. I'll get the coffee and fix us a special breakfast." Martha pushed the men toward his parents' sitting room.

"What made you decide to come home this weekend?" Douglas asked as they sat down.

"I have a free weekend, so it seemed like a great idea."

"It's an excellent idea," Douglas said enthusiastically.

Martha came in with mugs of coffee and placed them on the coffee table. "Doug, show him the pictures from Greece." She tapped Dean's knee. "I know we've emailed you some, but we took so many. It's a majestic place, honey. We enjoyed it so much."

"I'm glad you did," he said as his mother returned to the kitchen.

Douglas reached into the open shelf below the coffee table and took out a series of photo books.

"Here you go." He handed them to Dean. "Your sister helped me put those books together with the photo app. I sometimes still can't get over how you can take pictures without film these days. And within days, you'll get a professional-looking album like these."

"Amazing, isn't it?" Dean retorted with a smile and started going through the photos.

His seventy-year-old father, a retired engineer, was always fascinated with the speed of technology. This wonderment had rubbed off on Dean as a child. He'd followed the growth of technology closely and seen opportunities to use it with every turn. It was what had led him to where he was.

"Your sister and Matt are coming for breakfast," Martha announced.

"Did you call Gene, too, Mother?" Dean said with a half-joking reproachful tone. "It's barely past eight on Saturday morning. Let the doc sleep in."

"He's at the office already," Martha said in a mock defensive tone. "He has morning appointments today."

"Gene's practicing on Saturdays now?" Dean asked. "I didn't know that."

"The population has grown, kid," Douglas said. "Doctor's time is more in demand. So, Gene started seeing patients every other Saturday, but only for half a day."

"They'll come around lunchtime," Martha said. "Oh, lunch. We should do something for lunch."

"Mom," Dean said. "We haven't even had breakfast yet."

"It's coming." She threw him a smile.

"I thought Dad and I could run out to the store after breakfast and get some steaks. We could fire up the grill for a cookout," Dean said.

"Great idea, son," Douglas said. "I haven't had a good steak in ages."

"Douglas," Martha's voice was full of warning. "Remember your cholesterol."

"It's a special occasion, Martha. I'm going to have a piece of steak."

Listening to his parents made Dean smile. He did miss them very much. He was glad he'd decided to come.

Not long after, Kat burst through the door, followed by her husband. "I didn't believe mom when she said you were here, so I had to come and see for myself."

Remembering what Rae had said about Kat, Dean replied, "Well, I have that beautiful house. It's a shame to just let it sit there, right?"

Kat came to him for a big hug. "Glad you're home, Dean."

"So, you're visiting for the weekend?" Matt shook his brother-in-law's hand.

"I just happen to have a free weekend."

"You should've waited for Labor Day weekend, so you could stay longer," Kat suggested.

"That's still a few weeks away," Dean replied. "I miss all y'all, and I didn't want to wait. Besides, I can always come home then, too."

All eyes were on him like he had grown another head. Only his mother recovered fast enough to smile warmly at him. "That'll be wonderful, honey."

"You can always come to New York to see me, too, y'know." Dean bumped Kat's shoulder.

"Are you kidding?" Kat said. "You're so busy, we'd be with Tom the whole time. Not that he isn't nice, but I don't really want to hang out with your driver."

"Next time you come up, I'll take some time off," Dean promised. "I'll have Melanie scour for the best Broadway shows. How about that?"

Kat's eyes narrowed in suspicion. "Okay. Who are you, and what have you done to my brother?"

Dean laughed. "I've just been reminded what's important, that's all. And spending time with my family is one of my top priorities."

Now everybody looked at him like they didn't know who he was. Again, his mother was the first to recover and came over to him. She kissed his cheek lovingly and said, "I think that's great, son."

"You made them happy today." Kat handed Dean a beer bottle and stood next to him on the deck.

Breakfast was long gone. Preparation for the impromptu cookout was underway. Gene and family had joined the rest at their parents' house, and now, it was a party.

"Nah. Those boys make them happy." Dean watched his dad giving pointers to the twins on bocce, their family game, on the backyard lawn. "Look how animated Dad is with them. He was born to be a grandfather."

"That he is." Kat smiled. "We're hoping to make him a grandfather a third time."

Dean stopped at mid-swig and almost choked on his beer. "Are you...?"

"No." Kat shook her head. "We just decided a few weeks back. So don't hold your breath just yet."

Dean threw an arm around Kat's shoulders and squeezed her. "Wow, my little sister is going to be a momma."

She playfully pushed against him. "Don't jinx it!"

He laughed and let her go. "I know you're going to be a great mom."

"I'll sure do my best." She smiled. "Now, what about you?"

Dean played dumb. "I think I'd be a terrible father."

"Don't say that," Kat said. "You'll be a great father when the time comes. When you let yourself be happy, that is."

"I'm perfectly happy." Dean's left eyebrow rose in question. "What are you talking about?"

"You can be happier." His sister looked at him with a y'know-what-I'm-talking-about look.

"Okay, don't start," Dean warned her with an eye roll.

"Please, just once, listen to me," Kat pleaded. "Why wouldn't you move on and actually let someone in? If you keep your blinders on, you'll never see the right woman, even if she's right under your nose. Those glamorous dates for glitzy events don't count because I know they weren't really who you're looking for."

"Why is everyone harping on about this all of a sudden?" Dean shook his head in disbelief.

Kat tilted her head at him. "Everyone?"

"Yeah. Rae, now you." His mouth flattened in a mild annoyance. "She said I needed closure. You both need to believe me when I say I'm over Leighton. I hadn't thought about her in years until you brought her up. What other closure do I need?"

"Rae? Are you talking about Rae Allen?" Kat snapped to attention. "The woman who wrote the feature on your house?"

Shit. Dean had completely forgotten his promise to Kat.

"Yes," he answered.

Kat's frown got deeper. "Why did Rae Allen say you needed closure? And how?"

"Ah, long story short," Dean carefully started, "I bumped into her at an Aquarius event. Turns out, her best friend is the front man of one of Aquarius bands."

"Which one?"

"Canis Major."

"Get out!" Kat slapped Dean on the arm, her eyes wide in shock. "Wait. I think I might've known that from her posts. Anyway, he's a serious hottie."

Dean bristled at his sister's opinion of Brandon Rossi.

"That still didn't answer my question. Why was Rae Allen talking to you about getting closure?"

"Well..." Dean scratched his head. "We kinda hung out a couple of times since."

"Hung out?" Kat's scowl returned. "That doesn't sound like you."

"That's her word. Friends hang out. They chat over coffee or a meal. And we chatted over breakfast...then lunch. And dinner." Dean drank his beer, trying to appear nonchalant.

"Dean Rowland," Kat said, sounding scarily similar to their mom when she'd caught one of them in a lie when they'd been younger. "Tell me the truth. Really? Friends? I thought she didn't even like you."

"I am an acquired taste." Dean shrugged.

"I thought you didn't like her." Kat's voice rose an octave in incredulity.

"I never said I didn't like her."

"So you do like her?" Kat pushed.

Like—such a mundane word.

"She's interesting," Dean replied, choosing his words carefully. "Different."

"Different how?"

"She's not dazzled—for lack of a better term—by me, or rather by what I am," Dean answered honestly. "She's not afraid to take me down a peg or two when I deserve it. It's humbling and quite freeing."

"Huh." Kat looked thoughtful. "I do remember that about her. I liked her for standing up to your rude ass."

She then asked, "So, you're not dating?"

Dean's lips twisted in thought. Rae wouldn't say they were. "No." He didn't mean to sound begrudging.

"But you want to, don't you?"

Date—another unexciting word. I want to spend the weekend walking the city with her, grab some groceries, cook dinner together, joke over the meal, and make long, passionate love to end the night. And perhaps do some of those during the week, too.

Dean swallowed hard at the sudden idea in his mind. It might seem boring and ordinary, but it suddenly dawned on him how he'd enjoy boring and ordinary with Rae because she'd never bore him.

And his thoughts must've translated on his face because Kat smiled as she studied him. "I knew she was the right girl for you."

"What did you say?" Dean glared at his sister.

"There was so much current between the two of you that first afternoon you met, I swore I'd get electrocuted." Kat laughed. "And you just couldn't tear your eyes off her."

"Wait." Dean turned to face Kat fully. "Then what's with the hands-off warning?"

"A little reverse psychology." She wiggled her eyebrows proudly. "When an object of one's affection isn't easily available, the heart grows fonder."

"Don't you think your strategy has backfired on you?" Dean questioned. "I only saw Rae again by coincidence months after."

"Ah, but you don't believe in coincidence." Kat winked at him. "Months passed, and you ended up in the same place, at the same time. Again."

Dean eyed his sister with a skeptical look.

"I believed if you were meant to be, you'd find each other again. And you did." Kat grinned smugly.

"Not trying to burst your bubble here, but we're not exactly together, Kat." Dean added, "She thinks I'm still hung up on Leighton and what happened. She's only tolerating me because she believes she needs to help me find closure."

"Interesting." Kat looked thoughtful. "I agree with her, though."

"You agree with her?"

"Yes. I think you're still holding on to some residual feelings about the wedding fiasco, whether you realize it or not. But it doesn't mean you can't work it out while starting something new."

Dean thought of the kiss he and Rae had shared the other day. "Well, the jury's still out. We'll see if the lady's willing to start anything with me."

"I have faith in you, brother. You always get what you want."

Dean tossed his last bocce ball with just enough momentum to knock Gene's yellow one a foot away, leaving his red one the closest to the white pallino ball.

Gene's groan was drowned by the family's cheering.

"And that's how you beat the family's self-proclaimed champion, boys." Dean winked at his nephews. "Stick with me, and I'll teach you how to beat your dad at his own game."

"I'm pretty good, Uncle Dean," Andrew claimed with the same confidence as his father. "I beat Dad a couple of times already."

"Way to go, bud." Dean fist-bumped his nephew.

"Well, I beat Andrew most of the time," Graham claimed.

"Hey, hey. It's not about who's beating who or who's winning." Gene messed with Graham's hair. "The most important thing is we're having fun as a family. That's what Poppop always says. Right, Dad?"

"That's right!" Douglas called back.

"But it's always been your uncle's and my mission to beat your dad," Kat chimed in.

"And it took you how long to do that? Just thirty years?" Gene grinned.

"Y'know what, I'll be back in a few weeks just to beat your..." Dean remembered his nephews and changed his word choice, "butt again."

Gene laughed. "Bring it on. Let's do a one-on-one right now."

"No, no. It's time to put away the toys," Kat said, then she gathered the twins. "While your father and uncle do that, you boys come with me and help me set up the table."

"Yes, ma'am," Gene and Dean replied in unison.

The older set of brothers then started picking up the balls and putting them back into their case.

"Say, you're in a better mood than you were the last time you were home," Gene said as he closed the case.

"Was I in a mood last time?" Dean grimaced.

"You were a bit broody, which, I feel, has been your general mood in the past few years. I sense a lightness in you today that I haven't seen for a while."

Leave it to his big brother, the doctor, to give him a mental diagnosis. Gene was always annoyingly observant.

"Anything new with life?" Gene casually asked as they hauled the lawn-game case back to the garden shed.

Dean contemplated what to say to him. Not that he didn't want to tell him about Rae. He just wasn't sure where to start.

"Yes." He started with that answer.

"Work?" Gene prompted.

"No. Something I'm still trying to figure out."

Gene eyed him for a couple of seconds before nodding. "Something I can help you with?"

"Maybe."

They stored the case away and closed the shed door. But when they turned toward the house, Dean stood still, looking at the home they'd grown up in.

Their parents had never allowed Dean to buy them a new house. They insisted that too many memories were embedded in every part of it for them to leave it. They'd let the children chip in on the few updates and repairs the craftsman-style bungalow had needed, but the place had pretty much stayed the same.

And it was now creating more memories as the third generation of Rowlands set up the outdoor dining table for a meal. Their dad stood by the grill, looking proud as he supervised Matt grilling the meat. The ladies of the family came out of the house laughing with side dishes in their hands. It was all so idyllic.

"Is this why you moved back home instead of staying in Atlanta?" Dean asked.

Gene stood next to Dean, seeing what he was seeing. "In a way, yes. I wanted a quieter life, or just a life." Gene chuckled. "Working in an ER in a city like Atlanta didn't give me much spare time. Turned out to be the best move I've ever made."

Gene had bought the retiring Dr. Bloom's family medicine practice and moved back home. Soon after, he'd met his wife.

"How did you know Amanda was the one for you?" The out-of-nowhere question brought Gene's eyes to Dean.

Dean glanced at his brother with a tiny smile. "I'm just curious."

"I didn't, at first." Gene found his wife on the deck, helping Graham with the silverware, and smiled. "I just returned to town and wanted to concentrate on the practice. But, one day, this woman walked in."

"I know how the two of you met." Dean was amused by his brother's reminiscent tone. "I wanted to know how or when you knew she was the one."

"I'll tell you if you shut up," Gene reproached him. "It was Amanda who decided I was the one for her."

Dean's head spun to his grinning brother. "That's not the official story."

"She fell for me the minute I put my stethoscope under her paper gown." Gene laughed. "Do not repeat this to Amanda because she'll deny it, and I'll deny ever saying it."

"You're full of it." Dean didn't believe him.

"I'm serious. She was my patient, and there's a patient-doctor code that I have to live by. I wasn't going to pursue a patient."

Dean was still skeptical. "So, you didn't have any feelings for her when you first met, but you're claiming that she fell in love with you right from the start?"

"Well, I can't help the famous Rowland charm." Gene grinned. "Women can't resist it, as you know yourself."

Dean thought of Rae. Oh, she'd resisted him pretty well for a while. Though, he wasn't convinced that he'd completely won her over yet.

"But I never said I didn't feel anything when I first met her," Gene added. "I decided not to do anything about it."

"So, as the story went, you somehow changed your mind because here you are married for almost nine years. When did you know you wanted to spend the rest of your life with her?"

"I just knew when all I wanted to see was her face, and I couldn't wait to go home to her," Gene replied. "I couldn't and still can't see myself being happy without her and the boys."

Dean absorbed Gene's answer as he watched the scene before him. He couldn't stop thinking about Rae. And though he was having a great time with his family, he counted the time until he could see her face again. He kind of wished she was there with them. Like last spring, he could picture her blending in well with his family.

"Why do you ask?" Gene returned the question.

"There's this woman," Dean started. "She makes me think and question how I live my life lately."

"Really? Question it how?"

Dean shrugged. "That it could use a little shake-up, a bit more enjoyment, companionship, family connection. She made me realize how I haven't made enough effort to be with you guys. Phone calls are fine and dandy, but nothing beats moments like this. You know?"

"Yeah, I do know." Gene nodded. "What else does she make you think about?"

Dean half-grinned. "Well, a lot of those thoughts are unmentionable."

"Okay." Gene laughed.

"But in all seriousness, I want to spend all my free hours with her. Is that weird?"

"No." Gene shook his head with a large smile. "That actually sounds promising."

"I'm not sure she wants to do the same, but I'm trying to convince her."

"You're not together?" Gene sounded slightly confused.

"Technically, no."

"So, what are you technically?"

"We're friends."

"Friendship is a great foundation for a strong relationship. If you break down my marriage, at the end of the day, Amanda is my best friend. She's the person I want to tell about how my day went, my troubles, my victories. Physical attraction and passion are important, but for a relationship to last, it'll need more than that."

Dean thought back to his relationship with Leighton. He'd realized they'd been wrong for each other too late. He'd considered marriage as a goal. It was something he'd needed to do at that stage of his life to be completely successful. And he'd thought Leighton had filled the bill to be his wife.

"What were you looking for in a wife?" Dean asked.

This time, Gene turned fully to Dean with a frown. "I didn't have a list of qualifications, if that's what you're asking. I wasn't looking for a wife. I simply found my life partner, and she found hers. It's not about checking boxes, Dean.

"Look, I've never said this before because I didn't think you'd welcome my thoughts. But I'm glad you didn't end up marrying Leighton. It would've been a mistake."

Dean gave his brother a sharp look. "I know that."

"I'm not sure you do. I felt that when you looked at Leighton, you felt that she filled the necessary suitability to be your wife."

"She did. She was beautiful, intelligent, poised, and came from a good family." Dean suddenly felt the need to defend his decision.

"And that's all good, but there was no real connection between you. Let me put it this way. A relationship—a marriage, especially—is not unlike a business deal. It is a partnership where you need mutual respect, trust, and shared responsibilities, but the stakes are different. You both must put in an equal amount of love, affection, and passion. With all these, you'll be able to deal with whatever challenges every couple might face."

"You didn't think Leighton and I had that?"

"You didn't love her, Dean."

"How would you know that?" Dean suddenly felt he was in high school again, being reprimanded by his older brother.

"You didn't run to find her when she left you standing at the altar. If you loved her, you'd search every corner of the world for her."

"She ran off with another man, Gene!" Dean said through clenched teeth. "She betrayed me. She didn't love me. Why would I run after her?"

"Then you probably had no business getting engaged in the first place." Gene's voice stayed calm. "Why did you ask her to marry you?"

"I decided I was ready for it. That it was the obvious next step." Dean huffed a heavy sigh. "I realize how stupid that sounds now."

Gene gave Dean a brotherly squeeze on the shoulder. "Look, I'm sorry for bringing up a sensitive subject. But we tiptoed around it enough. You haven't been quite yourself since the wedding. Don't you think it's time to let all that bitterness go?

"Now, it sounds like you've met a wonderful woman with real potential. But you can't fully embrace the future when you haven't made peace with the past. It'd be a real shame if a good woman got hurt because you can't find a way to forgive what another woman did to you."

Dean forced a small smile and a nod.

"I'm gonna shut up now," Gene said and patted Dean on the back. "Let's eat!"

Twenty-Two

After a long day of work, Rae found herself sitting on a bench in Central Park on a glorious late summer evening. She was still basking in the satisfying feeling of a day well spent. The final agreement for the TV miniseries was all done, and she and the team had dove into the preparation immediately.

Yet, despite the busy day, Rae had found her mind taking occasional detours to a tall, dark, and sexy man who had been making her sweat all weekend. Granted, it usually happened in her dreams.

Rae could kill Dean for leaving her with that kiss to relive repeatedly in her head. It was the type of kiss that made one want more. It was the type of kiss that made one wonder about possibilities.

And Rae could kill Brandon for putting doubt in her mind about ghosting Dean. Though she really doubted it'd be easy to avoid Dean Rowland. He was very crafty. But then again, deep down, she was curious.

I must be crazy!

Perhaps sitting in the park on a beautiful day with the cheery sunshine peeking through the heavy canopy of green leaves looming above her made her a little hopeful. Perhaps the love quote carved on the plaque on the bench she was sitting on inspired her. Maybe Dean Rowland had some kind of crazy spell on her.

The sound of her cellphone's ring made Rae jump in her seat. A smile involuntarily formed on her lips when she saw the name on display. She quelled it because she swore he'd know she was smiling even if he couldn't see her.

Rae pressed the answer button. "Hi."

"Hi," Dean greeted from the other end of the line. "How are you doing?"

"I'm enjoying this fine summer evening sitting at the mall in Bethesda Terrace," she hinted. "So, I'd say, pretty good."

"Want some company?" he asked.

Rae counted three beats. "Sure."

"Don't move. Be there in..." Rae heard a quick muffled exchange, "ten minutes."

Rae laughed. "Really?"

"Fifteen tops. Tom's confident."

"I'll be here."

"Text me your location."

Rae filled the time by doing what she enjoyed best in the park—people-watching. On a night like this, the park was especially full of life. All kinds of workers had spilled out from their offices to cut across the park for a lovely commute home. A band of young men was playing a catchy tune in the middle of the promenade, inviting walkers to stop and listen for a while. She especially loved seeing older couples strolling hand-in-hand without a care while the busy bees passed them with their phones glued to their ears.

Some people found lasting love, Rae admitted. And she would never begrudge them their happiness. She just didn't dare to hope for love herself.

Brandon's words suddenly echoed in Rae's mind. *Be open to it, Rae. Even if you're not actively looking for it, don't close yourself to its possibilities.*

With that advice fresh in her memory, Rae turned her gaze to the other end of the mall and found Dean walking toward her. And her heart stuttered at the sight of him. It'd been four days since they'd kissed, but her toes still curled every time she thought about it. And now, seeing him in the flesh, her body hummed with anticipation.

Mentally preparing herself, Rae schooled her expression. *Don't want to appear too eager, or I'll never hear the end of it.*

She checked the time. Twelve minutes.

"How do you get here so fast?" Rae asked, half-awed, half-amused. She assumed he'd come from his office in Midtown. It would've taken him more than twelve minutes to get to the middle of Central Park during rush hour.

"Tom is a devil behind the wheel," Dean answered flippantly as he easily lounged next to her on the bench.

Rae scoffed. "You calling that sweet man a devil is laughable."

"What? I'm a simple small-town boy. Without Tom, I'd be lost in this city."

"I doubt that." She smiled. "And there's nothing simple about you at all."

Dean returned her smile and leaned in close enough to kiss her but paused, as if waiting for permission. Rae didn't retreat and held her breath. He closed the distance and gingerly touched his lips to hers. No teasing fingers on her nape or bodies crushed together. Just a few simple caresses, gentle and unhurried, leaving Rae breathless when he pulled slightly away.

"There's nothing simple about you, either," he whispered.

Rae hadn't been hot before—and it was August—but she was definitely warm now.

"Walk with me?" Dean offered her his hand.

Accepting it, she got up from the bench with him and picked up her leather tote bag.

"You look lovely, by the way." He eyed her appreciatively. "That shade of yellow suits you."

"Thank you." Rae graciously accepted the compliment. She was wearing a plain sunny yellow cotton strapless dress. She'd had a blazer on for her earlier meetings but had taken it off once outside.

"You look sharp, as always," she noted his suit. She loved that he preferred the slimmer European cut suit to the boxier American style. "But don't you feel stuffy in your jacket and tie?"

"Can't wait to undress me, huh?" He winked.

Rae burst into a laugh. If any other men had said that to her, she was sure she would've walked away. But she and Dean had crossed so many polite boundaries that the innuendo had become a game.

"I've seen what's under that suit." Rae gave him a knowing smile.

Two can play this game, buddy.

But Rae promptly changed the subject. "How was the visit with the fam?"

"It was fun and relaxing. It was good to see everybody," Dean answered as they promenaded toward the fountain. "Kat says hi."

"Oh?" She was surprised at the last bit because he'd mentioned her to his sister.

"Do you know how to play bocce?" he suddenly asked.

"The ball lawn game? Yes. Why?"

He just gave her a small side smile. "Do you like pulled pork?"

"I like all southern-style barbecue. Though I'm more inclined toward the sweeter sauce than the tangy vinegar of the North Carolina sauce."

"Excellent answer."

"You do know who you're talking to, right?" Rae grinned at him.

"Did you do what you did in Italy here, too? Work and travel?"

"From Minnesota to Florida, then to the southwest up to Washington before crossing through Wyoming and the Dakotas."

Dean looked at her as if she was crazy. "How long did that take you?"

"A few summers," Rae answered, but she refocused the conversation on his weekend. "So, how was your family?"

"Everybody's good."

Rae looked at him expectantly when he stopped. Dean raised a questioning eyebrow at her.

"Oh, you want details?" He laughed. "Well, I learned Kat and Matt are planning to get pregnant—"

"Are they? They'll be great parents," Rae claimed as if she'd known them all her life.

"I said that," Dean agreed. "My parents would be ecstatic."

He then went on to tell Rae everything about his weekend. She loved hearing every detail, even the dessert Amanda had made. Gene had claimed his wife's peach cobbler was the best in the county.

Rae had never experienced a family life like Dean's or Brandon's. But she enjoyed living through every bit of theirs.

"Is there any place in this world you haven't been to?" Dean asked as he walked Rae up to her apartment.

After their stroll in Central Park, they'd gone to a tiny hole-in-the-wall restaurant in Chinatown. Dean had considered himself worldly from traveling for business, but after hanging out with Rae, he'd learned he knew nothing about world cuisine.

Rae had ordered enough for at least five people. Dean had no idea what the dishes had been, but she'd told him they were closest to the ones she'd had in Hong Kong. He'd just eaten and enjoyed them. Now, they were carrying enough leftovers for another dinner for two.

"Tons. There are a lot of beautiful places that aren't deemed safe for a single woman to travel alone. I may be daring, but I'm not stupid."

"Did you ever feel unsafe?" Dean asked.

Rae sighed. "Of course. The world is a dangerous place for women, Dean. But I've been taking care of myself for so long, and I've learned to protect myself from harm. Now I've formed enough friendships and connections that I generally feel safe wherever I decide to go. Usually, I always have someone local or near enough to call for help if needed."

That eased Dean's mind. Though he knew he had no right to suddenly feel protective of her.

They reached the top floor and walked to her door. He handed her the leftovers bag. "We have enough for tomorrow's night dinner."

"We?" She unlocked her door. "You're assuming you're coming to dinner tomorrow?"

Dean stumbled for a response. It wasn't an assumption, but he'd felt so at ease with Rae that coming home to her for dinner seemed the natural thing to do. As if he already did it every day, when this was technically only their third "date."

"Maybe I should take the doggie bag so I can invite you for a leftover night," he said, taking the bag back. It wasn't a great save, but it was the best he could think of on the spot.

She eyed him with an amused little smile. "You're inviting me to your place to serve me leftover food?"

"I don't cook." Dean sheepishly replied. "So, what do you say?"

"I'll have to check my calendar." Rae opened her door and stepped inside.

Dean caught her hand before she completely cleared the threshold and tugged her back out and into his arm. "Why don't you do that," he told her as he looped his free arm around her waist and hauled her up to meet his kiss.

The sense of ease sizzled into a searing tension as soon as their mouths met. His whole body came to attention; he wanted to devour, feel, and fuse with her.

There was a thud like something dropped on the floor, but Dean wasn't paying attention to what it was. He only felt Rae's arms locking around his neck, her fingers running through his hair, and her tongue meeting his. She tasted like honey and spice, just like her personality.

And as abruptly as he'd started the kiss, Rae pulled back, but not away from him. Her chest heaving as she breathed, her clear blue eyes burned.

"Stay," she invited.

Rae made the invitation with a clear mind. What was the point of denying her desire? She had no expectation from their connection—most definitely not love. But there was this powerful chemistry between them. Why not embrace it and enjoy him while she could? After all, not every day a man would hold her interest as Dean did. And not every day a man could make her ache from wanting him with just one kiss.

For the first time in her life, Rae let desire rule over her head. She stepped out from his embrace, picked up her tote, and went inside. Without a word, he followed her into her apartment and closed the door behind him.

When she turned, the look in Dean's grey eyes echoed what was inside her. He was still in his suit—Rae had to admire his sartorial commitment—and looked sexier than any man needed to be. Even with the Chinese leftovers bag.

With a half-grin, Rae took the food from him to put into the fridge. She couldn't help chuckling at how even sexy thoughts didn't stop her efficiency. But she wasn't going to let good food spoil.

"What are you giggling about over there?" Dean followed her into the kitchen.

Rae bit her lips to curb her laugh. She closed the fridge door and found Dean looking at her with a bemused expression.

"Nothing. I just had to put the food away before we..." Rae chuckled and put her hands on her heating cheeks. "You must think I'm odd."

"Oh, I know you are." Dean's sexy smile returned as he backed her to her beloved vintage butcher block. "But that's what I like about you. You fascinate me, Rae."

"Do I?" she smiled, pleased by his words. "I thought I exasperate you."

"That, too." Lifting her by the waist, he sat her down on the block. He quickly eyed the thick legs where the block stood. "Is this thing sturdy?"

"I guess we'll find out." Rae laughed and circled her arms around his shoulders, drawing him to stand between her legs and pushing the skirt of her dress to ride up her thighs.

Dean put his hands on the block on either side of her hips and studied her face. "Tell me what you want."

Rae cocked her head to the side, eyeing him back. "You'd like me to spell it out for you?"

"I promised you I won't touch you until you ask me to."

"You've touched me plenty since." Rae thought of his kisses.

Dean gave a short shake of his head. "Not even a fraction of what I want to do to you."

"What do you want?" she reversed the question.

"I want you," he stated simply. "If I haven't made it completely clear."

"Then I'll make it easy for you. I want you, too."

The smile on his face made Rae's heart miss a beat. He seemed relieved and—dare she say—happy?

"You're the jump-right-in type, aren't you?" he said with a full-on grin.

Rae squinted her eyes slightly. "Not sure I follow."

"No tiptoeing into a pool once your mind is made up. You'll cannonball right in."

She shook her head. "Tiptoeing doesn't get me anywhere but doubting myself."

"No doubt?"

"No. I'll tell you a secret." Rae pulled Dean close until there was barely any distance between them. "I wanted you from the first time I laid eyes on you."

Twenty-Three

Any control Dean had left shattered. He somehow managed not to crush her against him as his mouth devoured hers. But then again, Rae was equally drowning in their combined passion.

As fast as he started their lovemaking, Dean soon gentled his kisses. His hand went to unbind her hair and let it cascade down her back. His lips trailed along the soft skin of Rae's jaw to the sensitive spot behind her ear, drawing a soft sigh out of her.

"I've wanted to do that all night," he whispered in her ear.

He pulled back slightly to look at Rae. Her skin was rose-tinted from the heat of their passion, her flowing hair framed her bewitching face, brilliant eyes unguarded.

"I've wanted to run my hands through your glorious hair since that dawn in Georgia." Dean brushed her hair off her bare shoulders, so he could plant butterfly kisses on them.

Rae's hands pushed his suit jacket off his shoulders, forcing him to break away from her. He threw the jacket onto the counter while she started loosening his tie.

"I swear you kept this on all night to drive me crazy." The corners of her mouth rose in a sensual smile. "I've wanted to do this all night."

"I knew it." Dean couldn't help grinning.

Rae glanced at his face for a second before returning to her task. She pulled the tie off his neck and continued to unbutton his shirt. She gently slapped his hands away when he started to help her with the buttons.

"I'm doing this." Rae undid the first three buttons and revealed the top of his chest. She brushed her fingers on his exposed skin as she slowly worked her way down. "Did you imagine me undressing you?"

Dean took a deep breath as he watched her hands. "No, not particularly. I thought about undressing you."

She flashed him an amused smile. She finally got to the top of his pants and unbuckled his belt and his pants button. Rae took his wrist and found his cufflink. Efficiently she worked it off his sleeve, then the other, before placing them into his pants pocket.

They'd be there all night at her pace, but Dean didn't mind. He suddenly found the simple act of being slowly undressed by a woman so erotic.

Next, she pushed the shirt off him, then leaned back to look at him. Dean held his breath as her eyes swept along his torso, and her palms ran lightly from his chest to his abdomen. His muscles tightened, responding to her touch.

When her hands went back to his pants, he stopped them. "My turn to play."

He wanted to take things slow. He wanted to focus on her, and he'd do anything in his power to ensure that tonight would be a night she'd never forget.

Rae expected Dean to rip her dress off, but instead, he cradled her face in his hands and kissed her. Achingly gentle and lazy. Her lips welcomed the seduction and opened in an invitation for him to taste her further. She didn't even realize when his fingers found the fastening of her dress and slowly undid it.

The light cotton fell off her torso and pooled around her waist. Already aroused from his kisses and undressing him, his large hands on her bare skin made her want to beg him for more. Encircling her arms around him, she let her head fall back as his lips traced their way down her neck to her collarbone.

"Bed?" Dean whispered in her ear.

Rae barely registered his question, but she nodded.

"Hold on to me." Quickly, Dean hauled her off the butcher block and headed to her bedroom. They tumbled softly onto her bed, where he reluctantly pulled slightly away, but Rae's hands around his neck stopped him from moving farther. She loved the feel of his weight on her.

"I'm not going anywhere." Dean looked at her. "I'm exactly where I want to be."

He dipped his head to the crook of her neck and trailed kisses until he found her earlobe to nibble, and Rae sighed. Dean's trained fingers found no difficulty undoing her bra, and the small item of clothing found its way to the floor. But all she was aware of was his mouth and hands caressing her, creating ripples of sensation throughout her body. When those two strong hands molded her breasts, caressing her sensitive skin, her eyes fluttered open to find him watching her reaction.

"You're beautiful," he said in his quiet voice. His eyes trailed down to where his hands were, and Rae felt more heat gather in her belly, knowing he was looking at her body.

"I've dreamed of doing just this," he whispered against her skin as he showered butterfly kisses on the valley between her breasts.

His fingers brushed against her sensitive buds, and a shiver ran through her body. When he captured one pink tip in his mouth and teased it with his tongue, she bucked under him, the fingers on his hair tightened their grip, and a soft moan escaped her lips. Encouraged by her response, he dragged his mouth into paying the tip of her other breast equal attention.

Rae's senses went wild with his mouth and hands on her. Never had her body liquefied with this intensity from a mere man's touch. Never had she wanted a man this desperately. With each caress, he just made her need more and more.

"I want to feel you. All of you," Rae demanded.

Dean brought himself up to kiss her mouth lightly. "Patience, sweetheart. I've been waiting for months to taste you. We're going to take our time."

Rae was impatient and wasn't willing to let him dominate her. With a show of strength, she rolled and reversed their positions.

He looked up at her with a shocked-impressed smile. "Is that one of your Krav Maga moves?"

She laughed. "Does that turn you on?"

"Absolutely."

Feeling confident in her power over him, Rae straddled him. She ran her hands down his torso and farther below to find proof that he was as aroused as she was. With her fingertips, she traced him through the fabric of his pants and was delighted to hear Dean groan with pleasure. Slowly, she unzipped his pants. She couldn't help wanting to stroke him, but after only a few delicate touches of her hands, he caught them in his.

"Don't," he said through his teeth as if he was in pain. "Keep touching me like that, and this will be over so fast."

Rae looked at his strained handsome face. She lowered herself, started kissing him along his jaw, and whispered in his ear, "I need you inside me now."

Dean responded to her request by rolling Rae over and pulling himself up to strip off the remainder of his clothing. He stood naked before her, giving her a full view of his leanly muscled body.

How? How do you make me so desperate for you? Rae was baffled by her body's response to his. And from the look of his rigid member, he was desperate for her.

After quickly taking care of protection, Dean pulled her dress and panties off her. Pressing her down on the bed with his body, he captured her hands in one of his, trapped them above her head, and kissed her thoroughly.

Yes! No more joking around. Patience was gone out of the window.

With his free hand, Dean caressed the length of Rae's torso down to the inside of her thighs. He found the center of her arousal, where she was hot and ready for him. She moaned into his mouth when he spotted the little nub hidden between the petals of the most intimate part of her body. Wanting to bring her as high as possible before joining her, he eased one and then two fingers into her tight channel.

Rae tore her mouth away from his and gasped for air. "Yes, more. Dean, please."

Dean needed to stay in control, or he'd burst. But when she called his name, he lost all control.

He released her hands and moved to fit himself inside her. The moan escaped from her throat at the sudden fullness of him replacing his fingers. Instinctively, her body bowed to meet his thrust, allowing him to bury himself deeper.

Pausing with his full length inside her, Dean buried his face against her neck, controlling his breathing while her arms clasped around him.

"Oh, god, Rae." He felt such pleasure just from entering her; without thinking, he said aloud, "Where've you been all my life?"

He started to move inside of her.

Rae matched his rhythm, and they both became lost in their lovemaking. All he could feel was being one with her and wanting never to let go. As they climbed toward the peak, Dean sought her hand and laced his fingers through hers. Watching her expressive face as she reached for her climax was ecstasy. He could hardly contain himself as he drove into her faster. He was straining to hold on to his own release when he felt her body tremble with hers, and a cry escaped from her lips. His own came while her climax was still soaring through her body.

And he felt as if the ground fell from under him, and he fell into the unknown to land on Rae's warmth.

Her limbs still tangled with Dean's, the world Rae knew shattered as she felt the last currents of her orgasm running from the center of her body to the tip of her toes. She knew a part of her would never be the same again after tonight.

She'd opened her eyes to look at him as they reached the peak. In those last seconds, he'd blinked his eyes open and locked with hers. There was something indescribable in his grey eyes, and something inside her echoed it.

Damn.

Twenty-Four

Sunlight streamed through the windows and brought Dean out of slumber. He blinked his eyes and blocked the offending light with his arm. He lay flat on his back for a minute to fully wake up.

What time is it? he wondered. He probably should shower. But strangely, his body felt so loose and relaxed that he didn't want to get up.

He felt the bed move, and something soft and warm snuggled into him. His eyes flew open, and he found why he was feeling uncharacteristically mellow this morning. Next to him, Rae lay on her side against him. Her dark auburn hair was strewn around her shoulder and his chest. Her breathing was slow and steady, indicating that she was still asleep.

Dean had fallen asleep in Rae's bed last night. After their second round of lovemaking, he remembered feeling content and wanted to lie there with her in his arms. A smile emerged on his lips as he recalled every moment of their night.

He hadn't expected her to invite him in. But he should've known that Rae would somehow blow his mind. The way his body responded to her amazed him. The way he responded to the woman next to him astounded him. The fact that he was still in her bed the morning after should've triggered his internal alarm. It'd been years since he'd spent a whole night in a woman's bed and still wanted to linger. Even with his ex-fiancée, it'd been sporadic. They hadn't even lived together.

Dean wrapped his arm around Rae's back so she would snuggle closer. He buried his nose in her hair as he spontaneously laid a soft kiss on the top of her head.

What's that fragrance? Floral, sweet, yet fresh and woodsy.

He inhaled her scent and felt something thawing inside him. Rae coaxed a change in him he didn't know he needed. She moved pieces around that hadn't fit well, and it filled him with an unfamiliar yearning. And he wasn't sure what to do about it.

Do you have to analyze everything, Rowland? Just take it day by day.

Shutting his eyes, he reveled in the feel of Rae naked and warm in his arms. He could get used to this, waking up with her next to him. Absently, he brushed his fingers on her arm, needing to touch her. He could feel when she started to stir. She slightly shifted her limbs, and her breath deepened.

Her arm slid across his chest and wrapped around him, pressing her body against his. "You're so hot," she murmured.

Well, that was an unexpected morning greeting. "Thanks." Dean grinned.

"I meant temperature-wise." She raked her fingernails on his pec, not painfully, but enough to convey her meaning.

Dean's chest rumbled with a chuckle.

Rae stretched her neck up to look at him. He shifted and met her halfway to kiss her.

"Good morning," he whispered onto her lips.

"Good morning." Rae studied his face with a soft light in her eyes, but a veil came over them in the next second.

"What are you thinking?" he asked curiously.

"Nothing," she replied. "I was just thinking that this morning you look more like the man I met in Georgia."

"I'm the same man."

"Without your tailored suit and groomed face, you look more relaxed." She rubbed his rough jaw. "Though not less intimidating."

"You never were intimidated by me." Dean scoffed, "Besides, who could be intimidating buck naked?"

Rae chuckled. "Oh, I don't know. I think you'd manage." She ran her fingers over the breadth of his shoulders. "I mean, anyone would think twice about challenging a man of your size. How does a CEO of a media technology company get broad shoulders like this anyway?"

"Swim team from grade school all the way to college." Dean shrugged. "I still swim daily."

"Of course." She had an I-like-what-I-see-smile on her face. "You were swimming when I first saw you. I remember thinking how sexy you looked slicing through the water."

"Really?"

"Until you greeted me so warmly, that is." Rae scoffed.

"I'm sorry." He eyed the heavens and argued, "I was startled. I don't get a gorgeous trespasser every day."

"Sure." She laughed, then pushed herself out of his arms. "What time is it? Don't you have to go to work?"

"I don't want to go to work," he replied, surprising himself.

Rae cocked an eyebrow at him.

Dean pulled her back onto the mattress and covered her with his body. With an inviting grin, he asked, "Play hooky with me?"

"It's your lucky day," Melanie said on the phone to Tom. "The boss is taking PTO. He won't need you until tomorrow."

"I know. He texted me." Tom sounded pleased. "In the five years I've driven him, I don't think he ever suddenly took time off."

"I was surprised myself. God knows he could use a vacation with how he works," she said thoughtfully. "He's different lately. He's been in such a light mood and smiling much more."

"I told you, Mel," he said smugly.

"You really think it's the new woman?"

"She's lovely, Mel, and kind. I've never seen Mr. Rowland look at someone the way he looks at Miss Rae."

"Miss Rae, huh?" Melanie wondered. "Well, I won't put too much hope into it. It's early yet."

"Sometimes it only takes a second to fall in love," Tom, the old romantic, pointed out.

"And it usually takes about two weeks for the boss to move on to another girl," Melanie, the skeptic, countered.

"When was the last time he took off work to be with someone?" Tom challenged. "He hardly even did that when he was engaged."

"That relationship was wrong from the start." Melanie huffed, remembering Leighton Heston.

"I say this one is promising," Tom insisted. "I never see him so eager to stroll in the park with a woman. And when they were in the car, they talked nonstop. Have you ever heard Mr. Rowland laugh out loud these past few years? Well, he does with Miss Rae. If I were him, I wouldn't want to leave her side, either."

"He stayed with her last night?" Melanie frowned, understanding what that meant. "And you think she's different from the other girls?"

"For sure. He *stayed*. He never stays," Tom emphasized. "Look, I can't tell you what he does or doesn't do when he's alone with a date, but I see what I see. Those gossip-mongers may make him seem like a womanizer, but you and I both know that's not who he is."

"I know that, but I'm not convinced your Miss Rae will be any different than the other women he dated."

"There's just something about the way they look at each other and how he is when he's with her."

"We can argue all day, but we'll never really know what's going on in the boss's head," Melanie said.

"Or in his heart," Tom added.

"Presuming it's still working properly," Melanie concluded.

Twenty-Five

The days flew by over the next two weeks. Dean's evenings were spent with Rae as work continued to fill his day. And he looked forward to each night he got to spend with her. Even when it was only for a simple dinner at her apartment, followed by an innocent goodnight kiss.

The first night she'd come to his apartment, she'd drooled over his spacious kitchen. And to his private pleasure, she'd made herself at home and cooked them dinner with the small staples his housekeeper had left. He'd proceeded to make love to her on the marble island right after.

Last weekend, she'd asked him to go to a one-woman show. It'd been a moving silent rendition of a noir movie acted by Rae's friend, Shelley. The audience had been encouraged to move around the set to capture the emotional performance from all angles. While Rae had circled the room, Dean had stood quietly in one corner. He'd been intrigued by the small production, but he'd been more captivated by Rae.

The emotions on Rae's face had equaled the intensity of the artist. There had been turmoil in those blue eyes, perhaps triggered by the performance. But he'd sensed it'd come from within.

I've experienced loss, too. Dean had recalled Rae saying that, but she'd never elaborated what it was she'd lost. He'd tried to coax her to tell him more about her past, but each time she'd only given him a vague answer before distracting him with something else.

For some nagging reason, he felt even though Rae had accepted him into her life, she was still holding a part of herself back.

Tonight, Dean had asked her to come with him to Chris Sullens' new club opening. She'd been reluctant and would only go if they'd arrived separately. He hated the idea but understood her disliking some tabloids' obsession with him. She hadn't wanted to be photographed with him and labeled his squeeze of the week.

It doesn't matter. As long she's here with me.

Dean tried to shake the annoyance and enjoy the evening instead. Chris' third club opening was in full swing. After selling his first one at a significant profit, he'd invested part of it into this smaller club targeting higher-end clientele who preferred quieter evenings with pricier vintage liquor and wines. He'd put the rest into a consortium of investors that bankrolled his actual passion project.

Chris was telling Rae all about it over glasses of wine in their VIP booth.

"The resorts are all about personalized service, unique locations, world-class food, luxury accommodations," Chris explained animatedly. "And my intention is to always keep the number of guests small. It'll be like staying in a spacious and luxurious B&B with world-class offerings."

"There are luxurious small hotels all over the world. What would make yours different?" Rae pointedly asked.

Dean suppressed a smirk as his friend tried to school his face. Most people in their circle who had heard Chris' spiel on his resort concepts tended to fawn over the idea. Rae had listened with interest, but she did bring up good points.

"Your first location, for example, is already well-known. There are numerous famous resorts there already, and it's not that big of an island," Rae said. "How do you compete with them?"

"I don't," Chris stated. "Those resorts are huge, with hundreds of rooms. There are no personalized services there. Guests will get lost. And they're all sequestered on one side of the island. Have you been to Bali, Rae?"

Rae nodded. "Yes. Though it's been a while."

Dean silently laughed at Chris' question and sipped his wine. *Of course she has.*

"Then you know most tourists flock to the northern part of the island, where the restaurants, bars, beach clubs, and shopping are." Chris took out his phone and pulled up some pictures. "Ours is on the still pristine eastern coast. Exotic black sand beach. Miles of unobstructed views of the strait. How spectacular is that?"

Rae looked through them and smiled. "It's gorgeous. I didn't go there. How far is this from the airport? Two to three hours' drive?"

"It is a long drive." Chris conceded. "But this is what I mean about personalized service. It starts from the moment you arrive at the airport or wherever you'd like to start your experience. We will pick you up in our comfortable car, with gourmet snacks and drinks provided for the long drive. And once you arrive, you'll never want to leave. We cater to those few who want to enjoy the quiet, the culture, the cuisine, the people, but without having to be in the tourist traps."

Rae now looked impressed. She touched Chris on the arm and said, "That sounds wonderful. I can't wait to see it."

Happy now, Chris beamed at the compliment and covered Rae's hand with his. "I'd love it if you come and visit. It's an open invitation."

Dean jumped into the conversation. "Let's talk about your current venture. This crowd seems to love the vibe here."

Dean took Rae's other hand on the table and held it. Chris saw the gesture and glanced at him with a slight grin. His friend understood the subtle message and released Rae's hand.

"Yes, this is lovely and low-key," Rae agreed. "Quite the opposite of your other club."

"Different target markets." Chris slid out. "These crowds like the personal touches, so, unfortunately, I need to leave you and pay my other guests some attention. Thanks for the discussion, Rae. I'll circle back to you guys later. Just ask any of my team to refresh your drinks."

And as smoothly as he'd greeted them, Chris slipped away.

"You two are good friends, you said?" Rae turned to Dean.

"Since the first year of college."

"I could see it." Rae had her analytical face on, amusing him. "Based on looks and demeanors, you can't be more different. You're dark, quiet, and controlled. He's light, all smiles, and charm—"

Dean narrowed his eyes at her. "You don't think I'm charming?"

"In your own special way, you are. And you choose when and to whom you turn on your charm. Chris seems to be on all the time. Look at him working the room."

"That's why he's in hospitality. It's in his blood."

Rae nodded. "You complement each other. But you wouldn't be friends unless you shared fundamental values."

"He's a hard worker. He might be the heir to the Sullens' hotel empire, but he wants to build his own legacy. And he's doing it."

"I sense there's a strained family dynamic," Rae said.

Dean frowned. "How could you tell?"

"I..." She hesitated. "Most people have daddy or mommy issues."

Now his senses were tingling. Dean was about to probe when he saw Gayle and a few people he knew approaching their table and had to shelve that topic for another time.

Rae blew out a long exhale when she entered the ladies' room. Like the rest of the club, this room exuded class—black marble, shiny fixtures, and lit vanity mirrors. And to Rae's approval, it was large with numerous full-door stalls. She hated those flimsy public bathroom doors with bottom cutouts and open slits on each side that anyone could see through. What was the point of having a door?

Taking her time in the relatively quiet bathroom with only a few other ladies coming in and out, Rae went to stand in front of a mirror to touch up her makeup. She didn't care about her face, but she needed the time to recompose herself. Being with Dean and being introduced to numerous people who had come to their table made her acutely aware of their speculative stares.

They had been mostly cordial and courteous, but some—the women, especially—were covertly hostile. It could all be in her head. But she had the impression that Gayle

Harris, one of Dean's top executives and good friends, didn't like her very much.

Rae had no basis to justify her feelings because Gayle seemed friendly enough. She asked questions about Rae's work and was particularly interested in her connection with Canis Major. She'd claimed the social-media coverage of the Canis Major indie tour was one of the reasons her team had signed the band. But for some unspecified reason, Rae had felt Gayle had underplayed Rae's role in it.

I don't care. It had been her idea, and her audience had boosted Canis Major's numbers. The boys knew, and that was all that mattered.

The main bathroom door opened, and a tall, long-limbed woman walked in. Rae locked eyes with the incoming woman in the mirror, and the other woman started toward her. Rae suppressed a groan and braced herself for unpleasantness.

"You've been in here for a while." Fiona Underwood's sickly sweet voice made Rae's skin crawl. "We're not making you uncomfortable, are we?"

Rae put away her compact and looked at the other woman with feigned confusion. Fiona definitely didn't need to know she had a low tolerance for people like her. Her experience working for the glitzy rich on that superyacht in Italy had taught her how to deal with them. They were like any other people: Some were decent, others were dicks. Fiona fell into the latter category.

"Why ever would you think that?" Rae asked.

Fiona pulled out a Chanel lipstick and applied it to her pouty lips with precision.

"Oh, a few of Dean's former dates didn't exactly..." she paused for a dramatic effect, "fit in. It's really not their fault. A man in Dean's position needs a woman who can keep up with his lifestyle."

"I see. And you think I don't fit in?" Rae kept her voice amiable.

"It's not really my place to say, is it? It's more about, do you think you fit in?" Fiona's eyes swept over Rae slowly down to her shoes and again to meet her eyes.

Wow. This woman is a viper. Though that might be an insult to real vipers.

Earlier, Fiona had inserted herself into the small group surrounding her and Dean. The conversation had been relatively benign—some business, current politics, and travel. Until Chris had brought up Rae's trips and shone the attention on her. Fiona had attempted to belittle Rae's style of traveling as the poor-people way.

Fiona then had turned her body close to Dean, put her hands on his arm and chest, and with a laugh, said, "Can you imagine having to fly in coach and work for your dinner?"

Dean had stepped away from Fiona and put his arm around Rae's waist to indicate where he stood. "I don't have to imagine it. I've done it. You should try it sometime, Fiona. Maybe you'll get a better appreciation of how most people live."

People like Fiona tended to conveniently forget that Dean hadn't come from money. But of course, as out of touch as the daughter of a New York real estate mogul that she was, Fiona had laughed off the comment. She'd then doubled down on never flying coach.

Rae hadn't flown coach for several years now. First, she could now afford it, and second, she knew how to upgrade to first class without buying it. But she wouldn't engage in Fiona's game.

Now Fiona had brought the battle into the ladies' room. Obviously, the viper saw Rae as a threat, and for some reason, Fiona thought she had a chance with Dean.

"Tell me, Fiona. You think you'd be a better choice for Dean?" Rae held the other woman's gaze.

"I know I am."

"Okay." Rae just shrugged, gave Fiona an I-don't-give-a-fuck smile, and turned to walk away.

"I managed to stop him from marrying Leighton. You'll be much easier to rid of," Fiona hissed.

Rae wasn't sure if Fiona had meant for her to hear what she'd say, but she did. She spun around and glared at the blond woman. "What the hell did you do?"

"Nothing sinister." Fiona acted innocent. "I only nudged Leighton toward the man she actually wanted. I was doing her a favor, really. What happened after that was not my doing. Perhaps you should think twice if you have any fancy thoughts about winning Dean Rowland."

Fiona leaned in as if they were two girlfriends sharing secrets. "You've heard that nobody has seen Dean's ex-fiancée since before the wedding, have you?"

"What are you saying?" Rae hated that Fiona managed to hook her.

"How do you think Dean gets to be where he is? I heard he's ruthless in the boardroom and the bedroom. He doesn't like to lose. So, who knows what really happened to Leighton? It is weird that she just disappeared."

Rae reeled back in disgust at Fiona's vile lies. "And why do you want him if you believe that?"

Fiona laughed. "Oh, honey. I can handle a man like Dean Rowland. Leighton Heston never had a chance, and neither do you."

Gathering her composure, Rae pulled back her shoulders, took a deep breath, and coolly replied, "Then you have nothing to worry about."

She stormed out the door without allowing Fiona another chance to bait her further.

"Pardon me," Rae brusquely apologized as she almost crashed into Gayle at the ladies' room door.

Gayle watched Dean's new girlfriend rush onto the main floor with an arched brow. *What has put her panties in a twist?*

She couldn't decide what she thought of Rae Allen yet. She seemed to be everything that Chris Sullens had advertised. And Gayle could see Dean was smitten with the woman. But Rae didn't seem to return the feelings. In fact, Rae looked anxious just before she'd excused herself to the restroom. The bathroom break didn't seem to have improved her mood.

Gayle walked down the short hall into the main floor of the marbled room and ran to Fiona Underwood. Oh, boy, what had Fiona done now? The woman was trouble, but Gayle couldn't say what it was about Fiona that made the hair on her neck stand up. And because of her father's connections and money, she showed up at every event that would give her a spotlight.

"Hello, Gayle." Fiona flashed him a smile.

Gayle could imagine fangs peeking through the other woman's red lips. "Hey. Did you say something to Rae?"

Fiona eyed her as she patted her nose with a compact. "Why?"

"She seems upset."

Gayle saw the sly grin Fiona tried to hide. But Fiona shrugged. "I just gave her friendly advice."

"About?" Gayle skeptically questioned. Fiona wasn't one to give out advice.

"You're one of Dean's most trusted friends." Fiona pronounced the word 'friends' as if gesturing air quotes. "Do you think Miss I-travel-the-world is a good fit for our Dean?"

Gayle restrained herself from rolling her eyes. The jury was still out as far as Gayle's concern, but she wasn't going to tell Fiona that.

"Because I don't." Fiona didn't wait for a response. "If I were her, I'd stick with Brandon Rossi. I think he's more of her class."

Gayle narrowed her eyes at Fiona without responding. Sometimes silence resulted in more info.

"I did a quick search on her." Fiona winked. "I'm so tired of hearing Rae traveled here. Rae did that. She's nothing but a common social media climber. First, she used Brandon Rossi to boost her popularity. And now she's setting her eye way higher.

"We got to protect our boy, don't we, Gayle?" Fiona eyed Gayle as if they were in on this together.

Gayle pursed her lips as she listened to Fiona. She knew she couldn't trust a word out of Fiona's mouth, but she might be on something.

Twenty-Six

Dean checked his watch as he walked out of the conference room. It was almost noon. After their weekly meeting, he'd stayed and chatted with his executive leadership team, but he now had to rush and pick up Rae for their weekend trip home.

Yup, he was introducing Rae to his parents. His palms sweated just thinking about it.

A pair of high heels fell into step next to him. Dean glanced to his side and found Gayle grinning at him.

"Going somewhere for the long weekend?" she asked.

"Home. As should you and everybody else." Dean asked, "Planned anything special with the family?"

"We might visit Greg's parents. By the way, Rae is an interesting woman."

Dean's eyebrow rose at Gayle's lack of segue.

"I enjoyed meeting her the other night," Gayle added. "Where is she from again? I thought I heard a hint of an accent."

"Minnesota," Dean answered, eyeing his friend.

"Minneapolis? St. Paul?"

"Just outside of the city, I think."

"You think?" Gayle frowned. "Are her folks still there?"

"I don't think so. She told me she hasn't been back to Minnesota for a while."

"Well, where does she go for the holidays then?" Gayle pushed.

"She usually travels during the holidays or celebrates with friends," Dean answered, wondering what was with the interrogation. "But this time, she'll be coming home with me."

Gayle stopped in her tracks. "Are you serious?"

"Yes." Dean faced her. "In fact, she's coming home to Georgia with me tonight."

"Meeting the family so soon?" She looked shocked.

"Rae already met the family, just not my parents. They're excited to meet her."

"Really?"

Dean's lips flattened as he heard Gayle's disbelieving tone. "Do you have a problem, Gayle?"

"No." Gayle quickly said. "I was just surprised, that's all. It's rather new, isn't it? I mean, you don't even know much about her."

"I know enough." Dean, more than annoyed now, headed for the elevator banks. Why did it matter to Gayle whether he was introducing Rae to his parents this weekend or a year from now?

Keeping up with Dean, Gayle said, "She seems like a nice enough girl. But is she the kind of a girl you'd want to bring home to your parents?"

"First, she's a grown, independent woman, not a girl." Dean punched the elevator call button. "Second, she's a brilliant and successful entrepreneur and author. Third, she fascinates me and gets me. Are any of those answers a good enough reason for you, Gayle? Or is a certain last name or a well-recorded pedigree also a requirement?"

Dean's sarcasm should've warned Gayle, but she didn't take the hint.

"All of those are fine and dandy." She brushed Dean's reasons aside. "You sound like a besotted man. But how does she feel about you? Because I don't see it."

"You don't see what?" Dean questioned.

"The other night." Gayle shrugged. "I felt she was a little cold."

Dean huffed a breath. His patience was running low. "I don't think she was."

"Do you know about her relationship with Brandon Rossi, Canis Major's front man?" Gayle kept pestering him.

"What is this about, Gayle?" Dean demanded. "What's your problem with Rae?"

"I just want you to be careful. I don't want you to get hurt again." Gayle touched his arm. "You know I'm just looking out for you."

The elevator door opened, and Dean entered before replying, "Rae is not Leighton. If that's what you're worried about."

"Just be sure before you do anything drastic," Gayle advised as the door closed.

Dean rode down with his mind replaying the confounding conversation. It tainted his excitement for the weekend.

He'd asked Rae to come home with him earlier in the week. He figured there was no reason for him to delay introducing her to his parents. She'd argued it was too soon, but he didn't think it mattered whether it'd only been three weeks or three years. He'd never felt more alive than he was in these past weeks with her.

In the end, Rae had agreed to come. But now, Gayle had made him question everything.

Goddamn it, Gayle.

Rae put her always-ready toiletry bag into her carry-on and zipped it close. Dean was picking her up in an hour to fly to Georgia for the Labor Day weekend. When he'd asked her to come, Rae had been apprehensive. She'd never met a man's parents before—except for Brandon's parents, but that had been a different circumstance.

Though the idea of meeting Dean's parents and spending a weekend with his family was still daunting to Rae, it wasn't what currently weighed on her mind.

Fiona Underwood's allegation against Dean still bothered her. She might've entertained the idea when she'd first read that one outlier gossip rag's article featuring the same theory, but not after knowing him personally. Dean Rowland might not be the easiest man to understand, but he was a good man. No ruthless man inspired the kind of respect and affection he had from his family, friends, and even employees.

Rae didn't care what Fiona had said. But it bothered her that Fiona had had the nerve to talk about Dean that way. She'd wanted to punch her big mouth, but she knew better. Someone like Fiona would use any ammunition she got.

I need help. I need someone who knows what happened back then.

Heading back to her closet, Rae took the clutch she'd used on the night of the club opening. She dug out a business card. She dialed the cell number jotted down on the card's backside.

Chris Sullens answered on the third ring. "I wasn't expecting you to call this soon. Have you decided to take me up on my offer?"

"I'm actually calling for another reason." Rae hesitated but decided she had already made the call. "I need your help. And since Dean trusts you, I feel I can do the same."

There was silence on the other end for a few beats. "What can I do for you, Rae?"

"It's more for Dean. I need to find Leighton Heston."

Chris blew a breath. "That's treacherous territory. I find it hard to believe that Dean is in on this. What's really going on?"

Rae considered what she should tell Chris. She took a chance that Chris had no love lost for Fiona Underwood. In fact, she felt most people tolerated Fiona's presence due to her father. But she was still taking a risk trusting him. People from Chris Sullens' level of society tended to have each other's back. She just hoped he was as good of a friend as Dean said he was.

She relayed what Fiona had said to her.

Chris swore under his breath, "That fucking malicious—" He cut himself off. "I'm sorry."

"No. I have a few choice words for her, too."

"I can't stand her, but I considered her harmless so far. I didn't realize she's so devious."

"I don't believe a thing she said about Dean. But imagine what else she's said to other women Dean dated. She might've manipulated Leighton to leave Dean. And if that was the case, what happened shouldn't have happened. They'd be married three years—"

"No." Chris interrupted her. "I don't think so. Leighton was never right for Dean. Or Dean for her."

"You can't know that."

"I was there when they met and when she disappeared."

"He's never gotten over her." Rae looked out the window of her apartment.

"Rae—"

"Do you have any idea where she might've gone?" Rae asked.

Chris hesitated. "No. Dean told me she'd eloped with another man."

"Yes, he told me Leighton had asked him not to look for her."

"So, why do you want to find her?"

"At first, because I thought he needed closure. I still do. He's not over her or her betrayal. But now, it's to stop Fiona from spreading these lies."

"Nobody believes those rumors."

"You're certain of that?" Rae asked.

Chris went quiet, then sighed before asking, "What do you need from me?"

"A lead. Think back to three years ago. You know everyone in that circle. I've seen the way you work through your guests. You might've met this man Fiona had pushed toward Leighton. Maybe at your clubs or private parties. Any event that both Fiona and Leighton would've attended."

"I'll try."

"Do you have the Hestons' address?"

"They declared bankruptcy and sold every asset. The last I heard, I think they moved upstate. I can find out where."

"We can start from there. Her parents must know something."

"From what I remember, they had no idea where she went."

"It's been three years. Something might've changed." Rae's phone pinged, indicating an incoming text. She briefly glanced at it. It was Dean. "I have to go. Dean's picking me up in a few minutes."

"Have you told him about this?" Chris asked.

"He'd just confront Fiona to protect me. I don't need that. I can handle Fiona."

"What about you looking for Leighton?"

"I don't think he'd like it. That's why I came to you for help."

"Why should I trust that you have Dean's best interest at heart?" Chris questioned. "I've only met you."

"That's fair." Rae nodded, even if Chris couldn't see her. "I suppose I can't ask you to trust me. I know you care for him. You're his best friend. I have a best friend, too, and I love him like family. I would do anything for him. Finding Leighton will do Dean good, whether he believes it or not."

Rae waited for a few beats.

"Give me a few days. I'll let you know what I can find out," Chris finally said.

"Thank you, Chris."

"Don't thank me yet. I'm still not sure if this is a good idea."

"I guess we'll find out."

Twenty-Seven

"I never thought I'd see this house again." Rae walked through the front door of Dean's lake house. "Should I go around back and reenact my first time here?"

Dean carried her suitcase in with a suggestive smirk on his face. "Somehow, that scene turns out very differently in my head now."

"You'd be nicer this time?" Rae headed to the kitchen to drop off the grocery bags she was toting.

"Oh, I'd be real nice." Dean followed her after setting the carry-on down.

"My god." She laughed, hearing the innuendo in his voice. "Men."

Dean came up behind her as she put the bags on the counter. "Didn't you tell me you wanted me the first time you saw me?" He wrapped his arms around her waist and kissed her on the neck.

"I knew telling you that was a mistake." Rae started pulling items out of the bag, even as Dean dropped kisses on her shoulder. "Help me with the groceries. I don't know where things go."

"Your guess is as good as mine." But Dean released her, grabbed the other bag, and started putting a few perishables like eggs, cream, and cheese into the fridge.

"I feel I need to bring something to your parents' tomorrow." Rae looked through the stuff they'd bought. "What do you think? I've never done this before."

Dean smiled at her. "You don't need to bring anything."

"What if I make something? For dessert?"

"Amanda has that covered, believe me." Dean closed the fridge and came to her. "Look, nobody is expecting you to bring or make anything. They know we're just arriving this evening. Relax."

But Rae couldn't relax, thinking about going to his parents' house the next day.

"Come on." Dean held her hand and led her out of the kitchen. "Let's watch the sunset."

They walked out onto the deck and settled on the outdoor couch just in time to see the sun go down. The blue of the sky started bleeding in with the redness of the evening rays, creating purple-pink hues across the horizon.

"It's so gorgeous here." Rae marveled at the sight. "I don't know why you still live in Manhattan. If I were you, I'd live here full time."

"You'd leave Manhattan to live in a small town like this?" Dean asked, sounding doubtful.

"I meant you. You'd be close to family and get to watch your nephews grow up. You could go to your family's Sunday dinner every week."

"What about the company?"

"You're a smart man. You'd figure it out. Atlanta is only an hour away."

Dean looked thoughtful for a minute, as if he was actually considering it.

"Tell me more about your parents," Rae asked.

Glancing at her, Dean had this little smile that only appeared when he was talking or thinking about his family. "My mom is a retired grade school teacher. She's mellowed out when it comes to discipline now that she's a grandmother, but she always has a warm way about her. Her former students never forget Mrs. Rowland taught them how to read.

"My dad is also retired. An engineer. Loves tinkering with anything with a machine and is fascinated with technology. He now builds classic model cars in his workroom. It keeps him entertained and out of my mother's hair most of the time," he finished with a chuckle.

Rae loved hearing the way Dean described his parents. There was this particular fondness in his manner, not just love. And this was the man Fiona had described as ruthless?

She wasn't so naive to think that a man couldn't be cruel in some aspects of his life and love his family at the same time. Mobster stories were famous for that archetype of a character. And she imagined Dean would have to make some tough decisions in business that were not received well by some, but she doubted he'd be unethical or dictatorial.

From what she knew, Dean mostly trusted a group of executive leaders to run the various business groups under Aquarius Media Corp. The key to their success had been investing in like-minded people with visionary outlooks and letting them take the lead.

"So, they're still quite active in their older age?" Rae prompted Dean to keep talking.

"Mom still tutors special-needs students. Dad has his buddies. They go fishing or work on each other's cars."

"I'm glad. I think staying engaged is important to health, both physically and mentally."

"Are you speaking from experience?" Dean asked.

"Are you calling me old, Rowland?" She gave him a side-eye.

He rolled his eyes at her. "No. I meant experience with your own family."

Rae averted her eyes back to the lake. "I was speaking generally."

"Why don't you talk about your family, Rae?" Dean asked. "You ask tons of questions about mine. Why won't you share with me about yours?"

Looking back at him, Rae didn't have a good answer.

He stared at her, his grey eyes probing. "I'm starting to think sharing information in this relationship is one-sided, where you get to ask questions while I know almost nothing about your family."

Although Dean's voice was steady and calm, Rae's first reaction was to get defensive. "You ever consider that perhaps I don't want to talk about them?"

"I get that. I didn't want to talk about Leighton, but you insisted I did. Why won't you extend me the same courtesy? You still don't trust me?"

Rae heard the hurt in his tone and heaved a sigh. He was right. She wasn't being fair.

Finally, she said, "I don't talk about them because they're all gone."

Darkness had descended, so Dean lit the fire pit low for illumination. The night was surprisingly pleasant—dry with a slight breeze blowing away the remaining heat of the day.

Dean handed Rae a glass of chilled rosé and sat down next to her. He'd thought she could use something to help her relax. Between them, they'd discussed all kinds of topics, but when it came to her family, she'd always retreated. Now that she finally cracked the door, Dean wanted to encourage her to open it all the way. He waited until she'd taken a few sips of her wine before asking her to continue with her story.

"I told you my grandparents raised me after my mother passed," Rae started. "She died when I was thirteen."

"I'm so sorry, Rae." Dean took her hand in his.

I've experienced loss, too. Her words from their walk-about-the-city echoed in his memory. He couldn't imagine losing one of his parents at that young age.

"She wasn't well for as long as I remember." Rae absently squeezed his hand as though she needed his strength. "I only remember seeing her smile less and less, and the light in her eyes faded with time."

"Was she ill?" Dean asked.

"She was. Chronic depression." Rae looked far into the night. "She was beautiful and happy once. I have pictures of her with me when I was a baby and a toddler. She was full of smiles. I'd like to remember her that way, but what's imprinted in my mind is how she'd looked the day she died. Defeated."

Dean regretted pushing her to talk—not because of what he'd just learned, but because she had to relive her grief.

"You must've been devastated, losing your mother at that age. I mean, it'd be devastating, losing a parent at any age."

"I was in therapy for a long time." Rae chuckled without humor. "This is why I don't talk about my family much. It drags the conversation. Nobody wants to hear a sob story."

Taking her chin in his fingers, he turned her face to him. "I want to hear your story."

Rae's gaze was soft as she smiled at him. "See, I rather listen to your family stories. They make me happy."

"You'll hear about them enough tomorrow. Tonight, I'd like to hear more of yours, if you'll share with me."

After looking doubtful for a few seconds, Rae then shrugged. She burrowed herself against his side, prompting Dean to put his arm around her shoulders. "There are parts of my childhood I'd rather forget, but there were wonderful times, too.

"There were moments when she was her old self. Those moments gave me false hope because my illusions shattered when she went down the rabbit hole again. I know now that I can't blame her for it, but as a teenager, I was angry at her for letting herself be consumed by depression. I told myself I'd never put myself into a situation where I'd—"

Rae abruptly stopped and huffed a breath.

"Where you'd what?" Dean looked at her.

"I just never want to be in her situation." She shook her head. "Anyway, my grandparents took me in, giving me as normal an upbringing they could. They became parents quite late, so raising a teenager in their late sixties wasn't easy. But they did."

"And they're gone, too?"

"My grandpa a while back, and my grandma only two years ago," Rae replied.

Dean tightened his arm around her and kissed her hair. His heart ached for her loss. It made him more determined to share his family's warmth with her.

"And before you ask, I don't have aunts, uncles, or cousins." Rae injected cheerfulness in her voice, but Dean heard the loneliness in it.

"You never mentioned your father," he realized.

Dean wasn't sure if he imagined it, but he felt Rae stiffen in his arm.

"I don't have a father," she flatly said.

"What do you mean? Did he..." He trailed off when he saw her face.

"I don't have a father." She repeated firmly. "My friends are my family now. And that's enough."

Sensing it wasn't the time to push for more, Dean reined in his curiosity. It was obvious Rae's father was an even more sensitive subject. He'd have to bide his time and give her space until she was ready to tell him that story.

"I'm here," Dean suggested, wishing she'd included him in her definition of family. But maybe it was too early to express it.

Rae gazed at him in the dim light, and slowly her smile appeared. She straightened to circle her arms around his neck and kiss him.

She murmured against his lips. "Yes, you are."

Twenty-Eight

Slicing through the water in smooth strokes, Dean reached the edge, flipped underwater, and pushed off the wall to do another lap. He'd done twenty-five laps so far, but the house pool was much smaller than the lap pool at his apartment building. The swim was still energizing and always got his system going in the morning.

Though when he woke up next to Rae some mornings, the pool had become his second exercise choice. He'd left her sleeping because she looked so peaceful in his bed. And he couldn't help but think that she belonged there, that it felt right to have her there at his house, in his hometown.

He didn't care about what Gayle had said before he'd left the office yesterday. It wasn't too early if it felt right. From the second they had met, he'd gravitated to her. Distance, time, and resistance hadn't mattered. In the end, their magnetic field had attracted them toward each other. And after last night, he'd never felt closer to her.

Dean caught a glimpse of Rae walking out onto the deck as he pushed off for another lap. He covered the length of the pool in a few seconds and emerged at the edge near where she stood. He brushed water out his face and hair, then looked up at her.

Wearing only one of his T-shirts with her legs bare, Rae made him drool. But her phone was at her ear, and she put a finger out to signal she'd be done in a minute.

Who is she on the phone with this early?

"Hey B, sorry for cutting this short. I got to go. Someone's waiting for me." Rae gazed at Dean with a smile. "Yeah, you go do your sound check."

Whatever Brandon's response was, it made Rae laugh. "Give my love to the boys. I'll see you next week. Love ya. Bye."

Hearing Rae say that particular "L" word to another guy gave Dean an unpleasant jolt. He recognized what it was and didn't like how it felt. It brought some old, bad feelings to the surface. He quickly shook it off as Rae squatted down by the pool's edge.

"Déjà vu." She leaned in for a kiss. "You're supposed to snap at me right about now."

Dean pushed himself off the pool enough to reach her lips. "I'd rather rewrite that whole scene. Was that Brandon on the phone?"

"Uh-huh. I hadn't talked to him since he left. We'd texted but not really talked," Rae said.

"How's the tour going?"

"It sounds like they're having a great time."

"They have a great following in Europe." Dean nodded. "Does he know where you are?"

"It didn't come up." Rae shrugged.

Dean thought it was odd, but he decided not to dwell on it. He didn't want to talk about another man anyway. What he wanted was Rae.

"I'd put that phone away if I were you." One corner of his mouth tilted in a slight warning.

Rae backed away a step. "You're not pulling me in."

"Wouldn't dream of it." Dean innocently grinned. "Get in. The water's nice."

"I don't have a suit on."

"It's just you and me here. Swimsuits are optional." He gave her a come-hither look.

Her cheeks turned pink as she bit her lower lip, considering his invitation.

Dean pushed off his own swim trunks and threw them by her feet. "Don't tell me miss solo-adventurer has never skinny dipped before."

Rae raised her brows at his challenge, stood up, and put down her phone on the nearby table. She turned her back on him and shimmied out of her panties. She glanced at him and paused when she saw he was watching her every move. Realizing he wouldn't look away, she finally just peeled off the shirt.

Dean blew out a slow exhale as his eyes swept over her nudeness. Rae Allen standing naked by his pool bathed in the morning light was his ultimate wet dream. He felt himself harden even in the relatively cool pool.

But, unaware of her power over him, Rae had a different idea. Unceremoniously, she ran and cannonballed into the pool. Splashed out of his lustful thoughts, Dean laughed and dove after her. He caught her by the waist, and they emerged from the water together. Her laughter filled the morning and his heart.

"That wasn't the most graceful entry." Dean held her against him and swam them to shallower water.

Rae locked her arms around his shoulders. "Were you expecting something more mermaid-like?"

"I should've known better who I'm dealing with." He chuckled, then kissed the grin off her lips. "How do you make me laugh when I'm all hard for you?"

"You have your superpower. I have mine." Rae wrapped her legs around his hips and rubbed against his hardness. "Goodness. Talking about superpower."

Dean gave a short bark of laughter. "Sweetheart, that's all you."

He calls me sweetheart.

Rae's heart fluttered inside her chest even as Dean gazed into her eyes before capturing her mouth for a kiss that melted the rest of her body. When she'd decided to embrace her desire for him, she'd never imagined she'd be back in this town, about to meet his parents. She hadn't expecting to grow this attached to him.

When he touched her like this, it was easy to tell herself there was only passion between them. Passion would sizzle out eventually. But when he'd held her last night as she'd told him about her mother, she couldn't lie to herself anymore. Her heart had gotten involved. Who was she kidding? It had always been involved.

"Do you remember the last night you were here in the spring?" Dean whispered into her ear. "We were sitting on that couch, discussing some details for the article. Man, you were feisty. I so wanted to kiss you right then and there."

"No, you didn't. You were being such a hard-ass." Rae giggled, but the laughter died as Dean backed her against the pool wall.

His warm gaze locked on hers, while a small smile formed on his lips. "Why do you think I acted that way? Do you know how bewitching you looked at sunrise in your silky robe? Even then, you pulled at me." Dean absently brushed her wet hair from her face. "There's something about you,..."

The look in his eyes as he studied her made her heart thud so hard against her breastbone, she was sure he felt it. Any teasing was lost from her tongue. She longed to hear more, but he didn't finish his thoughts. Instead, he kissed her, leaving her wondering what he meant and wanting more.

Dean hauled her out of the water and sat her down on the infinity edge of the pool. Though the morning temperature had quickly risen into the low eighties, Rae felt goose bumps prickle her skin. But she quickly warmed up as Dean cupped her breasts in his hands, kneading them gently. Nimble thumbs brushed against her nipples in a rhythm that forced a moan out of her.

Replacing one of his thumbs, he sucked a tip into his mouth, circling it with his tongue, sending high frequency current into Rae's whole system. Needing more of his warmth, her torso arched like an offering to a god. With equal eagerness, he took her other breast and feasted.

There was no denying that passion ran high between them. Plus, they genuinely enjoyed each other. That might be all there was, and that would be enough.

Enjoy each moment life offers you. Rae reminded herself of her own motto. Her mother's death had always compelled her to live life to the fullest. She never wanted to waste any opportunity to feel alive. And Dean made her feel alive like she never had before.

When Dean trailed his mouth down the center of her belly, Rae could only sigh. When he went farther down and brushed his lips against her folds, she surrendered. She lay back on the hard, wet ground, not feeling discomfort. She could only feel him, doing unbelievable things with his tongue.

Her soft moan mingled with the singing of the morning birds. As if encouraged by it, Dean teased and sucked her clitoris harder. Her body shuddered, and Rae buried her fingers in his hair, pleading for him not to stop. He didn't until her whole body convulsed in ecstasy.

While she was still on cloud nine, Dean pulled himself out of the pool and carried her jelly-like body to a pool lounge chair. He lay her down and hovered over her with a grin that only a man who knew he'd satisfied his woman could have.

"Do you want more?" he teased.

"Yes," Rae answered and entwined her leg with one of his, bringing him close.

Dean entered her with his eyes locked on hers. His hardness fit perfectly inside her, as if he was made for her. And when he moved slowly inside her, building heat within her again, Rae whispered in his ear, "More."

She just didn't realize she wanted a lot more.

Dean quickened his pace to the demand of their joined bodies. Their lovemaking was electric; he could almost see sparks flying around them.

Explosive.

He always felt he would fully combust and disintegrate into nonexistence when they made love. Yet, when he looked at her face, even more striking at the brink of her climax, he held himself together to drive himself fully into her once, twice, or thrice more.

Rae's silent scream of ecstasy triggered Dean's own groan as he let himself erupt inside her. He half-collapsed onto her as his climax abated. His breath was shallow and heavy, racing along with Rae's. Then he felt a rumble of laughter underneath him.

Dean opened his eyes to find Rae laughing with glee.

"I never got that reaction before." He grinned at her.

"You weren't with me before." Rae ran her fingers through his wet hair.

She got that right.

Dean had never been with a woman like Rae, who filled his life with her infectious laughter. He hadn't realized how much she'd brightened his days. Who would have thought she had such a bleak childhood when she shined so brightly?

Enfolding Rae into his embrace, Dean kissed her, needing her glow to continue feeding light into his heart. Each day, his need for her grew instead of diminishing. He wanted more of her. He wanted her to be his.

All his.

Twenty-Nine

"She is lovely, Dean." Martha squeezed Dean's side as the two watched Rae roll a green bocce ball toward the jack on the other side of the backyard.

Dean and Rae had arrived at his parents' house before the rest of the Rowland clan. He wanted his parents to have private time with Rae before the whole family descended on her. As he predicted, his mom and dad were immediately taken with Rae. He'd never seen his dad this energetic as he gave Rae a pointer at bocce. And Rae was so sweet to pretend she didn't already know how to play the game. Dean bet she'd played it plenty with the Italians.

"She makes you smile again," his mother said.

Dean couldn't help but smile at that statement. "I was just thinking the same thing this morning."

"I'm glad you brought her home. It's about time you open your heart again."

"I hope I don't screw up this one, too."

"You didn't screw up, honey." Martha patted his arm. "Don't dwell on the past when the present is full of promise. If you keep looking back, you'll second-guess every step you take. And you're smarter than that."

Dean's lips twisted in a wry grin. "I'm not good at figuring out women."

"Then it's lucky that you found a woman who tells you how it is. At least that's what Kat told me."

"What did she say?" He glanced at his mom.

"Oh, she told me how Rae wouldn't take your crap even knowing who you are. Kat thinks Rae is the female version of you: a go-getter, independent—"

"She's better than me. She has a kind soul that sees past your flaws. She has a strength that keeps her going even after facing deep loss. She laughs with everything she is. I wish I could be more like her."

"You know all that about her in the three weeks you've been together?"

His mother stared up at him with a knowing look on her face.

"What?" Dean asked. "Why did you say it that way?"

"I think you know what. Or if you don't, you'll figure it out soon enough." Martha kissed his cheek. "I'm happy for you, son."

"Martha, it's your turn," Douglas called out. "Let's show these kids how this game is played."

"I'm coming." Martha started toward him.

"Don't strain yourself, Mom," Dean reminded her.

"Don't you try to psyche me out, young man." She winked at him. "I still have one or two tricks to show you."

Yes, you do. Dean wished she'd tell him what she seemed to have figured out. His mother seemed to know things before anyone did. But, being the teacher she was, she tended to let you work out the answer on your own.

His mother picked up her ball and aimed. Watching Rae amidst his parents on the lawn made him happy. He somehow knew Rae would fit right in. He couldn't help to compare today to the time he'd brought Leighton home. She'd been courteous, but Leighton had never been able to connect with his parents. Their relationship had been at best polite, but it lacked actual warmth.

Focusing on the present, Dean made his way to the three people huddled around the balls on the grass. Through the spaces between their heads, he spotted two of their opposing balls neck and neck. The trio was trying to figure out which one was closest to the jack.

"Move aside, people." Dean picked up the last of the green balls. "It doesn't matter whose ball is the closest because I'm going to knock your red one off the lawn."

His dad straightened up and with mock outrage. "You dare not!"

Dean smiled his winning smile and nodded as he aimed. "Oh, yes, I dare. I don't know how to lose. Do you think I'll go soft on you because my girl is here?"

He thought Rae's eyes widened slightly at his use of the possessive term. But he was trying not overanalyze everything Rae did on this trip. He focused on rolling the ball with laser-sharp precision. It hit his parents' red ball sideways with his trailing behind it but leaving Rae's ball the closest to the jack, thus making their team the winner of that round.

Groans of frustration erupted from Martha and Douglas while Rae and Dean shouted triumphantly.

Rae went to him for a victory hug. "You're damn good at this game."

"You're not too bad yourself...for a 'first-timer.'" He winked at her, then whispered, "Thank you for indulging my dad."

"He's a papa bear." Rae chuckled. "I love him. I love your parents."

Dean knew her words were expressions, but they meant a lot to him. He kissed her hair and said, "And they love you."

Dean's siblings and families arrived later in the afternoon, bearing more food and adding further amusement into the mix. Rae witnessed the friendly rivalry between Dean and his brother, Gene, as they played another round of bocce. Kat egged her older siblings to one-up the other, but everything was all in good fun.

It was so entertaining for Rae to see Dean in this setting again. It was a wonderful afternoon, and her nervousness about seeing Dean's family had evaporated. Martha and Douglas had welcomed her with warmth, and the rest of the family had hugged her as if they were all old friends.

She'd thought the Rowland family was wonderful when she'd first met them. Today, the sentiment doubled. She was envious of their bond, but she was glad to join in their weekend and, for a moment, felt a part of their happy family.

When Rae traveled, she'd met many beautiful souls who had invited her to their family dinners, parties, and even weddings. They all gave her a taste of a wholly functional family. They were not devoid of conflicts or issues. Still, there was always an abundance of affection, love, and trust that helped them overcome any problems.

Rae's issue was that she always fell in love with the families she'd met during her travels, and then it was always time for her to leave. Today, she'd fallen in love with Dean's family. It'd break her heart to leave this family.

With her phone camera, Rae took candid pictures of the family in their leisure for her memories. She'd asked permission to take photos of the display of succulent smoked pork and all the side dishes Martha and Amanda had put together on the outside dining table. Wildflowers in small vases and Martha's colorful choice of platters and dinnerware brightened the table.

Kat looked over Rae's shoulders at her phone display. "That's gorgeous. How did you make our humble table look like it came out of *Southern Living* magazine?"

Rae laughed. "I only took the picture. Your mom and Amanda did all that."

"You're going to include these pictures in your next book?"

"If you let me." Rae nodded. "My next book is about the families I've encountered throughout my journey. Conventional families and not-so-conventional ones."

"What do you mean by not-so-conventional?" Kat asked.

"As you know, not everybody in this world was born into a happy family like yours. Some may be absorbed into one if they're lucky. Some form their own family, with friends or similar-minded people. I once stayed at a commune of young adults without traditional nuclear family support. They found each other, and they now live together, helping each other with their young ones."

"Like a cult?" Kat frowned.

Rae laughed. "Not quite. There's no leader or crazy philosophy they follow. They're committed to their own partners if they have one. They're just there for each other. It was tempting to stay."

Kat tilted her head in curiosity. "You were tempted to stay?"

"I'd just lost my grandmother then." Rae thought back. "She was the last blood relative I had. But then I realized I had my own nontraditional family back home in New York."

"Oh, I'm sorry to hear about your grandmother, Rae." Kat looped an arm through Rae's elbow. "You can always be a part of this family."

Kat turned them back to the lawn where the men and boys gathered the games equipment to store away. Dean was jostling around with his nephews. His handsome face was bright with laughter.

"You make my brother laugh again." Kat squeezed Rae's arm gently. "That makes you family in my book."

Rae's heart expanded at Kat's sentiment. Yet she was afraid to let hope bloom. She'd entered this thing with Dean, always thinking everything about him was in the moment. But he already made her break the few rules she lived by.

Never get involved too deep, especially if it risks your heart.

She was already in too deep. She was sure her heart was already at risk. Was it foolish of her to think there might be a happily-ever-after future for her after all?

Thirty

"Hey, gorgeous," Brandon greeted Rae as she met him at Katz's Delicatessen for lunch.

"Welcome home, good-looking." She hugged and kissed him on the cheek before sitting at their small table, already laden with food and drinks. "Digging the new haircut. It suits you. You look good, B."

Brandon grinned as he raked his fingers through his shorter hair. "Thanks. I got you your kosher dog and root beer."

"Thanks." She eyed their lunch.

"I missed their pastrami sandwich." Brandon didn't wait to bite into his thick sandwich.

"And I love their kosher dogs." Rae slathered mustard on her lunch. "So, tell me about the tour."

She was about to take a bite and ready to listen, but Brandon didn't roll into a story as he usually would. She found him staring at her with a little squint in his eyes and a peculiar smirk on his face. "Why are you looking at me like that?"

"You look different." He gestured with his sandwich.

"I do?" Rae raised a brow, confused.

"Your eyes sparkle. Cheeks, naturally rosy." Brandon grinned widely. "You got laid."

Rae's face instantly reddened, and Brandon burst into laughter. "So? You're not the only one who can get some action."

"Of course not." Brandon's amusement subsided. "I've recommended it to you many times. I'm glad you finally took my advice."

Rae glared at him and deliberately took a big bite of her hot dog to avoid replying.

Brandon ceased his teasing but didn't stop smiling. "Seriously, though, you look good. 'Happy' might be the word."

"I'm a happy person in general." Rae shrugged.

"This is different," he pushed. "I gather things are still going well between you and this guy Dean. The two-week countdown has come and gone?"

"Yes," Rae grudgingly admitted.

"That's great. So when am I going to meet him?"

"I don't know. We'll set something up."

"Bring him to Brady's this weekend," Brandon suggested. "We'll have some beer, some food. Shoot some pool."

"I'll ask him." Rae twisted her lips, thinking about how to break the news to him. "I probably should warn you before you meet him."

"Warn me about what?"

"About who he is." Rae grimaced. "I've been seeing Dean Rowland."

Brandon's face was blank, not registering the name. He chewed his food as he studied her face, pondering why he should recognize the name. Rae saw the moment it hit him. He swallowed too soon and almost choked. Rae pushed his drink to him.

He downed half of it before he looked at her with round eyes. "Damn, girl. Give me a warning before you drop a bomb like that."

"I didn't realize you'd be that shocked." Rae took a sip of her root beer.

"When...how?" Brandon stammered. "Spill!"

Rae told him the condensed story of how she and Dean met and started seeing each other. Brandon listened without interrupting except for some expressive facial movements here and there. Until she got to last weekend.

"Hold up." Brandon held out a hand. "He took you home to Georgia to meet his parents?"

Rae nodded.

"You've known each other for four weeks?" he asked for confirmation.

"Well, technically, we've known each other since April."

"Don't throw technicality at me. You told me you weren't sure about seeing him again just before I left. In fact, you told me you didn't want to."

"You're the one who told me to give him a chance," Rae retorted. "'Be open, Rae. Let things take you where they may.' All that romantic crap."

"I didn't think you'd take my advice." Brandon grinned. "And see how great it's going? Jeez, meeting the parents within one month of dating. That's serious."

Rae took a tiny bite of her food and chewed slowly.

"You look worried." Brandon leaned in. "Is something wrong?"

Rae shook her head.

"Ah." He sat back in his chair with a little twist on his lips.

"What?"

Brandon sighed. "You're doing the Rae thing again. Don't do it."

"What are you talking about?" Rae demanded.

"Things are going well, and now you're thinking of an excuse to end it."

Rae's jaw dropped at Brandon's assessment. "I'm not."

"You do this with every guy you date. Granted, this is the longest you've ever dated anyone. Usually, you'd find an excuse to let the guy down easy by the second or third date, or you'd friend-zone the guy."

"That's not fair, Brandon. I never had a connection with those other guys." Rae's brows drew together, thinking of Dean. "Not like this."

"Then what are you worried about?"

"I'm worried I'll fall for him."

Brandon's eyes went wide at Rae's words. "That's a good thing. That isn't something to worry about. Falling in love is a beautiful thing."

The look Rae gave him was full of skepticism. "Maybe for some. But me?"

"Why do you fight it, Rae?" Brandon shot straight to the issue. "You shouldn't project your mother's life onto yours. You are two different people."

Rae gave a short snort. "You never knew my mom. She was full of life before my father happened to her. Things could change very easily with the right trigger."

"It won't happen to you."

"How would you know that?" Rae returned. "Studies indicate that major depression is forty to fifty percent hereditary."

"Did your grandma or grandpa have severe depression?" Brandon rallied back.

"No. But—"

"So, there's also fifty to sixty percent chance you won't get it."

"Yes, because I've made sure I have nothing to be depressed about." Rae pointed her finger at him with an I-know-what-I'm-doing look.

"People will argue falling in love is the best way to produce endorphins—the happy hormones. It fights off depression."

"Sex is. Or exercising and eating."

"And what do people in love do the most?" Brandon pulled up his hand and started ticking off with his fingers. "Eat, sex, and exercise. Well, maybe not the exercise."

Rae laughed. "This is ridiculous."

"I agree." Brandon ate his sandwich while he thought of a different way to prevent Rae from sabotaging herself. Though maybe he should get to know Dean Rowland before he pushed Rae to jump into love. Perhaps there were other reasons she didn't want to fall in love with him.

"Tell me about Dean. What is he like in person?" Brandon started. "I've only met him briefly once."

"What was your impression then?"

"He exuded confidence. It was rather intimidating, actually," Brandon recalled. "Didn't say much, but I could tell he was absorbing a lot."

Rae smiled. "Sounds like him. He's not so quiet with me. He actually talks a lot once I get him going."

"What do you talk about?" Brandon was curious.

"Anything. Our days, work, current events, travel, food, friends, families—"

"Families?" Brandon knew how sensitive Rae was about her family. He'd gotten a chance to meet her grandma and heard more stories than Rae had shared herself. She'd been devastated when her grandmother had died in her sleep.

"I told him about my mom. My childhood with my grandparents." Rae's lips twitched.

Brandon was surprised and impressed at the same time. Rae hadn't shared that part of her life until at least a year into their friendship.

"That says a lot, Rae," Brandon said. "That says you trust him."

His friend paused and stared at him, looking perplexed, as if it hadn't occurred to her. One corner of his mouth rose in a pleased smile. "You trust him enough to be vulnerable. You're a good judge of people, but you don't trust just anyone when it comes to your family."

"He's a good man." Rae nodded, agreeing. "I can't tell you why, but I feel something continue to draw me to him. The more I resisted, the stronger it got. And when I finally surrendered to it, the more intense it became. I don't just want him. I can't wait to see him at the end of the day. I want to tell him about what's going on with my project. He pops in my head throughout the day. It's really distracting."

She sighed in frustration. "When is this going to let up? Tell me that this will go away eventually."

Brandon felt a tiny pang inside from listening to Rae, because it meant he'd lose some of his best friend privileges. But it also made him smile.

"Here's a newsflash for you, kid. You're already falling in love."

Thirty-One

After having Rae mostly to himself for the past month, Dean finally got to meet her best friend now that he was home. Dean recalled meeting Brandon and his bandmates when Aquarius signed them.

Brandon wasn't what he'd expected a typical front man of a rock band would be. He looked the part with his tattoos, good looks, and style, but he was a soulful songwriter, articulate, and intelligent. Dean also learned Brandon was a visual artist—a talented one, too—and a protective friend.

Tonight, after a quick pizza dinner at Lombardi's, Rae had taken him to a cozy little pub to meet up with Brandon Rossi and Curtis Bisset for beer and a game of pool. He wasn't much of a pool guy, but Rae once again amazed him by dominating the game over the three men.

"Finally, I found something you're not excellent at," Rae teased him. "It kinda worried me that you're that perfect."

"I'm as flawed as any man." Dean flashed a smile at her. "I'm costing you the game, partner."

"You're welcome to play anytime," Curtis said from one corner while Brandon aimed at the eight ball for the win. "If not, Rae always kicks our asses."

Brandon sunk the eight ball into the far right corner.

Curtis shouted toward the bar, "Brady, another round here!"

Rae was already reaching for some bills from her jeans pocket and walked to the bar. "I got it."

Dean watched as she leaned over the bar and chatted with the new bartender who arrived as the bar got more crowded. There was a familiarity between Rae and the bartender. He wondered whether he was crazy or if men were just drawn to her. Even his male friends he'd introduced her to at the few events they'd attended together automatically flocked to her, including Chris. It didn't sit well with him.

"That's Brandon's brother at the bar, Brady." Rae handed him a fresh bottle of beer. "He and his wife, Teresa, own the place." She pointed at the woman on the other side of the bar.

Suddenly he felt like a jerk for having wayward thoughts about her. Dean nodded and thanked her for the beer.

At the pool table, Curtis already had the balls set up again. Brandon handed Dean his cue back. "Want a chance to redeem yourself, Rowland?"

Dean sensed the challenge in Brandon's casual words. He accepted the cue. "I'll play. I think Rae enjoys saving me from humiliating myself."

By then, Dean had gotten past some of his rustiness. He aimed and made the shot. The balls scattered. Rae's cheer elevated his ego when two balls plunged into the far corner pocket. For his second shot, he aimed more carefully, wanting to continue impressing her. One ball was situated precariously at the edge of the left middle pocket, and he got just the right angle. The ball went in smoothly, earning him another cheer.

He didn't succeed at the third shot, but Rae gave him a high five, looking pleased. That was enough for him. The second game was more even, especially when it was her turn. The balls seemed willing to do all her bidding. Fortunately for the other team, she didn't manage to finish them off at her last turn, giving Curtis a chance to shoot.

Rae's eyes were on Curtis when Brandon went to stand next to her, elbowed her arm, and made a little head gesture toward the bar. Curious, Dean followed the direction of their gazes. She and Brandon were checking out a couple of girls that had just walked in. When he looked back at Rae and Brandon, she was nodding her approval while Brandon chuckled at her response.

The nonverbal interaction showed Dean that Brandon and Rae weren't just close. There was an obvious bond between them that could only occur when two people really cared about each other. Sparks of jealousy singed his brain. It irked him that Rae was that close with another man while they were still getting to know each other.

"Hey, don't mind them." Curtis suddenly was at his side. "They're like twins separated at birth. At first, I got so pissed at Rae for stealing my best friend."

Dean looked at the laughing tall guy. "Rossi's your best friend, too?"

"Since first grade. But I'm used to having to share Brandon. He has this thing with girls. They just love him. For the longest time, he was the only person who could calm my sister. She had major anxiety issues."

"What happened to them?" Dean frowned at him.

"Nothing. She left for college. Now she lives in Paris." Curtis shrugged.

Puzzled, Dean asked, "What are you trying to tell me, Curtis?"

Curtis looked at him with a frown. "That they're tight, that's all. They'd been inseparable from the first time Shelley hooked them up."

"Rae mentioned they went on a couple of dates." Dean vaguely remembered.

"Yeah, a couple of dates or a month, whatever," Curtis distractedly answered as he spotted Brady coming with some plates. "Here comes my favorite dude!"

A month? Dean's brain so zeroed in on the word that he overlooked Brandon's brother joining them.

"You're the big man. I heard Rae was bringing you around." Brady stuck out his hand to Dean. Brandon's older brother shared his boyish good looks. But instead of Brandon's careless rocker style, Brady sported a buzzcut and Dean would bet he'd played football in college.

Dean accepted the big guy's hand. "You have a great pub here, Brady."

"Thanks, man." Brady shook his hand vigorously. "This is probably a bit late, but thanks for giving these guys their big break, man. I'm honored to have you here with us."

Uncharacteristically embarrassed, Dean gave a short nod. "They're a great band. I have little credit for their success."

"Humble man. He's a keeper, Rae." Brady winked at Rae, who had rejoined them with Brandon.

Rae looked at him with a little smile. "What have you guys been gossiping about over here?"

"Curtis was just telling me how you guys met." Dean put his arm around her back.

"Oh?" Rae eyed him as if she detected an odd tone in his voice.

"Ah, I remember the first time Brandon took her here," Brady said with a big grin. "Our whole family loves her. Too bad these two didn't become a couple. I'd always thought Brandon should marry Rae and keep her in the family."

Curtis and Brandon laughed at Brady's teasing.

"You know Rae would never have me," Brandon quipped. "She knows too many of my secrets."

"I'd marry her myself if I wasn't taken already." Brady patted Rae's shoulder. "You're always family, either way."

Rae just rolled her eyes at her friends.

Dean knew his face didn't show the sudden surge of jealousy filling his brain. But he wasn't laughing along with them, either.

"Why are you so quiet?" Rae looked at Dean in the dim backseat of the cab on their ride back to her apartment. He hadn't said a word since they'd left Brady's bar.

"I'm thinking." He continued to stare out into the night.

"About?"

"That it's interesting what one can find out from someone's friends."

Rae sensed Dean's mood had dramatically changed in the middle of their night. But even this was a bit too cryptic for him. "What do you mean?"

"You told me you didn't date Brandon."

"What?" The statement was so out-of-blue that Rae didn't know how to respond.

Dean finally turned to her. "Curtis said a friend hooked you two up, and you hit it off from the start. The word he used was inseparable."

His cool, quiet voice didn't waver, but she was perplexed by the unexpected accusation she sensed in his demeanor.

"I told you we went out on a couple of coffee dates four years ago. Why does it matter?" Rae asked.

"It matters when his whole family still dreams about marrying you two off."

"That was just one of Brady's old jokes," Rae said in disbelief. "What has gotten into you? This is ridiculous."

"Did you sleep with him?"

Rae was outraged by the question. "I'm not going to even dignify that with an answer."

"I'll take that as a yes."

"How dare you ask me that question," Rae hissed. "Even if I did sleep with Brandon, it isn't your business who I slept with before I met you."

"It is my business when you're still in a close relationship with that man." His voice finally rose.

"In a close *friendship*!" Rae emphasized the word, trying to get it into Dean's head. "Should I start questioning you about your friendship with Gayle? She's quite possessive over you. It was obvious she didn't like me when we met. Why is it, huh? Did you sleep with her and dump her like your other dates?"

The man had the gall to look offended. "Gayle's been my loyal friend and employee for seven years. I've never touched her. She's married, for crying out loud."

"Oh, so you can have female friends, but I can't have male friends?"

Rae could tell when Dean's common sense started to return to his brain. But he stubbornly clenched his jaw even when he didn't have a comeback.

The cab stopped in front of Rae's building.

"Don't even think about coming up. My apartment isn't big enough to accommodate you and your ego tonight." Rae slid out. "Call me only when you stop being this big of an ass!"

She slammed the cab door.

Crap!

Rae flew out of the cab so fast that Dean had no chance to think. His temper flickered as he watched her slam the door of her building.

"Where to next?" The cabby asked reluctantly after witnessing the fight. Dean told the cabby his address.

All he could think of throughout the ride was Rae and Brandon in bed together. It twisted him inside, and all the old feelings he thought he'd buried came back with double force.

When Dean got into his apartment, all he wanted to do was to run his fist through the wall. Sleeping wasn't an option. He went into his study and poured himself a good serving of bourbon. For most of the night, he sat there nursing the drink in the dark, only the moonlight shining in.

He reran tonight's events, watching Rae and Brandon's interactions and finding out they'd dated. He felt the jealousy flare up again, and he didn't like the feeling.

Dean didn't recall feeling the same intensity when he'd found out Leighton had stood him up at the altar to run off with another man. He remembered feeling extremely betrayed, but not this searing jealousy that burned inside. Still, there it was, the other glaring difference. Leighton had betrayed him. Rae had not.

A long while later, he had to admit that he'd let his emotions get the better of him. He still didn't care for Rae's friendship with Brandon and didn't believe Brandon's platonic feelings for Rae, but he'd crossed the line tonight. Guilt rushed in as he replayed his words to her. He'd acted like a righteous prick when he hadn't exactly been the poster boy for celibacy himself.

Rae had called it right. He was an ass.

Thirty-Two

He hasn't called.

Rae rechecked her phone. To her disappointment, Dean hadn't reached out to her right after their fight. She hadn't expected him to, but she'd hoped he would. Come Monday morning, fueled by leftover annoyance, she tried to go about her day as planned.

Chris had called and informed her that he'd found the Hestons' address upstate. They'd made plans to drive up today. He'd insisted on coming along, reasoning with Rae that the Hestons didn't know her. They'd surely be more open to him. But Rae had a feeling Chris wanted to accompany her because he didn't completely believe her motive.

Rae understood that. She would've insisted on coming, too, if they'd been talking about Brandon. Because that was what you did for your friends. She wished Dean could see that.

"Waiting for an important call?" Chris asked from the driver's seat, glancing at Rae.

"Sorry." Rae put away her phone. "Just checking if Dean called. We had an argument last night."

He raised a brow but stayed focused on the road. "Regular argument or more serious?"

"I don't think he trusts me." Rae decided to confide in Chris. He, after all, knew Dean well. And she thought the fight might prove why she needed to do what she was doing.

"What happened?" Chris asked. "I might be able to give you some insights."

"He met my closest friends last night. My best friend is a guy."

"Brandon Rossi from Canis Major," Chris interrupted. "I know. I follow your stuff, remember?"

"Then *you* can tell Dean that that's all we are. He got upset when he found out that Brandon and I went on a couple of dates when we first met. We had coffee, for crying out loud. We knew we made good friends from the start, but we had no chemistry."

"I disagree. I've seen the videos you did with the band. You definitely have chemistry," Chris stated. "I could see why Dean might get a little jealous."

"A little?" Rae scoffed. "It was out of proposition. I never hid the fact. I didn't think two coffee dates years ago were significant."

Chris looked thoughtful. "Like I said, I've seen the videos. Even if you say there's nothing romantic or sexual between you, there is a definite vibe. Or you wouldn't have your fans commenting about how much they shipped your relationship."

Rae rolled her eyes with a little groan. "Don't start me on that. I don't get it. Why can't people accept that a woman and a man can be just friends? The regular people I can understand. They don't really know us. But I expect more from Dean. We've been together for..."

Chris glanced at her when she trailed off. "For? A few weeks?"

"A little over a month." Rae realized that it hadn't been that long. "It seems like forever."

"Is that a bad or a good thing?" Chris questioned.

"I don't know." Rae sighed. "I just thought he'd know me and how I feel about him by now."

She shook the depressing thought and concentrated on her mission today. "This is why I need to find Leighton. My gut tells me that Dean will never trust any woman until he works out his feelings about Leighton."

"I don't think he has any more feelings for Leighton, Rae." Chris turned the car into the gravel driveway of a large nursery. "I hadn't seen him this lighthearted before he met you. You have an impact on him. Maybe give him a little break to figure things out."

Rae nodded. "He might not have feelings for Leighton anymore. But what she did affected him more deeply than he'll admit. There are ghosts in our lives that could haunt us for the rest of our days if we don't deal with them. Believe me, I know."

"What haunts you?"

"Today isn't about me. We're here for Dean."

Chris parked the car. "Well, here we are. Let's hunt some ghosts."

Chris and Rae walked into Square One Nursery.

"This is beautiful." Rae looked around the lush garden. Late summer blooms still dominated the grounds while workers put in fall flowers and plants. The landscape design of the place would make anyone who walked in sign up for service.

"The Hestons aren't doing so badly." Chris looked around the property.

They stopped and asked a groundskeeper where they could find the Hestons. They were directed to the office area in a cottage behind the nursery plots, where they knocked on the "Staff Only" door. It was opened by a smiling lady in her late fifties, dressed in jeans and a white T-shirt, topped with a light chambray shirt.

"Yes? Can I help..." Her smile froze when her eyes landed on Chris.

"Hello, Debra," Chris greeted.

Debra Heston stepped out and recovered her smile. "Chris Sullens, is that you? What a surprise."

From his expression, Chris hadn't expected a cordial welcome. But he returned the smile with one of his own. "How are you?"

"I'm very well." Debra held out a hand to him. "It's so good to see you. I never thought to see you in our neck of the woods."

Chris squeezed Debra's hand. "This place is beautiful, Debra. I assume this is your handiwork. I remember your garden in the city. It was always spectacular."

"Oh, that garden was much easier to handle compared to the size of this one, but I do love it." Debra's smile was bittersweet. She then offered her hand to Rae. "And this is...?"

Rae shook Debra's hand. "Hi, Mrs. Heston. My name is Rae Allen. I'm a friend of Chris."

"Oh, we're not formal here. Debra, please." She clasped her hands together. "Did you just come from the city? Or are you up here for a vacation? Please, please, come in."

"Actually, Debra." Chris stopped Debra. "We were wondering if we could talk to you and Samuel. And maybe Petra."

Chris had told Rae that the Hestons had two daughters. Petra was a few years younger than Leighton.

Debra studied Chris' face. "This isn't a social visit, is it?"

"It is, but we do have some questions for you, if you don't mind talking to us," Chris said.

"Come." Debra led them between rows of plants. "Samuel should be somewhere in the back."

As they followed Debra, Chris continued chatting her up. "I didn't know you moved up here until just recently."

"Yes. After Samuel had to declare bankruptcy three years ago, we sold whatever we still could and left the city. We didn't feel it was our place anymore. I personally always feel more at home here in Rhinebeck." Debra's tone was light, without a trace of regret.

"We put what we had into this land and started over. This time, we built on my passion. It took a while, but with Samuel dealing with the business side and me on the plants, we started making it work. Then Petra started taking an interest in landscape architecture, and here we are."

"You built this in three years?" Rae asked, impressed.

"More like a little over two years. It took a while to sort things out in the city." Debra glanced at Rae. "How did you know Chris, Rae?"

"We have a mutual friend," Rae answered.

"Someone I'd know?" Debra asked Chris.

Chris hesitated, but he answered truthfully. "Dean."

"Oh." Debra's bubbly demeanor dropped a level. "How is he?"

"He's doing fine," Chris said simply.

Rae was too impatient to continue with all the social niceties, so she pointedly said, "I'm actually here for Dean. I'd like to ask if you've seen your daughter, Leighton, since she disappeared before their wedding?"

Debra's face blanched slightly at Rae's question. Instead of answering, her eyes darted ahead.

"There's Samuel." Debra picked up her pace and approached her husband, who was talking to an employee.

Chris held Rae back. "Take it easy, okay? Let me handle the talking."

"I'm not here to chitchat, Chris." Rae looked at him impatiently.

"And how do you think you'll get them to talk?"

"She's talking openly now," Rae argued. "Can't you see she's at peace here? Debra doesn't look or sound like the ousted society dame that some of you've made her out to be."

"It doesn't mean she'll talk about her daughter to a perfect stranger," Chris replied.

"I think she may." Rae softened her voice. "She sounds like a lovely woman. I doubt a woman like that would disown her child like the gossip said."

Chris considered her words. "I guess we'll find out."

When they reached the older couple, Samuel shook Chris' hand. "Chris. Good to see you."

"Likewise, Samuel. You look good. Both of you do. It seems small-town life agrees with you," Chris said. "I told Debra how wonderful this is."

"We are doing well. Thank you." Samuel nodded. "So, Debra said you're here about Leighton. You know about what happened as much as we do. We haven't heard from her since the morning of the wedding."

Chris was taken aback by Samuel's directness. He gave Rae a side-eye in annoyance. But the woman ignored him and addressed Samuel herself.

"Mr. Heston, my name is Rae Allen. If you just give us a few minutes to ask you about what happened that day, perhaps we could figure out where Leighton is."

"And who are you, Miss Allen? Why do you need to find Leighton?" Samuel demanded.

"I'm just trying to help a friend to find closure," Rae answered.

"Did Dean send you to do this?" There was still a trace of bitterness in Samuel's voice. "It's three years too late."

"Samuel," Debra touched her husband on the arm. "It wasn't Dean's fault."

"Perhaps it wasn't anyone's fault," Rae said gently. "I have a hard time believing that one person is at fault in that situation."

Samuel scoffed. "We wouldn't have had to liquidate everything we owned if Dean hadn't pulled out of his intention to give me a loan after the marriage."

"You know that was legal and part of the prenup, Samuel. Dean had no obligation to honor that intention when the marriage didn't happen," Chris jumped in to defend his friend.

Samuel grumbled. "So, you're saying it's Leighton's fault to run away, right? Perhaps it would've turned out differently if Dean knew how to control his fiancée."

"Samuel!" Debra snapped. "Leighton didn't love Dean. You and I knew that, and we continued pressuring her to save us from our financial problems. It wasn't her responsibility to bail us out of your mistakes!"

Chris and Rae exchanged glances.

Well, that was unexpected.

"We are fine now. We are happier than we've ever been. Why can't you let go of this?" Debra stared daggers at her husband. "I want my daughter back!"

"Debra..." Heston turned to his wife wide-eyed.

Debra Heston ignored her husband and faced Chris and Rae. "It was my fault. I couldn't let Leighton marry a man she didn't love. Dean is a fine man, but they didn't have any business getting married. I told Leighton the morning of the wedding that she didn't have to go through with it. I helped her get out of the city to meet up with Nick—"

"You did what?" Samuel gasped the words in disbelief.

"She's my little girl, Samuel. And I know you would disapprove of Nick, but he loves her," Debra said evenly.

"Who's Nick?" Chris inquired.

"They met in college. He moved abroad for work after they graduated, and they lost touch. When they reunited, Leighton had already agreed to marry Dean." Debra sighed. "I've said too much. But I'm going to ask you to please leave Leighton alone. She is happy and doesn't need this back in her life."

"Are you saying you've known where Leighton is all this time?" Samuel demanded.

"Yes."

"And you've kept it from me all these years?"

"Just listen to how angry you still are at her," Debra said. "She doesn't need that from you."

"Perhaps this is the chance for everyone to heal from that episode," Rae chimed in kindly. "Don't you think it's time to forgive your daughter, Samuel? And at the same time, for you to apologize to her?"

Samuel just glared at Rae. Obviously, he wasn't ready.

Rae turned to Debra instead. "I understand you want to protect Leighton. But I think you understand that what you and Leighton did also affected Dean. I don't think he ever processed his feelings about what happened, and I'm afraid it's affecting his chance at happiness. As Leighton deserves to be happy, don't you think he deserves it, too?"

Debra studied Rae. "Why is he looking for her now?"

"He doesn't know we're here. He probably won't be happy when he finds out. Leighton asked him not to look for her, and he has honored her request. I'm looking for her, hoping somehow she could provide the closure Dean needs to move on."

"Why are you doing this for him?" asked Debra.

Chris watched Rae hesitate. But she straightened her spine and looked straight into Debra's eyes.

She answered, "Because I'm in love with him."

Thirty-Three

The drive back into the city was relatively quiet for the first hour. They didn't get what they needed, but Rae didn't think the trip was a complete failure. They'd uncovered some new details, even if Debra wouldn't betray Leighton's confidence. Rae wished they'd gotten a new lead to find Leighton on their own.

"Well, at least we know Leighton is alive and well," Chris broke the silence. "We can squash those unsavory lies Fiona has been using to scare women off Dean."

"Yes, at least we got that straightened out," Rae agreed. "Now, how do I shut her up?"

"You can only ignore a woman like Fiona. The more you fight her, the more vicious she gets. And you don't want to lower yourself to her level."

"That's wise advice, Chris." Rae added, "But I can't promise I won't scratch her eyes out the next time she comes at me."

Chris burst out laughing. "I figured you'd put her in a choke hold or something. Dean told me you do Krav Maga."

"Krav Maga actually involves a lot of legs, arms, and elbow strikes. And I learned to protect myself from physical attacks. Fiona requires a different approach."

"Trust me, nothing works better against Fiona than showing her that she can't get to you."

Rae huffed a breath. "I don't care about her, but if Debra wouldn't change her mind, Fiona is the only other person who knows who Nick is. And I really don't want to ask her for any favors."

"How hard is it to find a Nick who graduated the same year as Leighton Heston?" Chris mused.

"Where did she graduate from?"

"Wellesley." Chris grimaced as he said the name of the prestigious women's liberal college outside of Boston.

"Oh, so that only leaves Northeastern, Babson, Harvard, MIT—just to list a few—as possibilities of schools that Nick graduated from." Rae threw up her hands.

"Let's hope Debra changes her mind." Chris glanced at Rae. "Hey, here's an idea. Why don't you tell Dean how you feel?"

"I'm not ready." Rae shook her head. "I'm still getting used to it. This is unfamiliar territory for me."

"Haven't you been in love before?" Chris looked at her as if she was from another planet.

Rae just gave another headshake. She didn't want to talk about it with Dean's best friend. Quickly changing the subject, she said, "Thank you for doing this with me, Chris."

"Yeah, of course. I'm glad we did it. I feel I got to know you a little better, too."

Rae looked at the New York skyline in the distance. The sun hit the skyscrapers, and the city seemed to shine.

"Hey, if you're worried that Dean is still hung up on Leighton, don't. Okay?" Chris said. "Believe me, he didn't love her, either. Debra was right. I didn't think he should've asked her to marry him, but he seemed to be on a mission."

"Dean is a goal-oriented man. He's always working toward something. And I think in his head, after reaching his success, the next goal was to start a family. His brother was married with children, and he was next in line. It was the natural progression to him."

Rae scowled as she listened to Chris. Is that why he introduced her to his parents so soon?

Her heart sunk.

Am I only another means to a goal?

Chris had dropped Rae off at Washington Square Garden. She'd gone to meet with her project team and put in a couple of hours of work. Grateful for the companionship, work, and energy she'd received from her friends, she'd managed to clear her head. At least for a little while.

On her way home, her overthinking head was full of things she'd never worried about before. What a mess a day could bring, for crying out loud. First, the fight. Then, the Hestons. She hadn't started the fight, but she definitely had brought the Hestons on herself. Now, she wondered if she'd been foolish. Chris' words also didn't sit well with her. Dean had another thing coming if he thought she'd take Leighton's place so he could tick another to-do box.

Rae stomped to her floor, more frustrated with how the day turned out. What welcomed her on the landing was staggering.

The wall along her apartment door was lined with flowers of different colors. Roses, tulips, orchids, lilies, and other flowers whose names she didn't know formed a mini garden.

Amazed, Rae approached the arrangement closest to her door and looked for a card but didn't find any. Though she knew who was excessive and bold enough to send her a whole store of flowers. Her earlier displeasure dissolved. What woman could resist such extravagance?

Looking at the rows of blossoms, she heaved a heavy sigh and unlocked her door. Grabbing the small vase of tulips on her left, she paused to admire them before walking inside.

"I just realized I don't know your favorite flower." A familiar quiet voice stopped Rae in her tracks. A smile spontaneously emerged on her lips at the sound of Dean's voice, but she quickly quelled it before she turned to him.

Dean was standing by the stairs, watching her with those sharp grey eyes. Always looking like he could conquer the world in his business suit, but he also looked tired for a change.

"This is over the top." Rae gestured to the colorful display.

"Maybe, but necessary." Dean took a step toward her.

"They don't erase what happened last night."

He nodded as he moved closer. "They're not meant to erase anything."

"What are they meant for then?"

"For softening you up when I apologize."

"A simple 'I'm sorry' would've sufficed." Rae tried to control the smile that wanted to break out.

"If you haven't figured it out yet, I don't do 'simple.'" Dean stood toe-to-toe with her. "So, are you softened enough to accept my apology?"

"I haven't heard one," Rae pointed out.

"I'm sorry I was an ass. I really don't have an excuse for what I said."

Rae studied his face and saw that he meant it.

"Gardenia." She smiled. "My favorite flower is gardenia."

His smile matched hers, but then his eyes swept the rows of flowers.

"You missed that one," Rae informed him.

Turning his eyes to Rae, he took the vase of tulips out of her arms and kissed her softly. "I'll get it right next time."

"I don't know about you, but I don't think I want to make fighting a habit."

"Neither do I." He picked up another bouquet with his other hand. "Let's go inside."

It took them a few minutes to get all the vases inside. When they were done, her apartment looked ridiculous. Rae couldn't help but chuckle at the man standing before her.

I love this man.

The admission felt bittersweet because Rae didn't know what to do about it. But she knew they needed to discuss what had happened.

"We need to talk about last night, Dean."

He took her hands and brought them to his lips. "I know what I did was wrong. That's that. We don't have to rehash it."

"You were so upset. I want to settle the issue."

"There's no issue." He shook his head. "Not anymore."

Rae didn't believe he'd just let go of his jealousy that easily.

"Dean," she tried again. "I want you to listen. Brandon is a dear friend, but that's all he is—a friend."

"I don't want to talk about Brandon." He gathered her in his arms.

"Dean, I..."

Rae wanted to tell him that her feelings for Brandon differed from what she felt for him. Both strong and unyielding, but while one had grown out of years of building a friendship, the other had sneaked up on her and caught her off guard.

"We don't have to talk about it anymore." He trailed kisses from her ear to her chin.

"Dean..." Rae started to stop him as she struggled with what she needed to say.

"Talk can wait," he whispered as he maneuvered her into her bedroom.

Rae's struggle ceased when he captured her mouth and started peeling her clothes off her. Her last coherent thought was the talk could wait.

Thirty-Four

Just got into the car. My place or yours tonight? Dean texted Rae.

He put down his phone and looked out the window of his car. Tom had just pulled out from the Newark Liberty airport domestic arrival terminal curb. He just returned from a quick trip to California to touch base with the head of Aquarius Productions, their newest expansion. After the success of his other media businesses, investing in making their own content had been the natural progression.

"How was your trip, sir?" Tom inquired from the driver's seat.

"Productive," Dean said. "But can't say I enjoy L.A. It's good to be back."

"Perhaps you miss a certain lady, sir." Tom's grin was visible in the rearview mirror.

"Do you ever mind your own business, Tom?" Dean tried not to roll his eyes.

"Of course, sir."

"Yes, I do miss her." Dean checked his phone. "She hasn't answered my text yet."

The rush-hour traffic on the turnpike slowed to a crawl. They'd be in the car for a while, so Dean checked his emails and other messages.

A text came in.

Rae wrote, *Welcome back! I'm having dinner with Brandon's mom tonight. She came into the city to help with his surprise birthday party. I can come by your place after if you'd like.*

Dean's jaw clenched in irritation. He started texting back, *Why did you make plans when you knew I'm coming home tonight?* His thumb hovered on the send button.

I sound like a dick.

He erased what he'd typed and waited for a beat to text back. *That's all right. I'm tired anyway. Have fun. Dinner tomorrow?*

Her reply was immediate. *It's a date. I miss you.*

Dean stared at their text thread, but his sudden bad mood stopped him from telling her he missed her, too. Since her best friend had returned from Europe, Rae's time had been more divided. Apparently, Tuesday night was her and Brandon's predetermined weekly dinner. She also made time during the week to cook for the boys when they were all in the city.

Rae had invited him to join the dinner last week, but Dean had declined, claiming he'd had work to do. He actually hadn't wanted to see more of her interacting with Brandon. Avoidance seemed to keep his jealousy at bay, up to a point.

Between their work and separate social life, they hadn't seen each other as much as they had the first month. Dean wondered if she was pulling away from him now that Brandon was home. She claimed there was nothing remotely intimate between her and Brandon, but it was getting more difficult to believe.

As if he didn't torture himself enough with his doubts, Dean pulled up Rae's social media page. He scrolled through posts updating her upcoming trip and fun candid shots of her with the crew, and he stopped at the latest post from last Tuesday night. It was a picture of her and her BFF having sushi. She'd written a little caption, "#TuesdaydinnerwithRossi is back."

Rae had never posted anything about her dates with Dean. She'd been so quiet about their relationship to the point of avoiding being seen together in some of his more public social commitments. He'd thought she wanted to keep parts of her life private, but now that she had many "friends" posts, he was thinking twice.

Dean scrolled through her older posts and saw more #TuesdaydinnerwithRossi posts. He quickly closed the app. He didn't need to go down that rabbit hole tonight.

"So, where to, sir? The Village or—"

"Home, Tom." Suddenly, Dean felt tired. "We're going home."

Thirty-Five

"Are you all right?" Rae studied Dean across the table from her.

They met for dinner at a restaurant tonight. Rae wished they could be private in either of their places, but today had been hectic. She'd suggested picking up pizza and bringing it to her place. Still, he'd instead picked one of New York's top restaurants with a reservation waiting list months ahead.

Dean looked up from his food. "I'm fine. Why?"

"You're quiet tonight. More than usual." Rae put down her utensils. "I've been talking nonstop about my day. I'm sorry."

"No, I just have some things in my mind, that's all."

"Thank goodness it's Friday night." Rae flashed him a smile. "We can just be lazy in the morning."

Dean smiled back. "I'd like that."

"I have to meet Linda at Brady's bar in the afternoon to assist with the birthday cake baking and putting up some decorations for the party," Rae said. "But I'll come home first to clean up and change. Justin's scheduled to bring in Brandon around eight-thirty. We should be there by eight at the latest."

"I..." Dean avoided her eyes. "I can't come."

Rae tilted her head with her brows scrunched together. "What do you mean? I told you about the party two weeks ago."

"Something came up. I have a few important guests in town that I need to entertain." Dean finished his dish and sat back in his seat. "I'd like you to come."

"You know I can't." Rae sat up, her frown deepened.

"Surely you can be a little late seeing your friend. You've seen him plenty this week." Dean's voice was blasé, but his meaning was anything but.

"What are you talking about?" Rae's eyes widened with puzzlement. "It's his surprise birthday party that I'm organizing. I can't be late."

Rae knew Dean was aware of the party. She'd been talking about it for the past two weeks. And he just chose to think it wasn't as big a deal as his guests.

This is about Brandon.

It boiled down to that first fight. Rae decided they'd ignored the issue for too long.

"You still have a problem with my friendship with Brandon," she shot straight to the point.

Dean lifted his eyes to meet hers but didn't say a word. His silence was enough confirmation.

"Why?" Rae asked. "Because we had two dates?"

"This is neither the time nor the place to have this conversation," he finally responded.

"This is as good a time or a place as any. Stop avoiding the subject." Rae refused to be shut down. "Let's hash it out. What is the problem, Dean? This is more than just about Brandon and me having been on a couple of dates, isn't it?"

Except for a slight tightening of his jaw and his eyes growing colder, Dean maintained his voice even. "I don't trust him."

"How could you when you haven't even tried to get to know him?" Rae said through clenched teeth.

"No man can be friends with a woman like you without ulterior motive. I just don't buy it."

"I guess he's been biding his time all these years, huh? I suppose Curtis, Ram, and Justin too?" she ridiculed. "Why can't you see a friendship as it is?"

Rae studied the hard-faced man before her. This was the man she'd fallen in love with. A man whose polished exterior hid a certain vulnerability that endeared him to her, but she hardly recognized him as he put up a wall between them.

"If you don't trust him, do you trust me?" Rae held on to her last shred of composure. "No, you don't have to answer that. I know the answer. I should've known better. No, I actually did know better."

Rae stood up and gathered her stuff.

"Where are you going?" Dean demanded.

"Home. I don't know what we're doing if there isn't trust or at least a willingness to try." Rae walked away from the table.

Dean caught up to her within a few seconds. He held her elbow to slow her down. She jerked her arm away from him.

"Rae, do not make a scene," Dean warned.

"I'm not making a scene. You are. Let go of me," Rae hissed.

When he released her arm, Rae stormed out of the restaurant straight onto the crosswalk toward the park.

"Rae." Dean went after her. "I'm not chasing you down Madison Avenue."

"Nobody's telling you to." The crosswalk light turned green.

"Rae, please." He stepped in front of her, stopping her short, while other people walked around them.

She glared at him under the streetlight. "What is it, Dean? Has anything changed in the last two minutes? Because unless you suddenly feel you can start trusting me, we don't have anything else to say to each other."

"This isn't a conversation I'd like to have on the side of a street."

"Is it a conversation we could honestly have?" Rae searched his eyes. She thought she saw a softening in his eyes despite his quiet turmoil, but the same doubt stayed.

At that moment, his car rolled in, and without answering, he opened the door for her. "Get in."

Rae should've refused, but she held on to a tiny hope that they could work this out. She slid into the car. But instead of joining her, Dean said to his driver. "Take Rae home, Tom."

Her heart cracked when he shut the car door without even a goodbye. She was sure her face showed how wrecked she was. Gone was her anger, replaced by disbelief. How could one moment change one's life? she thought.

"Are you all right, Miss Rae?" Tom's soothing voice filled the silence in the car.

Rae tried to compose herself, but she didn't think she could hide what she was feeling. She looked at him briefly to give him a smile. "Don't worry about me, Tom. I'll be fine."

"Are you sure, miss?"

"Definitely." Rae turned her eyes to the side window. She repeated mostly to herself, "I'll be just fine. I have to be."

Thirty-Six

Friends and family crammed Brady's bar to celebrate Brandon's birthday. The atmosphere was festive, with expressive artists, down-to-earth Jersey folks, and eccentric New Yorkers mixing together. Music blared, but the party's mood was chill. It was very Brandon Rossi.

The delight on Brandon's face when he'd walked into the bar had made Rae happy. She'd never known an adult man who enjoyed his birthday like Brandon. It was one of the things that she loved about him.

From across the space, Rae spotted the birthday boy holding court by the bar. He had an easy way with people, and his personality made them relax around him. It was probably what had made her feel comfortable with him from the beginning and how they'd become such close friends.

In her eyes, there was nothing strange about their relationship. They were just two people who had bonded over time. Was there a romantic attraction in the beginning? Maybe. But she didn't think she'd been open to it, and they'd fallen into friendship naturally. He'd been the person she would share things with, turn to for advice, and run to when a problem surfaced for the past four years.

Rae tried to put herself outside, looking in to see what Dean might've seen. People had mistaken their friendship for something more, but she couldn't understand how Dean would think that. Couldn't he see she yearned for him? Couldn't he see how she missed him by the end of the day when she just saw him in the morning? Maybe he couldn't. Perhaps he didn't want to see it.

Her chest constricted as she remembered the way last night had ended. She hadn't heard from him since, and she wasn't sure if she ever would again. She didn't know how they could go on if he didn't trust her. She knew this was what eventually would happen between them.

Curtis emerged at her side, offering a glass of wine. "What's with the gloomy face? You're bringing down the vibe."

Rae glanced at Brandon's childhood best friend and bandmate as she accepted the glass. "Thanks, Curtis."

He was always the comical one in the group, who sometimes didn't think before he spoke. His mixed Chinese and European heritage gave him an exotic complexion, and his deep brown eyes were always mischievous.

"What are you doing standing here alone?" Curtis asked. "Where's Dean?"

"He's got somewhere else to be."

"Well, he's a busy dude." Curtis threw an arm around Rae's shoulders. "Don't worry. I'll take good care of you."

Rae smiled, appreciating his company. "Where's your date?"

"Introducing her girlfriend to Ram right there." He gestured to the middle of the room.

"She's cute," Rae acknowledged, but her mind wasn't entirely on the party, though she tried. "Hey Curtis, you know I love Brandon like a brother, right?"

"Sure." He nodded.

"Why do people keep thinking we're more than friends?"

Curtis shrugged. "You look good together."

"What?" Rae's eyes were huge with shock.

"You do. But that's all most people see. I lived with you both, so I know you treat him like the little brother you never had. And Brandon is..." He trailed off. "Let's just say he's looking for something he's lost."

"He is?" Rae frowned. That was the first she'd heard of it after being friends for years.

Curtis rolled his eyes to show how silly he thought it was. "That's my guess. If he'd found it in you, he wouldn't have settled on just being your friend. Not again."

"Again?" Rae was perplexed now.

"Anyway." Curtis grinned as if he hadn't dropped a bomb on her. "What's with the questions? Is Dean jealous about Brandon?"

"Jealous is an understatement."

He patted Rae's shoulder in understanding. "Brandon's ex-girlfriends got jealous of you, too."

"What are you talking about?"

"Frances gave him an ultimatum to stop being friends with you. You can guess how that went." Curtis chuckled.

Rae's jaw dropped. "Brandon never told me."

"Oh shit. I probably shouldn't have told you, either." Curtis quickly added, "Look, Brandon didn't want you to feel bad, 'kay? Obviously, those girls were insecure if they couldn't see your friendship for what it was. I get it, though. Who wouldn't get a bit jealous of a beautiful woman like you?"

Rae was speechless.

"But why would a guy like Dean Rowland be jealous of Brandon?" Curtis murmured.

Rae wished she knew the answer to that.

Dean shook several hands and excused himself from the private booth where Leon, his head of International Relations, was hosting their guests from South Korea. He'd spent the last hour making polite conversations with their future investors. It was all a part of the business, but he hadn't needed to be there tonight. Leon had it under control.

Bringing the guests to Chris' new club was a good idea. The bar boasted a stellar whiskey selection, and the Korean guests enjoyed themselves. Dean left them to sample their drinks in peace to find his friend. He could use an ear and another perspective on what had happened last night.

Dean couldn't help but berate himself about what had transpired. He'd thought he'd had his jealousy under control. Still, whenever Rossi's name was mentioned, an image of him and Rae together appeared in his mind. It drove him mad. Rae had also made it harder for him to contain his resentment when she'd openly chosen Rossi over him.

He'd wanted her to pick him. Instead, she'd called him out. *Do you trust me?* Rae had asked.

Dean had thought he could trust her. He wanted to. But he couldn't stop the gnawing suspicion that her loyalty would lie with her friend in the end.

Sitting in another private booth, he ordered a new drink and asked the server to get Chris for him. Deep in his brooding, he didn't see a particular blond sashaying her way over to him until it was too late. Unable to avoid the encounter, he groaned silently and braced himself by chugging the remainder of his drink.

Why does she always show up?

"Hey, lover. I can't believe I spotted you alone." Fiona Underwood slid into the half circle booth right next to him.

"Fiona," Dean said with forced politeness and scooted away from her.

She looked at him through her lashes with a voracious smile. "Have I missed the news again, or are you once again available for the rest of us poor, lonely women?"

Dean tasted bile in his mouth. "The last I checked, you're neither poor nor lonely."

"So you've been checking up on me." Fiona deliberately misunderstood his meaning, her fingers reaching out to caress his hand. "I must say it's about time we get together."

She eyed him with the look of a hungry feline that he detested.

"I don't think so." Dean pulled his hand away, curtly smiling only not to be openly rude.

The spark of outrage in her eyes shouldn't satisfy him, but it did.

"So, you're still in the clutch of that common redhead?" she hissed maliciously.

"Watch yourself, Fiona." Dean's voice grew icy.

Quickly recovering her smooth visage, the two-faced woman adopted a concerned tone. "Oh, I didn't say it to be mean. I just don't want you to get hurt again. The way Leighton hurt you."

At the mention of his ex-fiancée's name, Dean didn't flinch. "I'm not sure what you're getting at."

"I know what really happened, Dean. Sure, it was announced that Leighton had a change of heart, which was true and bad enough, but I know she eloped with another man."

Dean's grip on his glass got tightened from wanting to strangle Fiona. Still, he refused to indulge the vulture with any response. She took it as a signal to go on.

"Now, here you are in the same old situation. Why would you put yourself through this again, Dean? You know that your girl is cozy with some musician, don't you? I didn't realize you like to share your woman."

"Are you done?"

Dean's tone would've made any man back off, but Fiona didn't waver. She took out her phone. "You know who else she's been cozy with?"

Fiona turned her phone to Dean. A zoomed-in picture of Rae coming out of a moss green Porsche. He knew one person who drove that particular car.

"See, I know you and Chris are close, but I didn't know you're that tight." Fiona's smile was almost devilish.

Dean clenched his jaw so hard that he could feel all the veins on his temple bulging.

"Oh, you didn't know?" She didn't even bother to cover her pleasure. "I'm sorry, darling. I'm just looking out for you."

His vision turned red.

I have to get the fuck out of here.

Chris skipped down the stairs to the main floor when he saw Dean storming out of the club. Dean didn't usually storm anywhere. Even in the chaos of his canceled wedding, he'd been unruffled.

Where the hell is he going?

From his peripheral view, Chris spotted Fiona Underwood getting out of a booth with a self-satisfied smile. Unexpected wariness crawled up his spine. He rushed to catch Dean, but he had already disappeared when Chris got to the exit.

Chris was about to call his friend when he bumped into Fiona.

"You just missed Dean," Fiona said with an I-know-something-you-don't-know smile.

"Did he say where he was going?" Chris asked.

"No. But he was enraged."

"What did you say to him?" Chris accused, not bothering to stay polite.

Fiona laid a hand on her chest, sounding offended. "Why do you think it's something I did?"

"Call me psychic." He crowded Fiona and asked again, "What did you say to him?"

The woman wasn't intimidated but seemed to enjoy his small display of aggressiveness. "I only gave him a little advice to watch where his common girlfriend has been spreading her favor."

Chris frowned. "What the fuck are you talking about?"

"Oh, I think you know exactly what I'm talking about, Chris." Fiona ran her finger on Chris' suit lapel. "I'm sure you know the real reason Leighton didn't show up at the wedding. How do you think Dean feels knowing he's being cuckolded again by his best friend?"

Chris froze as he stared at Fiona. "That's a blatant lie."

"I have proof." She showed him the picture on her phone.

"How the hell did you even get that?"

Fiona shrugged. "I have my ways."

"Why are you doing this, Fiona?" Chris genuinely wanted to know. "What's with the obsession with Dean?"

"I saw him first." Fiona cocked her chin in defiance. "Not Leighton. Not those other women he dated. And definitely not miss travels-on-coach."

"You need help," Chris told her. "Even if he wasn't with anyone, you'll never have him. I suggest you find something better to do than obsessing over a man whose heart is with someone else."

Fiona lost a bit of her bravado but still held her spine straight and her eyes spiteful.

"Obsessing over someone unavailable to love you won't ever make you happy, Fiona. Trust me. I know," Chris said, not unkindly. "He loves someone else."

"Love is overrated, Chris Sullens." Fiona strutted away. "I doubt love is what drove Dean out of here like a bat out of hell."

Fuck.

Chris dug out his phone and dialed Dean. Call declined. He dialed Rae next. It kept on ringing.

Thirty-Seven

"My mom's red velvet cake is the bomb." Brandon brought two enormous pieces of cake and handed one to Rae.

"I helped bake it," she claimed with a smile.

Brandon noticed her smile didn't quite reach her eyes, and she didn't cut into the cake with as much enthusiasm as she normally would've. He couldn't pinpoint what, but something wasn't right.

"I haven't talked to you all night," Brandon said, trying to gauge Rae's mood. "You're awesome, by the way, for organizing this."

"Just want to welcome you to the thirties club. You're officially old. Your bones will start creaking when you wake up in the morning."

He laughed. "Men don't get old. We become distinguished with age."

"Right." Rae rolled her eyes.

Brandon looked around the bar. "Is Dean here?"

"No," she answered shortly.

That was it. But before he could probe, Rae spoke first.

"Did you and Frances break up because of me?"

The question came out of nowhere, and he stopped chewing the cake in his mouth and swallowed it whole. "What?"

"Forget it. I shouldn't bring that up tonight."

"Wait a minute. You can't just ask me a question like that and tell me to forget it."

"I'm sorry. It's your birthday." Rae shook her head as if trying to shrug off her mood.

Frances, his ex-girlfriend, broke up with him a few months ago, saying he wasn't there enough for her. She'd claimed he devoted most of his emotional availability to Rae. And she told him to stop being friends with Rae. That had been a deal-breaker, but Rae didn't need to know that.

"You're not the reason Frances and I broke up," Brandon assured her. "We had issues. Insecurity, distance, and we didn't feel strongly enough about each other."

His explanation didn't seem to relieve Rae. Besides, he doubted his relationship with Frances was the cause of her agitation.

"Hey, what's wrong?" Brandon set their plates aside and took her hands. "Talk to me, Rae."

"Nothing's wrong." Rae smiled brightly at him, but it felt false. "We'll definitely talk, just not right now. Tonight we celebrate." She squeezed his hands. "Let's dance!"

Brandon was concerned about Rae's mood changes. It wasn't like her to be gloomy, and she wasn't one to pretend something was okay when it clearly wasn't. But if she wanted to dance, he'd dance. They joined their friends grooving to the lively song on the floor. Rae looked determined to enjoy herself.

"I love this song!" she exclaimed with a laugh when it ended. She cupped his face and gave him a peck on the cheek. "Happy birthday, B."

Brandon chuckled and was glad to see her laugh was actually genuine. But her face tensed in a blink of an eye, and she broke away from him. Before he knew what was happening, Rae bolted and weaved her way through the crowd.

"Rae!" he called, trying to go after her. "Hey, where are—"

"Having a good time, bro?" Brady suddenly stood in front of him.

"Absolutely." Brandon looked over his brother's shoulder to see where Rae was heading. "I'll be right back."

He left his brother talking and made it to the door just in time to see Rae running up the stairs to the sidewalk. He stopped in his tracks on the steps as he heard Rae's voice.

"Dean, wait!" she called out.

Rae was about to quicken her pace, but she stopped instead.

What am I doing? If he wouldn't chase me down a street, I won't either.

"Dean Rowland, stop and talk to me like a civilized person," Rae called out loud enough. "You came for a reason. This silent treatment doesn't work for me. If you have something else you want to accuse me of, then say it to my face."

The few people strolling the street did a double take at her but continued walking.

"I suppose you can go into your fancy car, drive away, and pretend nothing happened. Just like Leighton didn't happen. I didn't happen."

Even as she said it, Rae wished it'd be easy to pretend he never entered her life. This was precisely why she'd avoided entanglement.

Dean spun around and stalked back to her. He loomed over her, his eyes piercing.

"You have some nerve, Rae," Dean said through grounded teeth. "You're still going to deny it even after what I saw in there?"

Rae glared back at him. "What did you see in there? People, having fun? It's a damn party."

"Then go back to your party. To your best friend," Dean jeered. "You'd never see me kissing my best friend the way you did."

"What the hell are you talking about?" Rae looked at him like he was from another planet. "I've seen you kiss your sister and mother the same way. How else would you kiss someone you love?"

"You must think I'm blind." Dean smiled bitterly.

"No, but something is definitely obscuring your vision. I couldn't figure out what I did to make you unable to trust me and why you see things that aren't true."

"I saw you dancing merrily with him, Rae. Kissing him." For the first time in their time together, Dean's voice rose. "And I saw a picture of you getting out of Chris' car. How are you going to explain that one, huh? Your best friend isn't enough for you. You have to fuck mine, too?"

Rae stumbled back in shock at his crude accusation, as if he'd physically pushed her.

"Did you have someone following me?" she asked in disbelief.

"So you're not going to deny that one?" Dean challenged.

"You're an idiot if that's what you think," Rae spat. "You learned nothing about me in the past two months, did you? And to accuse your friend along with me? You need to get your facts right.

"I'll admit I'm guilty of not telling you about what we did," Rae explained, despite being hurt from more accusations. "I asked Chris to help me find Leighton because you wouldn't do it. To his credit, Chris didn't want to out of respect for you. But after hearing the lies Fiona Underwood told me, he agreed it was best to try to find Leighton ourselves."

"Don't try to spin this around. Fiona was the one who alerted me about you and Chris."

"What did she say to you? How would she know anything that we did?"

"She had a picture of you coming out of Chris' car. What's your excuse for that?" Dean's tone was so damning.

"You're so quick to believe Fiona, a woman you despise. But you can't give me the benefit of the doubt?" Rae laughed wryly. "If nothing remotely good came out of this, the least I could do is warn you to watch your back with her.

"She implied you made Leighton disappear after she left you to scare off any potential women in your life. And you know what, *I* didn't believe her." Rae looked straight into his eyes, showing her conviction in his character. "That was why Chris and I went to see the Hestons in Rhinebeck. Debra Heston told us enough that she's been in contact with her daughter, and she's happy.

"Leighton moved on, Dean. When will you get over her and move on with your own life?" Rae questioned.

"Oh, she moved on? That's great." Dean's laughter sounded harsh. "She made a fool of me after two years of a so-called relationship, a long engagement, and a shamefully extravagant wedding. And what did I get? Courtesy? No. All I got were lies and a Dear John letter telling me she'd run off with her lover, and you expect me to just move on with my life?

"And what else? You expect me to believe what you have with Rossi is just friendship? When I saw you cozying up in his arms? You expect me to trust either of you? I won't play the fool again! Not for you, not for anyone!"

"Can't you see that he's my family?" Rae yelled in frustration. "You have your parents and siblings. Those people inside are my family! I won't choose between the two of you. I can't. I will not be punished for something another woman did to you."

"Then go marry him already," Dean hissed. "You've obviously made your choice."

"If that's what you think, then you are a fool, Dean."

Rae felt drained. She had no more fight in her. She turned back and left Dean standing on the side of the street.

This time, she held no more hope.

Brandon could almost hear Rae's heart breaking as she said her parting words. She walked back toward the bar and froze when she saw him waiting at the stairs, realizing that he'd listened to the whole fight. She looked emotionally drained, though not a single tear was on her face. But he knew she was in pain.

Without hesitation, Brandon pulled her in for a hug. Around the corner, Brandon saw Dean as he turned to leave, his face hard. He knew he should've been angrier with Dean for hurting Rae. He should probably go after him and give him a piece of his mind. But somehow, Brandon pitied him. He was sorry that Dean couldn't see love when given so freely.

Brandon agreed with Rae. He was a damned fool.

Thirty-Eight

Melanie kept a watchful eye on the boss as he listed tasks he needed done. Documents from various departments, arranging meetings, and dodging calls from specific people—such as Chris Sullens—were only a few things she had to do. It was all part of her job and wasn't more than her usual responsibilities.

It was the pace—his pace. Dean had been working nonstop, forcing people around him to keep up with him. Melanie remembered the last time the boss had been on a working rampage. It'd been right after the wedding. And it was happening again.

Tom had told her about the quarrel between Dean and Miss Rae. It had come to a head last weekend, and the boss hadn't been right since. When Tom had insisted there was something different about Miss Rae, Melanie had been skeptical. But when a month had gone by, she started believing that Dean had found someone special. He'd been happier. He'd continued to work hard, but when it was time to go, he'd left with a smile. His social calendar had decreased dramatically because he'd rather spend his free time with Miss Rae.

Melanie had never met Rae Allen, but she'd heard enough from Tom that she'd started feeling grateful for her presence in her employer's life. Now she wondered what had happened between them that caused this abrupt change. It was frustrating and sad when you had to watch someone you cared about wasting away in his work like this.

"What are those?" Dean suddenly gestured to the stack of envelopes on her lap.

"These are end-of-year invitations from various partners and organizations. I'd like to go through them with you real quick," Melanie answered.

"Decline all holiday parties," Dean dismissed.

Melanie nodded, but there was one particular international aid organization that had sent an invitation for their annual gala, accompanied by a handwritten letter addressed to her. She'd debated what to do because she really didn't want Dean to be hurt further. But her instinct told her there might be a reason why that letter had come now.

"Dean, if I may propose something. I think this wonderful organization is worth looking into," Melanie started carefully, handing him the small book showing the group's programs. "It'd help them greatly if you'd attend their annual gala and pledge your support."

Dean looked up and fixed his eyes on her. Her suggestion wasn't out of the ordinary. A man in Dean's position got numerous invitations from nonprofit organizations all the time. One of Melanie's jobs was to filter these invites and run them through either Robert's team in Communications or Aquarius Funds, which handled the company's charity work. But this time, she went directly to Dean.

He could tell her to go to the usual channels or—with his mood lately—reject her proposal on the spot. To Melanie's relief, he simply said, "Tell me who they are."

It didn't hurt that Melanie actually liked what the organization was doing. She explained how the programs focused on providing equal education to disabled children worldwide, especially those with hearing, visual, and speech impairments. She didn't have children, but one of her nephews was blind.

"You really believe in this organization's missions, don't you?" Dean sat back in his chair, studying Melanie. "Buy a table. You don't have to run it by Funds; I'll pay out of my personal account. Check with Robert who would be best to attend the gala. Save three seats for me, you, and Gary if he'd like to join."

Melanie was pleasantly surprised. "That's so generous of you to include me and my husband at your table, Dean."

"You don't speak up about these things very often, Melanie. You convinced me to participate in this event. I think you should be there."

"Thank you. We'll be delighted." Melanie quickly added, "The gala takes place the week before Christmas. Do you have any holiday plans that are not on the schedule yet that may coincide with the event?"

"No." Dean returned his attention to whatever he'd been reading.

"Should I save another seat for Miss Rae?" Melanie asked.

Dean's head whipped up so fast that Melanie's eyes rounded in alarm.

"That'll be all, Melanie." Dean delivered the order evenly without an uptick in his volume, but the message was clear.

Melanie quickly beelined for the door. But before she escaped from the office, Dean gave a final warning.

"Stay out of my personal business. That goes the same for Tom. Make sure you pass it along," he said. "Do I make myself clear, Mrs. Swanson?"

Dean had never referred to her so formally that it effectively put her in her place. She left his office in a flash and picked up the phone after making sure the coast was clear.

"You're right, Tom. Something is definitely amiss between the two of them. When I mentioned her name, the boss warned us to keep our noses out of his personal life. You better keep your mouth shut," Melanie relayed the info.

"I haven't said anything to him since the last time he saw Miss Rae," Tom grumbled.

"Good. Keep it that way."

"I wish I knew what happened. They were good together."

"It's none of our business," Melanie warned him again.

"I know. But I can't stand seeing the boss all brooding and unhappy."

"Then it's all your Miss Rae's fault!"

"You didn't see her, Mel. They're both hurting. What a waste."

"Well, there's nothing we can do," Melanie said. "Dean will get over it soon enough. Let's just do our jobs and not worry about it."

"I can't help it, Mel. I know it's silly, but I thought Miss Rae would be the one for him."

"I understand your sentiment, Tom. I want him to find love, too."

"I wish we could help. But what could we two lowly employees do?" Tom sighed.

"I just did something that might help him close up a long-abandoned chapter," Melanie mused. "Or it might get me fired."

"You have a sec?" Gayle asked Dean as he finished shaking and congratulating his other heads of department for an excellent annual performance.

He gave her a short nod while wrapping up his conversation with Leon. "The Korean deal capped the year. We'll celebrate next week with the rest of the team."

After Leon waved to Gayle and walked out of the boardroom, Dean turned to her. "What's up? Did I miss something from your department?"

"No. We've covered everything. Can't do better but topped last year by tripling profits, doubling talent into the pool, and gaining two-hundred percent more subscribers on our streaming platforms."

"You and your team earn your bonuses." Dean gave her an impressed smile.

"Yeah, and the projection for next year looks promising, too. That's why I'm willing to do some cuts."

Dean narrowed his eyes at her. "Cuts for what? We don't need to cut anything."

"For personal reasons." Gayle took out a folder and handed it to Dean.

"What is this?" He opened it, and his jaw locked when he saw the contract.

Gayle gauged his reaction to see if she had made an error.

"Why are you giving this to me?" Dean lifted the folder between them.

"I heard what happened," Gayle said carefully.

"Enlighten me. What did you hear?"

"That Brandon Rossi screwed you over a woman. I can't let our talent humiliate my boss."

Dean's face hardened further. "When did my personal life become a company issue?"

"You're the founder of this company, Dean," Gayle said with more force than she intended. "I knew that woman could be a problem when I first met her. She's ambitious. She couldn't ditch the rock star when she hooked a bigger fish?"

"Don't talk about her that way. You don't know her, Gayle," Dean warned quietly.

"I don't understand how you could say that so calmly. If I were you, I'd want to teach Rossi who he was fucking with. You gave him and his band their chance."

Dean tossed the contract on the meeting table. "They're one of your best assets. As the head of Aquarius Music, you would cut them loose, Gayle?"

"No. But as your friend, absolutely."

"This is business."

"And there are other assets that won't cross you this way," Gayle stated. "Just so you know, I've called their representation to discuss their contract. Give them something to think about."

Dean's lips flattened in response to her announcement. He didn't look as pleased as Gayle had thought he would.

"I didn't start this company to throw my weight around, Gayle." Dean's sharp grey eyes focused on her. "I've trusted you to run Music because I respect your musical instinct and business savvy. I wouldn't usually question how you run your department, but I can't let you do that. You'll risk us a big lawsuit."

Gayle blanched. That possibility, of course, had occurred to her. But in her moment of weakness, she'd indulged that they could afford a payout if it came to that.

"I'm sorry, but I couldn't help myself." Gayle lost her conviction. "I don't know how you can still be level-headed after what they did to you. I just hated seeing you hurt again, Dean."

"That's not how we do business, Gayle." Dean shook his head. "I can't let my personal feelings about Rae and Rossi affect this company. It is more than me."

"I've already made the call with the veiled threat, but I won't take further steps," Gayle informed him. "Good thing the band couldn't all make it for a meeting when I requested it. Apparently, Rossi just left for Italy."

"Did you say Italy?" Dean's expression took another turn.

"That's what their manager told me." She eyed her boss curiously. "Why?"

A trace of displeasure and—would Gayle dare say regret?—flitted over Dean's face. "Rae's in Italy."

Thirty-Nine

Rae waved at her crew as they drove away in their van. After a long, full week of shooting, they all had earned a bit of R&R. From the time they'd landed in Milan, they'd worked nonstop. They'd had a great time meeting people, exploring vineyards, and eating beautiful food while driving to Piedmonte. Now they were in Tuscany, and the crew wanted to spend their day off checking out spots not on their filming list. There were so many beautiful things about Italy, they couldn't cover them all.

Italy is always a great idea.

With a smile, Rae walked back into the little courtyard of the charming *pensione* they were staying in. Brandon was still sitting at their breakfast table, sipping his coffee. He'd arrived in Florence two days ago and joined them for the ride to Siena. He'd even made a guest appearance in a few shots where Rae was reunited with the family who taught her to cook Tuscan-style dishes. Brandon had loved every minute of it. He was three-quarters Italian, after all.

His presence had boosted her spirit. It'd been hard keeping up a peppy appearance for the shoot when you were still nursing a broken heart. She'd thought she'd shake it off as soon as she stepped on Italian soil. Traveling had never failed to fill her with joy before. This time, it couldn't quite fill the void Dean had left.

Rae sat next to Brandon and picked up her cappuccino. "Where should we go today?"

"You're the expert. But..." He finished his coffee. "I don't get to see the countryside on tour, so I'm game for driving around."

"My favorite way to explore. Let's get lost." Rae drank the rest of her coffee. "And eat our way through the day."

Brandon chuckled. "I second the eating part."

"I'm glad you're here." Rae squeezed his hand briefly.

He eyed her. "How are you holding up?"

"I'm good." She flashed him a smile.

"You don't have to hide it from me." His eyes were direct even under his sunglasses.

With a sigh, Rae set her finished cup. "I'm coping. Most days I'm fine, but there are moments when I feel overwhelmed by...grief, I suppose."

'You did lose someone you love. You are grieving.'

"Will it go away? This hollowness in my chest?"

"I don't know." Brandon looked blankly at the fountain in the middle of the courtyard. "Time might numb the pain. Other things, friends, new people, and lovers will help fill your heart again, but you have to let them."

Rae watched her friend's face curiously. "Did Frances break your heart when she broke up with you?"

Brandon thought for a few beats before answering. "No, I don't think so. But yeah, I've had my heart broken. It was a while ago."

"Curtis told me you're looking for something you lost. What did he mean?"

Brandon turned his gaze to her with a frown. "I have no clue. Did I lose a key or something?"

"I think he meant a lost love."

"This is Curtis you're talking about, right?" Brandon scoffed. "You know he isn't exactly a perceptive person."

He had a point: Curtis wasn't the type to dive into someone's thoughts and feelings. He was a loyal friend, but no one went to him when they needed to talk about something serious. Now, if they needed cheering up, he'd be the man.

Rae shrugged. "He made a point I wished Dean could hear. You know how Dean's convinced you had a secret motive to be friends with me. But Curtis was positive I wasn't the one you're looking for because if I were, you wouldn't let yourself be friend-zoned."

"So, you admit you friend-zoned me," Brandon pounced with an "aha" grin.

"You friend-zoned me, too!" Rae pushed his shoulder.

Brandon made a more-or-less hand gesture. "I would've given us a few more weeks."

"Why extend the inevitable? We're meant to be friends." Rae rolled her eyes. "But I must say life would be much simpler if we'd fallen in love with each other."

Brandon smirked. "Wouldn't that be something?"

For a second, they eyed each other, then they laughed.

"You're ready to go?" Rae stood and hauled her backpack onto her shoulder.

"Lead the way, baby."

Life would be simpler if she'd fallen for Brandon a few years ago. They got along. They understood each other. They knew they could rely on each other for support. But something was missing. Dean triggered an extreme response from her—both emotionally and physically. It was unexplainable. Her heart had expanded when they'd been together. She'd thought she couldn't contain it in her chest at times. But now, every time she thought of him, her chest constricted.

Rae tried to shake the feeling as she followed Brandon to the car he'd rented. She couldn't help to think that it'd be nice to be reborn, as depicted in Botticelli's *Birth of Venus*? She felt like she needed to start anew with a blank slate. She simply wanted it all erased because she wouldn't have to feel any of this if she didn't have the memory.

The sky was clear, the air crisp.

Just my kind of day.

Brandon maneuvered the zippy car on the empty country road. He and Rae had picked a route and let the road take them where it might lead. They'd stopped for an early lunch in a town called Pienza, known for Pecorino cheese. The little old town boasted vast, gorgeous farmland he'd itched to capture on canvas.

They were now on a large loop back toward Siena. Brandon noted a sign that said Pievasciata when Rae suddenly sat up.

"What's that? Turn around." She twisted her body, trying to look back.

Brandon slowed to a stop on the side of the secluded road. "What is it?"

"I think it's a sculpture garden." Rae sounded excited. "Let's check it out."

He did a K-turn, drove into a driveway, and stopped in front of a locked gate. "It's closed."

Being the curious traveler she was, Rae got out and walked to the signage. "They're closed off-season, but we can still enter. We just have to go to the art gallery across the street."

The artist in Brandon hummed at the prospect of seeing some art. Soon, the gallery curator opened the gate for them, and they had the park all to themselves to enjoy.

"Look at this gate. It's exquisite." Brandon studied the iron gate in the form of delicate leaf veins. He didn't do three-dimensional artwork, but he always admired people with that talent.

They walked down the path and started marveling at different works created by international artists. Canopied by tall trees, it was more woods than a garden. It was so peaceful.

"Do you mind if I take a short video?" Rae asked. "This place is so cool."

"Sure." Brandon stopped at a wooden footbridge designed with railings resembling waves going in opposite directions. "We have something like this in Jersey, y'know. Grounds for Sculpture in Hamilton. It's pretty cool.

"I love this bridge. It's so simple, but you get this visual sensory effect when crossing it." Brandon ran his hands along the planks.

Rae smiled as she followed Brandon with her camera. He continued with his commentary on the sculptures. Then they traded off, with her giving her takes on stumbling on the garden while getting lost on purpose.

"That was good." Rae put away the camera. "Do you mind if I post that tonight?"

"Of course not." Brandon had appeared on Rae's pages numerous times, but she always asked before she posted anything with him in it. "People probably will comment we're on our honeymoon."

"Oh, god." Rae blew a breath as she rolled her eyes. "If I had a dollar for every time a person told us we should get married already."

Brandon chuckled. "You ever heard about friends making a pact to marry each other if they still haven't found their soul mates when they turn forty?"

"Wasn't that from a movie?" Rae raised her eyebrows at him. "Why? You think we should make a pact? But what if your soul mate didn't show up until you're forty-two? Then you'd be stuck with me."

"Back up the truck." Brandon held up his hands. "You don't even believe in soul mates."

Rae smiled. "But you do. I wouldn't want to deprive you of spending your life with the woman of your dreams."

"I think you started believing there might be something to this love thing. I hope you won't let this experience with Dean stop you from giving another guy a chance, Rae."

"Oh, no." Rae shook her head. "He just proved to me what I believed all along: love isn't for me. It might be for you or others, but I think I'm good."

Brandon turned to her. But when he was about to say something, Rae stopped him.

"Not everyone needs to be in a relationship, B." She looked at him earnestly. "I get all the love I need from my friends."

She was right. Not everyone needed to be married with two children and a dog to live a fulfilling, happy life. But he was worried Rae was choosing to do that over fear. If she'd avoided potential love interests before, this time she'd altogether rejected it.

Suddenly feeling impulsive, Brandon grabbed Rae's hand. "Well, I'm your friend. I love you, and people already want us to get married anyway. Maybe we should explore that."

Rae looked at him as if he'd grown another head. "What?"

Brandon wasn't sure what he was doing, but he didn't want Rae to live a loveless life. Maybe they could learn to love each other more intimately.

"How many couples have you heard say their spouse was their best friend?" Brandon asked. "We're already there."

"Are you nuts?"

"I think you're a beautiful woman. It won't be hard to...uhm, y'know." Brandon looked her up and down.

"Oh, gee, thanks."

"And I'm not that bad, right?" Brandon scrunched his face.

"What you're suggesting is practically incestuous."

"C'mon..."

Rae came close to him and looked him in the eyes. "Kiss me."

"What?" Brandon's eyes widened at her request.

"Let's test it out. Kiss me." She stared at him expectantly.

Brandon swallowed, feeling unsure. He moved forward. His hand hovered around her waist, but he didn't quite know where to put it.

Rae placed a hand on his shoulder and encouraged him to close the gap. When their faces were about an inch from each other, he stopped. He didn't even know where to look.

"Are you going to kiss me or not?" she asked.

"I am. Give me a sec." He concentrated, then he touched his lips to hers.

After two beats, he pulled back. "You're supposed to kiss me back."

"That was you kissing?" Rae retorted.

"Hey!"

Rae grinned. "Try again."

"You're going to kiss me back?"

"We'll see."

Brandon tilted his head this time and tried to relax. He closed his eyes and felt his way to Rae's lips. They felt soft. He focused on her lower lip and felt it trembling.

That's a good sign. Except for the giggling that came with it.

"I'm sorry. I can't do this." Rae covered her mouth with her hand. Her eyes were apologetic.

Brandon sighed. "Me, neither. That was awkward as fuck."

They looked at each other, then both burst into laughter. When the hilarity subsided, Rae put a hand on his arm and looked at him with love—a friend's love.

"I'm sorry," she started. "I know you were half-serious in suggesting we get married, but that was your protective instinct talking. And that would be wrong for us. I can't let you sacrifice your own possibilities. You need a woman who can give you her whole heart. You deserve nothing else. I gave mine away." Rae gave a little shrug of acceptance. "And I'm not getting it back."

"I know you did." Brandon gathered her into his arms and gave her what he could: comfort.

He felt a twinge in his chest for his friend for the love she missed. He just wished he could help her gain her heart back.

Forty

The traffic heading downtown was still bumper to bumper, but Dean barely noticed it as he sat in the comfort of his car, scrolling through Rae's posts from the past few weeks. He stopped at a picture of her with the filming crew with Lake Como in the background. She had a smile that brightened her whole face, and a longing automatically rushed at him.

He couldn't deny it. He missed her.

It was foolish to think he could get over Rae easily. She wasn't like any other women he'd casually dated. However short-lived their relationship was, she'd shaken up his monotonous existence. He'd been back to that life, burying himself in work, even skipping going home for Thanksgiving, so he wouldn't have time to think about her. But however busy he was, his mind occasionally conjured up her expressive face. Then, each time, he'd think of her with Brandon and feel as though he had just taken a hit in the gut.

Like a masochist, Dean tapped on a video Rae had recently posted.

Her sparkling voice came on, "Hi, guys. We're taking a detour from our schedule to do what I love best: get lost on purpose. As you might've noticed from my last update, Brandon decided to join us for a bit on this trip. So this morning, we randomly picked a route and found a gem. Look at this place. How magical are these woods?"

The camera did a slow three-sixty turn, showing modern sculptures among the tall trees with leaves falling amid them like a golden-red shower. Rae said a bit more before the video focused on Brandon for a minute while he gave his impression of a wooden bridge. The video ended with the two of them together in the frame, encouraging people to throw caution to the wind while exploring.

Dean ground his teeth.

She apparently didn't have a problem forgetting him.

He really should delete the app. Why was he torturing himself? But he tapped on the hundreds of comments and started reading.

"Aww, you guys are so cute together!" one commenter said.

"I don't know why you're fighting it. You two belong together," said another.

"Wait, did we miss the announcement? Did you get married, and now on your honeymoon?" another asked.

Even the world wanted Rae to marry Brandon. He wasn't crazy.

With a swipe of his thumb, Dean closed the app.

Enough.

Tom, who had been blessedly quiet, finally pulled in front of his building. He got out after thanking him and headed in. He'd just tapped his electronic key onto the reader when another person rushed in as the door closed.

Dean's gaze locked with the newcomer.

Chris smiled at him. "Hi, buddy. We need to talk."

"You can't avoid me forever." Chris crossed his arms as he stared at Dean.

His friend's expression was as unreadable as usual. "I have nothing to say to you."

"I beg to differ." Chris matched Dean's level tone. "You've been fed lies, Dean. You know that."

"So Rae wasn't in your car that day?" Dean narrowed his eyes at Chris.

"It's not what you think."

"What was I supposed to think, Chris? You barely knew each other."

"I expected you not to think the worst thing you could imagine!" Chris threw his arms in frustration. "We've been friends for over a decade. You know I won't ever poach your woman."

The elevator dinged open. Dean walked into his apartment without a word.

Chris quickly followed. "I might've run into her somewhere and offered her ride, for all you know."

"But that's not what you were doing, was it?" Dean dropped his bag and suit jacket on the couch.

"I took her to see the Hestons."

To Chris' surprise, Dean didn't react to the announcement.

"That much she told me." He went to his liquor cabinet and poured himself some bourbon. He didn't offer Chris one.

"Wait. You knew all this time? Why the hell are you giving me the cold shoulder then?"

"You went behind my back."

"Look, I'm sorry for that. Rae wanted to be the one to tell you, but—"

"Well, she didn't say anything until I confronted her."

"We weren't sure what was the point of telling you what we learned."

"You're supposed to have my back, Chris." Dean stood with his drink in one hand, the other in his pocket—the picture of a calm, collected man. But Chris knew his friend was furious about something Chris considered trivial.

"That's why I went with Rae," Chris explained. "I told her you wouldn't be happy when you found out. But she was determined to find Leighton. She felt it was the only way to shut Fiona up. She's been using lies to keep women away from you. Even now, she's playing you. You're letting her win by distrusting Rae.

"Rae cares about you, Dean," Chris told Dean, itching to reveal what he knew about Rae's feelings. Though he wanted to be completely honest with his friend, it wasn't his place to tell him what Rae felt about him.

Dean gave a short, humorless chuckle. "She sure showed it in a strange way. She's gallivanting in the Tuscan valley with her best friend."

A shadow cast over Dean's stoic face. "I was going to meet her. We were planning a road trip after she finished filming. If you've seen her latest video, you could see how easy it is to replace me."

"They're just friends, you know that."

"Is that what she told you, too?" Dean looked at him as if he was gullible. "They're such good friends that everyone sees them as the perfect couple. There wasn't a day since Brandon Rossi's return from the tour when I didn't hear someone or another saying they should be together."

Chris studied his friend and got annoyed. "And you know what? She was worried you couldn't let go of your ghost—Leighton's betrayal. And she was right. You accused her of cheating on you based on internet comments and Fiona Underwood's manipulation. I'd leave your ass, too."

Dean's eyes sharpened. "Screw you, Chris."

"You expect me to be real with you. This is me doing that." Chris walked to the elevator and hit the call button. "Get your shit together, or you'll always be lonely."

The door opened, and he got on.

"Perhaps you'll get lucky, and she'll forgive your stupid ass when you get your good sense back."

Forty-One

The holiday season was in full swing in Manhattan. The display of lights on Fifth Avenue, the Christmas tree at Rockefeller Center, and the decked-out store windows were all competing to make the city bright and merry. Rae loved December in Manhattan and was determined to enjoy it as she browsed for a few additional presents for her friends.

She'd released her second book and been busy with promotional events since her return. Between work and her social calendar, she would be busy until Christmas. She was grateful for her life and her family of friends. If she kept her focus on those things that mattered, she'd be content.

After her holiday shopping, Rae crashed Brandon and Curtis' dinner since she happened to be nearby.

"Done with your Christmas shopping?" Curtis eyed the bags Rae set down.

"I did." Rae then said to Brandon, "I picked up the thing you asked me for you know who."

Before Brandon could say thanks, Curtis demanded, "Ooh, what did he get me?"

Rae laughed. "What are you? Twelve? It's for Linda."

"Aren't I getting anything?" Curtis made a face. "I just got your new book for my parents and sister." He pulled out several copies. "Sign this one, 'To my most handsome, funniest friend ever, Curtis.' And the others just write something profound. They'll love it."

"Is your sister coming home?" Rae took the stack with a smile. "Will I finally meet the elusive Callie Bisset?"

Curtis' eyes darted to the unusually quiet Brandon. Rae noticed Brandon seemed to anticipate Curtis' answer.

"No, not that I heard." Curtis scratched his temple. "She doesn't get along with our mom."

"That's too bad." Rae felt sad when she heard about parents and adult children not having a relationship. It was a shame to take one's family for granted.

"Why are you so quiet?" Rae addressed Brandon after they'd ordered.

"Just thinking about something," Brandon brushed the question off.

"We've got to tell her, Brandon." Curtis looked serious, which was unusual unless he was in music mode.

Brandon glared at Curtis as if he wanted to strangle his friend, which wasn't uncommon between the two buddies. Rae frowned at the change of mood at the table.

"Tell me what?" she asked.

"Nothing," Brandon replied without taking his eyes off Curtis. "It's just band stuff."

"She deserves to know what kind of an asshole he is," Curtis ignored Brandon's attempt to shut down the subject.

Who's the asshole?

Confusion and curiosity filled Rae's voice. "Just tell me."

"We may not be with Aquarius much longer," Curtis said.

"What do you mean?" Rae straightened in her seat.

"We don't know anything yet," Brandon jumped in. "It's just speculation at this point."

"Speculation? Gayle Harris herself called Martin," Curtis scoffed. "That's pretty much decided."

"What are you talking about?" Rae asked, even if she was sharp enough to put two and two together.

"Your boyfriend is terminating our contract." Irritated, Curtis slammed his hand onto the table.

The force of it wasn't too loud, but it jolted Rae. Or maybe it was the news that shook her?

"Shut up, Curtis." Brandon covered Rae's hand. "Nothing is happening yet. Gayle Harris called for a meeting to discuss our contract. That's all."

"Right, that's all," Curtis said sarcastically. "That's why Martin suggested bringing our lawyers in."

Brandon gave Curtis an irked side-eye.

"This can't be right." Rae's voice was merely a whisper.

"They haven't followed up since the initial call," Brandon said. "Can't be that serious."

"Or maybe they're just waiting after the holidays before dumping our asses," Curtis deadpanned.

"I swear to god, Curtis. Shut up." Brandon slapped Curtis on the arm.

Rae slumped in her seat, not knowing what to say. Thankfully, their drinks arrived, giving Rae a second to process.

This is all my fault.

As if he read her thoughts, Brandon said, "Rae, it's not your fault."

"Oh, shit. I'm not blaming you, Rae. I just want you to know what he's doing," Curtis added sheepishly.

But Rae wasn't listening to them. "I can't believe he'd do this."

Brandon had never seen Rae's face that pale. He wanted to kick Curtis for blurting the news to Rae like that. What did he expect she'd feel?

From her expression, he didn't think she was hungry anymore. So he looked for their waiter, but he was nowhere in sight.

"I'll get the check," Brandon announced.

"What? We haven't gotten our food yet," Curtis protested.

"You think anyone except you still has any appetite after that?" Brandon practically hissed at Curtis.

Ignoring Curtis' response, Brandon left their table to find someone. Curtis wasn't the only one who was worried. Hell, everybody was concerned, but it wasn't something they couldn't handle. They'd gained a large base of followers and critical acclaim for their two albums. It wouldn't be challenging to get a deal with a different label or go back to being independent.

Brandon was arranging to have their meal boxed and paying their bill when he heard Curtis' voice calling Rae. He spun around to see Rae's back disappearing through the restaurant door. Without thinking, he took off after her.

It took him a few seconds to spot her among the evening crowd on the sidewalk. She'd flagged a cab and was about to disappear into it before he could get to her.

How the fuck did she get a cab that fast at this hour?

"Rae!" He called out.

Rae turned her head his way, and Brandon could see fury on her face. He knew it wasn't aimed at him, but he was definitely troubled about what she would do to vent that wrath. She got into the cab and vanished into the heavy traffic when he finally got to the curb.

"Damn it!"

Forty-Two

Come on, come on. Pick up!

Rae impatiently waited for her call to be answered.

"Tom Wilkins," came the voice at the other end.

"Tom, this is Rae Allen. Can you tell me where Dean is?"

Tom sounded surprised. "Miss Rae?"

"Please, Tom. I need a word with him."

"He's still at the office, miss."

"Thank you." She abruptly ended the call and directed the cab to Aquarius.

Rae couldn't keep herself from shaking, thinking about what Dean was doing to her friends. It'd never occurred to her that he would punish his friends for what he believed she did. When Fiona had told her Dean was known to be ruthless, she hadn't bought it. She'd fiercely believed he was a good man. She couldn't be that wrong.

It seemed like it took forever to get to her destination in the traffic. She'd already declined Brandon's call several times when the taxi dropped her off.

Rae marched into the building with a purpose and was almost immediately confronted by an anxious Tom.

"Miss Rae, what are you doing?" he questioned.

Rae didn't stop walking but managed a smile for the kind older man. "Hello, Tom. I need a word with your dear employer."

"Does he know you're coming?" Tom walked with her and nodded at security at the front desk. "I'll walk up Mr. Rowland's guest, Barney."

The tall person returned the nod and cleared them through the security gate. Tom led Rae to an open elevator and punched the twenty-fifth-floor button.

"Thank you, Tom." She hadn't thought about the building's security measures in her rush. Without an appointment, she probably wouldn't have passed the front desk. But her stars were lining up tonight. The universe must know she needed to let that man know what she thought about his despicable action.

"I hope you're here to work things out with Mr. Rowland," Tom said. "He hasn't been happy since you last talked."

"He doesn't want to be happy, Tom."

"That's not true, Miss Rae." Tom looked at her. "I've driven Mr. Rowland for years. I've never seen him happier than when he was with you. He hasn't been the same."

Listening to Tom made the emotions in her chest churn. Her eyes burned as Rae tried to keep it together.

"Dean did this to himself, Tom," Rae bitterly said. "I wish we never came to this."

The light in Tom's eyes dimmed. "Miss Rae, please forgive an old man for being intrusive. It breaks my heart to see you both so unhappy. Maybe it's the old romantic in me, but I could see that you were meant to be together."

It felt like a boulder was crushing her lungs, listening to Tom's words. "Unfortunately, he doesn't, Tom. I don't think he's capable. And after what he did, I don't see it, either."

Tom's face fell at her words, and he didn't say anything else when the door opened. He led her through Aquarius' main entrance, an empty lobby and hallways accented with polished cherry wood and clean lines. One thing she couldn't blame Dean for was his classy taste. Unfortunately, his latest action didn't reflect any class at all.

They reached the end of the hallway, and Tom opened a door leading to an office suite.

A woman in her late fifties stood behind a desk, looking puzzled. "Tom, what are you doing up here?"

"Is Mr. Rowland in there?" Tom eyed the connecting door to Dean's office.

"Yes. He just dismissed me." The woman studied Rae with a scowl. "Who is this?"

"This is Miss Rae," Tom introduced them. "And this is Melanie, Mr. Rowland's faithful executive assistant."

Looking shocked, Melanie hissed low at Tom, "Why did you bring her up here?" Abruptly, she turned to Rae. "I don't mean to be rude, Miss Allen, but what are you doing here?"

"I'm sorry to put you in a difficult position, Melanie." Rae understood the protective stance of a mother hen. "But I need to talk with Dean."

"He's right in there, miss." Tom gestured at the door. "Melanie and I will be on our way out."

"Tom!" Melanie ran around the desk to stop Rae. "I'm sorry, Miss Allen. I can't allow you to go in there."

"Come, Mel. Let the two of them talk." Tom put a hand on the woman's shoulder. "You were about to leave."

"You're going to get us fired!" Melanie said under her breath.

Rae wasn't listening anymore. Her path was clear, and without hesitation, she walked in.

Dean's office was spacious and designed with the clean lines the rest of Aquarius was, except that this particular office had a fantastic view of the city. She found the man she was looking for standing by the floor-to-ceiling glass wall, looking down at the Christmas lights and traffic flow below.

"What is it, Melanie?" Dean didn't turn when he heard the door. "I thought you'd gone home."

The weariness laced in his voice surprised Rae. But she didn't let it deter her.

"Melanie left."

Dean turned when he heard the voice echoing in his mind manifested into real life. And there she was, standing in his office. Or was she just a figment of his imagination?

"What are you doing here?" The question finally left his mouth.

Rae walked toward him, her eyes assessing him. He could smell her scent, flowery with a hint of spice.

She's really here.

"Nice digs you have here." Rae casually glanced around. "So this is where you make all of your important decisions."

Dean followed her movement until she stopped before him. This close, he couldn't mistake the fire in her eyes. The blue usually reminded him of the warm and inviting Caribbean water. Every time he'd made love to her, he'd wanted to immerse himself in them. But tonight, they looked as if they could burn him.

"Is it here where you decided to screw my friends over their contract?" Rae maintained a casual tone despite the fury Dean felt from her.

Unprepared for the accusation, he blurted, "What are you talking about?"

"I've misjudged you." Rae's gaze didn't waver from his. "All this time, I thought you were respectable, brilliant, and decent. But I'm wrong. Petty is what you are."

The insult went straight to his pride and lit his temper. Her mocking was a punch straight to his heart. He involuntarily balled his fist at his side as he tensed at the attack. "Is that why you came here for? To call me names?"

"I'm here to tell you what you're doing is despicable!" she spat. "If you need to punish me for something I didn't do, then punish *me*. Brandon and the band had nothing to do with whatever happened between us."

"Always so protective of your *best friend*." Dean couldn't help the bitterness in his voice. Crossing his arms over his chest, he studied the angry woman shooting daggers at him.

When was she ever so mad for him?

"Do you enjoy playing with people's lives, Dean?" Rae stood taller, crowding him without closing their distance. "Is it not enough that you've projected your insecurities on Brandon when he doesn't deserve any of it? You need to destroy his career, too? Along with my other friends for my momentary stupidity of letting you into my life?"

Even after all this time, Dean felt her apparent allegiance to Brandon like a stinging slap. But it became clear what she was talking about. Dean remembered his conversation with Gayle.

Goddamn it, Gayle.

"I thought you were more of a man than this. I never thought you'd stoop this low."

Dean ground his teeth, trying to keep himself calm while she condemned him. "Of course you'd believe the worst of me."

Rae laughed at his face. "You believed the worst of *me*. How does it feel, huh?"

Before Dean could respond, she continued, "The difference is I didn't do what you accused me of. On the other hand, you know exactly what you're doing."

"I'm not doing what you think I'm doing to your friends, Rae."

"Are you denying that Gayle Harris threatened their manager about their contract?"

"No. But she acted on her own, and I put a stop to it."

Rae smirked in disbelief. "Like anything happens in this company without your direction or approval."

"What do you think I am? I don't run this company like the mob," Dean hurled back. "Music is under Gayle's purview, but when I learned about what she did, I told her to stand down. You and your friends can relax. Their contract is safe."

He broke away from their standoff in disgust. "Unlike Rossi, I don't need a woman to fight my battle."

Turning his back to Rae, he shoved his fists into his pockets and stared into the dark sky.

"Thanks for stopping by and showing me how you feel about me once and for all," Dean said. "I should've known I was simply a placeholder while Rossi was away. How stupid was I to think there was something special between us?"

"There was something special between us. *You* chose to put Brandon between us."

"*I* chose to put him—?" Dean abruptly turned to her. "*You* chose *him* over me. And every time I see you have a grand time, frolicking in the woods of Tuscany with him, I was reminded you'd always choose him."

"I'm not here to defend my friendship with Brandon." Rae shook her head. "You believe what you want to believe, Dean. I don't have to prove anything to you. Not anymore."

Disappointment shone in her eyes and gave him pause. He should feel satisfied that she sounded defeated, but it made him feel small. He struggled to keep himself still from needing to erase that look from her face.

"I can't understand why you could do this to my family. I suppose you never truly cared about me, or you'd see the truth by now." Rae retreated and turned toward the door.

This time he really reached out to her. Dean wanted to shout that he did care. That he still couldn't get over losing her to another man. But his hand met air.

"This is the last time you're going to break my heart." Rae walked out of his office and closed the door with a quiet slam, leaving Dean numb.

He felt like a tank had hit him. That look in her eyes had chilled his blood. The look that said he'd failed to measure up to her expectations. Once again, an awareness of his failure overwhelmed him.

As if moving with its own will, his hand grabbed the closest thing and threw it hard against the wall. The impact was deafening, and the cut crystal paperweight shattered. But it didn't make him feel any better. He'd held on to his emotions so long to stay in control when a moment with Rae made him want to break out and beg her to stay.

And now that she was gone forever from his life, Dean could only stare at the pieces of broken crystal sparkling across the floor when he really wanted to do was to pummel something.

The door slammed open, and there stood the person he'd really wanted to knock down.

Forty-Three

Brandon stormed into Dean's office with dread on his face. Within the split second he'd entered, he searched the room with his eyes but only saw Dean looking at him predatorily. Rae was nowhere in sight.

Brandon could think of only one place where she might've gone in her state of mind. When he'd walked into Aquarius' office and heard a bang, he'd feared the worst.

"Where is she?" Brandon demanded.

To his shock, Dean rushed at him and threw a punch at his face. Brandon was quick enough to avoid Dean's fist fully meeting his nose. He recovered from the initial blow fast. He saw something in the other man's eyes and almost laughed.

What happened to the famously calm and collected Dean Rowland?

Brandon was relieved that Rae wasn't in the room or the object of Dean's fury. He was also glad to find himself in the position to finally confront Dean for what he'd done to her.

"I guess we've avoided this long enough." Brandon tweaked his nose, making sure it was intact. "I'd prefer to talk about your issue with me, but if you want to let off some steam first, I'm game."

Brandon charged at Dean's midsection without warning. They both hit the floor hard.

Neither man remembered they were two civilized people who should've been past this type of aggression. Fists flew, punches missed, elbows connected with vulnerable body parts. After a brief struggle and without any obvious winner, they broke away from each other winded.

Brandon rubbed his side as he caught his breath. Dean got in a couple of good blows, and Brandon would be sore until Christmas. Though, looking at Dean, he knew his opponent didn't come out unscathed either.

"Had enough?" Brandon asked between painful breaths.

Dean glared at Brandon as he wiped the blood from his split lip with his knuckle. Brandon noted that, even if his ribs hurt like hell, he was in a much better mood.

Dean's demeanor didn't improve. "I can give you a couple more cracked ribs."

"I'm done. I still want to enjoy my Christmas dinner, thanks."

"Get out of here, Rossi," Dean dismissed him, irritated. He went to a cabinet and took out a bottle of bourbon. "How the hell did you get up here, anyway?"

"I have my ways." Brandon watched Dean pour himself a generous helping of the liquor, take a swallow, and curse as the alcohol burned his lip. "I have a few things to say to you while we're here."

"I've listened enough for tonight."

"You'll listen anyway."

"I don't need to listen to you!" Dean barked.

"You broke my friend's heart. I'd say you do," Brandon countered. "I didn't want to be that guy who had to warn you that you'd answer to me if you broke her heart. And even after you did, I was hoping you'd get over yourself and realize you made a mistake."

Dean stood there rigidly.

Brandon glanced at the broken crystal. "What happened here?"

"What else but her standing up for you?" Dean said resentfully. "Must be nice to have her fight your battles, huh?"

"Was she the one who gave you that bloody lip, Rowland?" Brandon mocked. "I never asked her to fight for me, but she'd do it because she's my friend. That's what people do when they care about each other."

"Are you done bragging?"

Brandon eyed the other man. "Man, was I wrong about you."

"I guess everyone was," Dean jeered.

"Look, I don't care what you do to me. You can rip our contract in half right now, but understand this: it won't be me you're hurting. I'll bounce back somehow, but Rae won't recover from what you're doing as easily."

"You can stop worrying, Rossi. I never had any intention to terminate your goddamned contract. Like I told Rae, I shut down Gayle's attempt to punish you on my behalf. Unlike you, I don't need a woman fighting my battle for me."

Brandon, for some reason, found it easy to accept Dean's explanation. "Is that right? Then why didn't you fight for her instead? Why did you let your stupid jealousy take over your supposedly brilliant brain?"

"Fighting a battle I know I already lost and will continue to lose?" Dean mocked. "Why am I even talking to you? She made her choice, and tonight once more, she showed me which side she's on."

"That's where you're wrong, you jackass!" Brandon snapped. "She never had any choice. It was never about a choice between you or me. She loves me because I've been her friend. But you, she loves you because...hell, I don't know why she loves you. I just know she does."

What did he say?

Dean must've looked like he'd been struck by lightning.

"Are you really that blind, man?" Brandon approached Dean. "How could you not see she's in love with you? Didn't you see how hurt she was when you doubted her? She didn't give her heart away easily, and you threw it in her face."

Dean dropped slowly into a chair, dumbfounded. He let Brandon's words sink in. "Why didn't she tell me?"

"Would you believe her? You were determined to see what wasn't there."

"Wasn't there?" Dean turned his gaze back to Brandon. "I saw how she was with you. So comfortable, so trusting—"

"But she doesn't look at me the way she did at you," Brandon interrupted. "Look, I'll make it plain: I love Rae, but I'm not in love with her. She's my friend and always will be, whether you like it or not. You just have to trust me that friends are the only thing we'll ever be."

He'd been convinced Brandon harbored deeper feelings for Rae. It was tough to believe him.

"If you don't believe me, read it in Rae's own words. Her new book is out. Maybe it'll enlighten you, and you'll finally see what you're missing." The look on Brandon's face echoed Rae's earlier expression—disappointed. Except Brandon's also seemed to say, *You're an idiot.*

Dean couldn't think. Everything churned inside him.

"I hope you'll figure it out, Dean." Brandon headed to the door. "I hope, for Rae's sake, you'll step up to the plate and show her you're worthy of her love. Don't be another person who takes it for granted. Something to think about."

Forty-Four

Dean woke up the following morning with a splitting headache and a throbbing jaw. The memory of the stupid fistfight came back to him, and he wondered what the fuck had he been thinking.

I wasn't.

When he saw the clock blinking eight-twenty-eight, he groaned and dragged himself to the bathroom. He stared back at the disheveled reflection in the mirror. Bruises had bloomed and deepened in color. Great.

He took some ibuprofen with a large glass of water and grabbed an ice pack from the freezer. Holding it to his jaw, he dialed Melanie's number.

"Are you okay?" Melanie asked urgently when he told her he wasn't coming in.

"I'm okay. I just need to clear my head."

"I'll rearrange your schedule today. But will you still be attending the gala tonight?"

The gala. Right.

"Yes, of course." He couldn't disappoint Melanie, too. "I'll see you there tonight."

After he hung up, he brewed some coffee and checked the fridge to see if his housekeeper, Carol, had left any food. He had no appetite, but he knew enough to feed his hangover. He found some bagels and cream cheese. As he closed the fridge door, his eyes caught an unopened box of oat milk creamer that Rae liked. His housekeeper must've replaced the last one she'd left.

Dean remembered she would pour the sweet stuff until her coffee turned creamy white. He didn't understand how she could drink the concoction, but the face she made after that first sip always made him smile. He was smiling now, just thinking about it.

With a sigh, Dean prepared himself a quick breakfast. While he sat, drinking his own coffee and carefully chewing his bagel, he thought it probably wasn't the best meal choice for an aching jaw.

Not smart, Rowland.

He hadn't been making smart decisions lately. Three people had basically called him an idiot in the past month: Rae, Chris, and Brandon. He was sure his sister would agree with them when he gave her a chance. He'd been avoiding his family like the plague since things had gone awry with Rae. Maybe because he knew, but wouldn't admit, that he was a fool.

When people tell you you're being an idiot, perhaps the problem is you, not them.

Dean picked up his phone again and dialed a number.

Chris answered after four rings. "You've come to your senses yet?"

Chris studied Dean with a raised eyebrow as he approached him in front of the bookstore they'd agreed to meet at. He eyed the bruise and smirked.

"What the hell happened to you? Did Rae finally Krav Maga your ass?" Chris chuckled.

"Don't start. I had a rough night." Dean entered the bookstore.

Chris followed Dean inside. "You didn't get into details on the phone, but it looks like someone beat the sense back into your head."

"It was Brandon Rossi."

Chris' eyes rounded. "How did that happen?"

Dean gave Chris a short rundown of last night's event.

"This morning, I woke up feeling like an ass. I'm sorry I doubted you, Chris," Dean apologized.

His easygoing friend simply held up his hand for a bro-handshake. "All good, buddy. So, what are we doing here?"

"I've made a mess of things. I gotta fix them."

Dean had phoned Gayle earlier and asked her to apologize to Canis Major for any misunderstanding. Though he'd told Rae and Brandon that Canis Major's contract was safe, he felt it was necessary to right the wrong they'd started.

Just now, he'd mended his friendship with Chris. He'd better take a lesson on friendship from Rae or end up alone in this life. He and Chris had had each other's back since their freshman year in college. Dean should've known better.

"Here we go." Dean found a stack of hardcovers of Rae's new book displayed under Holiday Gift Recommendations. He picked one up. "I'm not sure how to fix this."

"What's wrong with apologizing?" Chris grabbed a copy, too.

"She won't take my call. I think I totally screwed up with Rae, Chris."

"I won't argue that point," Chris said as they headed to the cashier. "We'll think of something. How about groveling?"

"I'll do anything."

Forty-Five

Dean headed to the banquet room where the Gala For Vulnerable Children took place. He rubbed his jaw and felt his rough two-day stubble. Good thing he could grow a decent beard, so tonight's look sufficiently covered the evidence of last night's idiocy.

Earlier, Dean and Chris had hunted for gardenias for Rae, but he hadn't realized how tricky it was to find the white blooms in December. Not that he thought flowers would make her forgive him. He needed a chance to tell her that she'd pegged him right from the start, that he was an arrogant ass who wouldn't admit he had issues. But most importantly, he had to tell her how he felt for her.

"Mr. Rowland." Melanie was beelining toward him. In public, she'd always insisted on referring to him formally. It was decorum, she'd told him.

But it wasn't decorum that made her sport that serious face as she stopped in front of him.

"You look very lovely tonight, Melanie," Dean noted.

"Thank you. Is this your new look?" Melanie studied him critically.

"You can say that." He rubbed his jaw absently, reminding him about the wreck he'd left last night. "I'm sorry about the state of the office."

"I've taken care of it. The carpet has been cleaned. The furniture is back in its spots. The wall will be fixed by tomorrow. But I don't think I can salvage the crystal."

"You are amazing, Melanie." Dean appreciated her efficiency and discretion.

The worried look on her face didn't fade. "Please pardon my impertinence, but what happened last night? It's none of my business, but I know Miss Allen came to see you, and everything was fine before then."

That answered how Rae could just walk into his office.

Melanie hesitated, but she pushed through, "I know you wouldn't have hurt her, but the mess indicated that there was—"

"I didn't hurt Rae. Not physically, if that's what you're asking."

"I never doubted that." She then eyed the cut on his lip. "Did she hurt you?"

"No. This and the mess happened after she left." Dean was touched by her concern, but he wondered why she'd let Rae in. "So you knew Rae came to see me."

An alarm showed on her face. "I probably shouldn't have let her through, but…"

"It's okay. She needed to blow off some steam, and I deserved it."

"Is everything going to be okay between you and Miss Allen?"

"I don't know. I screwed up really badly."

"May I give you a little advice as someone who has spent more than a decade working for you closely?"

"Of course," Dean said. "You know I respect your opinions."

"I've always kept my thoughts on your private life to myself. It's been difficult for you, hasn't it? Being without Miss Allen?" Melanie asked.

"Have you and Tom been gossiping about me?" Dean tried to keep things light.

"The two of us see you closer than anyone who works for you. And we're two old folks who can't mind our own business." Melanie chuckled. "It's obvious that you were much happier when Miss Rae was a part of your life. I don't know whatever it is that's keeping the two of you apart, but I'd suggest you try to have an open conversation with her if you haven't already. Let it all out in the open. And listen. Without anger. Without judgment. Without preconception. Without a doubt."

"That's very sound advice, Melanie." Dean nodded. "But she doesn't want anything to do with me right now."

"Do you love her?" Melanie pointedly asked.

"Yes." Confirming it came easily, though it weighed like a boulder on his chest.

"Then don't give up. Find a way," Melanie tapped his arm affectionately. "You've never been a quitter."

Dean let Melanie's advice sink in. Suddenly, everything felt overwhelmingly heavy. The lights, the chattering, the expectation of him to be sociable. He told Melanie he'd meet her at their table after he circled the room. But what he needed to do was to get away and compose himself before facing all these people.

He found a quiet hallway and headed to the window. Looking down at the chaos of the traffic below somehow eased him when he felt overwhelmed. Strange, but traffic always resolved itself, and it assured him that things would be okay. He just needed to find the choking point, and the problem would clear itself up.

Right now, the choking point of his problem was that he couldn't get through to Rae. She didn't answer his calls or texts, and her neighbor told him she was probably gone on one of her trips. But she was just in town last night. How fast could she disappear? Knowing Rae, in a blink of an eye.

"Dean." A voice he hadn't heard for a long time brought Dean out of his reverie.

For two nights in a row, he turned in surprise to a woman. This time, someone from his past stood before him, wearing a smile and a blue maternity dress.

"It is you." She came closer. "I almost didn't recognize you."

Dean's back reflexively went rigid despite her warm smile.

The woman noted his reaction. "I see you're still upset with me."

"That's an understatement," Dean replied coolly.

Her smile didn't waver. "I was hoping you'd forgive me and be happily married by now. You were quite intent on getting married."

"Until my fiancée eloped with someone else and disappeared." Dean's mouth flattened into a line.

The smile dimmed on Leighton Heston's pretty face, but she looked at Dean steadily. "I'm sorry for leaving the way I did. I wish I could turn back time and go about things differently."

"That's thoughtful, Leighton. But a bit too late."

"Is it really too late to apologize?" Leighton asked.

"No," Dean reluctantly said. He couldn't be hypocritical when he was hoping it wasn't too late for him to apologize to Rae, either. "I wish you had talked to me. We could've parted ways in a more civilized fashion."

Leighton pursed her lips in a little grimace. "I suppose that was what I ran away from—our civilized relationship, if you understand my meaning."

Dean didn't take offense to her reasoning. That was what their marriage would've ended up being: cordial without passion.

"Did you find your happiness then?" Dean gestured to her. She didn't resemble the Leighton he'd known, who had been pampered and aloof. This Leighton had a calm and joyful air emanating from her.

"I did." Leighton's smile returned. "Being away from everything I knew was rough at first, but I learned so much. The past three years have opened my eyes to the world. Thanks to Nick and this organization you're supporting. Thank you for accepting the invitation, by the way."

"You sent it?"

She nodded. "I got a reminder that the mess I left behind had lasting effects on some people, namely you, my father, and my sister. Now that I'm expecting my own baby, it's time for me to mend some fences, or at least try. My dad still refuses to see me, but Petra and I have started talking again."

"I'm sure Samuel will come around when his grandchild arrives." Dean truly hoped so. "When are you due?"

"He's ready to pop out soon enough. We came home to give birth and spend some time with family. Then Nick and I will bring our son back to Nepal."

"Nepal?" Another surprise.

"That's where I've been," Leighton explained. "Beautiful country. You'll hear what kind of programs we have there."

"You're working for this organization?" Leighton kept surprising him with her news.

"Yes, along with my husband."

Dean must look dumbstruck because she chuckled. "I've finally grown up and become the person I wanted to be, Dean. It took almost four years of living in a foreign country, an understanding, loving husband, and a kid on the way. It's bound to happen, right?"

Leighton touched Dean's arm. "How about you, Dean? Have you found what you're looking for? Because from what I heard, a woman went out of her way to find me so you could get closure. Thanks to her, I was forced to face my past mistakes and came out of hiding to make things right. She sounds like someone who cares a lot about you and can keep up with you."

"Yeah, she is," Dean agreed. He wished he'd figure it out sooner.

"Is she here tonight?"

Dean gave a short shake of the head. "Unfortunately not."

"Oh." Leighton's face fell a bit, understanding his meaning. "Well, I hope you'll find your happiness with her, Dean. You deserve it."

A woman popped into the hall, spotted Leighton, and signaled her. Leighton gave her a nod.

"I have to go in." She stepped back. "I'm glad you're here. And thank you for listening to me. This may be a poor excuse of an apology and way overdue, but for what it's worth, I'm sorry for the pain I caused."

She turned to the ballroom.

"Leighton," Dean called.

She looked back at him.

"I'm sorry you felt you couldn't come to me then. But I'm glad you're happy."

Her smile was warm. "It's good to see you, Dean."

Dean watched Leighton go and was surprised to find the resentment he'd harbored against her vanish along with her. He'd thought of a few different scenarios of when he'd find himself facing her, but none of them were even close to what had just happened. He thought he'd still feel anger. Instead, he felt light. Lighter than he'd been in a long time.

Forty-Six

"Hey, let's take a walk." Brandon handed Rae her coat.

"Right now? It's freezing." She frowned.

"It won't be in the sun. Come on, it'll be nice to get some exercise before sitting down for dinner."

"I should be helping," Rae mumbled but accepted the coat and put on her knit hat, scarf, and gloves.

"Don't worry about it. My mom and Brady have it under control. You know how they are about Christmas dinner. Better stay out of the way." Brandon led Rae out into the crisp and clean December Jersey air.

When they heard New Jersey, most people thought of the gritty industrial part of the state but forgot why it was dubbed the Garden State. Where he'd grown up—near Princeton, not too far from the Delaware River—it was beautiful, with historic homes and scenic farmlands.

Brandon loved coming home for the holidays. And he loved sharing it with his friends. Rae had joined his family holiday events whenever she could since her grandmother had passed away.

"How are you doing?" Brandon walked down a path behind his parents' home that he knew like the back of his hand. There was a dusting of white on the ground from an earlier snow shower. He hoped for more snow tonight.

"I'm okay." Rae gave him a look.

"We haven't talked much about what happened with Dean," Brandon prompted.

Rae huffed. "Nothing to talk about. That short chapter of my life is done."

"It doesn't seem done on his end. Was that gardenia from him?" He referred to the small plant he'd seen in Rae's trash when he'd picked her up for the drive to Jersey. Rae loved gardenias.

"If he thinks flowers can make up for what he did, he can think again." Rae flattened her lips in annoyance.

"What did he say?" Brandon pushed.

"Nothing." Rae shrugged. "I got home from New Mexico, and the plant was at my door."

"No card?" Brandon frowned.

"Oh, there's a card." Her tone said it was a doozy.

When Rae didn't volunteer the content, he impatiently asked, "What did it say?"

Rae pursed her lips. "'I'm sorry. I'm a fool.'"

Brandon paused and raised an eyebrow. "That's it?"

"I'm done talking about this, Brandon. Dean Rowland is out of my life. Period."

"But why? He apologized, Rae. Don't you think you should give him a chance to at least talk to you in person? He might not—"

"What part of 'I'm done' don't you understand?" Rae glared at him. "I gave it a try like you suggested. It didn't work out. Let it go."

"Well, I'm not letting it go just yet. You were distraught the last time I saw you. But I know you went to see Dean. He told me as much."

Rae eyed him. "He told you?"

"I went to see him. You think I'd just let you confront him on my behalf? You didn't need to do that. We would've dealt with it. Besides, Gayle Harris called the next day with an apology for the misunderstanding about her last call."

"A misunderstanding? That's what they're calling it?" Rae laughed.

"I believed Dean when he said Gayle acted out of loyalty, and he stopped it as soon as he found out."

"You're a much more generous person than me, Brandon." Rae shoved her gloved hands into her coat pockets. "I can't easily forgive someone who openly wants to hurt my family."

"But he didn't."

"What do you want me to do, huh?" Rae stopped walking and faced him. "You want me to talk to him? I did. He would never trust me as long he believed you were a threat. And I'm not sacrificing you to be with someone.

"I am good the way I am—the way I was. I don't need a man to be happy. Succumbing to the idea of love has only led to heartache in my family. I won't fall for it anymore. I've had enough of putting hope on men—my father, Dean." Rae shook her head stubbornly. "No more."

"Rae, you can't compare Dean to your father," Brandon argued. "People make mistakes—even a man like Dean. He's not perfect. The gardenia proves he's trying to make up for his mistakes. If you love him, you need to have faith in that love and that it will heal you both. I saw him that night, too. He's hurting as much as you are."

His friend just scoffed in disbelief.

"Rae, you need to talk to him. You never even told him how you feel about him. Knowing you loved him might've made a difference in how he saw things. But that's in the past. What you do now will decide the trajectory of your life. Will you choose love and take that leap of faith? Or will you throw it all away?"

She put up her hands to stop Brandon. "I don't want to talk about it anymore, Brandon. I'm going back to help your mom with the food."

Rae turned and rushed away. Brandon was stunned into silence for a moment, then he trailed behind her in dismay. He couldn't make her listen when she wasn't ready. But it pained him that his friend was shutting out love.

He was sure it was her defensive mechanism. He couldn't blame her. Dean would need more than a plant to prove his worth. He had his task cut out for him because Rae wouldn't be easy to persuade.

When they got back to the house, the aroma of lasagna and pork roast was in the air. Dinner would be ready soon.

Ignoring Brandon, Rae hung her outerwear and took off her boots. She went straight into the kitchen and asked if she could do anything. His mom never had issues assigning tasks, and soon Rae was busy setting the table.

Meanwhile, Brandon was still preoccupied with how he could prevent Rae from going down a lonely path.

A buzzing began nearby. Brandon checked his phone. It wasn't his. He looked around and saw Rae's coat was vibrating. He knew Rae had blocked Dean's number, so it couldn't be him.

Impulsively, Brandon fished the phone out of the coat pocket and checked who was calling. His mouth formed a grin at a solution that might've just presented itself.

Without hesitation, he tapped the green button.

Coming home was always a great idea.

Dean looked at the faces he loved encircling him with support. As he'd expected, Kat had rolled her eyes at him when he'd first arrived, then hugged him tightly and told him things would work themselves out. He wished he had her conviction.

He'd just finished relaying what had happened in the past few weeks. He hadn't edited any part of it, starting from his unfounded distrust to the fistfight with Brandon, however embarrassing it was. He'd only made sure it was the PG version since his nephews were also listening. They couldn't be too young to learn from their uncle's mistakes.

"You should've told Rae you love her, Uncle Dean." Andrew, one of the twins, chimed in.

The look on his face was so serious that Dean could hardly contain his smile. "You're right, kid. I should've."

"Should've, could've, would've," Kat said. "You need to tell her. What are you waiting for?"

Dean glanced at her sister. "It's not like I haven't been trying, Kat. I can't force myself back into her life if she doesn't want me in it."

"He needs a plan to get him in," Gene interjected. "Calling and texting aren't options anymore. Showing up at her place might get him arrested. What can he do?"

"He needs an inside man," Matt pointed out. "Someone Rae trusts who can get you alone time with her."

"That's brilliant!" Kat patted her husband's leg enthusiastically. "I knew there was a good reason why I married you."

"Maybe that Brandon fella will help you," Dean's father added. "He is your best chance."

He is.

Dean sighed heavily at the prospect of having to ask Brandon for his help.

Apparently, his mother saw his hesitation. Martha squeezed his hand and advised, "Dean, you need to learn to trust him if you want a future with Rae."

Looking at his mother's face, Dean knew she was right.

Forty-Seven

"It took you a while." Brandon stepped aside to let Dean into his loft. Despite his low-key sarcasm, Brandon was glad Dean finally came to his senses. This would make Brandon's mission easier.

"You're a bourbon guy, aren't you?" Brandon offered a drink.

Dean hesitated, then nodded. "Neat, please."

Brandon fixed their drinks and handed Dean his glass.

"Thanks." Dean looked as if he was bracing himself to do something difficult. "I owe you an apology. I made a big deal out of your friendship with Rae and hurt your friend. I hope you can accept my apology."

Brandon gestured Dean to a seat. "I would if you could convince me that you really cared about Rae."

The guy gave a short laugh of irritation, but he took a beat before answering. "How do I do that? Do you want me to tell you how I don't sleep at night, wondering where she is, if she would ever talk to me again? Or how I ache inside knowing there's a huge possibility I will have to go on without her in my life?"

"Do you?" Brandon studied Dean with scrutinizing eyes.

"Yes, damn it!" Dean cursed. "Rae was that left hook I never expected coming at me. She blew me away from the first time I saw her. She literally took my breath away. And when she convinced herself that she was meant to help me find closure over my past, neither of us realized that she was the key to it."

Dean inhaled deeply. "I regret I broke her heart in the process, when what she was really doing was rescuing me from a lifetime of loneliness."

Brandon nodded his approval. "Apology accepted. Now, we must work together to rescue her from falling into the same pit you were in."

"What do you mean by that?" Dean scowled.

"Did you read her book?"

"Yes." Dean looked troubled. "I didn't realize her mother took her own life."

"Officially, it was believed to be an unintentional antidepressant overdose, but Rae thought otherwise. Though she was thirteen when it happened, she must've seen more of her mother's condition than any child should."

Brandon continued, "I'm surprised Rae revealed as much as she did in the book. But I supposed it shows why she values her friends so much. We are her family now. Not just me. A whole network of people love Rae and are loved by her. I'm just one of them.

"Now, you don't have to love me to be with her, but you'll need to be able to handle our relationship. I will expect the same from my future partner someday. Now, if you love Rae, you just need to accept that you'll be stuck with the rest of us. We're not that bad once you get to know us."

Dean smiled thoughtfully. "Just like any family."

"That's right." Brandon nodded.

"How do I win her back, Brandon?" Dean looked desperate. "She won't give me the time of day. If I could just get an hour, hell, I'd take a few minutes—"

"It'll take more than an hour to win her over again." Brandon eyed Dean. "How much do you know about Rae's father?"

"Nothing. When I asked her about him, she told me she didn't have a father."

Brandon gestured at Dean's untouched drink. "You might want to brace yourself."

"Whatever it is, just tell me." Dean leaned his forearms on his thighs, focusing on Brandon.

"All right." Brandon took a sip of his drink as if preparing for something unpleasant. "Well, Rae does have a father, and he's alive. He walked out on Rae and her mother when Rae was only six. Her grandmother Alice told me this story when I accompanied Rae to visit her before she passed. Rae never talks about her father, not to me, not to anyone.

"The only reason Rae's grandma said anything was because she knew she wouldn't be around much longer. She wanted to make sure someone would look out for Rae and remind her not to cloister herself away. See, I always thought what happened to her mother was one of the reasons Rae hardly dated, and when she did date, she always found reasons to end it early on. She didn't want to fall in love and risk the same pain her mother had felt. When she met you, I started seeing these sparkles in her eyes, even if there were still doubts lurking. I thought you succeeded in curing her fear."

"Until I fucked up." Dean filled in what Brandon wasn't saying.

"After you split, she seemed to be dealing with it quite well, relatively speaking. She accepted that it wouldn't be easy to get over you. Still, considering how heartbroken she was, she was doing okay."

"Yeah, I watched her videos. They cemented my suspicion that I was never that important to her."

"That's her survival mechanism," Brandon explained. "Rae has a big fear of ending up like her mother. Heartbreak sent her mother to her death. Rae is determined not to follow in her mother's footsteps, so even when she's torn inside, she'll find laughter and joy wherever possible.

"But after she confronted you before Christmas over the contract—"

"I explained to her I would never stoop that low."

Brandon shrugged his understanding. "I know."

"Fuck! Over one phone call." Dean rubbed his hand over his face. "I can't get over this overwhelming sense that I've disappointed her so deeply. I saw it in her eyes as she walked out of my life."

"Yeah. Her father was the ultimate disappointment to her, and unfortunately, she's put you on the same bracket now." Brandon grimaced as he delivered the news.

Dean stared at Brandon, aghast. "He abandoned a wife and a child. I mean, what I did wasn't right, but—"

"Rae felt you attacked her family, and she would protect us. She couldn't do that for her mother."

"So, you're telling me I can't make this right?"

"I'm saying it's going to be a tough battle to regain her trust. See, Rae found her father, and what she discovered caused her to scrub him completely out of her life."

"What did she find out?"

"He's married with two children about the same age as Rae. And he claimed Rae was a distant cousin instead of his daughter."

"God. I can't imagine being abandoned by my father and then rejected again when I just found him. I don't blame her for erasing him from her life." Dean processed the information and concluded, "She's doing the same thing to me?"

"Unless we can do something about it." Brandon smiled conspiratorially. "I promised Alice I won't let Rae lock herself in out of anger or fear. And you will help me to fulfill that promise."

"How? Rae won't even talk to me." Dean was desperate for ideas. "Tell me how, and I'd do it."

"We just have to make her talk to you. You eased your way into her life once. You simply have to do that again."

"It's not so simple. Rae didn't hate me then."

"And she doesn't hate you now. She's too softhearted to hate another person, especially someone she fell in love with," Brandon dismissed Dean's negativity. "But you need to give her time to cool down. Everything's still too raw for her now."

"Okay." Dean understood that and clammed down on his instinct to take action. "How much time?"

"Just back off for now. I suggest you get away for a week or two so you won't be tempted to bombard her with apologies."

"A week or two?" Dean didn't know if he could wait that long.

"In the big picture, two weeks is nothing." Brandon then asked, "When was the last time you had a vacation?"

Dean remembered Rae asking him the same question. And the answer was a long time.

"My buddy Chris did invite me to his resort in Bali," Dean mused. "Maybe I'll take him up on it."

"Perfect." Brandon beamed satisfactorily.

Dean narrowed his eyes at him, suddenly feeling dubious.

As if sensing it, Brandon looked straight into Dean's eyes. "Trust me. I just want to see my friend have a chance at happiness."

And for some odd reason, Dean believed him.

Forty-Eight

There was something about Bali that took the mind away from troubles. As soon as Rae stepped out of the airport and into her awaiting car, she felt lighter. Perhaps finally planting her feet on solid ground after twenty-four hours of flying had something to do with it. But as the car drove through acres and acres of newly planted rice paddies, the weight on her shoulders started to lift one tiny bit at a time.

Rae hadn't wanted to take the project Chris Sullens had offered. He was a connection to Dean, but she also felt guilty that she'd caused a rift between Chris and Dean. It wasn't Chris' fault that she had issues with his friend. Besides, they'd discussed her coming to the resort before everything had gone to hell.

Being thousands of miles away from Dean Rowland had appealed to her. She'd failed to cleanse herself of him. It was difficult when she could see him in every corner of her apartment. A paid getaway to paradise sounded like the perfect solution.

The drive to the island's eastern side took two hours on tight country roads weaving through fields, villages, and temples. She was so excited when they finally arrived. From the moment they'd picked her up at the airport, the service had been incredible, and it only continued as they welcomed her to the resort. She couldn't wait to finally see her haven for the week.

When she'd accepted the project, Rae made Chris promise that the staff wouldn't know she was there on his behalf. She didn't want to be treated extra special. She had to experience the boutique resort like any other guest.

Rae walked through the doorless main entrance into the open-air lobby with the most incredible view. Beyond the cliff where the resort stood, a vast sleepy sea and a never-ending blue sky greeted her. She was in awe. Her feet stepped to the edge of the lobby to take in the view, breathe the sea air, and let go of all her burdens.

It's going to be an unforgettable week.

"This place is incredible, Chris." Dean rested his arms on the pool's infinity edge, looking at green lawns peppered with tall coconut trees. Beyond the greenery, the sight of a deep blue ocean released any tension he'd brought when he'd arrived yesterday.

The pictures Dean had seen were beautiful but merely hinted at the place's tranquility. Though he didn't exactly forget his troubles, he could breathe again at this moment. New York had felt so cold and suffocating. In the end, he was glad he'd agreed to Brandon's suggestion. And Chris' invitation came at the perfect time.

"Thanks." Chris saluted him with a tropical drink from the lounge chair nearby. "We had a great soft opening. Straightened out some kinks, and now we're running smoothly."

"You should be proud. This has been your dream for the longest time."

"I am." Chris grinned.

"What did your dad say?" Dean asked carefully.

Chris' smile dimmed. "He's reserving judgment."

Dean rolled his eyes. "Your grandparents and mother would've been proud."

"I know." Chris segued, "How do you like your villa?"

"It's luxurious. You're wasting it on me." The villa Chris had assigned to him boasted a king-size bed with an indoor-outdoor bathroom, a prep kitchen, a large patio, a smaller rectangular pool, and a great view.

"I thought you'd enjoy the pool."

"I did. You know I love to jump into the water first thing in the morning." Dean grinned. "But I must try the other three public pools on the grounds."

"Tomorrow, you'll get to swim with the fish," Chris told him. "I've made arrangements for you. A driver will take you to our dock at seven-fifteen in the morning. Don't be late, don't be early. Breakfast will be served on the boat. It'll take you to some of the best snorkeling spots in the area."

"You're not coming?" Dean frowned.

"I have things to take care of. I want you to enjoy yourself. The boat ride itself is energizing."

"You didn't have to do that."

"You're my guinea pig. Enjoy the service. Let me know what you think after."

Dean nodded. "I can do that. Thanks. And thank you again for getting me out of New York. I didn't know I needed that."

"Yup." Chris smiled. "Sometimes, when we're stuck, it's time to pull back and regroup before we try again."

Dean thought it was sound logic.

Chris left Dean at the lower pool to check on his other special guest. As he walked back up to the lobby, he typed a message on his phone, *Dove One is settled and relaxed. Just heard Dove Two has arrived. The mission is now officially a go.*

Not expecting a direct reply, Chris put his phone away. But the vibrating in his shorts' pocket indicated he had received a message. Though it was five in the morning in New York, Brandon wrote back, *Awesome! Dove Two just sent me a picture. Gorgeous view. Wish I were there to witness this. Keep me updated.*

Chris grinned. *I better say hi to Dove Two and make sure everything will go as planned.*

He just hoped their mission wouldn't blow up and bite them in the ass.

Forty-Nine

Rae woke up at the crack of dawn due to jet lag. She jumped out of the large comfortable bed and opened the sliding doors to her front patio to find a magnificent view. Her suite was located at the resort's highest point, but the vista was well worth the climb. Before her, the sun had just started rising over the horizon, spilling its rays across the sea's calm surface. It was breathtaking to witness.

As the sun rose, Rae's mind wandered to a similar experience on one memorable morning in Georgia. A sunrise, mist over water, and a conversation with a captivating man. That morning she hadn't known that she'd fall deeply in love with him and be in the state she was in today.

Rae let the memory wash over her, and she braced for the tautness in her chest whenever she thought of Dean. She closed her eyes and let herself feel the ache. After four breaths, she opened her eyes to the beautiful scene unveiled before her and focused on the now.

This resort was exactly what Chris had told her. They'd ensured the view was the focal point, and the resort was designed around it for maximum enjoyment. Though size-wise it covered significant ground, the place oozed intimacy. There were no wall-to-wall rooms. Each suite was its own spacious room with an indoor-outdoor bathroom and a patio overlooking the sea. She knew there were also a couple of larger pool villas and one villa for a bigger group.

Rae loved it so far. The staff was personable and knew the guests by name. The handwritten welcome card from the manager with the welcome basket in her suite had been a nice touch. When she'd first walked in, she'd immediately noted the understated luxurious décor. Earth tones and muted marble floors dominated the suite but framed the view outside perfectly. There was also a daybed on the patio, which would be a perfect place to write while enjoying her surroundings.

She could just laze around in this luxury, but Chris had already planned an excursion for her this morning. He'd come by her suite to welcome her yesterday. He'd told her that starting her first morning with breakfast on a boat after a refreshing swim in the ocean was just the cure for jet lag.

Rae quickly donned her new blue two-piece suit and topped it with a white filmy shirt. Well-armed with a bottle of powerful sunscreen, a large-brimmed straw hat, her camera, and notebook in her beach tote, she made her way to meet her car. She got there right on time at seven.

The ride didn't take long. The boat attendant greeted her with a broad smile and led her to a long pontoon boat, customized with two open-air wood decks. The top deck was a giant daybed perfect for sunbathing, while below was where the breakfast would be served later. It was a no-brainer: Rae opted for the upper deck to enjoy the mild morning sun.

"Please make yourself comfortable, miss," the attendant said. "We'll depart as soon as our other guest arrives."

Rae nodded, made her way to the far side of the deck, and got busy with the sunscreen. She didn't even realize the other guest had come on board until the boat started moving. They didn't join her on the upper deck, and Rae was happy to have it all to herself. Soon, she was absorbed by the exhilaration of sea air whipping against her skin and hair.

After about twenty minutes of cruising the calm water, the boat stopped. An attendant asked her to come down to the main deck to be equipped with fins and snorkel and get instructions from the guide. Rae didn't need any instructions, but she was too excited to get into the blue water and check out the coral reefs to care. She quickly came down and found herself face-to-face with the one person she was running away from.

His grey eyes froze on her face, as did hers on his.

As if lightning had struck him, Dean could only stare at the woman who had just come down from the top deck.

"What are you doing here?" Rae recovered faster than he did.

He was as shocked as she was, and he reacted defensively. "What are *you* doing here?"

"Aah. Do you know each other? Excellent." The boat steward beamed at them.

"No. Not excellent." Rae turned her gaze at the steward. "What is he doing on this boat?"

"Um, Mr. Rowland is a guest of the resort just like you, miss."

Rae's head whipped back to Dean with an accusatory glare. "You set this up."

"I did not." Dean glared back at her.

What the hell?

They looked at each other, trying to make sense of what was happening. Dean was still processing that the woman he'd been looking for had suddenly appeared in front of him.

"Chris!" He and Rae came to a conclusion at the exact second.

"When did you arrive?" Dean asked as the situation sunk in.

"Yesterday," Rae answered shortly.

"I got here the day before." Dean huffed. "Chris didn't mention you were coming."

"Shocking. He failed to mention you were here when he saw me yesterday."

They exchanged glances. Hers was filled with annoyance while he absorbed everything about her face. Her skin was flushed with outrage, her blue eyes sharp as knives, and her lips flat as a line. But boy, was she beautiful.

She's here. On a boat in the middle of the ocean with me.

Dean belatedly realized what his friend had done for him. And he suspected it wasn't Chris' handiwork alone.

"Is everything good?" the steward finally asked.

"No. I want to go back," Rae told him.

"But we just got here, miss." The steward gestured to the snorkeling guide waiting with fins and snorkels. "*Bapak* Windu is ready to show you the coral reefs."

"I'm not doing this." Rae shook her head.

Dean had to think fast. "You'll stop these fine men from doing their job?"

"You can do whatever you want, but I refuse to participate in this setup." Rae waved her hands in irritation.

"I did not set this up, Rae," Dean reiterated. "But this proves you and I will always converge, however hard we fight it."

Rae crossed her arms, turned her back on him, and refused to listen.

Okay, this will not be easy.

"I know you don't want to be near me, but I'm here. And I'm going to enjoy myself." Dean changed his tone. "This is my first full vacation in four years. I won't let you ruin it for me."

"Excuse me?" Rae spun to face him. "I'm ruining this for you? I woke up in an excellent mood this morning, but that all went out the window because of *you*!"

Dean shrugged and sat near the guide, who watched their conversation with wide, confused eyes. "If you want to go back, you'll have to wait. I'm going snorkeling."

With a challenging smirk, Dean accepted a pair of fins and a snorkel, then put them on. He ignored Rae and asked the guide to tell him what he needed to know.

"Will you go into the water, miss?" asked the attendant.

"She won't." Dean waved him off before Rae could answer.

"You don't speak for me," Rae snapped.

Dean gave her a quick smirk. "Just trying to be helpful."

He went to the rear of the boat and fell back into the ocean. The cool seawater felt heavenly. As if he were home, he kicked away from the boat and started swimming in the direction of the corals the guide had shown him.

His body moved in the water on instinct while his mind raced. He hoped he didn't make a mistake. He'd reverted to his old tactics, hoping Rae wouldn't let him have the last word. If he just pushed the right button, maybe he had a chance in challenging her to stay.

A hand touched him on the arm. Dean found the guide at his side, signaling him to follow. Nodding, Dean changed direction and caught another form on the other side of the guide.

If he didn't have the mouthpiece in his mouth, he would've smiled at the sight of Rae snorkeling in her delectable blue bikini.

She ignored him and kept her distance. It didn't matter to Dean, as long as she was there. Soon, they were consumed by the ocean floor, where colorful fish swam around the reef. It was spectacular down there.

Dean could tell when the reef life started to absorb Rae. She didn't seem to mind having him nearby. And when he dived to the bottom to gently touch a giant pink starfish, he might've been showing off a bit. He knew it would make her look at him. It was hard to compete with tropical reef life. But he'd enjoy it while he could. He knew the peace wouldn't last.

Rae handed her fins to one of the crew members and climbed the ladder back into the boat. She didn't know how long they'd stayed in the water, but she could've stayed longer if not for hunger. She covered herself with the towel handed to her and sat at the table set up nicely with tropical fruits, baked goods, juices, and coffee. She was famished. She didn't care that she had to share with Dean.

The devil himself dropped on the wooden bench across from her after barely drying off, not bothering to cover up. His face was light with a hint of a smile. He was always in a better mood after a swim. And he always looked too delicious when wet.

Rae couldn't help but sweep her eyes over his naked chest behind the protection of her sunglasses. He reached for a muffin, and his pectoral muscles flexed with the movement, making her stop chewing her banana bread and have to swallow.

"Coffee, miss?"

Rae jumped and looked up at the attendant, smiling at her expectantly.

She spotted the coffee thermos he was holding. Coffee. "Yes, please."

When she returned to her food, Dean had a big grin on his face. God, how the hell did he still have this hold on her?

Just ignore him.

But Dean Rowland wasn't an easy man to ignore, especially when he was sitting in front of her half-naked.

"What do you think of the reef?" he asked casually.

Rae sighed and looked away.

"You're just gonna ignore me?" He drank his coffee. "Come on. We're in this gorgeous place. There's no reason why we both can't enjoy it. Can we have a truce and forget what happened between us while we're here? You're the one who told me I needed a vacation."

"Forget what happened?" Rae asked in disbelief. Did Brandon hit him too hard when they had that stupid scuffle over her?

"You can go back to hating me once you're back in New York if you want," Dean suggested nonchalantly. "Or you may decide to accept my apology."

"It wasn't me you needed to apologize to," Rae scoffed.

"I've apologized to everyone I wronged in that whole episode. You're the only one who hasn't accepted it."

"Your company apologized to Canis Major, not you."

"I personally apologized to Brandon if that's what you meant. Who do you think suggested I leave you alone and take a vacation to get my mind off you?"

Rae's brows scrunched at what he was saying. Brandon?

"In fact, I wouldn't be surprised if he and Chris had planned this whole scheme together," he added.

Brandon had encouraged her to accept Chris' invitation and laid out why she shouldn't punish Chris based on association. Her mouth fell.

"That sly—"

"They mean well, Rae."

"By manipulating us?" she retorted. "What did they think forcing us in this situation would do?"

"Well, I for one hope we could talk."

Rae gave a short laugh. "Talk? We're past talking. We don't have anything else to discuss."

"I disagree. A lot has happened since we last spoke." Dean looked at her with a silent plea.

This was why she hadn't wanted to see him. He still had the power to persuade her to do his bidding.

Rae tore her eyes away from him. "I don't want to hear it."

"Don't you want to know that you succeeded in your mission to find me closure?" Dean asked. "Your trip to Rhinebeck paid off. Leighton contacted me. We talked."

Rae held her breath as she listened, but she didn't respond.

"It was what you suspected. Seeing her again after all this time opened my eyes. I didn't realize I needed that. But you did," he continued.

"Good for you." Rae gave a slight nod. She was glad he did get that closure.

"Thank you. It wouldn't have happened without your effort. Leighton is now also trying to reestablish a relationship with her family. She wanted me to convey her thanks."

"Unnecessary."

Rae also didn't want anything from the woman whose one selfish act had become the catalyst of the end of her doomed affair with Dean.

"Rae—"

"I can't do this, Dean." Rae abruptly stood.

"Rae, please give me a chance to say what I need to say."

"I'm out of chances, Dean." Rae shook her head. "I need space, okay? I'll consider accepting your apology if we agree to stay out of each other's way. The resort is big enough for both of us. We must learn to exist knowing that we might run into each other once in a blue moon. But it won't mean anything. Contrary to your belief, coincidences do happen."

Rae left the unhappy-looking Dean and headed to the top deck. She'd rather risk sunburn than have to take a risk on Dean Rowland again.

Fifty

"Well, your brilliant plan sucked," Dean stated sarcastically. "You should've warned me. I was unprepared."

He was having breakfast at his villa with Chris. Brandon was on speakerphone with them. Dean had refrained from chewing out the two after the boat trip with Rae. He understood they were trying to help, and it could've worked, but Rae wasn't being cooperative.

"We wanted you to have deniability," Brandon said. "Rae had some chosen words for me when she called. Now I'm in the penalty box, too."

"She'll forgive you eventually." Dean set his fork down. His appetite vanished. "I think it's hopeless for me. She's been hiding from me since she got off the boat. That was two days ago."

"She's been keeping herself busy, checking everything the resort offers," Chris chimed in. "At least she's not avoiding me, but she is definitely putting a professional wall between us."

"You must try talking to her again before you leave," Brandon urged. "The week's almost up."

"She asked me to give her space." Dean sighed.

Chris eyed him from across the table. "I've always admired your strategic mind, but is this really the time to give her space? We got her here so you could be in the same space."

"Have you told her you love her?" Brandon asked pointedly.

"She's not ready to hear it."

"Are you joking, dude?" Brandon's voice rose in frustration. "What is with you two? Why won't you just tell each other how you feel?"

"What if I told her, and she just threw it back in my face?" Dean felt his stomach churn at the thought.

There was a pause before Brandon replied, "Rae won't do that."

"You hesitated. You know there's a chance she'll never forgive me."

"Of course, but do you want to live the rest of your life wondering 'what if'?" Brandon asked. "I promise you, it's torture."

The regret in Brandon's voice was apparent.

"And how would you know that?" Dean inquired.

"That's a story for another time." Brandon sighed. "Listen. You've just gotten over one ghost. Losing Rae, if you love her the way I think you do, will haunt you for the rest of your life." He painted a terrifying future.

"If I were you, I'd rather know I tried," Chris advised.

"I've tried, Chris. Before I could even work myself up to tell her how I feel, she shut me down." Dean slumped in his seat. "How can I tell her when she won't give me a chance?"

"Desperate times, you need to create the chance, not ask for it," Chris said.

"You're right," Dean agreed. It was time to act, not wait.

"Better do it soon, 'cause time is running out. She's leaving in two days," Brandon reminded.

"Yup." Chris picked up a folder he had brought earlier and got up. "I got to get moving. Let me know if I could be of help."

A piece of paper slipped out of the folder. Dean picked it up and handed it back to his friend.

"Wait. What's this?" He read what looked like a schedule. He pointed at a specific event happening at dusk.

"Ah, that's a special show of traditional dance we're presenting tonight by the main pool," Chris explained.

"Rae would love that. She won't miss it." The gears in Dean's brain were finally moving again. He glanced at Chris with a smile. "I need some assistance."

"Name it."

The sound of the *gamelan*—Balinese percussion instruments made of bamboo and metal—filled the air.

Oh no! I'm late.

Rae flew down the stone stairs to get to the main tiered pools by the lobby. She'd been looking forward to the traditional dance performance after the staff had told her about the special event. But she could've sworn they told her it started after sundown. She'd deliberately avoided the happy hour before the dance so she wouldn't have to run to a certain someone. She'd still risk seeing Dean, but she didn't want to miss the event because of him.

She'd seen the *Barong* dance about a battle between forces of good and evil and the *Kecak* dance at the Uluwatu temple on her first trip to Bali. It had been an awe-inspiring experience. The *Kecak* depicted the bravery of the monkey soldiers who helped fight in the battle of *Ramayana*. And apparently, tonight's performance was going to be a condensed version of *Ramayana*.

Almost there!

Rae could see the pool area had turned into a mystical amphitheater. Candles in beds of white flowers floated on the water, while tall pristine white banners flapped lightly with the wind. A glimmer of sunshine peeked over the horizon.

The gamelan orchestra was arranged to one side while cushions were set on the long steps leading down to the pool for the audience. People were already sitting with drinks in their hands.

Damn it! She wouldn't get a prime seat now.

Breathless, Rae only had a dozen steps left. She lifted her long, light skirt and picked up her pace, simply to stop short at the last few stairs. At the bottom, Dean was looking up at her, waiting. There was a look in his eyes she hadn't seen before, as if a veil had been lifted. It caught her off guard and threw her off balance. Literally.

She stumbled on the second to last step and yelped as she fell straight into Dean's arms.

"I got you," he whispered as he straightened her within his embrace. "Are you hurt?"

Rae's face burned with embarrassment at her clumsiness, but she shook her head. "Did anyone see that?" she asked under her breath.

His chest rumbled with his chuckle. "I was the only witness to that bit of acrobatics."

She quickly broke away from him and composed herself. "Well, you, I don't really care about."

"Ouch." Dean rubbed his heart as if she'd punched him where it counted. Then, he offered her his arm. "Come. I saved you a seat."

Rae blew a heavy breath but took his arm and let him lead her to the front row. He handed her a flute of champagne from a nearby waiter before he sat next to her. It'd help her forget he was sitting so close for the next hour.

It'd been almost three days since they'd seen each other face-to-face, except when she'd caught him doing laps in the pool on the lower grounds on her way to the beach. She should've walked away, but watching him cut through the water so smoothly still mesmerized her as much as it had the first time.

Rae wished her feelings for him were limited to physical attraction. Then she'd be over him already. But as she couldn't tear her eyes from him in the pool, she acknowledged getting over Dean Rowland wouldn't be easy. Especially not after he'd stood at the foot of the stairs, looking devastatingly handsome and gazing up at her as if she were a goddess.

After chugging half of her champagne, Rae settled her nerves with a few deep breaths. Thank goodness the dance started, and Dean didn't get a chance to strike up a conversation.

Soon, Rae was entranced by the Indian mythology-inspired dance. *Ramayana* was a saga, mostly a love story, set in an ancient mythical kingdom. Rama, the King's son, was banished to the forest due to unfortunate circumstances. His faithful wife, Sita, followed him, even though he'd told her to stay.

Sita told Rama the forest would be a kingdom for her while he was in it, but a kingdom without him would be hell. But hell broke loose when the king of the giants abducted Sita to be his wife. She, of course, refused because of her love for Rama.

Attempts to save her took place, but she was only rescued when Rama defeated the giant himself. The unfortunate twist was that Rama didn't trust Sita when she told him she was untouched. He asked her to jump into a fire to prove her purity. She did it obediently and survived the fire unscathed, as she'd told the truth.

Years went by. Rama came to the throne but succumbed to the public's questioning of Sita's purity and banished her from the kingdom. Heartbroken, she left for the forest, bore Rama a pair of twins, whom he wouldn't discover until they were older, when Sita was dying. In the end, due to Rama's unfortunate decisions and constant distrust of his wife, he'd missed out on what could've been the happiest time of his life.

It was a beautiful but heart-wrenching dance. A love tragedy where one was devoted, and the other took it for granted. It wasn't unlike her story or her mother's, Rae thought. The difference was Rae wasn't as gullible as Sita. Or was she?

When Dean had turned on his charm, she'd quickly fallen in love with him. When he'd pushed her away, she'd pined for him. He'd hurt her, she couldn't completely expunge him from her heart.

And here he was, sitting next to her like nothing had happened. Once again, she opened up for more pain, just like Sita.

What am I doing?

Fifty-One

Dean barely followed the dance. He was more enthralled by the woman next to him. The emotions on her face as she watched the performance fascinated him. When it came to a close, she was almost in tears.

"Are you all right?" He handed her a napkin he'd snatched from a waiter.

Rae started at the question as if she had just woken up from a dream. "Yeah. I'm fine."

Dean studied her as she dabbed on her eyes. In seconds, she seemed herself again.

"Ready for dinner?" He offered his hand as they followed other guests vacating the stairs and moving to the restaurant for dinner.

Ignoring his hand, Rae got on her feet and smoothed her dress. "I have dinner plans."

"I know." Dean smiled. "Chris invited me, too."

"Go figure." Rae headed to the stairs.

"So, how come you're being cordial with Chris after knowing he tricked you?" he asked as they climbed the stairs to the villa.

"I'm doing business with him. But if he keeps meddling in my personal life, I may have to rethink our agreement."

"Don't you think if my best friend and your best friend joined forces to get us together, there's something we need to discuss here?"

"They don't know everything that happened between us."

"I'd say they know more," Dean retorted. "Like Brandon knows you're shutting me out because you're afraid."

Rae laughed. "I'm afraid? Of what? Of you?"

"You're afraid you won't be able to resist me." Dean half-smiled.

She glanced at him. "Still the same arrogant asshole I first met, I see."

"The same one you fell in love with."

Rae stopped in her tracks and spun to face him. Her eyes were ablaze. "Why, you're so full of yourself."

"You're not denying it." Dean smiled, pleased by her reaction.

A gate opened, and Chris appeared. "There you guys are. I thought I heard an argument."

"I'm not in love with you," Rae hissed stubbornly as she moved past Dean.

"You could've fooled me," Dean retorted as he beat her to the gate.

Dinner was delicious, as expected. The resort's restaurant definitely featured a group of talented chefs. Tonight, they had an array of Balinese delicacies of *Babi Guling*—pork from a whole roasted pig, *Sate Lilit*—grilled ground meat wrapped around skewers, *Urap*—vegetable salad dressed in toasted shredded coconut, and fragrant steamed rice.

With Chris between them, Rae and Dean managed to go through dinner without touching personal issues. Though it was challenging to respond to anything Dean said without having her irritation color her answers.

"I heard your second book is doing well." Chris poured them a little more wine as wait staff cleared the table.

"It's doing remarkably well, yes. "Rae smiled proudly.

"Just in time for the debut show." Chris saluted her with his wine glass. "Things are looking great for you, Rae. Congratulations."

Rae smiled gracefully. "Thanks."

"She's amazing." Dean openly stared at her with this big smile as if he was proud of her.

It irked Rae more. *He doesn't have any right to be proud of me.*

"You know Dean must've bought a whole bookstore's worth at Christmas." Chris grinned.

"I did not," Dean assured her when she narrowed her eyes at him. "I bought a few for my family. They wanted me to tell you they're all enjoying it."

Feeling both pleased and sad at the news, Rae nodded. "Thank you. Kat texted me about it. That's really sweet. I'm surprised they'd read my book."

"Why wouldn't they? They love you. And they all told me what an idiot I was for hurting you."

Rae glared at him, speechless. Really? He'd go into this in front of Chris?

And as if on cue, Chris pushed back his chair and stood. "Well, I think it's time for me to go. I'll leave you to talk."

"What?" Feeling ambushed, Rae jumped from her seat. "If you're leaving, I'm leaving."

"Rae, I'm speaking on behalf of the best friends." Chris opened his arms in a calming gesture. "For our sakes, please sit down and have a conversation. Whatever the outcome is, this will be it. We'll leave you two alone. But we're tired of watching both of you mope around, not admitting that you miss each other."

"I do not mope." Rae straightened indignantly.

"He does." Chris gestured with his head to Dean. "And it really isn't a good look for a CEO of a huge company."

Dean's brow rose at the dig.

"So, if not for you, do it for Brandon and me," Chris implored. "Please, don't leave here without resolving what this is between you. You both deserve happiness or, at the least, closure."

Chris started walking to the door but stopped to lean into the flabbergasted Rae. "Please, hear him out, Rae."

Then, it was just her and Dean. Alone.

Fifty-Two

Rae finally looked at Dean again after Chris had been gone for a few minutes. They'd sat there at the dining table in silence. Dean hadn't realized how long mere minutes could feel.

"Well, here we are." She demanded, "What else is there for us to talk about?"

"Plenty."

"Like?"

"I love you," Dean said straightforwardly, with his heart in his eyes.

Rae's pupils dilated as she registered the three words. "What?"

"I love you," he repeated. "With everything that I am."

Dean could hear her breath hitch as she stared at him. Doubt clouded her eyes, and she pushed out of her chair. He quickly stood, caught her wrist, and pulled her to him.

"Please, don't leave," he pleaded. This was his last chance. "I've given you your space. I'm only asking for you to give me a few minutes and listen."

He eased his grip from her wrist to hold her hand instead. She could easily pull away if she wanted to. But she only took a step back, still looking like a trapped animal.

"No, you listen," said Rae. "You don't get to tell me you love me and expect things to return to normal."

"I don't." Dean shook his head. "I'll spend the rest of my life earning your love back if that's what it takes, but I don't want to go on living without you, Rae. You're like air to me, and I could barely breathe these past months."

He closed the distance between them and stood before her, reaching for her other hand. This time she didn't fight him.

"I didn't realize how essential you are to my existence until I truly lost you." Dean squeezed her hand gently. "I know now why you came into my life. You breathed colors back into my days. You brought smiles to my lips and warmth back into my heart. You came into my world to rescue me from myself. I was too caught up in my own stupidity that I couldn't see it."

Tears and doubt pooled in Rae's eyes as she gazed at him.

"I was so afraid of the past repeating itself that I made it happen," Dean pushed on and put his vulnerability in her hands. "I see it now. My eyes are wide open. I beg you, forgive me."

Damn you, Dean Rowland.

Rae looked into his smoky grey eyes and could only see the sincerity in them. How did he do this to her? He said those three little words, and her heart thawed. But this must be how her mother had felt for her father.

She vaguely remembered her parents had fought, then made up, before fighting again. It was a vicious cycle Rae didn't want to live in.

"I'm not sure you won't break my heart again," Rae stated.

"I'm not your father, Rae," Dean said as if he knew what she was thinking. "I won't take you for granted ever again."

Rae reeled back as tears spilled freely now. "You don't know what you might do in the future. He told me he'd come back that last time, but he never did."

"I know, sweetheart." Dean wiped the tears from her cheeks with his thumbs. "I'm sorry for what he did to you. But I—"

"Don't promise me anything. You walked away from me once. What would prevent you from walking away again?"

"Love, Rae."

"My father told us he loved us. Love isn't always enough!"

"No, it isn't. You also need faith in that love and each other." Dean smiled assuringly. "Your best friend taught me that. I can't tell you what the future might hold, but a few things I know: I know I love you, and if things get rough, I'm going to fight with everything I am for us. I know you love me, and you're not the type of person who will back down from a fight. So, fight for us with me."

Rae wanted to believe in everything Dean said. But the risk was her sanity.

Dean cupped her face in his hand. "Rae, look at me. Stop running. Look into my eyes and see the possibilities when things go right, not the other way around. We can't let fear stop us from trying something. You and I both know that."

He stepped back and let go of her hands. "What do you say?"

Rae held his gaze as she let images of their future run through her mind. She saw arguing because they were both too headstrong not to butt heads sometimes. She saw them making love because they lit each other like tinder. She saw them traveling the world with kids in tow. But she also saw them cuddling in bed, sharing laughs with friends and family, and simply living. And loving.

"So are you going to tiptoe around fear?" Dean asked, holding out his hand.

Rae took a deep breath and wiped the tears out of her eyes.

"Or are you going to cannonball into love?" he challenged with a knowing smile.

She laughed and threw herself at him with an impact they knew would change their lives forever.

"God, I missed your laugh." Dean squeezed her deeper into his body, and she never felt more right.

"I love you." Rae's heart was made up and full as she said it. She finally breathed fully again.

"And I love you." Dean leaned in to capture her lips in a kiss that would seal their faith in each other.

"Take me inside. Make love to me." But she stopped short and pulled back. "Oh, this is Chris' villa, isn't it?"

"It's actually mine." Dean scooped Rae into his arms. "Who do you think planned this? I can't let our friends do all the scheming to win you over. You are the love of my life, Rae. I didn't plan to let you out of this villa until you forgive me, even if I had to seduce you for it."

Rea locked her arms around his neck. "Well, don't you have a lot of faith in yourself. You thought I'd just melt as soon as you touched me, didn't you?"

He maneuvered around some furniture and stepped inside the bedroom.

"I know you would, and I was ready to play dirty to hear you tell me you love me." He smiled mischievously as he set her down on his bed. "Because any other outcome is unacceptable."

Rae's smile echoed the promise in his. She grabbed a fistful of his shirt and pulled him down on her. "I should've let you grovel a little longer."

Fifty-Three

Dean's eyes darkened with passion as Rae pulled him into her warmth. But instead of succumbing to the urgent release of passion, he laid soft kisses on her lids, temple, nose, cheeks, and finally her lips, drawing sighs from her.

He trailed slow kisses along her jaw and throat while his hands slowly undressed her, stopping only to caress the skin he exposed. He took his time while she impatiently pulled at his pants and shirt. Feeling her frustration in failing to undress him, he pulled back to stand. In an unhurried movement, he shed his shirt, unbuttoned his jeans, and let them drop at his feet.

When Rae pulled him back to her, he laughed. It felt so good to laugh with her again.

"What's your hurry?" he teased her. "Are you going somewhere?"

"Nowhere without you," Rae answered.

"Then relax." His smile was full of promises as he peeled her dress off her and unveiled her breasts for him to feast. Brushing a thumb over a peak, he suckled the other into his mouth, gaining a moan from her. "I've missed you like crazy. Let me love you thoroughly. We have the rest of our lives to do this."

Rae wanted to drop her head onto the pillow, surrendering herself to his torturous lovemaking. But this was a new chapter in her life, where she'd take equal charge of their happiness. So instead of letting him get all his way, she pushed him onto his back and pinned him down with her legs on each side of his hips.

"Why don't you let me love you for a change," she told him.

She got her fill of his body as her hands explored the contours of his chest, down along his defined stomach, feeling his muscles get taut wherever she touched. Her mouth followed wherever her hands had caressed as if she was starved, and he was the only one who could fulfill her appetite.

Dean's response to her touch emboldened her. She felt playful and daring, and she loved it. That was how declaring her love for him made her feel. This was how being free to love felt to her. She pulled herself into a sitting position on his lap to look at his face. His eyes met hers.

"I've missed how I am with you," she said. "You always bring out extreme feelings in me."

"Like when you got extremely mad at me?" he teased.

"Yes." She laughed. "But also like how I can do anything."

Dean pushed himself to a sitting position and wrapped his arms around her. "You make me feel like an entirely new person. I never want to be apart from you ever again."

Rae noted every angle of his face and the look in his eyes. "I think I can go along with that."

"Can you?" A slow smile emerged on his face as he kissed her again. "Then marry me."

She pulled back and looked at him, stunned. Dean took her left hand from around his neck and dropped kisses on her fingers, palm, and pulse before he put her hand on his heart and held it there. "I don't have a ring to offer right now. Just my heart and all of me."

Rae's heart stilled as she felt the steady, strong heartbeat under his skin.

"I realize I'm a cannoballer, too, when it comes to you." Dean smiled. "Take a leap of faith with me."

Rae took a calming breath as she searched his eyes and found nothing but his love and their future together. She nodded her answer. "Only with you."

The look on his face echoed everything that she was feeling inside. In the next second, Dean's arms crushed her against him as her words sunk in, and his joyous laugh was infectious. This was no time for tears, even happy tears.

"Now love me, please," she pleaded.

"Always, my love," he answered as his body urged hers to open for him.

Her body sparked alive when his hard parts brushed against her soft ones, and she liquefied with every touch and stroke. Soon, she was lost in their lovemaking as the man she loved lost himself inside of her. All of her senses burst and all of her past troubles evaporated from inside of her.

And when Dean held her close in his arms and whispered his love for her, she could see their future possibilities together. This time without a trace of worry clouding it.

Fifty-Four

Gainesville, Georgia—three months later

Their small, understated, beautiful wedding took place in the lake house backyard. Only family members and close friends had witnessed the exchange of vows between Dean and his bride with sunset over the lake as the backdrop.

The night air was nice and cool on that spring evening as they gathered in celebration of love. It was the perfect night. At least, it was for Dean. And when he looked at his stunning and radiant wife, he knew Rae felt the same way.

Dean swept his gaze around the elegantly decorated tent and took note of the laughing faces of his family and their friends as they celebrated the nuptials. He smiled at Melanie and Tom, whose meddling played a part in his finding happiness. Even Gayle danced happily with her husband. She'd humbly apologized to Rae for her erroneous judgment and was fully supportive of their relationship since.

He then scanned the dance floor where his parents were dancing cheek to cheek, not far from his six-month-pregnant sister and her husband. He remembered when he and Rae had broken their news to his family. Kat had added to the celebration by announcing that she was three months pregnant. He didn't know how much happier he could possibly get.

Suddenly, an elbow nudged him on his side and brought him out of his reverie. He turned his head to see his brother, Gene, grinning at him.

"You're happy this time?" Gene asked.

Remembering that Gene had asked him a similar question about his previous experience standing at an altar, Dean gave him a knowing smile.

"Beyond words," he replied without a doubt.

Turning his eyes to the dance floor, Dean found his newly wedded wife as she swapped dance partners from Chris to Brandon. He saw the smile she bestowed on her best friend, and Dean noticed the lack of bad feelings that had usually come up when seeing them together.

Brandon had walked Rae down the aisle and represented her family when he'd given her hand to Dean. It had taken heartache for him to see Brandon as what he was to Rae and not as a threat. However, after what the other man had done for him and Rae, he could see why she considered him family. Dean himself could always use a good friend.

As if she knew Dean was watching them dance, Rae looked over Brandon's shoulder and met his gaze. She gave him a dazzling smile before returning her attention to her partner to say something.

With a last twirl on the dance floor, Brandon escorted Dean's bride to him. Her off-the-shoulder long-sleeved French lace wedding dress made her look like a redheaded deity coming home to him.

"Your lovely wife, Rowland." Brandon handed Rae's hand to him.

"Thanks, Rossi," Dean replied.

"Will the two of you stop calling each other by your last names?" Rae laughed as she dropped lightly onto Dean's lap. "We're all family now."

"I suppose we are." Dean nodded at Brandon.

"Then I suppose I don't have to remind you to take good care of my friend," Brandon said.

"You can count on me." Dean offered his hand.

Brandon gave him a smile of approval and shook his hand. Then with a playful tap on Rae's cheek and a grin, he walked away. "The night is young, lovebirds. I don't know about you, but I'm gonna steal someone's date for a dance. Maybe your mom, Dean. I think she has the sweets for me."

Rae's laugh triggered Dean's own smile. "I say you're in a good mood."

"I'm in an excellent mood," Rae gazed into his eyes, and all Dean could see in hers was happiness. "I've never been in a better mood."

"Really?"

"Yes." Her expression turned serious. "I think I know what my next book will be about."

"What?"

"Well, the first one was an exploration of family in the places I visited," she prefaced. "Then I wrote about the relationships I formed on my travels and the nontraditional family I found through them."

Dean nodded. "And the third?"

"It'll be about finding a home in you. How we're planting a root, tending it to grow. In the past decade, I've bounced through life, borrowing other people's families, homes, and happiness. And I love them for being generous in sharing those with me, but I can't explain how it makes me feel now knowing I will always come home to you."

Dean was mistaken if he thought he couldn't be happier when she'd said "I do" earlier. Moments like this would add to his joy.

"You know I'm planning to join you on as many of your trips as possible in the future." Dean mused, "Does that mean I'll be a mobile home then?"

Rae burst into her infectious laughter. "Why, Mr. Rowland, when did you acquire such a sense of humor?"

"Since you trespassed into my life, my love."

From the Author

Dear Readers,

The love story of Dean and Rae was the first full novel I've written. I started it more than a decade ago when I lived in Nepal. It had been overhauled completely since then to reflect the changes in time and the way my writing has evolved. I find this newer version to be more lighthearted and hopeful, without sacrificing the angst and heat that I also love in a good story. I hope you enjoyed it!

If you did, I'd appreciate a review on Amazon, Goodreads, BookBub, and Allauthor. It'll help other readers to find the book and a tremendous help for me as an Indie author. If you haven't already, I'd also like to invite you to subscribe to my newsletter, so I could share with you updates of upcoming releases, freebies, and other recommendation. You can also keep in touch with me on Instagram.

Keep flipping for a sneak peek to *His Forever Muse*, the second book in the Echo series. Thank you for reading and all the support.

Love,
C. R. Alam

About the Author

C. R. Alam was born in Jakarta, Indonesia. She grew up reading western novels and was inspired to write her own love stories from a young age. She used to handwrite her stories on legal pads that she still keeps in the attic. Her first novel, *Echoing Hearts*, has its seeds from one of those old writings. After a satisfying but demanding career in the communications world, she decided it was time to pursue her longtime dream of being a romance writer. She loves crafting heartfelt love stories with strong yet vulnerable characters. And whenever she can, she'll entwine her love of travel and food into her books. After living in Jakarta, the Midwest, and Nepal, C.R has now made a home in Durham, North Carolina, with her husband, daughter, and cat.

a amazon.com/C.-R.-Alam/e/B07JW81XG3

f facebook.com/CRAlamauthor

instagram.com/https://www.instagram.com/c.r.alam_author/

BB bookbub.com/authors/c-r-alam

Sneak Peek–His Forever Muse

Even among the enlightened elites, monsters lurked—because where light existed, shadows were never far behind. One even hid in plain sight, standing tall, golden, and magnificent. He moved with elegance and spoke of beauty with *savoir faire*. He enthralled his prey with promises. They all ignored the glint of wickedness in his eyes and fell for the spell in his smile.

One

Paris, The City of Light, France—Spring, three years earlier

The classic brass handle of the heavy apartment door slipped Calliope's damp, shaking fingers, and the door slammed shut. She froze, petrified she'd aroused the devil himself from his slumber. But nothing stirred in the night's silence except for her racing heart.

Only an explosion would wake him up from his drunken stupor—perhaps not even that—she'd made sure of it. The ground anti-anxiety pills she'd mixed into the cognac had knocked him out, but not before he'd knocked her about first.

With a suitcase in her left hand and a large leather tote hoisted over her right shoulder, she limped down from the third floor and out of the gilded cage that was her prison. Once outside, she breathed again, the chilly air easing into her straining lungs.

She swept her gaze along the empty lane lit with pale golden light from the cast-iron street lamps. The residents of one of Paris's most prestigious neighborhoods were sound asleep and oblivious to anything sinister happening behind these elegant walls. Or perhaps they knew but chose to turn a blind eye.

It didn't matter. Survival was her only goal now.

She forced her battered body to move into the safety of darkness. Focusing her willpower on taking step after step with her weakened legs, she had no more strength to contain her tears.

These were not tears of sadness but rage. She seethed at herself for getting caught in his web of charms and deceit. But most of all, she was furious at herself for staying. Too long.

The trembles intensified as a wave of fear, anger, and adrenaline flooded her bloodstream.

With another deliberate breath, she steeled herself. Too much was at stake now. She wasn't the only one at risk anymore.

There would be time for a breakdown, just not now. She had one goal in mind at the moment—to put as much distance as possible between herself and the man who had made her life a living hell.

Two

Gainesville, Georgia—Middle of May, present day

"We're almost there!"

Brandon Rossi glanced away from the road to check on his passenger. His friend, Rae Allen, puffed short pants of breath, one hand clutched to her enormous belly while the other was almost white from gripping the car door's armrest.

Thirty-two and still a bachelor, Brandon had never thought he'd be racing a woman in labor to the hospital. He came from New York City to visit his friends and paint a mural in their nursery. A nursery for a baby who wasn't supposed to arrive for a few more weeks.

"This is not how I planned it. This isn't supposed to be happening yet," Rae said breathlessly as the contraction abated.

"I guess your baby has other plans." Brandon made the next right as prompted by the GPS lady. "It's going to be fine, Rae."

"No, it's not fine. Dean's supposed to be here with me."

"Look, he was already on his way home when I talked to him. He'll meet us at the hospital."

"Did you call Martha?"

"Dean said he'd call his mother."

Brandon checked his blind spot before changing lanes, passing the annoying slowpoke driving in the left lane. Conscious of his anxiety level, he took a deep, calming breath. He didn't need to get into an accident and risk both mother and baby.

"I haven't read the manual for the car seat yet." Rae gasped. "It's still in the box. Shit, the crib is not done—"

"Rae," Brandon stopped her without taking his eyes off the road. "Don't worry. Just focus on yourself and the baby right now."

"I'm not ready, Brandon."

The tremble in Rae's voice made Brandon turn his head to assess her. He'd never seen her like this. Nervous, of course. Devastated, yes. But terror in her eyes? No. She wasn't talking about the half-done crib or the car seat anymore. He reached for her hand and held it tight, trying to transfer any calmness he had to her.

"I don't know how to do this," Rae whispered, near tears.

"The doctor and the nurses will help you through, Rae. You and Dean have taken classes. You'll be fine."

Brandon tried to sound as convincing as he could. Truthfully, what did he know? He had limited knowledge of birthing or babies. His two nephews, Eric and Alex, were the only kids he had dealt with. And though he considered himself a damn good uncle, he'd been little help to his brother Brady and his wife Teresa when it came to changing diapers and all.

Rae shook her head. "I don't know the first thing about being a mother. What if I screw up this baby?"

Understanding where this new fear was coming from, Brandon squeezed her hand. Rae hadn't grown up in a typical family. Her mother suffered from chronic depression until the day she died, while her father had been MIA most of Rae's life.

"My mom didn't exactly leave me a manual on being a mother," Rae went on. "What if this is the one thing I will fail at?"

"You will not fail at being a mother," Brandon assured her.

"How could you be so sure?"

"If this is the one role in life that scares you the most, I know you'll do anything to conquer it. Because that's just how you work, my friend."

Turning the car into the hospital entrance, Brandon kept his eyes open for a sign to the birthing center. It was easy to spot as he found Rae's husband, Dean, pacing a hole into the cement by the main door. Gone was the suit jacket and tie he'd worn to work earlier, but not his management skill. As soon as Dean spotted their car, he gave a signal and an orderly ran out with a wheelchair.

Brandon rolled to a stop and turned to his ashen-faced friend. "And you've got to remember, you're not doing this alone."

The level of panic in Rae's eyes eased when she saw Dean rushing to the car. Brandon witnessed color return to her face, and tension in her muscles melted as trust and faith took over when her husband held her hand in his and helped her out of the car.

"I owe you one, brother." Dean looked into the car at Brandon. "Thank you for getting her here."

"Glad to be of service. Go be with your wife. I'll see you in there." Brandon waved him off and gave Rae a thumbs-up for good luck.

Brandon watched them roll Rae away before he put the car back into drive and found a parking spot. Rae's expression when she looked at Dean stayed in his mind. That complete trust only came with a strong bond.

Rae and Dean had found each other three years ago. Their love story hadn't been smooth at first. Two years into their marriage, with their first child arriving any minute, they'd pulled through complicated challenges in the beginning. Perhaps that was why they were so solid now.

Brandon coveted the love they had. It was the type of love that could withstand anything life would hurl at you. It was the kind of love that inspired songs, poetry, and paintings.

A smile broke on his face.

If Rae had heard his musing, she'd tell him he was a romantic. Maybe he was, though a romantic without his own love to inspire him. And if she'd heard that one, she'd tell him to go find it. In fact, she'd been telling him to do something along those lines just before her water had broken.

Two hours earlier

"Ethereal!" Rae marveled at the scene painted on one of the nursery walls. "That's the word I've been looking for."

Brandon leaned in close to the wall. With tiny strokes of his brush, he created the illusion of thick fluffy fur on the polar bear cubs play-wrestling in a magical playground ensconced on the softest white cloud. Satisfied, he stepped back to study the mural he'd been working on for two days.

Enchanting creatures were busy at play—furry ones, plump ones, winged ones. Some resembled cute kittens with angel wings. Others were covered by white fur that equaled the fluffy cloud they bounced on. Cheeky monkeys climbed and leaped from the limbs of the tall trees that canopied the playground.

"They look so happy. Thank you." Rae came to stand next to Brandon and bumped his side with her shoulder. "I'd say you've got your mojo back."

"Maybe," Brandon doubted. "But I must say it feels good to paint again."

The mural was his first creation in months. Lately, inspiration was hard to come by. The empty canvases and torn sketches scattered in his loft proved that.

Rae gasped and rubbed her belly. "Oof, don't kick Mommy, darling."

"Is that the baby?" Brandon watched with awe the subtle movement visible on the surface of his friend's stomach.

"Yeah. The baby's restless. I swear this kid will be a strong swimmer like their daddy. Here." Rae grabbed Brandon's free hand and placed it on the swell of her belly. "Feel that?"

Brandon's eyes widened at the resounding kick against his palm. "Oh yeah. You got a lively one."

"Imagine getting kicked in the ribs several times a day."

Brandon chuckled, but his laughter died when he felt Rae's stomach tighten. She sucked in her breath and her face tensed.

"What's wrong?" he asked.

Rae waved off his worry. "Nothing. Just Braxton Hicks—false contractions. I've been having them on and off since I woke up."

"Are you sure you're okay?"

"Yeah. My back hurts, that's all."

Brandon put away his brush, then led her to the nursing chair in the corner of the room. "Here, get off your feet."

"I'm fine," Rae insisted but sat nonetheless. "It'll pass."

Brandon dropped on the ottoman at the foot of the chair, unconvinced.

Rae relaxed her shoulders a few seconds later and leaned back on the chair. "See, it passed."

Brandon thought she looked a little pale but kept it to himself.

"I'm so glad you're here, Brandon. I miss having you only a few subway stops away. Did I see you last at your exhibition?"

"Yup, just before Christmas," Brandon confirmed.

"That's crazy." Rae shook her head in disbelief. They used to see each other at least once a week before she and Dean moved down to Georgia.

"We've both been busy. You had your book tour, the big move, and the baby coming."

A travel writer and best-selling author, Rae had stayed active throughout her pregnancy. Whereas Brandon had nothing new to show since his last art exhibition. No new artwork. No new music.

He wasn't sure how often he'd sat with a sketchbook and a piece of charcoal in his hand, watching the world buzz by through his windows, waiting for inspiration to strike. Most times, he'd walked away with a blank page.

"This is my first completed work in months. I haven't even written a verse since the boys and I returned from our world tour," Brandon said.

"You're on a break. You were going nonstop. Seems normal to me if your brain is on strike."

It was true. His band, Canis Major, had released their most recent album last year, and it was their most popular yet. They'd played all over the country right after the release, followed by a world tour last summer that lasted into the fall.

And in between, Brandon had painted and held his first art exhibition. To his surprise, it was a huge hit. Riding high on his success and the inspiration from the world tour, he'd painted like a madman. His second art exhibition had capped the whirlwind and exhausting year.

"Maybe you're right." Brandon sighed. "Nothing is pulling at me lately, though."

Rae pointed at the mural. "I'd say something pulled at you."

"But I have nothing else. I feel tapped out." Brandon raked his paint-covered hands through his messy hair with frustration.

Rae's brows shot up. "I think you're in a funk."

"A funk?"

"Yes. Everyone goes through a funk sometimes in their lives."

"Hah." Brandon mulled the word *funk*.

Rae had succinctly stated what he'd been trying to wrap his mind around for weeks in one word. Here he thought he was going down a rabbit hole with some kind of depression he couldn't explain. And trying to analyze the word *depression* had stressed him out even worse. A funk he could deal with.

"Forget painting or music for now. Just live your life," Rae suggested. "When writer's block hits me, I walk away for a little bit. Living always brings the words back to me."

"Maybe that's the problem. I have this full life that I'm crazy grateful for, but I feel something is missing."

"Then go find it."

Brandon threw up his arms in frustration. "Go find what? I don't know what it is."

"Why don't you start an adventure and see what you find? Nothing is stopping you. Take it from me, the professional traveler. A good trip will help you gain a new perspective on life."

Brandon snorted skeptically. "I was just on an epic world tour last year."

"And you painted your heart out after that tour, remember? Perhaps another trip would trigger new inspirations. I'll tell you, solo traveling is a whole different experience. It's helped me understand more about myself, people, and the world around me."

Brandon contemplated the suggestion. Rae had a point. Playing music and meeting their fans from other parts of the world had been more than inspirational to him; it'd helped him grow as an artist.

"Maybe you're right," Brandon said.

"Oh, I know I'm right. Give it a thought, then pick a starting point. Wherever you want to go, I can help you plan it. But now, I need you to help me up."

Brandon belatedly noticed Rae struggling to get out of the chair. With one easy pull, he helped her stand.

Rae stared up at him with wide blue eyes. "I think I'm leaking."

"What?"

Rae looked back to the chair, and sure enough, there was a small wet spot.

"Did you pee on yourself?"

"No, smartass," Rae retorted. "I think my water broke. I mean, I could be peeing myself. God knows I haven't had control of my bladder for months. I'm gonna check."

Brandon watched Rae go and waited. He was sure Rae was fine. She'd come out laughing at herself for peeing her pants. He wouldn't let her forget that one for a while.

After what seemed like a long while to Brandon, Rae reemerged. "I called my doctor. She said it might be my water. And those contractions I've been having might not be Braxton Hicks after all. Since I'm not due for another three weeks, she wants me to go to the hospital."

The unexpected information rendered Brandon mute. Rae didn't wait for a response. "I need to clean up before we go."

"Clean up?" Brandon found his voice. It came out croaky and high. "We need to take you to the hospital now!"

Brandon rushed Rae to the door, but she stilled him with a hand on his arm.

"Brandon, listen. The doctor said not to rush, just to get there soon. She wasn't worried but wanted to be cautious. It can be a false alarm. I need you not to freak out on me, okay? I'm barely holding it together myself."

Noting the tension on his friend's jaw, Brandon forced himself to take a deep, calming breath. "Okay, got it. I'm cool. Go clean up. I'll let Dean know to meet us at the hospital. I'll get your go bag and the car."

Rae nodded appreciatively and started for her bedroom.

"Hey, Rae," Brandon called out. "It's going to be okay."

Also By

this author

Fated Together
(a prequel novelette to the Echo series)
Free when you subscribe to the author's newsletter

His Forever Muse
(Book 2 of the Echo series)

Book 3 & 4 in 2023

Made in the USA
Columbia, SC
10 February 2025